WESTERN

Rugged men looking for love...

Redeeming The Maverick
Christine Rimmer

The Right Cowboy
Cheryl Harper

T0363176

MILLS & BOON

Christine Rimmer is acknowledged as the author of this work
REDEEMING THE MAVERICK
© 2024 by Harlequin Enterprises ULC
Philippine Copyright 2024
Australian Copyright 2024
New Zealand Copyright 2024

First Published 2024
First Australian Paperback Edition 2024
ISBN 978 1 038 91751 5

THE RIGHT COWBOY
© 2024 by Cheryl Harper
Philippine Copyright 2024
Australian Copyright 2024
New Zealand Copyright 2024

First Published 2024
First Australian Paperback Edition 2024
ISBN 978 1 038 91751 5

MIX
Paper | Supporting
responsible forestry
FSC® C001695

Published by
Harlequin Mills & Boon
An imprint of Harlequin Enterprises (Australia) Pty Limited
(ABN 47 001 180 918), a subsidiary of HarperCollins
Publishers Australia Pty Limited
(ABN 36 009 913 517)
Level 19, 201 Elizabeth Street
SYDNEY NSW 2000 AUSTRALIA

Cover art used by arrangement with Harlequin Books S.A.. All rights reserved.

Printed and bound in Australia by McPherson's Printing Group

Redeeming The Maverick

Christine Rimmer

MILLS & BOON

Christine Rimmer came to her profession the long way around. She tried everything from acting to teaching to telephone sales. Now she's finally found work that suits her perfectly. She insists she never had a problem keeping a job—she was merely gaining "life experience" for her future as a novelist. Christine lives with her family in Oregon. Visit her at christinerimmer.com.

Dear Reader,

Can you believe it? This year, the beloved Montana Mavericks series is celebrating thirty years of engaging, emotional Western love stories. And to mark this exciting milestone, we are introducing a whole new Montana Mavericks hometown.

Tenacity, Montana, lives up to its name. It's a hardscrabble ranching town smack-dab in the heart of Big Sky Country. You have to work hard to make it in Tenacity.

Hayes Parker grew up there. But he left right after high school, vowing never to return. For years, he's kept that vow. But trouble at home draws him back. And right away he runs into the girl who broke his heart all those years ago.

In the decade and a half since Chrissy Hastings had to walk away from Hayes, she's left town, too—and loved and lost a second time. Now she's returned to Tenacity to start over. Neither Chrissy nor Hayes has any intention of fanning the embers of their long-ago love.

However, when she needs a helping hand, Hayes reaches out. They agree to keep it strictly friends only. But their yearning hearts have other plans.

I hope this story grabs you and won't let you go till the very last page. And thank you for making the Montana Mavericks series a reader favorite for three decades and counting.

Happy reading everyone,

Christine Rimmer

DEDICATION

This book is dedicated to Susan Litman, our fabulous lead editor for this long-running, much-loved Montana Mavericks series. Thank you, Susan, for so smartly and conscientiously guiding each Montana Mavericks story all the way from conception to publication—and somehow always managing to tackle every challenge with skill, patience and heart.

CHAPTER ONE

THEY SAY YOU can't go home again, and that was just fine with Hayes Parker. He'd left the End of the Road Ranch on the day he graduated from Tenacity High School vowing never to return. For fifteen years, Hayes had kept that vow.

But hey. Never say never.

In early June of his thirty-third year, Hayes's older brother Braden called.

"The ranch is in big trouble," Braden said flatly. "As for Dad, he's worse than ever, barking orders right and left. Nowadays, the man is incapable of a civil conversation. He's just plain unbearable to be around."

Hayes was thinking that none of that was news, but he took the high road and kept the snarky comment to himself.

Braden wasn't finished. "Miles is off in the service and unreachable." Miles was the youngest of the three brothers. "As for Rylee, she's engaged, and living in Bronco."

Hayes felt the sharp pinch of regret. Rylee was the youngest of the four of them, their only sister. And Hayes had never kept in touch the way he knew he should. He drew a slow breath. "Rylee's engaged..."

"Yeah. To Shep Dalton."

"Wow." Rylee and Shep had been friends in school—just friends, the way Hayes remembered it. "The years do go by..."

Braden said, "She's got herself a big-time job in Bronco."

A hundred miles from their hardscrabble hometown of Tenacity, Montana, Bronco was bigger, greener—and for some families, richer. "I'm telling you, Hayes, no way Rylee has time to deal with Dad, let alone to take on the near-impossible task of saving the ranch."

"I hear you," Hayes replied. Because he did and he sympathized. But that didn't mean he'd be headed for Tenacity imagining he could save the day.

"I'm done," Braden said darkly. "Finished. On my way out the door. I've stuck it out as long as I can stand to. But no more. I'm leaving."

Hayes tried to find the right words. Too bad there were none.

"Hayes? You still there?"

"I'm here. And, Braden, I get it. And I wish you well. But I'm not going home to try to deal with Dad. I gave all that up when I was eighteen. You have to know that."

There was a silence, a silence weighted with grim understanding on both their parts.

Braden asked in a hollow voice, "Not even to save the family ranch?"

Hayes felt a tug deep down inside him. He hated that ranch. But he loved it, too. Even after fifteen years, it was all tangled up for him, the hurt. The frustration. The clear knowledge that he needed to get out or there would be no hope for him. "Uh-uh," he said quietly into the phone. "I'm not coming back. No can do."

Braden let out a heavy sigh. "I understand."

"Sorry, brother."

"Hey. It was worth a shot. You take care now."

"Let me know where you end up," Hayes said.

"Will do." Braden said goodbye.

Hayes hung up the phone determined to stand his ground. Yeah, the very idea that the ranch might fall out

of Parker family hands…it got to him, it hit him deep. True, he'd vowed never to go back there. But that didn't change the way he felt about the ranch. It was Parker land. And it damn well ought to remain that way whether Hayes ever set foot there again or not.

He told himself to let it go, that he wasn't going back and there was no upside to stewing about it.

But over the next couple of months, thoughts of home nagged at him. There had been good things back home. He'd found first love there, deep and true. At least for as long as it had lasted.

Since then, he'd been married—and widowed. He'd loved his wife with all his heart. And yet sometimes he still thought of Chrissy Hastings, his high school sweetheart. Of her long brown hair and big brown eyes, her sweet laugh and kind heart. It had cut him deep, losing Chrissy. But still, he'd moved on.

In the past fifteen years, he'd worked on ranches all over the Western states. Now, he was top hand on a fine spread called the Bar-M up in northern Montana near the town of Rust Creek Falls. The owner's son on the Bar-M was ready to step up as top hand, so Hayes knew he'd be leaving here soon anyway—and when he did, he would finally buy his own land and build his own spread. He refused to go backward. Why in hell should he help out the father who'd rarely given him anything but grief?

But then, on the last day of July, his mother called.

He considered not answering. Over the years, he'd let most of his mom's calls go to voicemail. She was such a good mom. He still missed her every day—and talking to her just made him long for the home he'd left behind.

She was the easy one to love, always gentle, thoughtful and full of understanding. The truth was, he'd always

hated hearing the pain in her voice. It hurt so bad when she said how much she missed him.

He'd missed her a lot, too. But overall, it just worked better not to poke at a deep wound.

This time, though, he couldn't stop himself from taking the damn call. "Hi, Mom."

Norma sighed. "Hayes. It's so good to hear your voice."

He had to swallow to loosen the sudden tightness in his throat. "How are you?"

"I'm okay, honey. Doing well…" The words trailed off into silence. Finally, she spoke again. "I'm just going to go ahead and put it out there."

He rubbed at the space between his eyebrows where tension had gathered. "Mom, look—"

"Please, honey. Hear me out."

He should say he had to go and then hang up quick.

But he did no such thing. "What, Mom?"

"Your father, well, he's sick. And he's been sick for a while now."

Sick? Not possible. Lionel Parker was too ornery to get sick. "Sick with what, Mom?"

"We're not sure. For months, he's been having horrible bellyaches with fever, and his stomach bloating up. Up till now, he's always gotten better for a while, at least—but then he ends up in bed, sick and in pain with a fever all over again."

"What does the doctor say?"

"Hayes." Her soft voice held the patience of the ages. "I can't get him to go to the doctor…"

Hayes rubbed that spot between his eyes a little harder.

Of course, Lionel Parker refused to find out what was wrong with him. Lionel Parker didn't get sick. Getting sick would prove he was only human like everyone else.

His mom continued, "He says he'll be fine, that we can't

afford to 'throw money away' on doctors. And honey, the hard fact is we're dead broke." She hesitated. And then she laid it on him. "We haven't lost the ranch yet, but it could happen if things don't turn around." Her words only confirmed what Braden had said two months ago. As though she sensed the direction of his thoughts, she added, "Braden picked up stakes and left."

"I know, Mom. He called me before he took off. Tell me you at least hired someone to help out."

She didn't answer. Her silence felt weighted with reproach.

"Right," he muttered. "You already said there's no money."

"Rylee has offered to take a leave from the great job she loves. She's director of marketing now for the Bronco Convention Center." His mother's voice was full of pride. But then she added wearily, "Hayes, it's just wrong to ask her to give up the job she's worked so hard to earn."

"I get it, Mom. I do."

"Did you know she's going to marry—"

"Shep Dalton. Yeah. Braden told me. I'm glad for her."

"Oh, Hayes…"

At his feet, his dog, Rayna, made a low, anxious sound. He shifted his gaze down to her. She'd sensed his mood. Now she stared up at him through worried eyes. He gave her a quick scratch on her furry head.

And his mom finally hit him with the big question. "Do you think you might possibly see your way clear to come on home for a bit?" Hayes could hear the tears in her voice. She was trying so hard not to cry.

Those unshed tears broke him.

He found himself thinking that he really needed to get over himself. He was no longer an overgrown boy with a

heart full of grievances. Uh-uh. Now he was a grown-ass man who'd loved and lost—twice.

It was about time he tried to put the past behind him. "Okay, Mom. I'll be there tomorrow."

She burst into tears then.

He soothed her as best he could, offering reassurances that everything was going to be all right while at the same time wondering if he'd somehow lost his mind.

When he hung up with her, he texted Braden to let him know what was going on.

And the next morning, as dawn painted the purple sky with streaks of orange, Hayes packed up his crew cab, hitched up his horse trailer and clicked his tongue for his dog. Rayna jumped right up onto the passenger seat. She was a big girl, a hundred-pound Bulgarian shepherd, long-haired and bred to live on the land guarding and protecting livestock. His late wife, Anna, had raised her from a pup, treating her like one of the family. As a result, Rayna was more pet than guardian dog.

"You ready to go?" he asked.

Rayna gave a low whine in answer.

"All right. Let's hit the road."

It was a seven-hour drive to Tenacity—seven and a half counting a stop to let his horse stretch his legs. They rolled into Hayes's dusty hometown at 1:30 in the afternoon. He drove down Central Avenue thinking that things hadn't changed all that much.

The local watering hole, the Grizzly Bar, still had that flat roof, like most of the commercial buildings in town. And it still had a big orange door with weather-beaten benches to either side and a rough façade of bricks made from natural stone. Directly across the street from the Grizzly was Tenacity's one bus stop complete with a bench, a sign and a plexiglass shelter where you could

catch the Trailways bus that rolled by twice daily going southwest toward Bronco, or northeast to the North Dakota border.

And if he drove on a few more blocks, he'd be leaving town. In no time, he'd find himself rolling onto Hayes family land.

But he wasn't ready for that. Not yet.

Instead, he went left at the next intersection and then left again. That had him ending up not far from where he'd turned off the highway in the first place. Pulling into the parking lot of the Tenacity Inn, he stopped beneath the porte cochere next to the lobby doors.

The way he saw it, he needed someplace to escape to, just in case. A room for the night would do just fine. That way, if his dad really drove him up the wall, he'd have a place to hole up for a few hours—after he put his horse out to pasture, somehow managed to get his pigheaded father to visit the damn doctor and saw to the evening chores.

Did they allow pets as big as Rayna here?

One way to find out.

He let the dog out. She promptly peed on a big, rounded landscaping rock. Luckily it didn't look like she'd hit any of the decorative plantings. Hayes decided to call that a win. From the trailer his sorrel gelding, Roscoe, nickered softly.

"Won't be long now," he called to the horse. Roscoe snorted once and let it go at that.

Hayes ran up the steps and pulled open the glass door to the lobby, ushering Rayna in ahead of him. Inside, the Tenacity Inn was nothing fancy, but it was clean with a nice, big lobby and plenty of windows to let in the afternoon light.

He led Rayna straight to the front desk, where he swept off his hat and asked for a room. The pretty blonde desk clerk said that she could reserve him a room, but he

couldn't check in until three—and yes, he could have his dog with him as long as the dog was quiet and well trained.

Rayna could bark with the best of them whenever she sensed a threat. She was bred to guard livestock, after all. But Hayes kept his mouth shut about that.

"Yeah," he said. "She's a good dog, easy-natured and well behaved. Sit, girl." Rayna tucked in her low, furry tail and dropped to her haunches. She was something. She sat there looking nothing short of regal, waiting for his next command.

The blonde nodded approvingly. "She's a calm one, I can see that," she said as she took Hayes's credit card.

The clerk had just handed him his room key when someone behind him gasped—and somehow, right then, just from that one sharp, indrawn breath, he *knew.* "Hayes?" the woman behind him asked in complete disbelief. "Is that you?"

He'd been in town for a matter of minutes. And somehow, already, the past had caught up with him.

He made himself turn to face her.

Damn. She looked great. Beautiful as always, but not the same girl he used to know. She was all woman now.

Her face was a little thinner, her cheekbones more pronounced. Her seal-brown hair was pulled back and anchored in a thick knot at the back of her head. Her eyes were exactly as he remembered them, deep brown around the iris, raying out to amber and green rimmed with gray. He saw sadness in those eyes—pride and grit, too.

"Chrissy," he said rough and low.

Those soft, full lips were slightly parted in surprise. "What are you doing here?" She asked the question quietly, her voice carefully controlled.

He took his time answering because he needed a moment to catch his breath. Even though she'd spoken to him

in a soft and civil tone, to have her standing right here in front of him felt like a slap in the face.

It was bad enough he was about to go try to deal with his old man for the first time in a decade and a half. But Chrissy...

That was a punch to the gut all over again.

She glanced down at Rayna. "Who's this?"

"My dog. Her name's Rayna."

"Hey, Rayna," Chrissy said. Rayna tipped up her big head, awaiting strokes. Chrissy gave her what she wanted.

He explained, "My dad's sick and there's no one to help out. You could say I drew the short straw. What about you?"

"I'm the catering manager here at the inn."

"I heard you got married," he said, playing it casual for all he was worth.

She lifted one shoulder in a sad little shrug. "I'm divorced now."

He'd had no idea. "Sorry to hear that."

"Uh, thank you," she replied stiffly. *God, this is awful,* he thought. And then she asked, "You?"

He gave her the truth. "I was married. My wife died..."

Those big eyes got shiny. She looked like she might cry. "Oh, Hayes. I'm so sorry..."

Way to go, Parker, he thought. He'd developed a real knack lately for making women cry—yesterday, his mom. Today, his first love.

With a tiny sniff, Chrissy glanced away, out toward the porte cochere and his truck and horse trailer waiting beneath it. He looked her over some more. Because he couldn't stop himself.

She had one of those word tattoos in a delicate font wrapped around her left forearm: *Be Bold. Be True. Be Free.*

That tattoo surprised him. The Chrissy he used to

know wasn't the type to get inked. He wondered so many things—like why the tattoo and how she had ended up divorced.

His brothers had never said a word about her in all the years he'd been gone—probably because they knew the subject of Chrissy was a painful one for him. Now and then, though, he would check in with his buddies in town. From them, he'd learned that Chrissy had finished college with a degree in hospitality, that she'd married a successful accountant. The last he'd heard, she and her husband were doing great over in Wonderstone Ridge, a resort town down the road toward Bronco.

Was it the divorce that had her choosing to move back home?

Not that it was any of his business.

"Well," she said, drawing her shoulders back, her lips tipping up in a cool smile, "I should get to work…"

"Good to see you, Chrissy." It was only halfway a lie.

Her smile wavered just a little. "You too, Hayes. Take care."

"Thanks." He tipped his hat to her as he settled it back on his head. And then, clicking his tongue for his dog, he turned for the door. Chrissy made no effort to slow him down.

He went out into the bright August sunlight reminding himself that he was bound to run into her at some point and it was just as well he'd gotten that over with quick.

His pulse roared in his ears as he opened the passenger door of his truck and clicked his tongue at his dog. Rayna jumped up to the seat.

And then, for a minute that seemed to stretch into eternity, he just stood there with the door open, staring blindly at his dog, his heart beating like a wrecking ball in the cage of his chest.

AT THE RANCH, things were every bit as bad as he'd expected.

The iron sign above the main gate had come loose on one side. Both the barn and the house needed repainting. The tractor shed and the chicken coop cried out for a fresh coat of whitewash. A quick glance around showed him that shingles were missing from just about every roof. A rusted pickup with two flat tires sat in the dirt next to the rough rail fence that surrounded the house.

And other fences were clearly down. Chickens scattered, stirring up dust, as he drove in. By the rail fence, a black Angus cow nibbled at Norma Parker's wilted roses while a baldy calf stuck his nose under the bottom rail to crop at the fringe of grass on the other side.

Hayes pulled to a stop by the low gate that opened onto a natural stone walk leading up to the front porch steps. For a long string of seconds, he just sat there, engine idling, dreading getting out, not wanting to face what waited inside.

And then the front door opened. His mom, looking worn and weary beyond her years, stepped out. With a cry, she rushed down the steps.

That got him moving. He shut off the engine and jumped from the cab in time to catch her when she threw herself into his arms.

"Hayes! Oh, honey... I'm so glad you're here." She stared up at him, dark circles beneath her eyes, tears on her cheeks. "Look at you. More handsome than ever..." A sob escaped her.

"Hey, Mom. Hey..." He pulled her in for one more hug before asking grimly, "How is he?"

She sniffled and swiped at her eyes with a work-roughened hand. "It's bad, honey. He won't listen to me. We have to do something."

He clasped her shoulders. "I need to take care of my horse. I'll be quick. And then I'll be in."

She squeezed his arm. "Hurry."

"I will."

Fifteen minutes later, he instructed Rayna to wait on the porch and went inside, where everything looked pretty much as he remembered—only older and more worn out.

"No damn doctor!" It was his father's voice, rough, angry and full of pain. The sound came from the master bedroom across the great room and down a short hallway.

His mother answered, "But you're ill, Lionel. You're sick enough that you're scaring me." She said something else, but Hayes couldn't make out the words.

"No, Norma," blustered his dad. "I'll be all right. Just leave me be!"

His mom started shouting then. "Lionel Parker, you are spiking a fever of a hundred and two! This cannot go on!"

His dad launched into more objections as Hayes started walking. His boots echoing on the worn wood floor, he strode toward the bedroom.

The door was open. He hesitated at the threshold, shocked at what he saw.

His dad lay on his back on the old iron-frame bed, his belly enormous, his face heavy, unshaven, his scruffy beard dead white, his skin yellowish and his eyes red-rimmed.

Those eyes locked right on him. "Well. If it isn't the prodigal son coming home at last…" Lionel Parker's insult died on his lips as he pressed his hands to his belly and moaned in pain.

Hayes swept off his hat. "Hey, Dad. Real good to see you, too. I'm here to help Mom get you to the hospital."

"No!" Lionel clutched his stomach even harder and groaned again. "We can't afford—"

"You're going, Dad."

"Do not call me any damn ambulance!"

"Okay, I won't." Hayes spoke to his mother. "Let's get him in my truck."

"I'm not going anywhere," growled Lionel.

"That's what you think, Dad."

Lionel kept saying no, but somehow Hayes managed to sit him up, put his slippers on him and drag him to his feet. From there, Hayes slung Lionel's beefy right arm across his shoulders. Norma pulled Lionel's left arm around her neck so she could support the old man on his other side.

They started walking. Lionel objected with each step. More than once, he almost got loose. But he was in bad shape and could barely stand on his own. Hayes kept a strong hold on his wrist and around his swollen middle as they went.

Somehow, they got him out the front door, where Rayna was waiting.

"Stay," Hayes commanded. Rayna sat.

With his dad sagging between them, Hayes and his mom staggered down the steps and across the walk. Norma ran around the truck bed and got in the crew cab's back seat on the far side. Hayes boosted Lionel up as Norma did the best she could to pull him into the cab.

"I'll stay back here with him," his mom said as she gently hooked up his seat belt for him.

Hayes glanced at his dog, who sat watching him from the porch. He hoped the rail fence would be enough to keep her close to the house. "Stay!" he shouted once more.

She gave him a worried-sounding whine.

Hayes shut the front gate, then ran around and got in behind the wheel. As he buckled himself in, his mom said, "I put in a little fountain in the backyard a few years ago. Your dog will have water when she needs it."

"Thanks, Mom. That's great." He started up the truck and headed for Bronco. Once they reached the highway, he kept the speed just over the limit while constantly fighting the urge to floor it and get them there quicker.

His mom called Bronco Valley Hospital from the back seat to let them know they were bringing Lionel in. As the miles rolled away beneath the crew cab's wheels, Lionel stared straight ahead, a grim scowl on his face. Hayes appreciated the quiet. But every time he glanced in the rearview mirror and met his mother's worried eyes, dread marched like cold fingers up and down his spine.

His father was in bad shape. Hayes was not a praying man as a rule. But he was praying now.

CHAPTER TWO

A WOMAN AND a man, both in scrubs, were waiting with a gurney when Hayes stopped at the curb twenty feet from the doors to Emergency.

Norma went in with Lionel while Hayes parked his truck. He was worried sick for his father—yeah, he and his dad shared a boatload of animosity between them. All that anger and resentment wasn't likely to be resolved anytime soon.

But for Hayes, at least, the love was still there. His dad had been a good dad until Hayes reached his teens. Until then, Lionel was a strict father, but he moderated his toughness with patience and affection.

And then times got harder, money got tighter, and Lionel got worried. His worry translated itself into harsh words and unreasonable demands. Especially when it came to Hayes.

Hayes had never really understood why his dad had seemed to turn against him, in particular. He wasn't even the oldest. But whatever the reason, Lionel had picked out his middle son as the one to pile the heaviest load of resentment on.

No, Lionel had never laid an angry hand on any of his kids. But he was harsh with his words, and he was merciless with his rules, and he never let up with that behavior once he started.

So Hayes had left as soon as he had his high school diploma.

Blinking, he looked down at the key in his hand and realized he'd been standing there by his parked truck for a few minutes at least, just staring off into space, lost in the past.

He locked the doors with his key fob then turned and jogged back to the building.

An hour later, the ER doctor diagnosed Lionel with acute pancreatitis caused by gallstones. He needed immediate laparoscopic surgery to remove his gallbladder.

As the nurses got to work prepping the old man, Hayes slipped outside to take a call from Braden.

The first words out of Braden's mouth were, "I'm at the ranch. Nobody's here except a great big hairy dog that will not let me in the yard—and brother, I have to tell you. The homeplace looks a lot worse than when I left two months ago. What is going on?"

In spite of how bad things were, Hayes almost smiled. "The dog is mine—and you came, after all."

"I'm not staying long," Braden grumbled.

"Fair enough. And here's the thing…" Hayes quickly filled his brother in on the situation.

"That sounds bad."

"It is. It's serious."

"Are you sure he's going to make it?" Braden spoke in a hushed voice.

"Are you kidding? He's too ornery to roll over and die."

Braden grunted. "You got it right about that."

"I should go back in."

"Rylee there?" Braden asked.

"She was at some sales meeting up in Great Falls when Mom called her. But she should be here soon."

"Good. I'm on my way."

Rylee and her fiancée, Shep Dalton, showed up before they wheeled Lionel into surgery. The old man was pretty

out of it by then. He spoke gently to Rylee, which lifted Hayes's spirits a little. Lionel was capable of kindness to his daughter, at least. Maybe there was hope for the old man, after all.

They all four—Norma, Rylee, Shep and Hayes—sat out in the waiting area, hoping for good news. After a tense half hour or so, a nurse emerged to inform them that the simpler, less-invasive laparoscopic surgery wasn't going to do the job. Lionel required an open surgery.

"Doctor Bristol will fill you in on the details later." The nurse spoke directly to Norma then. "Your husband will be in the OR for another hour at a minimum but be prepared for two."

"Is he okay?" Norma asked in a tiny voice.

The nurse gave her a nod and a firm, "Yes. He's in good hands."

Rylee put her arm around their mother and whispered something in her ear.

Norma said, "I know, I know. You're right, honey. Your dad's a tough one."

They all nodded at that, even Shep.

"I hate this," whispered Norma.

Rylee tightened her arm around their mom, hugging her closer as Norma reached out a hand for Hayes. He took it. Shep took Rylee's free hand.

For a while they just sat there, the four of them, no one saying a word, holding on to each other for dear life.

THAT EVENING, CHRISSY Hastings left the inn a few minutes early. She longed to go home to her cute little condo on First Street, to fix herself a simple dinner of pasta and salad, maybe stream something on Netflix and try not to think about Hayes Parker, which was going to take serious effort. Because Hayes, in his worn boots and weath-

ered Stetson, remained as lean, tall and broad-shouldered as ever. Even his faded jeans fit him the way no jeans had a right to do.

And so much for not thinking about Hayes.

With a weary sigh, she got into her Chevy Blazer and headed for her parents' house. Because when she'd begged off on dinner with them last week, she'd promised she'd be there for the evening meal tonight.

Five minutes later, she was pulling up to the curb in front of the meticulously maintained Craftsman-style bungalow where she'd grown up.

Her mom, Patrice, was waiting at the front door in crisp jeans and a red Western shirt. "There you are! Come in, come in." She grabbed Chrissy close in a too-tight hug. Chrissy breathed in the familiar flowery scent of her mom's favorite perfume. The smell of that perfume made her feel equal parts cherished and smothered. "Your father's in the living room…"

"How's my girl?" Her dad folded his copy of the *Billings Gazette* and set it on the arm of his worn leather chair. "So good to see you." He got up and gave her a hug.

She hugged him back good and hard. Her dad owned Hastings Tractor and Supply right there in town. He sold farm machinery, tools and fencing, along with clothing and anything else you might need to keep your farm or ranch going. He was highly respected, and for good reason. Mel Hastings was kind, thoughtful, patient and helpful. He was also a longtime town councilman.

As for her mom, Patrice was good as gold, yet somehow she always managed to get on Chrissy's last nerve.

Tonight was no exception. They no sooner sat down to dinner than her mom started in.

"Sweetheart, I got a postcard from Sam!" her mom announced gleefully. Sam Shaw was Chrissy's ex-husband.

Patrice had always adored Sam. "He says he's doing really well down there in Key West. He says he hopes we're all fine." She leaned in. "Sweetheart, in my heart I just know he misses home—and you."

Chrissy had explained a hundred times that she and Sam had had fertility issues and Sam couldn't deal with that. And so, in the end, they divorced. But her mom still didn't get it—not why Sam would leave her *or* why in the world he would want to go live on a boat in Florida.

"Oh, sweetheart. I just know that someday soon, he will be coming back to you."

Chrissy passed the platter of air-fried chicken thighs to her dad. "Mom, Sam always liked you a lot. It's nice that he sent you a note. But he and I are divorced. It's over between us."

Patrice gave her a look of infinite patience and a sad little sigh. "Of course. You're right. I'm sorry to bring it up."

Chrissy put on a smile. "This chicken looks amazing."

"It's the best," said her dad.

"Life just…moves on so fast these days," said Patrice. "I mean, you and Sam are divorced. And here *you* are, back in town, working at the inn…" She puffed out her cheeks with a hard breath, as though life were just too convoluted for her to comprehend. "I can't keep up with all the changes, with Sam off in Florida *finding* himself or some such. And what about you, going off to one of those tattoo parlors to get words written on your arm that will never wash off?"

Patience, Chrissy thought. "Come on, Mom," she replied in a mild tone. "Enough about the tattoo." Patrice had burst into tears the first time she saw it. "I thought you said you were over it."

"Well, sweetheart, it's only that it really is so…*permanent*, isn't it?" Chrissy said nothing. The silence went

on for several seconds. Finally, Patrice added sheepishly, "Though the sentiment is, er, lovely, sweetie. It truly is."

"Thank you, Mom." For no reason whatsoever, Chrissy thought of Hayes right then. Today, he'd looked older and just possibly wiser. But he still had that smoking hot intensity in those green eyes of his.

As though Patrice had the power to read her daughter's mind, she said, "I suppose you've heard already that Hayes Parker is back in town. I ran into Millie Stafford at the grocery store. She said she saw him driving down Central Avenue in a big, black crew cab with a horse trailer hooked on behind…"

Chrissy stifled an eye roll. "Word does get around fast in this town."

Her mom peered at her sharply. "You knew already that he was here, didn't you?"

Why lie? Her mom would know it if she did. "Yeah, I knew. Hayes stopped at the inn this afternoon." When her mom just looked at her, waiting, Chrissy added, "We spoke for maybe a minute and a half. You know, *Hi, how are you? Have a nice life.* He has a beautiful dog. Her name is Rayna." It could be spelled different ways in different languages. But it meant *queen*—and yeah, she'd looked it up. So what?

Patrice sipped her iced tea. "Well, it's no secret that the Parker ranch is in trouble. And now both Braden and Miles are gone. And Millie also mentioned that Lionel isn't doing well. He's been sick a lot lately."

Chrissy nodded. "Hayes did say that Lionel was ill."

"There you have it, then. *Somebody* had to come help out." Patrice shook her head. "Poor Norma. She must be at her wit's end…"

There was more in that vein. Chrissy tuned her mom out. Her mind wandered to thoughts of Hayes, back in Te-

nacity all over again, having to deal with his sick father, who'd been the reason he left town in the first place.

FORTY-FIVE MINUTES AFTER the nurse came and told them that Lionel needed open gallbladder surgery, Braden appeared. Norma let out a cry at the sight of him and grabbed him in a hug. They brought him up to speed on Lionel's surgery and then they all settled in to wait for the doctor to come and tell them how bad things were.

An hour after that, Dr. Bristol finally came out to report that Lionel was out of surgery and resting comfortably.

"Can we see him?" asked Hayes's mom.

The doctor nodded. "One at a time and very briefly."

Hayes went in third, after his mom and Braden. His dad was pretty out of it—which at least meant that Lionel didn't have the energy to say anything mean. Hayes patted his hand and said, "I'm heading back to the ranch in a bit to handle evening chores."

The old man gave a slow nod. "Good." He said the word so quietly, Hayes had to bend close to hear him. "Real good…"

Hayes went back to the waiting room and Rylee took her turn with their dad.

When Hayes dropped into the chair next to his mom, she said, "They're wheeling a bed into his room for me so that I can stay with him overnight—and for as long as he has to be here."

Hayes wasn't surprised. When his mom put her mind to something—like sharing her sick husband's hospital room—she usually managed to make it happen. Norma Parker was also a saint. She loved her husband through thick and thin, unconditionally and with her whole heart. Enough to spend her nights on a rollaway just to stay by his side. "Okay, Mom. I'll see to things at the ranch."

She eased her hand around his arm and rested her head against his shoulder. "Thank you, Hayes. It's good to have you home. I just wish you were here under better circumstances."

"Don't we all, Mom," said Braden, who was sitting on Norma's other side.

Hayes and Braden hung around until Rylee and Shep went home, and their mom was settled in with Lionel. By then it was getting pretty late.

The brothers walked out to the parking lot together. In the bright light beaming down on them from the LED lamps overhead, Hayes thought Braden looked older than his thirty-five years.

Hayes knew what his brother was thinking. "Go." Hayes clapped him on the shoulder. "It's okay."

Braden shook his head. "I'll go back to the ranch with you, help with the chores, stay the night."

"If you do that, you'll never leave."

They stared at each other. Finally Braden said, "Well, it *is* your turn."

"Damn right it is." Hayes said it with conviction, though they both knew coming back to Tenacity was the last thing he'd ever planned to do.

"Listen, Hayes. I mean this. I want you to call me if there's—"

"You know I will."

Braden stretched out his long arms. "Get over here."

They shared a quick hug and some back-slapping.

Five minutes later, Braden was gone, and Hayes climbed in his crew cab for the drive back to the ranch.

When he got there, he found Rayna waiting in front of the house. She was still inside the fence. He told her what a good girl she was, giving her plenty of scratches and strokes. Then he fed her. For himself, he heated up some

leftovers he found in the fridge. Once he'd straightened up the kitchen, he went outside again and headed for the barn to see what needed doing.

No surprise, it was a lot.

He was up past midnight feeding stock, putting at least a few escaped cattle back behind fences where they belonged and taking care of various other chores that should have been done long ago. He hadn't gotten anywhere near checking the books on his dad's old computer yet, but even in the middle of the night, with the moon beaming down on him, making everything softer and prettier, it was still painfully obvious that the End of the Road Ranch was in deep trouble.

At 12:45 a.m. when he finally climbed the stairs and settled, exhausted, into his narrow childhood bed, he couldn't get to sleep. As he rolled over on his back and stared up at the shadows on the ceiling, he reminded himself that nobody ever said ranch life was easy.

He crawled from the bed at five and headed out to tackle the morning chores—and to discover an even longer list of repairs and neglected tasks that had to be done yesterday.

At ten a.m., he knocked off, took a quick shower and drove into town to drop off the room key he'd never used. He was at the inn for maybe ten minutes total. The whole time he kept expecting to see Chrissy again, anticipating the moment when he'd turn around and find himself looking right into those big brown eyes.

That moment came just as he was leaving. He spotted her over by a potted ficus tree, discussing something with a tall, skinny guy—a hotel employee judging by his maroon slacks and vest. She glanced over and saw Hayes looking at her.

He nodded. She nodded back—and then she resumed her conversation with the other man.

Hayes went out the glass doors feeling lonely, wondering what might have happened if she'd had a minute to chat with him.

Outside, he shook his head at his own damn foolishness. What did he and Chrissy Hastings have to say to each other anyway? Nothing, that's what. He hardly knew her anymore.

Back at the ranch, he found his mom in the kitchen putting groceries in the fridge. "I ran into an old friend up at the hospital and I hitched a ride home with her to pick up the Suburban."

He teased, "Same Suburban you've been driving since before I left town?"

"That's right. It runs great and gets the job done and I'm holding on to it. We stopped at the grocery store in Bronco. I bought enough food to keep you from starving."

"That's all just for me?"

"Hon, I'm going back up to be with your father."

Hayes wasn't surprised. "How's he doing?"

"Well, he's not happy being stuck in the hospital…"

"Translation, he's crabby and short-tempered."

His mother granted him a gentle, accepting smile. "Doctor Bristol says your father will be staying right there at Bronco Valley Hospital for the next five or six days, minimum."

And there was more. It would be six to eight weeks before Lionel would be able to get around comfortably.

Norma went on, "Doctor Bristol says we have to be realistic. Given your dad's age and how sick he's been, it's going to be quite a while before he'll be out herding livestock and mending fences. How about a big, fat roast beef sandwich with my special potato salad?"

"Thanks, Mom. That sounds amazing."

"Hayes, I am sorry," she said when they sat down to eat.

"I should stick around today, take care of my garden, thaw some of the meat in the deep freeze and do some cooking for you. I should give you a hand with the mountain of work that has to be done around here, but I—"

"You need to be with Dad right now. Mom, I understand. I really do. I'm not an eighteen-year-old fool anymore. Dad needs you. As for me, I'll figure things out around here just fine."

She reached across the old pine table and put her hand on his. "You're a good son. The best. Your dad was always too hard on you. I love that man with all my heart, but he really messed up when he drove you away."

"Yes, he did," Hayes said darkly. But then he shrugged. "It was years ago. And we all know I was no saint."

Back then, the tougher Lionel was on him, the more Hayes had acted up. Once he'd gone "surfing" on the hood of a friend's pickup. At sixty miles an hour. Another time, he'd broken into the Grizzly Bar at four in the morning and helped himself to a lot of beer. A sheriff's deputy who'd once worked as a cowhand for Lionel had brought Hayes home in disgrace. Worst of all, Hayes was so drunk, he kept falling down any time the deputy let go of him.

And then there was the night he decided to run away after a fight with Lionel. It was cold out. He'd started a fire to keep warm and the wind had come up. A couple of acres had been burned to black ash before he, his dad, his mom, his brothers and his sister, too, had managed to put the fire out.

"Well, your father was too rough on you," his mother said, waving a wedge of dill pickle. "And you rebelled."

"Yes, I did."

"Sometimes I'm afraid you two won't make up before he…" She looked away. Her lips were pressed together, her chin quivering.

"Mom…" Now he was the one reaching across, squeezing *her* hand. "He'll be okay. He's tough."

She faced him then and whispered, "If you hadn't come home when you did yesterday, I never could have gotten him up to Bronco in time."

"You've got friends you can call, and you would've called them. And you could've called 911. Fire and Rescue would have come to deal with him—and anyway, he's getting the care he needs now. He's going to come through this. He's going to be fine."

She sniffed and straightened her shoulders. "You're right. Of course, you are."

Hayes rose and went around the table to her side. "You've got that look…" He held out his hand.

She took it. "Like I need a hug?"

"That would be the one." He pulled her up and wrapped his arms around her. "It will be all right, Mom."

"Yeah," she whispered, holding on tight.

Twenty minutes later, Norma headed back to Bronco. Once she was gone, Hayes called one of his high school buddies. Jake Marshall had been driving the pickup the night Hayes went surfing on the hood.

After they caught up with each other a little, Hayes laid the truth right out there. "So anyway. I'm back here in Tenacity because my dad's in the hospital and the End of the Road Ranch is nothing short of a disaster."

Jake chuckled. "Remember you used to call that place the *End of My Rope Ranch*?"

"Yeah, I remember. Because it was—and it still is, now more than ever…" Hayes hesitated. He was working up the gall to beg for help.

But then Jake said, "I'll make a few calls and be there in a bit."

"Man." Hayes swallowed a hard knot of emotion. "Thank you. I owe you."

"You'd do the same for me. See you soon."

Jake wasn't kidding. He showed up an hour later. And with him he had two of their other high school pals, Beck Douglas and Austin O'Connor.

The four of them went to work. By six that evening, they'd contained all the loose chickens, rounded up several head of wandering cattle, fixed a whole bunch of downed fences, cut a field of alfalfa and even repaired the drooping sign at the main gate.

Norma had left a couple of rotisserie chickens in the fridge, along with plenty of coleslaw and potato salad. The four men scarfed down the food and then took turns in the shower.

"It's Friday night," announced Austin, once they were all cleaned up and gathered around the kitchen table enjoying a beer. "You all know what that means."

Beck raised his can of Bud. "To the Grizzly!" he toasted.

Jake snickered as he reached down to give Rayna a good scratch around the neck. "Hayes, we've got good news for you."

"I could use a little of that. Lay it on me."

Jake said, "Ten years ago, old man Kelsy sold the Grizzly to a guy named Dale Clutterbuck. Dale has no memory of that time you broke in and guzzled all the beer."

Hayes actually smiled then. "Hold on a minute. Are you saying that the new owner won't shoot me on sight?"

Austin nodded. "That is exactly what he's saying. Finish your Bud. The Grizzly is waiting."

AT THE TENACITY INN, Chrissy was working late on what she had begun to think of as the Worst Day Ever in the History of Bad Days.

It was just one near disaster after another at work. The inn was full for once, mostly because of two mini-conventions, one for a local fertilizer company, the other a couples retreat.

The fertilizer group had somehow managed to turn in an incorrect head count. Instead of thirty employees, there were forty. As for the couples retreat, they were an emotional bunch. They huddled together in small groups, many of them crying, talking much too loudly about their personal issues and their unsatisfying sex lives.

Chrissy did her best to keep up with the situation, running herself ragged making sure all the meals and snacks were delicious, attractive and served on time.

Somehow, though, she made it work. She and the inn's small staff managed to get everyone fed and on to the next meeting without any major screwups. Ruby McKinley, who'd moved to town a couple of years after college and worked the front desk, came to Chrissy's rescue more than once, carrying messages back and forth to the kitchen while Chrissy tried to herd one group in and the other out of the main dining space.

By six, all the meals had finally been served. Chrissy supervised a swift cleanup and left the inn at a little before seven.

Looking forward to a giant glass of wine and a long soak in the bathtub, Chrissy drove straight to her condo on First Street.

But when she let herself in the door, she heard the strangest dripping sound. Bewildered, she stopped just beyond her small entry hall and stared, disbelieving, across the great room to the pretty kitchen area with its white

quartz counters, sage green cabinets and beautiful over-sized pendant lighting.

Her mind couldn't quite comprehend what she was seeing. Water was falling out of the ceiling…

CHAPTER THREE

IT TOOK HER a minute or two of standing there, stunned, with her mouth hanging open, to process what she saw.

Disaster.

That's what it was. Complete disaster.

Water flowed down the pendant lights, splashing onto her quartz countertops, spreading out from there, trickling down her gorgeous cabinets, dripping onto her cute little farm-style table, only to flow off of it and pool on the wood floor.

The building was small, containing four condos total, two up, two down. Evidently, the one above hers had an overflowing tub or a burst pipe.

First priority—flip the breaker. Then pack up what she could and get out.

Staying close to the wall, she darted to the side and through the square of hallway to her tiny laundry room. The breaker box was behind the door. She flipped the main switch, and her place went dark, though the small window over the laundry sink let in the early evening light.

Already the ceiling in there had darkened with a spreading water stain. The overhead light fixture was dripping. She pulled out her phone and called the association that managed the shared areas of the building. The call went to voicemail, so she left a harried message with her name and address, along with a brief description of the problem.

After that, well, what could she do but pack fast and get out?

Twenty minutes later, she'd filled two suitcases. Trying not to think of all her pretty things that would never be the same, she darted back into the great room. Moving as fast as she could along the wall, lugging her suitcases, she quickly reached her small foyer. From there it was only a few steps to the front door and escape.

Outside, she found Darren and Lily Kizer, the couple who owned the other downstairs condo. They stood huddled together, luggage and overflowing boxes waiting at their feet. Her neighbors looked as shell-shocked as Chrissy felt. Unfortunately, the guy who lived in the condo with the leak was nowhere to be seen.

"I went up there and knocked," Darren said. "I knocked hard and for a long time. Nobody answered."

Just then, the guy from the building management company drove up. Ten minutes later, he'd turned off the water and the power to the building and advised Chrissy and her fellow condo owners to call their insurance companies and arrange to stay elsewhere for now.

Lily dared to ask, "How long can we expect to be sleeping *elsewhere*?"

The man from the management company had no idea, but hedged a guess that it could be a while.

"Contact your insurance company ASAP—and your agent, too. The insurance company will send an adjuster out to assess the damage and then they should pay up within thirty days. Your agent should help you navigate the whole process. And the sooner you get to work drying things out, the better. You don't want mold and mildew on top of everything else."

Feeling nothing short of numb, Chrissy called her in-

surance company's hotline. They promised that an adjuster would contact her within the next three days.

"Three days?" She might have screamed those words. "Can't you get someone over here tomorrow?"

The operator made soothing noises but no promises.

Chrissy loaded her suitcases into the back of her Blazer—and then couldn't decide what to do next.

The inn was full, so she couldn't stay there—not that she really wanted to, anyway. She worked there at least forty hours a week and had no desire to sleep there, too.

She could call a friend.

But that seemed unnecessary. Because her mom and dad would be happy to have her stay with them tonight. And realistically, she was going to end up with them for the next several weeks anyway.

Chrissy cringed at the thought. Several weeks at her mom's house, sleeping in her childhood bedroom, listening to her mom's well-meaning never-ending advice. Did it get any grimmer than that?

Sometimes life just sucked.

Resigned, she got in behind the wheel, started the engine—and then let her head drop to the steering wheel. Sleeping at her mom's house...

No. She simply could not face that yet.

Maybe a drink would help—possibly two. Chrissy rarely drank. But tonight, she needed a little good cheer before making herself deal with her mother's relentless concern for her life and her future. Straightening in her seat, she put on her seat belt and eased out of her parking space behind her building.

At the Grizzly Bar on Central Avenue, warm light spilled from the windows on either side of the orange door. She could hear laughter and honky-tonk music coming from inside.

Her spirits lifted a little. A drink at the Grizzly. Just what she needed, lots of people around her having a good time. Was a good time contagious? She hoped so.

A block down from the bar, she found a parking space. Jumping out of the Blazer, she settled her purse strap on her shoulder and followed the sounds of laughter and music back to the saloon with the orange door.

Inside, the laughter was louder and so was the jukebox. Everyone seemed to be talking at once. Several people were shouting.

She felt a bit foolish, still dressed for work in her white shirt, maroon vest and skirt with practical pumps to match. Well, too bad. She'd had no time to change, given the immediate problem of grabbing her things and getting out before the flood brought a section of ceiling down on her head.

About then, she spotted Hayes, sitting in a corner booth with three of his buddies from high school. He locked eyes on her a second after she saw him.

Their gazes held and Chrissy wanted to throw her head back and scream her frustration at the antler chandelier overhead. She couldn't even have a drink at the local honky-tonk without running into the one man in town she really would rather avoid.

This was simply not her day or night. She wanted to spin on her heel and head right back out the way she'd come in.

But no. Her distressingly hot first love was not driving her out of the Grizzly. At least not until she'd had a drink to fortify herself against the reality of her current situation.

She scanned the packed room. There had to be a seat for her somewhere—and then she saw it. There was one empty stool at the bar.

Luck was with her for once, and she got there before anyone else did. She climbed on that stool with a sigh of

relief and hung her shoulder bag on the convenient hook down by her knees.

The big, bearded guy behind the bar came right over. "Welcome to the Grizzly. I'm Dale."

She recognized him. "Dale Clutterbuck, right? The owner."

Dale's smile was contagious. "That's me."

She offered her hand. He took it. "I'm Chrissy Hastings," she said.

"Mel's daughter, right?"

"You got it."

"What can I get for you, Chrissy?"

"Margarita, please."

Dale served her and headed back down the bar to fill other orders.

Chrissy drank half her margarita in two sips. It didn't help much. She still felt like bursting into tears of misery and frustration. But she kept a big smile on her face, sipped again and promised herself that she wasn't going to get weepy. She would drink her two-drink limit—slowly—and eventually she would feel ready to head for her folks' place.

A hand closed on her shoulder.

She stiffened and slowly turned her head. Now she was looking into the bloodshot eyes of a guy she'd never seen before. Clearly intoxicated, he gave her a woozy smile. "Hey there, gorgeous. Where you been all my life?"

"Take your hand off my shoulder please," she replied in a voice of velvet over steel.

It worked. The drunk let go of her shoulder. But he didn't step back. "Listen. I'm here and so're you." Breathing ninety proof, he leaned in even closer. "What does that tell you, baby?"

"That I suddenly wish I was somewhere else?"

The drunk scowled. "Huh?"

It was exactly the wrong response after Chrissy's terrible, awful, endless day. She took her purse off the hook, spun on the stool and faced him directly. "Sometimes when you see a woman alone it's because being alone is exactly what she wants."

The guy leaned closer and sneered, "Pretty lady, you got a bad attitude."

She clutched the strap of her purse tightly in one hand just in case she had to fend him off with it and matched her annoyance to his. "And you can't take a hint. Let me be perfectly clear. Leave. Me. Alone."

About then, she realized that the Grizzly had gone pin-drop quiet.

Down the bar, Dale called out to the drunk man who wouldn't go away. "What'd I tell you, Roger? Time to head on home!"

Roger sneered. "I got no wheels. You know that."

"It's not that far. Call a friend to come and get you, or start walkin'."

Roger grunted and held his ground. Worse, he grabbed Chrissy's arm.

HAYES HAD BEEN trying his best not to let his gaze wander in Chrissy's direction. But he'd known from the moment she came through the orange door that something was wrong. Yeah, it had been forever since she was his girl, but still. He'd known her so well. She might be all grown up now, but she was still Chrissy.

And tonight, for whatever reason, she was not happy.

When she first came in, their eyes had met for just those few seconds. Then she looked away and didn't look back.

He got the message. She was miserable. But as far as she was concerned, that was none of his business and he should leave her alone.

So he had.

Until now. Because no way could he let some drunk fool get up in her face like that—and worse, put his hands on her.

Hayes slid from the booth.

"Hayes, you want backup?" asked Beck.

He shook his head. "I got this."

He took two steps and then paused as Chrissy got down off her stool, drew herself up to her full five foot, seven inch height and smiled with her teeth showing. Pulling up even taller, she whispered something in the drunk's ear.

The drunk blinked and jerked back like she'd slapped him. "What'd you say?" he growled as he let go of her arm.

She leaned right toward the guy again and whispered some more.

Whatever she said worked. Roger put up both hands and backed away three steps. And then, staggering a bit, he turned and went out the orange door.

When the door swung shut behind him, the dead-quiet bar erupted in applause. There was also whistling and a number of shouts of "way to go" in appreciation and re-spect for the way Chrissy had shut the drunk down.

In response to the applause, Chrissy put on her big-gest, brightest smile. Yeah, Hayes knew that smile was fake. But it dazzled him, nonetheless. Finally, still smil-ing, Chrissy took a bow.

By then, Hayes was at her side. He asked quietly, "You okay?"

"I am just fine." She smiled on through gritted teeth.

"Look, let me buy you a drink and we can—"

"Maybe some other time." She said it softly, gently. He could see it was taking all the will she possessed to keep her brave smile in place. "I have to go." She hooked her

purse on her shoulder. "You take care, Hayes." And she started for the door.

Hayes glanced toward the table where his friends waited. He tipped his head toward Chrissy's retreating back. They got the message and remained in the booth. Chrissy went out the door. Beck tossed him his hat as he passed them. Settling it on his head, he followed Chrissy from the bar.

By then, it was dark out. The Central Avenue streetlights had come on. Hayes just stood there on the sidewalk for a moment, hanging back. Chrissy was halfway across the street by then, probably headed for the bus-stop bench in its plexiglass shelter. When she got there, she dropped to the bench, pressed her knees together, braced her forearms on her lap and stared at the sidewalk beneath her feet.

Still, he lingered by the orange door, watching over her from a distance just in case Roger reappeared. Eventually, Chrissy looked up and spotted him. For several seconds, she glared defiantly at him.

And then, blowing out her cheeks as if keeping up the animosity was just too much work, she dropped her gaze and stared down at her shoes again.

He crossed the street. "Mind if I share your bench with you?"

She slanted him one of those are-you-kidding-me looks. But then she sighed. "This bench is public property. I have no say as to who sits on it."

He swept off his hat. "I'm going to take that to mean, 'Sure, Hayes. Have a seat.'"

She gave him a dramatic eye roll, but she didn't object, so he sat as far away from her as the bench allowed and put his hat in his lap.

Neither of them spoke for several minutes.

Eventually, a guy came out of the Grizzly and headed

down the street whistling. Two women emerged, laughing, their arms around each other. They went the other way.

Hayes dared to slide a glance at Chrissy just as she snuck a quick look at him. Tears gleamed in her eyes.

Angrily, she swiped them away. "I don't know what I'm doing," she said, her voice low enough he had to lean her way to hear it. "My parents adored my ex-husband and sometimes I think that my mother still doesn't really believe that Sam and I are actually divorced. I'm just…well, I mean, I'm figuring things out slowly, but some days are hard. Today was the worst ever." She tipped her head to the sky and let out a groan. "Oh, why am I telling you all this?" she moaned.

"Hey," he suggested gently. "It's okay. I'm here and I'm willing to listen."

She laughed, but it wasn't a happy sound.

And then she turned those big brown eyes directly on Hayes. He felt that look like a shock of electricity shooting right through him. "That guy in the bar…?"

"Yeah?"

"He scared me."

"He was an ass, and you took care of him just fine."

She giggled then, wrinkling her nose at him like she had a secret at the same time as her eyes looked so sad. "Want to know how I backed that sucker off?"

"You bet I do."

"I confessed in graphic terms to having an STD."

He almost burst out laughing, but somehow he managed to play it straight. "Impressive."

"Thank you—but for a minute there, I didn't know what would happen. He freaked me out. It's just…my life, you know?"

"No, Chrissy. I don't know. What about your life?"

"My life is one disaster after another."

"Maybe it just seems that way today."

"Hayes. It *is* that way. Just take my word for it."

"All right. But I'm saying it again. What you did in there was perfect."

"Thank you," she replied in a small voice.

He shrugged. "It's only the truth."

She gave him a nod and said nothing else. He got it. She still wanted to be left alone. He should go.

But somehow, he couldn't bring himself to leave her sitting there alone.

CHRISSY REALLY DIDN'T want to lay all her troubles on her long-ago boyfriend.

But he was here, and he was being so great. And she really needed to talk to someone.

And so, sitting at the bus stop across from the Grizzly at nine thirty on that warm August night, Chrissy told Hayes everything about her terrible, awful, endless day.

It took a while, but he sat there and listened to all of it. He listened like he cared, like it mattered to him that her workday had been its own special kind of hell, that her cute condo was now a disaster zone, and she was about to move in with her parents again.

"Tell you what," he said when she finally fell silent. "Why don't you just come and stay at the ranch? My brothers are gone and my sister lives in Bronco now. That leaves more than one empty bedroom upstairs. You can take your pick."

She looked at him without speaking for a long time. He didn't try to break the silence. Finally, she said, "I couldn't." Although staying at the Parker ranch seemed a lot less depressing than moving in with her parents.

"Why not? I promise you, Chrissy, I'm not going to

get in your space or anything." He put up a hand, a witness swearing an oath. "Friends only, you have my word."

"I believe you." And she did, she realized as she said the words. "But won't your parents have something to say about your high school girlfriend moving in with you?"

"Nope. My dad's in the hospital after major surgery and won't be home for a week or so. And my mom made them wheel a bed into his room for her. She won't be home much in the next week or so either—not that it will matter to her. She's always loved you. For now, I'm alone at the house. You might as well use one of those empty rooms."

She set her purse on the bench between them. "I can't believe I'm actually considering it." But she was. Because right now moving in with her long-lost first love felt like a much better option than going back to her parents' house again.

She might be able to get a room at the inn once the weekend was over. But then she'd be living at her place of work, which made her uncomfortable—not to mention it could get expensive.

Who knew how long repairs would take at her place or how much her insurance would end up paying?

Yeah, she and Hayes had a painful history with each other. And he was still one hot cowboy.

Maybe too hot. Maybe that she was even considering staying at the ranch house with him was just asking for trouble.

Hot trouble, she couldn't help thinking.

And then she frowned because…how could she be thinking about having sex with her ex at a time like this?

She was losing it, no doubt about that.

"Look," Hayes said. "If staying at the ranch doesn't work out for you, your parents aren't going anywhere. You can ditch plan B and head for your mom's house."

The more she considered the idea of a room at the ranch, the more appeal it had—Hayes Parker's hotness aside. "I would want to pitch in, help with chores and with meals."

"Works for me. The ranch is a big job. I can use all the help I can get."

"And I would pay for the room."

"No. Uh-uh. You help out with the house, pitch in with groceries, do some cooking, that's more than enough."

"But I—"

He put up a hand to silence her. "Stop. You pitch in. That's enough."

She knew that look in his eye. He would not take her money for the room. "Thank you, Hayes."

For that she got a quick nod. Then he went right on to the next question. "You need to go back to your place tonight?"

She shook her head. "I packed some bags. The good news is I'm not on the schedule at the inn tomorrow or Sunday. So I'll have time this weekend to start dealing with the mess at my condo."

"So then. You have a plan."

"More or less, yes."

He laughed then. The sound was warm and somehow private—just between the two of them. That laugh stirred memories better left alone.

And apparently, Hayes thought so, too. The laugh faded. He asked briskly, "Where are you parked?"

"Up the street."

"I'm in the lot behind the bar. I'll get my crew cab and you can fall in behind me."

"Okay."

He rose. She looked up at him in his worn jeans and black T-shirt. All cowboy, lean and tall and ready for any-

thing—including coming to the rescue of the girl he left behind. He started to turn.

"Hayes?"

"Yeah?"

"I'll say it again. Thank you."

He touched the brim of his hat. "Anytime, Chrissy. You know that."

"BEST TO TAKE Rylee's room," Hayes suggested, pushing open the door to the bedroom at the end of the upstairs hall. "It's got that window with a view of the mountains—yeah, they're way in the distance, but on a clear night, they look real pretty under the stars." Rylee's room was also the farthest from his room—the one he used to share with Miles back in the day. He figured she'd be more comfortable off to herself.

She caught her lower lip between those pretty white teeth and worried it nervously. "You sure Rylee won't mind me moving her stuff around, taking over her space?"

"Rylee took everything she wanted when she moved to Bronco. It really isn't her room anymore."

"Well, then." Chrissy was nodding. "Okay. I'll take it."

"Great." He carried her suitcases into the room and set them on the blue rug by the bed. "There's only the one bathroom up here. I hope you don't mind sharing."

"No, of course not. This is so great." She tried a teasing smile. "I promise not to hog the bathroom."

"Just make yourself comfortable. I mean that."

"I will—and thank you again."

With a nod, he left her.

CHRISSY HAD MORE than a little trouble sleeping that night. She worried about her condo. How long would it be be-

fore she could move back in? Would her insurance cover all the damage? How much might it end up costing her?

And it wasn't only her ruined condo that kept her awake. She couldn't stop second-guessing her decision to stay here in this house with Hayes sleeping in the room down the hall. It was years ago, what they had. They were kids then. They were two different people now.

But still, it felt so…intimate. The two of them, sharing a house after all this time.

Way past midnight, she finally drifted off. And she woke to her phone's alarm clock, which she'd set for five a.m.

In the bathroom, she splashed water on her face, ran a brush through her hair and secured it in a low ponytail. Back in her room, she dressed in jeans and a pink T-shirt with *Cowgirls don't cry—but you might if you cross one* printed on the front.

Downstairs the coffee was already made. She poured herself a mugful and stood sipping it, staring out the window over the sink. There was a light on in the barn, which meant Hayes was already out doing morning chores.

It would be a few hours before she could try to get hold of her insurance agent and the water damage restoration people, so she ran back upstairs to put on an old pair of sneakers.

A few minutes later, she found Hayes feeding the horses. He said he was on top of things and that his friends would be there in an hour or so.

"Have you gathered the eggs yet?" she asked.

One side of his mouth lifted in a grin. She knew he was remembering the old days. He used to let her gather eggs in the evenings sometimes when she'd come over to hang out with him. Mostly, they tried to stay away from the house because his dad was constantly on his case. Lio-

nel Parker had always treated Chrissy like a queen—and his wife and daughter, too. But he was hard on the boys, Hayes most of all.

"All right," said Hayes. "You go on and gather eggs—and don't let those chickens peck your hands off."

"I won't. I've got a special way with the hens."

He gave a little snort of laughter. "Or so you always said."

Two hours later, she returned to the house ahead of Hayes and started cooking breakfast. She got lucky and found some potatoes in the fridge to brown in a skillet with onions and olive oil. She also fried up enough bacon and sausage and cracked enough eggs for Austin, Beck and Jake, too. The boys had driven up a while ago and gone right to work alongside Hayes.

She was standing at the stove turning the skillet potatoes, expecting the four of them to come in loud and hungry any minute now, when she heard the front door open and close. "Food's ready!" she called out over her shoulder. "And the coffee's fresh!"

Footsteps approached through the great room and stopped stock-still several feet behind her. "Chrissy? My dear, sweet Lord, is that you?"

Chrissy set down the slotted spatula in the spoon rest and turned. "Norma! Hey…"

Norma carried four plastic grocery bags, two hooked on each hand. She dipped and set them on the kitchen floor and then rushed around the high, narrow table that served as a kitchen island to grab Chrissy in a tight, warm hug. "Oh, my heavens," she whispered, tears in her voice. "I never thought I would see you in my kitchen again." Norma's hug got even tighter.

When Hayes's mom let her go, they just stood there

staring at each other. Norma's eyes were misty with emotion. Chrissy knew hers were, too.

Then Norma asked in a hushed whisper, "So then, you and Hayes...?"

Chrissy slowly shook her head. "It's not like that." Quickly, she explained about her flooded condo and Hayes's offer of a room at the ranch for as long as she needed it. "So, I'm staying in Rylee's old room as of last night, intending to help out where I can. From what I've been told, dealing with the water damage at my place is going to take a while. So once you bring Lionel home, well, we'll see how it goes."

Norma braced her hands on her generous hips. "And here I was hoping that you two had gotten back together again."

"No," Chrissy said firmly. "He's helping me out and I really appreciate it—as long as you're okay with my staying here, too?"

"Am I *okay* with it? Are you kidding me? I'm so glad to see you here." Norma beamed. "Even if you and Hayes aren't going to be getting back together, it sure is good to have you with us on the ranch again." She rounded the island to grab her grocery bags and started putting stuff away as she explained that she'd left the hospital early to buy groceries so she could stock the fridge. "Now that Hayes's friends are helping out, I want to be sure there's plenty in the pantry to keep their bellies full."

"You must have left Bronco before dawn."

"You know me. I like to get up early and get stuff done."

"But, Norma, it's a lot, driving back and forth from Bronco."

"It's not so bad."

"Listen, I'm going to pitch in with food, too. That way you don't have to make the drive as often."

"Oh, now, sweetie…"

Chrissy held up her slotted spatula for silence. "Don't argue. I have to do something to hold up my end here."

"There's chops, roasts, you-name-it in the deep freeze. And vegetables from my garden, too. Use them."

What could Chrissy say? "Thank you. I will."

"And let me give you some cash for—"

"Absolutely not. Norma, I need to contribute, and you need to let me."

There was more hugging before Chrissy went back to the stove.

The boys came in a couple of minutes later. They drank lots of coffee and shoveled in the food.

During the quick meal, Hayes said, "Chrissy, the boys and me are going to follow you to your place, deal with what we can water-wise and help you get more of your things out of there."

Chrissy shook her head—because no way was that happening. "I'll take care of my place. You guys have way more than enough to do here."

"Come on." Hayes gave her one of those looks of his, the kind that used to have her agreeing to any old thing he wanted her to do. "We can get a lot done," he coaxed. "And we can do it fast."

She stared him square in the eye. "You're letting me stay here. It's way more than enough. I have the whole day off to start getting a handle on the disaster at my place."

"But I—"

"Stop." She pointed a slice of bacon at him. "Thank you, but I've got this."

Hayes let it go. When the men were done eating, they cleared off their places. Then Chrissy and Norma shooed them back out to work.

Once they were gone, Chrissy started loading the dish-

washer. She was filling the top rack with coffee mugs when Norma asked, "Don't you have calls to make?"

"I do. And as soon as I clean up the kitchen, I'll—"

"Nope. Uh-uh. I'll take care of the cleanup. You need to get the water out of your condo today if at all possible. You know it doesn't take long for mold and mildew to set in and then all your problems are multiplied."

Chrissy groaned. "You're freaking me out, Norma."

"That is my intention. You need to get on top of the problem." Norma reached around her and shut the dishwasher. Then Hayes's mom took her by the shoulders and turned her away from the kitchen counter. "Now start making calls."

"Fine." Chrissy tried her insurance agent first. A woman answered the phone and promised that Chrissy's agent would call her back within the hour.

The agent reached out fifteen minutes later with numbers for the nearest highly rated water abatement companies—and to tell her she needed to get over to her condo and drain the pipes by turning on all the faucets and repeatedly flushing the toilets. "Wear rubber gloves and boots," he suggested. "I'm guessing it's wet in there."

"No kidding," she muttered.

"You have your list of all your household goods and equipment and their value, right?"

She was able to say yes to that. Her dad was big on being prepared. And when she'd bought and furnished her condo, he'd insisted she make a detailed list of all her things and their value. At the time, she'd thought going to all that trouble was a bit ridiculous. But right now, she kind of wished her dad was at her side so that she could hug him.

Before she headed for her condo, she called the water abatement companies. Both were in Bronco. The first call went to voicemail. An actual human answered the sec-

ond one. He asked questions about the damage and about her insurance company—because she needed to get the adjuster out immediately so the water damage company could create a plan and submit it for payment.

It all went around in a circle, and she was dizzy just thinking about it. Next, the water abatement guy warned her that mold and mildew would set in within twenty-four to forty-eight hours if she didn't get the water out of her home.

By then she was so frustrated with the impossibility of the task ahead of her that she got snippy with the poor guy. "Yeah, my high school boyfriend's mom already explained about the mold and mildew, thank you."

She hung up. Her last call was to the condo management representative who assured her she was cleared to get back into her unit. The power was still off, but in the daytime, that wouldn't be an issue.

When she told Norma where she was headed, Hayes's mom disappeared down the hall and came back with two big rolling suitcases, rubber gloves and rain boots.

Norma said. "Lionel and I were always planning to go on one of those cruises. Never has happened so far, but at least we bought the luggage. And there are a few duffel-type bags inside these big ones. Whatever you can carry that isn't wet, bring it back here—in fact, wet clothes should be fine too. You can just throw them in the washer. Take some big plastic trash bags to bring them back in."

"Oh, Norma!" Chrissy grabbed the older woman in a fierce hug. "Thank you."

Norma guided a loose swatch of hair behind Chrissy's ear—and said, "I'm coming with you to help."

Chrissy just shook her head. "I'm on it. Don't worry."

Norma clucked her tongue. "Your dad is the one with the clout in this town. He is on the town council, after all.

I'm betting he could really get things moving on the water abatement and insurance front. Just call him."

"I will."

Norma still wasn't satisfied. "Do it now." And then she just stood there and waited.

Chrissy gave in and made the call—to the number at her dad's store.

"Tenacity Tractor and Supply. This is Myron." Myron Betts had worked at the store for as long as Chrissy could remember.

"Hey, Myron. It's—"

"Miss Chrissy! How you doing?"

"Just great," she lied with enthusiasm. "Listen, is my dad around?"

"You bet. Hang on."

A moment later, her dad came on the line. "How's my girl?"

Her throat clutched, "Well, Dad, I..." Norma was watching her, those green eyes so much like Hayes's eyes urging her to tell her father everything. She gave in enough to admit, "I've got a big problem."

"Well, I'm glad you called, Sugar Bee." The endearment made her tear up all over again. Her dad had always loved Sugar Bee apples. He'd started calling Chrissy his little Sugar Bee when she was still in diapers. "If you've got a problem," he said, "let's get it solved."

It all came pouring out then—the burst pipe upstairs and all that happened after.

Her dad listened without a single interruption until she said, "That's it. That's my problem."

"Don't you worry for a minute," he instructed. "I get that it's bad. But you and me, we're going to jump right on this problem. I'm not going to promise you it won't take a while, but I'll see to it that everything is good as new

without you suffering a big gouge in your savings account. Now, have you got rubber boots and gloves?"

She gave Norma a wobbly smile. "I do, yes."

"Let's get after it then. Where are you?"

She considered trying to bypass that question. Not because her dad would make a big deal of her staying at the Parker place, but because he would tell her mom. There was no predicting how Patrice would respond to the news.

But then, who did Chrissy think she was kidding? It was such a small town. One way or another, her mom would find out where Chrissy was staying.

And that was not in any way a problem for Chrissy, she reminded herself. She was thirty-three years old. Where she slept was her business, and her mom would just have to deal with that.

"I ran into Hayes last night, Dad," she explained. "We struck a deal. I'm staying at the ranch and I'm helping out around the ranch house by way of saying thank you."

"Ah," said her dad. Then he added, "You know you're welcome to stay with us. Your mom would love the chance to fuss over you."

Exactly, Chrissy thought. "Thanks, Dad. But I'm fine at the ranch."

"Well, all right, then." He left it at that, which she greatly appreciated. "Meet you at your condo in twenty minutes?"

"I'll be there."

Her dad showed up at the condo in his big crew cab with a trailer hitched on behind. The two of them put on their rubber boots and gloves and made a quick pass of the rooms in her unit just to get an idea of the damage.

Her dad started making calls. Chrissy flushed the toilets and turned on all the faucets to get the water out of

the pipes. After that, she made a couple of trips out to her Blazer for the suitcases and the box of big plastic bags.

The insurance agent, the adjuster and the guy from the water abatement company appeared as she was filling the suitcases and bags. Because when Mel Hastings made the calls, stuff got done.

Around ten, a couple of burly guys from her dad's store showed up with another truck and lots of packing boxes. They carried her furniture out. Some of it was unsalvageable and would go to the dump. Everything else, her dad would keep in his warehouse until her place was back together again.

By late afternoon, Chrissy felt ready to drop. But it had been a very productive day. The water abatement crew had the standing water cleared out. Every window was open. They had their own generators in their enormous truck to run all of their equipment—including high-powered blower fans to speed up the drying process.

Also, the condo management company had contacted the owner of the unit above Chrissy's. Another abatement crew had worked up there for most of the day. From them, Chrissy's dad had learned that most of the building's walls and ceilings would have to be ripped out to the studs and replaced. Chrissy knew she wouldn't be moving back in for a while.

Late that afternoon, when Chrissy hugged her dad and thanked him repeatedly, he kissed the top of her head and promised her everything was going to work out fine.

"Just give it time," he whispered. "And call your mother," he added before he let her go. She promised she would.

Chrissy waited until she was back at the ranch to make the call. Stopping by the rail fence next to the front gate,

she turned off the engine and dialed her mom's number right there in her Blazer before she went inside.

Her mom answered on the first ring. "Sweetheart, I've been worried sick. How are you?"

"It's okay, Mom. Really. I'm fine. And I'm guessing Dad filled you in on the disaster at my condo?"

"Oh, yes, he did. I'm so glad you called him."

"Me too. He got right on it. He's the greatest."

"Sweetheart, why don't you come on home and stay with us until you can get back into your condo? Your old room is ready and waiting for you."

She'd known that was coming. And she had her answer ready. "I have a place to stay, Mom. But thank you for offering."

Right then, the front door opened, and Hayes emerged wearing his usual worn jeans and dark T-shirt. His thick brown hair looked wet. No doubt he'd just jumped in the shower after a long day of mending fences and feeding stock. She stuck her hand out her window and gave him a quick wave.

He came down the steps toward her, all lean, easy grace. True, they were over as a couple and had been for years and years. But looking at him now, well, she couldn't fault her younger self for falling head-over-heels for the guy. Even now, her breath came faster just at the sight of him.

Her mom said, "I want you to come home, sweetie. Let me spoil you a little."

"Thank you, truly. But I'm all set up at—"

Patrice cut her off. "I know. Your father told me. End of the Road Ranch."

Hayes came out through the gate, his big dog right behind him. A moment later, he stood by her open window, looking like the best kind of trouble, waiting for her to finish on the phone.

Her mom was still talking. "…because there is no reason for you to stay with the Parkers when you can—"

"Mom. Let's not do this. I'm staying at the Parker ranch and it's working out fine." Hayes raised an eyebrow at her through the open window. She wrinkled her nose at him, then held up her index finger and mouthed, *One minute.* He nodded.

Her mother asked, "But are you sure that's a good idea?"

"Yes, I am. And I have made my decision on this. So let's just leave this subject behind, all right?"

"You are so stubborn."

"I love you, Mom. Lots. But I really have to go now."

"Well, if you change your mind—"

"I won't. But thank you."

"Listen, I'll have dinner on the table in half an hour. Why don't you just come on over and eat. Then you can hang out here for a little while. I would love to see you."

"Sorry, Mom. I can't tonight."

"Soon, then?"

"Yes. I promise. And I have to go. Bye, now." She disconnected the call before her mom could pile on more pressure. "Whew." She dropped the phone on the dashboard.

Hayes leaned in the window, bringing the clean scent of soap from his recent shower. His mouth had that sexy quirk at the corner and those green eyes glittered. She smiled at him, her breath kind of tangling up on her chest. The man was a menace in the best kind of way. He asked, "Bad day?"

"Hellacious. But also extremely productive, so I'm not complaining."

"Well, I'm glad you got a lot done."

"Yes, we did."

He was eyeing the duffel bags piled on the passenger

seat as well as the suitcases, carryalls and plastic bags in back. "Let's get all this stuff inside."

"Sounds good. Then I'll get going on dinner."

He grinned again. "Dinner's handled."

"What?"

"There's no need for you to cook tonight."

Chrissy smiled in exhausted delight. "Wait. Don't tell me. Your mom cooked before she left."

He nodded. "Meat loaf, mashed potatoes, green beans with bacon. Cornbread, too."

She put her hand over her heart. "I love your mom so much."

"She's a wonder. No doubt about it." He pulled open her door and gestured her out with a flourish.

"Why, thank you," she said, playing it just a little bit coy.

"For you, anything."

Chrissy got out and knelt to greet Rayna who wagged her giant, furry tail at the attention. "The guys?"

"They took off already." He opened the rear driver's-side door and started pulling out bags.

Working together, it didn't take them long to get everything inside. They piled most of the duffels and suitcases in Braden's old room and carried the plastic bags of wet clothes and linens to the laundry room off the kitchen.

Once he brought the last suitcase in, she said, "I'm going to get a load of laundry going and then I really need a shower."

He gave her one of those smiles that seemed so off-hand and casual—and yet still managed to have her feeling a little bit giddy. He was truly that kind of man—the dangerous kind. The kind that got her all stirred up with just that bad-boy grin of his and the knowing gleam in his

eyes. "Go for it," he said, that smile of his somehow managing to get even sexier.

They'd agreed they were just friends and yet here he was, outright flirting with her. She should tell him to knock it off. But she didn't.

It wasn't until she was naked in the shower that she started to reevaluate her own reactions to Hayes.

Because really, she needed to watch herself.

She'd been in love with him once—deeply. Passionately. And he'd shattered her nineteen-year-old heart into a thousand pieces, laying down that ultimatum the way he had.

Marry me, he'd demanded. *Marry me now, or it's over.*

She didn't even like to think about how awful it had been to lose him. It had taken a long time to put herself back together again after Hayes Parker finished stomping on her heart.

She couldn't afford to let herself get worked up over him now. Her heart had been broken twice already. A third break might just finish her off. Yes, it was so kind of him to give her a place to stay when she really needed one.

But she had no business letting herself get too close or too friendly with him. She couldn't go getting all hot and bothered over his devilish grin or his lean, hard body or the smell of his aftershave.

Please. She was smarter than that now.

Quickly, she finished her shower. Leaving her damp hair to air dry, she toweled off fast and pulled on clean clothes.

When she joined Hayes in the kitchen, he turned from the counter by the fridge where he had the food dished up and ready for reheating in the microwave. He met her eyes.

And she knew that *he* knew. He saw that she had her guard back up.

That warm, teasing smile of his died on his lips.

And all of a sudden, she just felt sad. Drained. Exhausted from a long day's work—and let down, too. Because getting dangerously close to flirting with him earlier? She had loved it. Even though she knew it was flirting with disaster.

He asked, "You okay?"

She nodded. "Just tired, that's all."

"I get it, Chrissy. I really do."

They stood there in silence a few feet apart and stared at each other. Over by the table, Rayna whined, an anxious sound.

And then Hayes said, low and intently, "Just friends."

She nodded. "That's right."

"Look, Chrissy. I'm sorry if I—"

She didn't let him finish. "There is nothing you need to apologize for. You've been so terrific, helping me out the way you have. I'm grateful. And surprisingly, given the awful way things ended for us back in the day, I just, well, this isn't going as I expected. I didn't think it would be so easy to, um, like you again."

"I hear you. And I… I like you, too." He said it kind of bleakly.

She pressed her hands to her cheeks. They felt warm. She wasn't sick, so she must be blushing. Which was unacceptable. She ordered the blush to fade, dropped her arms to her sides and spoke carefully. "After the way it ended for us, I just didn't imagine how natural it would be to, you know, joke around with you, to have fun just being with you."

His nod was slow. Thoughtful. "Yeah. It's the same for me. So easy and natural…" His words trailed off. And then he added in a brisk tone, "So then, let's eat?"

She allowed herself a smile. "Yes, please."

CHAPTER FOUR

FOR THE NEXT few days, Hayes took extra care to give Chrissy her space.

Because she was right. They had to be careful around each other. They needed to avoid getting overly friendly.

The thing was, he did like her. A lot. Her face and body held the same magnetic appeal for him as back in high school.

And damn. Was she ever smart. That drunk at the Grizzly Friday night had not stood a chance against that quick wit of hers. With just a few choice words, she'd had him staggering out the door.

Hayes shook his head, grinning, remembering the past.

Back in high school, all the guys had liked her. And it wasn't only the way she looked that made her beautiful. It was also her goodness. Chrissy Hastings was one of those people who would always offer help and a kind word when either was needed. He'd known her since grade school and the two of them had always been friendly.

But by freshman year, she'd changed. She came back to school with curves and a womanly way about her. That first day back, she'd smiled at him—a special smile that told him she was seeing him in a new light, too. That smile had made him the happiest guy at Tenacity High. Within a week, they were holding hands in the hallways, meeting up between classes, inseparable. He'd believed they were forever.

Looking back, it still came to him vividly, how angry and hurt he'd been when she refused to marry him. He'd been furious at her then—for promising to love him forever, for making him believe in her. And then turning her back on him when things got too tough. Back then, he'd had his butthurt blinders on. Because he was nineteen and his forever love had walked away.

However, right now, as a grown man, he saw her choice in a whole different light. He realized he'd let the chip on his shoulder drive her away.

Hayes had wanted her to leave town with him.

She wouldn't. But she hadn't dumped him. After he left, she'd remained his girl long-distance.

For almost a year, he called her often, begging her to join him at the ranch down near Kaycee, Wyoming, where he'd hired on as a cowhand.

She'd loved him, she really had—loved him as much as he'd loved her. And finally, during her spring break in her freshman year at Montana State, she came to visit him.

As soon as he had his arms around her again, Hayes had taken her hand, slipped a gold ring with an itty-bitty diamond on her finger and asked her to marry him. She balked. She tried to make him see that she just wasn't ready for marriage. That they were both too young—and he lived in a tiny old trailer provided by his boss.

He remembered her standing by the rusty sink in that rickety trailer, begging him to try to see it her way…

"HAYES, WON'T YOU please try to understand? There's no room for me here. I love you. You know I do. And I don't see why we can't stay together long-distance. I promise I'm yours and I always will be. But I can't come live with you now. And really, it won't be so bad. We can visit each other every chance we get."

He saw red then. He was through with her telling him no.

Drawing his shoulders back, he stood tall. He wasn't having less than all of her—all of her, right now. "It's not enough, Chrissy. Marry me."

Those big brown eyes begged him and so did that soft mouth of hers. "Oh, Hayes, please try to understand. I can't. Please won't you wait for me? At least let me finish college before we go talking about getting married?"

He'd scoffed in her face. "Be with me. Now. Marry me. Or we're done."

TWENTY MINUTES LATER, he'd watched her drive away.

He'd hated her then. And for the next five years or so, he'd burned with fury every time he thought of her. Even when he met Anna and found himself wanting to get to know her better, he'd continued to think of Chrissy with fury in his heart.

That anger didn't fade until about the time he admitted to himself that he was ready to try love again—with the boss's daughter.

Looking back, he could see now how similar Anna was to Chrissy. Both of them were big-hearted and smart, quick to laugh and to find the joy in life. Anna was a rancher's daughter. Her dad had put her on a horse when she was barely out of diapers. Chrissy was a town girl. But deep down they were both strong women who knew what they wanted and went after it. He'd been happy with Anna, and he'd put Chrissy behind him.

Or so he'd thought.

But now, Anna was gone forever.

And the last thing he'd ever expected was to find himself sharing a home with Chrissy at the End of the Road Ranch and liking her a little too much, realizing that she

was every bit as strong, smart and desirable as she'd been at nineteen.

Even more so if the truth were told.

He needed to watch himself around her. It would be far too easy to start hoping for more than either of them were ready for at this point in their lives.

Austin, Jake and Beck showed up bright and early on Sunday. Chrissy cooked them all breakfast and then went off to work at the inn.

That evening, she got back to the ranch at five. Hayes's friends had gone home. It was just the two of them at the dinner table. She served spaghetti with meat sauce, garlic bread and a big green salad and then sat there eating in silence, strangely afraid that anything she might say would be overly friendly, somehow.

After several endless minutes of quiet interrupted only by the sound of Rayna's tags rattling as she scratched herself and the scrape of forks on plates, Chrissy took a stab at conversation. "So how was your day?" she asked, knowing it was arguably the most boring question ever. But hey. At least she'd tried.

He swallowed pasta and knocked back a big gulp of water. "Nothing special. We burned a bunch of ditches, baled the hay we cut on Friday and whitewashed a couple of sheds."

"Wow. That's a lot." She tried to think what else to say as he nodded and shoveled in another forkful of spaghetti. "At this rate, you'll have the ranch in tiptop shape in no time."

He scoffed at that. "Doubtful." And he forked up a big bite of salad.

As she watched him chew, she realized he really didn't

want to chat with her and she might as well give up trying to get a conversation going.

Hayes kept eating. He plowed through that meal at the speed of light. As soon as he'd devoured his second helping of pasta and meat sauce, he was on his feet. "I'm going to get after the evening chores. I'll probably be a while."

"All right."

"The baler needs a little housekeeping. It's been running hot, and I should probably blow out the oil cooler."

She smiled and nodded and off he went, Rayna at his heels.

As soon as he was gone, she felt bizarrely lonely, which annoyed her no end. She reminded herself for the umpteenth time that she was grateful to be here instead of staying at her parents' house until her condo was livable again. Hayes had no responsibility to hang out in the house keeping her company. In fact, it was better that he didn't, given that she had way too much of a tendency to fall back into old patterns when he was around. What they'd shared was years ago and they were never going there again.

As soon as he was out the door, she put the leftover spaghetti and garlic bread away for tomorrow night, cleaned up the kitchen, ran a bunch of clothes through the washer and dryer, and tidied up the house a bit.

The next day, Hayes's high school buddies were back again. Before she headed to the inn, they ate breakfast and went out with Hayes to work. That night, Austin and Jake stayed for dinner, which worked out great because there was plenty of spaghetti left for everyone.

Plus, Hayes's buddies kept the conversation going, which made the meal a lot more pleasant than the night before.

On Tuesday at work, Chrissy got a call from her mom.

"Sweetie, you mentioned the other day that you would

come for dinner soon. How about tonight? I'm making your favorite creamy herb pork chops."

Chrissy longed to say she just couldn't make it. She knew the topic for the evening would be something along the lines of what *could* she be thinking, to be bedding down at the End of the Road Ranch?

But why put off the inevitable? She'd promised to come for dinner soon, and she might as well get it over with. Plus, there were the pork chops cooked the way only her mom knew how. Her mouth watered just thinking about them.

When she called Hayes to back out on cooking for the boys that night, he said it was no problem. "The guys aren't staying for dinner. And I really need to drive over to Bronco and pay my dad a visit."

She stifled a laugh—but didn't hide it completely.

He grumbled, "What? You think that's funny? You know I don't get along with my dad."

"I do know, yeah. And that's why I laughed, because you sounded as eager to go visit Lionel as I am to spend my evening listening to my mother lecture me on my unfortunate life choices."

"What unfortunate choices have you made lately?" He sounded way too amused—and curious, too. Plus, they were having an actual conversation again, which was definite progress after the radio silence of the past two nights.

However, no way she was admitting outright that staying at the ranch was her bad choice *du jour* from her mom's point of view. "Got an hour? Because my mom has a whole bunch of my bad choices to discuss with me."

"Oh, I'll bet."

"See you tomorrow morning for breakfast," she said. "Drive carefully, Hayes."

"I will." And then he was gone.

And she ended up standing there in the inn's kitchen, holding her phone, smiling because she and Hayes had just exchanged a few friendly words.

That evening, the pork chops were every bit as good as Chrissy had known they would be. And her mom ran true to form.

As Chrissy savored her first yummy bite of the delicious creamy dish, Patrice started in on her. "Honestly, sweetheart. You should be here with us until the issues at your condo are resolved. I was thinking that after dinner, we could caravan out to the Parker place—you, your dad and me. I'm sure whatever things you have at the ranch house will fit into three vehicles. It'll be quick and simple and from tonight on, you're here with us, all comfy in your old room, until your place is ready for your return."

Chrissy enjoyed another bite of tender breaded pan-fried pork chop slathered in scrumptious sauce. "Mom. You've outdone yourself. This is so good."

"Thank you, sweetheart. What do you think?"

"Delicious. Absolutely delicious."

"Chrissy. You know very well I wasn't asking about the pork chops."

"Oh. Right. You mean your suggestion that I stay here instead of out at the ranch."

"Yes. What do you say?"

Chrissy slid a glance at her dad. Mel Hastings gave her a tender smile and then forked up a bite-sized wedge of beautifully browned oven-roasted baby potato. But as for coming to her rescue in the discussion with her mom, not a chance.

"Thanks so much, Mom," Chrissy said. "But I'm all settled in at the ranch."

Her mom frowned. "But should you be taking advantage of the Parkers that way?"

Chrissy tamped down a spike of irritation. Her mom had a way of pushing all her buttons. "There's nobody there, Mom. Hayes's brothers aren't at home right now. Rylee's engaged and moved out for good. It's just Hayes and me staying there—and I'm pitching in, doing my part, cooking and helping around the house while Norma is spending most of her time over at Bronco Valley Hospital with Lionel."

Her mother said just what Chrissy should have known she would say. "Hmm. Just you and Hayes. Is that wise?"

Shaking her head, Chrissy drew a slow, calming breath. "Don't, Mom. Just don't."

"You're right," her mom said sweetly. "You're an adult and your life is your own."

"Thank you for acknowledging that."

"And as for your helping out at the Parker place, of course you are. You've always been helpful, always happy to do your share. But the ranch is out of town. It's a longer drive to work for you, whereas we're right here, a few blocks from your job."

It went on like that for the rest of the meal, her mom coming up with new reasons why Chrissy would be better off moving back home for now, and Chrissy insisting that she intended to remain at the ranch.

At a little after eight when she finally left, she was promising herself she would avoid having dinner at her mom's until she was back in her condo again. From now on, even creamy herb pork chops wouldn't tempt her to change her mind.

HAYES WAS SITTING on the sofa staring blindly at the front door across the room when he heard a vehicle drive up outside.

At his feet, Rayna stirred. "Stay." He patted her head, and she settled back down.

A car door slammed. A minute later, he heard light footsteps on the porch. The front door opened.

"Hey." It was Chrissy in her work skirt and vest, with a stressed expression on her face.

"Hi," he replied without much enthusiasm.

Her low, chunky heels tapped the hardwood floor as she came closer. Setting her small shoulder bag on the big pine coffee table, she dropped into a chair across from him. "How's your dad doing?"

Rayna sat up and gave a questioning whine.

"Go ahead," he said to the dog. She went to Chrissy, who scratched her around the ruff and told her what a good dog she was.

Chrissy glanced up from petting his dog. "Hayes."

"Huh?"

"Your dad?"

He shook his head. "What can I say? He never changes. He hates being in the hospital. He's worried about the money it's costing for him to be there. The stress isn't good for him, and his bad attitude will probably keep him there longer—and anything I say flat out pisses him off. I drove all the way to Bronco and back and for what? Apparently, to listen to him complain about every little thing and remind me of all the things that need doing here, as if I didn't know."

"It's good that you went."

"I'm glad somebody thinks so."

Her eyes were softer than ever and full of understanding. "He's a good guy, your dad."

"I keep trying to remember that. But it's been so damn long since I saw his good side, it's way too easy to forget that he has one."

"Your dad was always friendly and sweet to me," she said with a tiny smile.

"He always liked you a hell of a lot better than he ever did me."

"Oh, come on. That's not true."

"Right. And enough about my dad." He leaned in and braced his forearms on spread knees. "How was dinner with the folks?"

She wrinkled her nose at him. "You had to ask."

"Sorry." He winked at her.

She scoffed. "No, you're not. As for how it went at my mom's, I'm looking on the bright side."

"Which is?"

"I got through it."

"So how *is* your mom?"

"Smart-ass," she muttered as she grabbed one of his mom's hand-hooked throw pillows off the end of the sofa and threw it at him.

Laughing for the first time since he left for Bronco that afternoon, he caught the pillow and tucked it under his arm. "What?" He pretended to look surprised. "Don't tell me you've got a problem with your mom."

"Ha. As if you didn't know. However, as I just said, I got through it. And by that I mean all the way through dinner and dessert. I even hung around afterward to listen to more of her unsolicited advice."

"Fun, huh?"

"That's probably not the word I would use. At least she didn't bring up Sam again, so that's a plus."

Hayes really wanted to ask her what had happened, exactly, with her ex. But how many times did he have to remind himself that he needed to keep things casual with her, not to delve too deeply into her past or her private life? They shared a slightly shaky friendship now and that was how it was supposed to stay. Which meant he needed to

keep all his personal questions about her life and her marriage to himself.

She went on. "Anyway, I had dinner at my folks' house and it's over and I got through it without saying anything I wish I hadn't."

"Sounds like a win to me."

"Yeah. Right. A win. That's what I'm calling it, too." She grabbed her purse and rose. "Okay, so I've got a couple of menus to tweak before I can finalize what I need to order for next week's events. See you in the morning?"

"You bet."

She went up the stairs. He flopped back in the chair and stared at the rough beams overhead and tried not to wish she'd hung around to talk with him a little longer.

Yeah, he and Chrissy were supposed to be keeping their distance from each other and he was trying his hardest to do that. But it didn't escape his notice that the only time he'd felt good about anything today was the past few minutes he'd spent with her.

THE NEXT MORNING, none of his buddies could get away to help out. After Hayes took care of early chores and chowed down on the excellent breakfast Chrissy prepared for the two of them, she headed off to work and he decided it was time to face the End of the Road Ranch's financial reality.

In the cramped office at the back of the house he booted up the ancient PC, typed in the password that hadn't changed since he left home and opened the accounting software.

The news was pretty much what he'd expected—not good. And the stack of overdue bills waiting on one corner of his dad's rollback desk needed attention ASAP.

The ranch had come down to Lionel from Hayes's grandparents, so at least they owned the land, the house,

the stock and the outbuildings. But they were definitely in arrears.

He'd been sitting at the computer, getting a handle on the grave situation for three hours when his mom spoke from the open doorway behind him. "Here you are…"

He turned around in the old oak swivel chair. Norma stood there, arms crossed, leaning against the door frame. "Hey, Mom. What's up? Need some help?"

"No. But thank you. I'm going to unpack the groceries I brought and do a little cooking. I can easily handle that myself." She pressed her lips together. "Going over the books, huh?"

He nodded. "We should talk, Mom."

She let her arms drop to her sides. "Yes. All right. I'll just put the perishables away and make some coffee."

Twenty minutes later, she set a full mug on the coaster by the old computer. "Here you go."

"Thanks." He took a sip.

She rolled the other chair over, sat beside him and put her hand on his arm. "You look as discouraged as I feel right now."

"Well, the numbers don't lie and the truth they're telling is not a happy truth."

"Honestly, we were breaking even until the past couple of months. Barely. But still. We were scraping by even after Miles left for the service. But your father was so worried. And when he gets worried, he gets—"

"Bossy and mean."

Her eyes were so sad. "That's not what I was going to say."

"But I don't hear you denying it."

"Yeah, well…" Her voice trailed off. Finally she added, "He's too old to be so frustrated all the time."

"You're right. It's making him sick."

She nodded. "Last night, when it was just the two of us in that hospital room, he admitted that he's got to get a handle on his attitude and his temper. He says he's trying, and he plans to try harder."

There were any number of snarky remarks Hayes might have made right then, but he kept his mouth firmly shut.

His mom said, "Your dad was extra hard on Braden after Miles left."

"It's what Dad does. You'd think at some point he'd start to realize that he's the one with the problem."

"He does realize, and he just feels terrible."

"Right."

"After Miles left, your dad and Braden were arguing constantly. At first, they would patch it up and move on. But the tension just escalated."

"Until Braden couldn't take it anymore."

A small, sad sound escaped her. "That's about the size of it. So then Braden took off and your dad and I, we tried to keep things going. Too bad we're not getting any younger. We should have hired a hand, but—"

"There was no money to pay wages."

"That's right. It's a vicious circle."

Leaning her way, he wrapped an arm across her shoulders. "And on the subject of wages, Jake, Austin and Beck have done more than enough to help out around here. They can't keep showing up, working for free. They've got lives and jobs of their own."

"I know. And I am so grateful for all they've done around here."

"I know you are and so do they. And now, I need to hire at least one capable, hardworking cowhand to keep this place running. With me and a good hand putting in full days, we could manage for now."

"We don't have the—"

"Money. I know. So don't worry about it. I have some money put aside. I'll pay the new hire."

She gasped. "Oh, Hayes. We can't ask that of you."

"You're not asking. I'm just saying I'm hiring a hand, and it will be on my own dime."

"You know your father is going to order you not to."

Hayes gave a low chuckle at that. "He's not really in a position to stop me right now. If he wants to make the decisions around here again, he should put all his effort into getting well."

She was silent. He figured she was marshalling more arguments against him spending his money to keep the ranch afloat.

But then she said, "He never did disinherit you, you know."

That shocked him. "The day I left, he swore that he would."

"He lied. He would never do that to any of you kids. But he didn't want you to go, he lost his temper, and he let his big mouth write a check his heart was never going to let him cash."

"Well." Warmth stole through him. His dad could be a pigheaded ass. But he did have a heart and an ingrained sense of what was right. "Okay then, Mom. When Dad's pride gets the best of him because I'm paying the new hand, I'll just tell him that I'm protecting my interest in the End of the Road Ranch."

"That conversation probably won't go well."

"Too bad. I'm doing it, so one way or another, he's going to have to deal." Hayes picked up the stack of bills. "And now we need to talk about paying what's due."

She snatched the stack from him. "I'll pay those."

He gaped at her. "With what?"

"My freedom money."

He puzzled over that for a minute before shrugging and asking, "What is freedom money?"

A sly smile twisted her mouth. "When your Grandma Tessa passed, she left me a nice chunk of change. She knew I would never leave your father, but she believed a woman should have money of her own, freedom money, so she would always have an option if things got bad or she wanted to treat herself to a little getaway. I put my freedom money away for the time when I really needed it."

"Does Dad know about this freedom money of yours?"

"Of course. He would never touch it, and he's not going to be happy I'm spending it on a stack of bills. I've tried more than once in the past month to convince him we need to use my money to help save the ranch. He said no, absolutely not. And up until today, I have backed down. But, honey, you have inspired me."

"What?" He wasn't following. "How?"

"The way I see it, if you can use your money to get us the help we need around here, I can use mine to pay bills. I love your father with all my heart. But Lionel does not get to decide what makes me free. I decide that. And having at least some of the bills paid—that's freedom to me."

For a moment, her eyes sparkled, and her smile was the bright, happy smile he remembered from way back when he was seven or eight, before things started to get tough at the End of the Road Ranch. But then, much too soon, the look of joy faded from his mother's face.

"Mom." He put his arm around her again. "What's wrong?"

She leaned against him. "The truth is, my freedom money isn't going to go all that far."

"We'll make it work."

She touched his cheek, a fond brush of her fingers against his skin. "Oh, honey. I'm so glad you're here—

and I hope we can find our way through this rough patch. But sometimes it feels like all we've had the past twenty years are rough patches."

"We will make it through," he said, shocking himself with how confident he sounded.

"I do hope you're right. I hope we can hold on, stick with it until we come out stronger on the other side. After all, they don't call this town Tenacity for nothing."

He scoffed. "No. They call it Tenacity because some early settler had a dark sense of humor."

His mom shook her head slowly, a faraway look in her eyes. "We *are* tenacious—tenacious and all those words that mean the same thing. We are stubborn. Obstinate. Determined. I mean, look at your father. Things just keep going from bad to worse and still, he swears he'll never give up, never sell."

"Because he won't, Mom."

"I know, I know. But, Hayes, to tell you the truth, lately it just feels like it's only a matter of time before we have no choice. And now there's the cost of Lionel's medical care on top of everything else."

"But you have insurance." He'd seen her hand over her insurance card that first day, when they rushed his dad to the hospital.

"Yes, we have insurance, and so far we've managed to keep up with the payments, but the insurance is not going to cover everything. Plus, well…" She glanced away.

"Just say it, Mom."

"All right. Your father *is* getting better. He's lost a little weight, and he will be losing some more with the diet he's on that he's promised to stick to when he's finally back home. But he's not getting better fast enough. It's been five days since the surgery and the doctor won't release him. Not for a while, the doctor says."

"What are you telling me? Is Dad okay?"

"Yes—or he will be, I'm sure. The doctor says so. But it's taking him longer than anticipated to be ready to come home."

"Mom. Just don't worry. He's going to be all right. And I will keep things going here. We won't give up. We'll make it through."

Hayes kind of marveled at the words coming out of his own mouth. After so many years of swearing he wanted nothing to do with the End of the Road Ranch, now he was seeing the truth he'd started facing two months ago when Braden called out of the blue to say Miles was gone and he was leaving.

The plain truth was, when Hayes had walked away, he'd never once doubted that his family would keep the ranch going. He'd sworn never to come back, and he hadn't. Not for fifteen years.

But for all that time, he'd had the sure and certain knowledge that home was there, that it always would be. That his mom and dad would grow old on the ranch, that his brothers and his sister would always be around to help out when needed. Together they would overcome any obstacle no matter what fate threw at them.

Well, there had been a lot of obstacles. Too many, as it turned out. His brothers had filled him in on all the challenges as the years went by.

Fate had not been kind to the Parker family. There had been years of drought followed by years of blizzards that tore across the land and froze the cattle where they stood. His dad had needed to change things, to be more flexible in order to stay in the black, but Lionel Parker had never been real big on change.

And now, it had gotten bad enough for his family that losing the ranch seemed inevitable to his mom.

"I'm sorry," his mom whispered. "I shouldn't be so negative."

He drew her close yet again. "It's going to be okay, Mom. We'll see it through."

"Oh, I do hope you're right."

"Count on it."

"You're a good son," she whispered. "I'm grateful for you, Hayes. So grateful for all four of you kids."

He hugged her closer as she sagged against him.

But Norma Parker was no quitter. Seconds later, she drew herself up. "Alrighty, then. Enough of this feeling sorry for myself. I've got lots to do and I may as well stop whining and get after it." She stood. "I noticed Chrissy's been cooking. There's a pot roast in the slow cooker. Smells good."

"Yeah, it does."

His mom scolded, "She works all day and also cooks for you."

"She insisted she had to help out or she couldn't stay here."

"I know, honey. She told me that, too. I'm going to pitch in a little on the cooking front."

"You know you'll just piss Chrissy off if you do that."

His mom grinned. "She's a spunky one, that girl." The stack of bills in her hand, Norma pushed her chair back where it belonged and left the small room.

Hayes shut down the old PC and then just sat there for a bit, staring at the dark screen, realizing all over again that, for him, there was no making peace with losing the ranch. He would do whatever he had to do. One way or another, he would see to it that the ranch remained in the family's hands.

CHAPTER FIVE

CHRISSY LEFT THE inn at a little after four that day. She stopped by her condo, where the workmen were ripping out ruined sheetrock. It looked like a disaster zone. She didn't stay long.

At the ranch, Hayes was apparently out somewhere on the land. She ran upstairs and changed into jeans and a T-shirt.

When she came back down, she discovered that Norma had been there. And she'd been cooking. A foil-covered squash casserole waited in the fridge, along with Swiss steak in a red-topped Tupperware container. There was mac and cheese, too. Chrissy shook her head at the sight of all that food. She wouldn't have to cook for a few days at least, that was for sure.

And tonight, the roast she'd put in the slow cooker before she left for work that morning was ready to go. All she really had to do to get dinner on was set the table for two, toss a salad and plate the food.

Hayes came in at five thirty and headed straight for a shower. She had the food on the table when he came back down. He seemed bothered, somehow. Preoccupied. The meal was mostly silent.

Afterward, he disappeared into the office in back, Rayna at his heels. Chrissy straightened up the kitchen and then headed for the mudroom where she'd left a pair of sturdy old shoes. She put them on, grabbed Norma's

gardening gloves and went out to the garden where the early evening shadows had pushed back the heat of the afternoon.

For an hour, she pulled weeds and picked green beans, peppers and broccoli. By then, it was getting dark. She went inside, took off her dirty shoes and Norma's gloves, and left them in the mudroom. Barefoot, she carried the basket of vegetables to the laundry room and washed them in the sink there.

The house seemed so quiet. She checked the office. Empty. Had Hayes gone up to his room already?

She considered going on up herself. Instead, she wandered into the great room and then out the front door.

Hayes was sitting on the porch steps, Rayna stretched out behind him. She stepped over the big dog and plunked down at his side.

"Your mom's been cooking," she accused. "Tell her I said to stop that."

He shot her a glance and then went back to staring out into the gathering darkness. Somewhere out there, a nighthawk let out its short, strangled cry. "I already told her you had the cooking under control."

"Well, she didn't listen."

"Sorry. Best I could do."

Bracing an elbow on her knee, Chrissy rested her chin on the heel of her hand. "So…what's up?"

Several seconds went by before he answered. "It's nothing too terrible. My dad's going to be in the hospital for a while longer."

"You're worried about him."

"Yeah. A little. My mom says he'll be all right, but he's not improving as fast as they'd hoped—and I'm also kind of down about the ranch's financial situation."

"Is it bad?"

"Bad enough." He turned his head her way. Their gazes locked. "Today I called a friend I met in Washington state. We worked together on the ranch that my wife's dad, Jacob Grantham, used to own. My friend, Arlen Hawk, will be here tomorrow or maybe Friday. I can use a good hand and Arlen's the best."

"Makes sense. I'll clear my stuff out of Braden's room tomorrow for him."

"No need. Arlen's got a fancy rig—a one-ton Chevy Silverado pickup pulling a combo trailer."

"He brings his living quarters *and* his horse?"

"That's right."

"Sounds like a good friend to have."

"He is. You'll like him."

"I have no doubt." She was still thinking about what he'd said a minute before. "You mentioned that your wife's dad *used* to own the ranch where you met her?"

"Yeah." He stared off to the west as the last rays of daylight slipped behind the low humps of the distant hills.

Just when she thought he'd said all he intended to say, he turned to her again. His eyes were full of shadows. She had no idea what he might be thinking, though she guessed he was about to say that he didn't want to talk about his dead wife's dad, and she ought to mind her own business.

But he surprised her. "My wife, Anna, was Jacob's only child. Anna's mom had died when Anna was a little girl. Jacob raised her on his own and Anna was everything to him. When she died, it broke him. He just didn't have the heart to go on running the family ranch. He turned the place over to his younger brothers and retired. A year later, he died of a stroke."

She hardly knew what to say. "Hayes. I'm so sorry..."

"Me, too." He looked down at his boots. "Jacob was a

good guy. The best. But the truth is, I think he was ready to go."

"And… Anna?"

He made a low, thoughtful sound—and fell silent. She accepted the fact that he wasn't going to answer the question she hadn't had the courage to ask clearly.

But then he said, "Car accident. Black ice. The Grantham Ranch is in eastern Washington. Anna was on her way home from Christmas shopping in Seattle. She hit that patch of ice and ended up wrapped around a Douglas fir tree. Died instantly, they said. People said that was a blessing. I don't know, though. Nothing about Anna's death feels like a blessing to me."

"Oh, Hayes…" She shouldn't touch him. She knew that. But she took his hand anyway and eased her fingers between his warm, rough ones. He didn't pull back, so she turned her body toward him. "I don't know what to say, except how sorry I am that you lost her."

"Thanks." He stared into the middle distance. "Anna was a happy person. Nothing got her down. It was hell losing her, but I'm grateful for the five years we had together."

Out in the dark, another night bird let out a lonely trill of sound.

Hayes said, "And now that we're sitting here talking about all the tough things…"

"Go ahead. I'm listening."

"My mom thinks it's just a matter of time until we have to sell the ranch."

"Oh, no."

"Well, it's definitely a possibility."

"You're saying that you think she's right?"

He didn't answer her question. Instead, he said, "All these years, I've told myself I didn't care about this place."

She whispered, "But you do."

"Yeah. Now that losing the ranch is a real possibility, I just can't stand for that to happen."

"So then, don't *let* it happen."

He laughed, a rueful sound. "Easy-peasy, huh?"

"Hey. If anyone can save this place, it's you, Hayes."

"Is this a pep talk?"

"Absolutely."

Behind them, Rayna stretched, yawned, and settled back down again with a long sigh.

Leaning sideways, Hayes bumped Chrissy's shoulder with his. "Your turn."

She faked a wide-eyed glance. "My turn for what?"

"I told you about Anna. Now, you tell me about Sam Shaw."

She let go of his hand and pretended to scowl at him. "I'm not sure I like where this is going, mister."

"Too bad. Talk."

She thought of how good Hayes had been to her, coming to her rescue last Friday night at the bar, moving her in here so she wouldn't have to live at her mom's again. Yeah, they were trying to straddle a tough line, be friendly but not *too* friendly.

But where was that line, exactly?

Right now, she wasn't even sure she cared. If he wanted to hear about Sam, she would tell him. "Sam is nothing like you."

He smirked at her. "Should I be insulted?"

"Please don't. What I mean is, Sam's a by-the-book kind of person. Or he was when I met him. He was one of those guys who had created a solid career that provided a good living so that he could get married and have kids. He defined himself by that, by his role as the man of the family. He is—or he *was*—a truly traditional kind of guy."

"And you liked that?"

"I liked that he was a family man at heart, that he wanted all the time-honored things, a good marriage and kids to see through to adulthood. I'd finished college and I had a job I loved. I was ready to get married at that point. But then, as soon as we got back from the honeymoon, he began pushing me to quit work and start having babies."

"But wasn't that what you wanted?"

"I did, yes, but not immediately. I wanted a little time just for the two of us. But he was so insistent. In the end, we agreed we would start trying right away, and I would keep my job until I got pregnant."

"And…?"

"Three years went by, and I never got pregnant. We finally went to a specialist about the problem and found out that we were not going to be having a biological child together."

Hayes studied her face. She waited for him to ask her outright if she was infertile.

But he surprised her. He let it be. Let her say what she was willing to say, tell the story in her own way.

She went on, "Sam couldn't deal with not being able to have a baby with me. He had this idea of what a family should be. A dad and a mom and children they made together. If it couldn't be that way, he wasn't interested."

"Whoa." Hayes said the word in a sympathetic whisper.

"I don't think he even imagined our marriage would be any other way than how he planned it. Not until the worst happened and he realized he wasn't going to get the life he'd always wanted. It threw him. He had no backup plan."

"So…just like that, you broke up?"

She considered how much to share. Despite the disaster that her marriage became, she still felt a certain obligation to her ex-husband. She still had sympathy for him. Sam always had such conviction about how things should

be. And when he'd suddenly found out life wasn't going to turn out as he believed it should, he just didn't know where to go from there.

"We didn't break up immediately. But things went from bad to worse. Sam spiraled into a depression. He started drinking. He was uncommunicative. He wouldn't even consider counseling, wouldn't put any effort into finding workable solutions to our problems. Two years after we went to that specialist together, Sam announced that he wanted a divorce."

Now Hayes was the one taking her hand, weaving their fingers together.

She gave him a misty smile. "By then, I was pretty much at my wit's end with him. I asked him—again—to go to counseling. He said no. He said that our marriage was over. There was no point, he said, in pretending there was anything left to save."

"Wow. Talk about cold."

"But see, by then, I agreed with him. I was ready to move on."

"So then, that was it for the two of you?"

"Yeah. That was it. We divided our assets down the middle and split up. Sam moved to Florida, bought a boat and set out to…find himself, I guess you could say. I moved back home and started over."

Hayes put his arm around her. She allowed herself to lean on him. "You're strong and smart and tough, too," he said. "You can do just about anything you set your mind to. You're going to be fine, Chrissy Hastings. You know that, right?"

She chuckled. "Going to be? Hayes Parker, I *am* fine."

"You certainly are," he agreed with a grin.

She grinned right back at him. "Why, thank you."

"Don't thank me. It's only the truth." His eyes gleamed jade green. And his lips were so close…

Uh-uh, she reminded herself. *Not going to happen.*

Gently, she pulled away from him. "I should go in."

His grin was gone now. "Got it. Night, Chrissy."

She rose. "Night, Hayes." She was careful not to glance back at him as she crossed the porch and went inside.

HAYES HAD WANTED to kiss her. He'd wanted that a lot.

But she'd stopped it.

And he respected her decision.

He was careful the next morning to be no more than casually friendly. She seemed to accept that he'd gotten her message. They were back on an even keel with each other.

That evening, the two of them had just sat down to eat when Hayes heard a truck pull in out front. "I'm thinking that might be Arlen," he said, sliding his napkin in by his plate and pushing back his chair. "Excuse me."

She nodded. "I'll set another place."

"Great. It'll be a few minutes. He'll need to put his horse in the pasture out behind the barn."

Arlen was coming up the front steps when Hayes opened the door. Tall and broad with mahogany skin and startling blue eyes, Arlen spread both long arms wide and kept coming. "Hayes Parker. It's been way too long."

The men met on the porch for a hug and some back-slapping. When they pulled apart, Hayes said, "Swiss steak tonight. You had dinner yet?"

His friend shook his head. "Not yet—and Swiss steak sounds grand."

"You got it. Let me show you where to take your horse and park your trailer, then we can eat."

Fifteen minutes later, Arlen's horse was free in the horse pasture, and his truck and trailer were parked just beyond

the backyard gate. He had his own generator and Hayes had shown him the outside faucet so he could hook up his hose for water. They returned to the house, where they washed up in the mudroom and then joined Chrissy at the kitchen table.

Hayes thought his friend and Chrissy hit it off nicely. Chrissy laughed at Arlen's funny stories of his years working on ranches from Southern California to the wilds of New Jersey.

Later, Hayes followed Arlen out back for a drink. In the trailer's small kitchen, they sat at the table. Arlen poured them each two fingers of the good stuff and then raised his glass. "To you, back home at last." They drank and set their glasses down. "Kind of proves that old adage, *never say never*."

Hayes moved his empty shot glass in a slow circle on the tabletop. "You're right. I always vowed I would never come back to this town."

"And yet here you are." They laughed together at that. And then Arlen said, "And not only did you come back, but you also have the one and only Chrissy Hastings living with you in your house."

Arlen was a few years older. Hayes used to confide in him, especially at first, before Hayes and Anna got close.

Hayes pushed his glass across the table. "Since you're saving my sorry ass here, I'm just going to let you yank my chain all you want."

Arlen refilled both their glasses. "I believe you once said that Chrissy Hastings ripped your heart out and put it through a shredder, that you would never let a woman get hold of your heart again."

"I was young. Young with a tendency toward embarrassing exaggerations."

"And yet, you found happiness with Anna—bless her sweet soul."

"To Anna—and Jacob." Hayes offered the toast. They both drank, after which they shared a moment of silence in honor of Hayes's lost wife and her big-hearted dad.

After such a solemn toast, Hayes dared to hope Arlen was done busting his balls.

No such luck. "And now you've got Chrissy sleeping in the same house with you, serving up the Swiss steak with that fine, glowing smile."

"We're friends now, Chrissy and me. That's all, nothing more."

Arlen folded his muscled forearms on the table and leaned across to grin at Hayes. "You're a goner for that girl, my friend. You might as well face it."

Hayes shot his friend a narrow-eyed glare. "I'm so happy to be a source of amusement for you."

"Go ahead. Blow me off. I can take it."

"Friends, Arlen. Chrissy and I are friends."

"Keep saying that, my friend. But the truth is the truth and in the end, a man can't hide from it."

THE NEXT MORNING before dawn when Hayes took Rayna out to tackle early chores, Arlen was waiting on the back porch. The men headed for the barn, the dog trotting at their heels.

Two hours later, Chrissy served them breakfast. They went back to work with full bellies and spent the day switching out mineral barrels, moving cattle and chasing down strays.

They were back at the house by five, going their separate ways to clean up. Chrissy served dinner at six. At a little after seven, Arlen retired to the trailer.

Through the window above the sink, Chrissy watched him go. "I like him." She loaded water glasses into the dishwasher.

Hayes rinsed the last plate and handed it over. "Yeah. Arlen's the real deal. Whatever needs doing, he's right on top of it. He knows horses and cattle. And he's always got a friend's back. He's the best. I'm hoping we can mostly keep a handle on all the work around here, just him and me. Which is saying something, let me tell you."

She loaded in that last plate, shut the dishwasher and started it up, then grabbed the hand towel and wiped her hands dry. "I'm glad you have help."

Damn. She really was way too pretty and always had been, with that sleek and shining coffee-colored hair, and those eyes that made a man feel like he could fall right into them.

"Hayes?"

He blinked. "What?"

"Nothing." She laughed. The sound curled down around inside him, warm and so sweet. "Seemed like you drifted away there for a minute."

Arlen was right, he though grimly. *I'm in big trouble with this woman. In big trouble all over again.*

He knew he should avoid her, say he had the accounts to go over in the office, or just say good-night and head up to his room, maybe read a damn book. He opened his mouth to say he had…things to do.

What he actually said was, "Want to sit out on the porch for a little while?"

Her smile was slow and sweet as honey—and maybe a little more than friends-only. "Sure."

They sat on the steps with Rayna sprawled out behind them and watched the colors of the sky change from orange and purple to darkest blue, the stars twinkling brighter as

each minute passed. She said her day had been hectic, but she'd managed to stay on top of things.

When he asked how the work at her condo was going, she shrugged. "As well as can be expected, I guess."

"You know, you don't sound all that happy about the progress at your place."

"Yeah, well. My dad says these things take time. And I know he's right. But I'm impatient."

"It's understandable."

She shot him a wary look. "Hayes, I have to ask you…" Her voice trailed off.

"Whatever it is, just say it."

"Okay. Am I wearing out my welcome here?"

He blinked in surprise. "Hell, no. Are you kidding? Don't tell me you're thinking of leaving now."

"No, I just…" Her gaze slid away.

"You just, what?"

"Well, I don't want to take advantage of you, that's all."

"Take advantage? You're not." He touched her knee. When she finally looked at him, he said, "Please. You are not in any way taking advantage. You work nonstop around here after working all day at the inn." He took her hand. Maybe he shouldn't. Maybe that was once again stepping over that invisible line between friendship and something more.

Well, too damn bad. She needed a place until her condo was livable again and there was no reason that place shouldn't be right here.

Chewing the inside of her lip, she gazed at him, wide-eyed, adorable in her uncertainty. "You really are sure about this?"

"You'd better believe it. It's working for me. When you go, my mom's going to insist on taking over, filling your shoes around here. Believe me she's got plenty going on

trying to deal with my dad." Right then, it occurred to him that maybe being here wasn't working out for her, so he made himself address that. "Tell me the truth. Does it work for *you*, staying here?"

"Yes. Of course. It does. It's just…" She eased her hand from his grip.

He studied her face. "Wait a minute. Did something happen today?"

She groaned then and tipped her head up to the sky. "On the way back here after work, I stopped in to check on the work at the condo. My mom was there. 'Just wanted to see how things are going,' she said in her sweetest voice. And then she started in on me again, that I was taking advantage of you, that I needed to come back home and stay with her and Dad because that's where I belong at a time like this."

"The question is do you *want* to go stay with your folks?"

She laughed. There was no humor in the sound. "Dear God in heaven, no!"

"Then what are we talking about? You're staying, and I'm damn grateful that you are." He took her hand again.

She didn't pull away that time—in fact, she held on. "Well, then. Okay. I'll stay."

"Whew. You had me scared for a minute there…" The sentence kind of trailed off. He realized he was staring at her mouth, remembering what it felt like, kissing her, holding her soft, curvy body in his arms. "I, uh…"

"Hmm?"

"Um. Good. Just… It's good that you're staying. Thank you. For staying."

She let out another trill of laughter. "Okay. You can stop now. You've definitely convinced me."

He grinned. "Finally."

"But still, I was thinking…"

Now what? "Yeah?"

"Well, I was wondering…" She seemed flustered, her cheeks pink, her eyes overly bright.

"Go ahead," he coaxed. "Hit me with it."

"Well, I was wondering if maybe you were free tomorrow night? I was thinking we could go to Castillo's, my treat." The small Mexican restaurant was a block down from the Grizzly, on the opposite side of the street. "I'll just come back here after I'm done at the inn. I can change out of my work clothes and then we can drive into town together."

Faintly, way in the back of his mind, alarm bells were going off. Wouldn't that be too much like a date?

Chrissy was still talking. "I mean, you know, completely casual—meaning, as friends. It's not much, just a dinner out. But I could really use a change of pace, to do something a little different, you know? And more than that, it's a way I can show my appreciation to you for giving me a place to stay."

We shouldn't. It's a bad idea. She really wants to keep it friends-only. And that place has dangerous memories. They used to eat at Castillo's, the two of them, back when they were a couple. The food was really good, and the prices were reasonable. It was the perfect date-night spot for a pair of high school kids.

So what? he reminded himself. *High school was a long time ago. This, now, is friends-only. Don't go making it a big deal when it's anything but.*

You're kidding yourself, he silently scoffed. *Look at you. Arlen's right. You're into her, you know you are. And look at her, with that soft smile, so hopeful and sweet. You know where this is going.*

To Castillo's, as friends. That's where.

Man. He was losing it, arguing with himself inside his own head.

It feels like more.

Well, it's not. So get over yourself and say yes.

No. It's a bad idea. He started to tell her that. But when he opened his mouth, he heard himself saying, "I would love to go to Castillo's with you tomorrow night."

"You would?" Her smile bloomed even bigger. That smile was everything. It reminded him that life was not only struggle, pain and disappointment. There was beauty, too. And good people, like Chrissy, good people just trying to do the right thing and get by day-to-day.

"Yeah," he said. "Come on back to the ranch after work and we'll ride into town together."

CHAPTER SIX

CHRISSY HAD ALWAYS loved Castillo's. Growing up, her parents used to take her there. She would order a chicken burrito and savor every bite. The small restaurant was cozy and a little dark, a narrow storefront with two rows of wooden booths, and a small bar in back.

Pablo and Yolanda Castillo owned and ran the place. They were in their early sixties now. Yolanda served the food. Their older son tended the bar and their younger son helped Pablo in the kitchen.

That night, Yolanda greeted Chrissy and Hayes with a big smile and led them to a booth back near the bar. They asked for frosty, delicious margaritas and quesadillas to start. The carne asada was the best, so they both ordered that, too.

"I love it here," Chrissy said, feeling downright nostalgic as they sipped their drinks and devoured the quesadillas. "It's just so…homey."

"You're right." He took a bite of quesadilla. "So good. Remember the times we came here together?"

"Oh, yeah. We always had beef tacos and tall glasses of Dr Pepper."

"Yeah. I felt so grownup and manly, taking my girl out to eat…" His big smile faded. He set down the wedge of cheese-filled tortilla.

"What's wrong?"

"It's just that I've been thinking about what you said

the other night, about your ex, about how he had an idea of the way things should be, how he couldn't cope when things didn't fit into his plans. And the more I think about it, the more wrong that seems to me. Because people ought to be able to work together, right? We should all try to roll with the punches when things get tough."

"I agree." She sipped her drink. "But Sam didn't seem to be able to do that."

"So he just walked away from you."

"In the end, yeah."

Hayes picked up his margarita and then set it back down without drinking from it. "I keep thinking about that. I keep thinking that I did pretty much the same damn thing to you. I said marry me now or it's over. And when you tried to explain that you weren't ready for marriage yet, I wouldn't listen. I said we were done, and I sent you away."

The regret on his face? It broke something open down inside her. She ached for him at the same time as she felt lighter, freer. Never in a hundred years would she have expected him to admit that he'd dumped her for not doing things his way. Even if it was the truth.

And he wasn't through. "I shouldn't have done that, Chrissy. Shouldn't have laid down that ultimatum, shouldn't have demanded that you marry me right then."

She wanted to reach across and lay her hand on his. But she held herself back. She'd taken his hand more than once last night and the other night, too. She had to stop doing that. Innocent touches could too easily lead to intimate ones. And they'd agreed they weren't going there. "Hayes. We were so young."

"Too young." He added, more softly, "Though I never would have admitted it then."

"You just…needed someone to be on your side, no matter what."

"I did. I needed someone willing to stand with me come hell or high water. I needed that so bad, Chrissy."

"And I couldn't be that for you then."

"Yeah. I get that now. You just weren't ready to leave everything behind for a mixed-up kid with no prospects."

"You're right," she answered honestly. "Except that it wasn't because you were kind of mixed up and not because you had no prospects, either. It was that I had things I needed to do, like get my degree, grow up a little. It wasn't about you, Hayes. I honestly wasn't ready to get married at that point. Not to you. Not to anyone."

"I should have waited. I should have had a little patience."

That made her smile. "It's so good to know that you can see my side of it now. But don't beat yourself up over it. You needed someone strong and sure to stand beside you then. I wasn't that person."

"I was so angry at you."

"I remember."

"And I've held on to that anger. When I first came back, when we ran into each other at the inn that first day, I still felt that way. I still saw you as having been the one in the wrong all those years ago. But tonight…"

"What? Tell me."

"Well, I'm starting to get that I was the unreasonable one."

"Now you're being too hard on yourself, Hayes."

"No. I'm just seeing the past in a different way, a more *real* way, that's all." He reached across the table and put his hand over hers.

She let him, though she knew she shouldn't.

A moment later, Yolanda appeared with the main course. Hayes pulled his hand away. They concentrated on the wonderful meal and left talk of the past behind.

WHEN THEY GOT back to the ranch, Rayna was waiting just inside the front gate. They stopped to greet her, and she followed them up the steps.

"It's nice out tonight." Hayes paused on the porch and turned to stare up at the starry, cloudless sky. He glanced down and into Chrissy's eyes. "Another great night for sitting on the porch…"

She should probably go in. But she didn't have to work tomorrow. There was no big push to get to bed or anything.

They perched on the porch steps as they had those other nights, with Rayna flopping down, getting comfortable behind them.

"Thanks for dinner," he said.

"You're welcome. Castillo's never disappoints."

"You got that right."

She brought her knees up to the first step and rested her arms on them. He stared out at the sky as she studied his profile—the strong, straight nose, the sharp cheekbones and sculpted jawline.

When he turned his head her way, they ended up staring at each other. It was no hardship, staring at Hayes Parker. Never had been.

"What?" he asked, one corner of that too-sexy mouth quirking up.

"You tell me," she replied. It came out sounding like a challenge, though she hadn't meant it to be—or had she?

Hayes leaned closer. She didn't back away. Her heart had set up a racket inside her chest. Her breath felt trapped in her lungs.

With some effort, she remembered to let the air out, to take in another breath.

Now everything felt slower, sweeter and a little bit magical.

The night around them seemed to hum and that hum was inside her, a yearning.

And a promise.

"I shouldn't," he said in a gruff whisper, his lips a breath's distance from hers now.

You're right. Don't. The words were there, trapped inside her mind, stilled by the hungry beating of her heart.

And then it happened. His mouth touched hers. A sound escaped her then, a sigh that got caught on a hint of a moan.

It was good. So good. After all these years. To feel his mouth on hers again.

At his gentle nudge, she parted her lips. His breath flowed into her.

It was so sweet, that kiss, full of tenderness and promise. It was all the good things they'd shared in the old days. It was the closeness, the soul-deep connection between them—the connection she'd severed by necessity so that she could get over him, get on with her life.

His hands clasped her shoulders. She sighed at his touch, expecting him to pull her closer.

Instead, very gently, he pushed her away.

She opened her eyes, stunned at what they'd just done. And even worse, at how much she'd wanted—still wanted—to keep right on doing it.

They stared at each other. He looked wrecked. She knew that she did, too.

"I'm sorry, Chrissy," he whispered, still holding her away from him. "I shouldn't have done that."

Her foolish heart cried, *Oh yes! Yes, you should have* at the same time as she knew very well that he was right. "Yeah," she said with a certainty she didn't feel. "I know. It's…not a good idea."

His grip on her shoulders loosened and his hands dropped away. "You okay?"

She tried on a smile as she lied outright. "I am. I'm

fine." Forcing her wobbly legs to straighten, she rose to her feet. "I think I'll go in."

"All right, then. Thanks again for dinner."

"My pleasure." It was far too true. "Night."

"Good night." She stepped over Rayna and made for the door.

"WHAT'S GOING ON with you and the ex-girlfriend?" Arlen asked the next morning after breakfast as they two of them mucked out the barn.

Hayes scooped up a shovelful of dirty straw. "No idea what you're talkin' about."

"Oh, really? You can't remember back as far as break-fast, with you and her being way too careful not to look at each other? And polite." Arlen let out a slow whistle. "Never seen manners like that so early in the morning."

"Let it go, Arlen."

That brought out Arlen's famous deep, knowing chuckle. "Never say I didn't warn you."

Hayes dumped the last shovelful of dirty straw on top of the pile in the wheelbarrow. "Pass me that broom, would you?"

Arlen handed it over and then clapped him on the shoulder. "You want to talk about it, you know I'm here for you, my friend."

Hayes longed to order the big cowhand to mind his own damn business. But then he'd only end up feeling more like a jerk than he already did. "Thanks," he said through clenched teeth and started sweeping up straw.

All that day he felt bad. He'd been the one who started it with Chrissy, leaning in, taking that kiss that he couldn't stop thinking about. She'd kissed him back and it felt so good, her lips opening, welcoming.

Her kiss had worked a certain scary magic. It threw him

back in time to all those years before, the two of them so in love they couldn't bear to be apart. Her mouth tasted like heaven. He'd wanted nothing so much as to haul her closer, kiss her more deeply, let the heat between them take control.

But they'd promised each other they weren't going to do that. So he'd stopped what he'd started—and yeah, he knew he'd hurt her feelings, running hot and then all of a sudden stopping things cold.

But it would be okay in a few days. The awkwardness between them would fade. They would get back to keeping it friendly, no pressure, no heat.

All he had to do was behave himself and the situation would work itself out. He could do that. No problem.

Except that later, at dinner, she remained so distant. So careful. He missed the new friendship they'd found.

And then, Monday morning, it was the same thing all over again. He left the breakfast table feeling like a stranger in the house where he'd grown up.

Chrissy was kind to him. She never once gave him a dirty look or raised her voice. But she was taking keeping distance between them very seriously. And by then, he'd started to wonder how long he could bear it, how soon he would break.

He just wanted their newfound friendship back, he kept telling himself. But then he would think about that kiss on the porch and a low, knowing voice in the back of his head would call him a liar for trying to tell himself that being just friends with Chrissy Hastings would ever be enough.

"THERE YOU ARE!" Chrissy turned at the sound of her friend Marisa's voice. Black-haired with beautiful brown eyes and lush curves, Marisa Sanchez stood in the open doorway of Chrissy's postage-stamp of an office at the Tenacity Inn.

"Hey, there! Right on time for lunch." Chrissy jumped up from her desk. Three steps later, she was hugging her friend.

Like Chrissy, Marisa had grown up in Tenacity. Marisa was younger, just twenty-six. But in Tenacity, everyone knew everyone, so they had always known each other, though they hadn't grown close until Chrissy returned to town after she and Sam broke up.

"This way." Chrissy took Marisa's hand and led her to the inn's dining room, where a light breakfast was served daily in addition to meals and snacks for events and the various mini conventions booked by local groups and businesses. She pulled out a chair at a two-top near a tall window looking out on a neatly landscaped section of the grounds. "Have a seat."

Marisa hesitated. "You know we could have gone to Castillo's or that little café next to the Grizzly."

The Silver Spur Café was mostly a breakfast place, but they served sandwiches, too. As for Castillo's? No, thank you. Not for a while. Right now, her favorite restaurant reminded her too sharply of Saturday night, of how absolutely great it had been.

Until it wasn't.

"Next time," Chrissy promised. Marisa took the offered chair and Chrissy asked, "Cobb salad, iced tea and crusty bread with sweet butter?"

Marisa laughed. "Okay, that sounds perfect. Some other time for Castillo's."

"Sit right there. I'll be back in a flash." Chrissy had assembled the salads ahead of time and put the crusty loaf in the warming oven a few minutes before. She quickly served them both.

They settled in to catch up. Marisa was a fine musician who taught piano to quite a few people in town, kids

and adults alike. She also had a real talent for organizing events. Nowadays, she was a local celebrity. Her video of the annual winter holiday choir right there in Tenacity had started out on TikTok and gone viral—as in all-the-way-around-the-globe viral. The choir's presentation was multicultural, funky and unique. Everyone in town had been thrilled that their small community had gained a moment in the spotlight.

"So what's new with you?" Chrissy asked.

Marisa set down her fork and clapped her hands together. "You won't believe it."

"What? Tell me!"

"You are looking at this year's director of the Mistletoe Christmas Pageant."

The Mistletoe Christmas Pageant took place in Bronco right along with the Mistletoe Rodeo, which was a very big deal. "Wow. Marisa. That's huge."

"I know! I can't believe they asked me. And I can still do our annual holiday show here in Tenacity, too."

"Right. Because the Mistletoe Christmas Pageant is in November and we do *our* Christmas show in December."

"You got it." Marisa beamed.

"This is fabulous!" Chrissy jumped up, ran around the table, pulled her friend to her feet and hugged her good and hard—yeah, they were huggers, the two of them. She loved that about their friendship. "You are brilliant," she said. "And I'm so glad you're getting the recognition and the great projects you deserve."

"Thank you. Me, too." Marisa hugged her right back.

Chrissy returned to her seat.

As she smoothed her napkin over her lap, Marisa asked, "So how are the condo repairs going?"

"Much too slowly if you ask me." Last week, when Chrissy called Marisa to invite her to lunch, she'd brought

her friend up to speed on the condo disaster. "As of now, my dad assures me that things are moving right along—but it's going to be another three or four weeks, and that's if I'm lucky. The whole interior had to be torn out to the studs. It's a major rebuild."

"But your insurance will cover it?"

"Yeah. Luckily I purchased really good coverage when I moved in. And now I'm so glad I did."

"Excellent."

They ate in silence for a minute or two. When Chrissy glanced up from her plate again, Marisa was grinning at her across the table. "Okay," Chrissy said. "What is going through that mind of yours? Tell me now."

"Hmm…" Marisa actually wiggled her eyebrows.

"What are you up to? Don't tease me. Put it out there, whatever it is."

"Well, I'm just wondering how it's going, you living at the End of the Road Ranch with Hayes."

Chrissy groaned. "What have you heard?"

"Well…" Marisa drew that one word out for way too long.

"Now you really are just teasing me. Spill it."

"Okay, fine. Rumor is, you were seen with him Saturday night at Castillo's."

"What? Two people can't eat at Castillo's without everyone talking? I cannot believe this town."

"Please. You were born and raised here. You know how it goes. Gossip spreads like a prairie fire."

"I should take out a billboard on Central Avenue. Two sentences. *I am not getting back together with Hayes Parker. We are just friends.* And then slap my signature on it."

Ice cubes rattled as Marisa sipped her tea. "That would definitely cause a stir. And then everyone could argue

about whether or not it's the truth, and if it is, how long you two will *stay* just friends."

"It's ridiculous," Chrissy muttered under her breath.

Marisa spoke more gently, "It's reality is what it is."

"I promise you, I'm just staying at the ranch temporarily while my condo is being repaired. And I am sleeping *alone* in Rylee's old bedroom. I mean, how many times do I need to remind people of that?"

"Oh, let me think… Hundreds? Thousands? And they still won't believe you."

"You are not reassuring me."

Marisa set down her fork. "Are you really upset?" When Chrissy let out a pitiful whine, suddenly Marisa was the one pushing back her chair. She stepped around the small table. "Come here. Come on." Chrissy got up. Again, they hugged it out.

"Thanks," said Chrissy softly when they were both sitting down again. "I needed that."

"Whatever happens, I'm guessing you two have made peace about the past?"

Chrissy nibbled a bite of bread and suddenly felt a little bit better about everything. "You're right. We have."

"And that's a good thing."

"Yeah," Chrissy agreed. "It's a good thing. It really is." And a change of subject was in order. "What's the latest on Winona? Tell me she's back."

Ninety-seven-year-old Winona Cobbs, who now lived in Bronco, but who was famous all over Montana for her psychic abilities and her talent at matchmaking any number of happy couples, had vanished from Bronco a couple of weeks ago, right before her wedding to Stanley Sanchez. Stanley was eighty-seven and madly in love with his bride-to-be. Everyone said he was devastated to have lost her.

Marisa shook her head. "Nobody knows why or where she went. She's still gone. It's scary."

"Oh, no. I really thought she would have reappeared by now." Chrissy forced a smile. "But she will. I mean, we have to stay positive, right?"

"That's right," Marisa agreed.

"Promise you'll call me right away if you hear anything."

"You know I will."

"Thanks. And you're the first one I'll call if I have news about her." Chrissy offered more tea.

Marisa accepted a refill. They chatted about happier subjects after that.

When her friend left, Chrissy cleared off the table and tried not to worry about the famous missing psychic—or to let her mind wander to thoughts of Hayes Parker.

THAT NIGHT, HAYES sat across the kitchen table from Chrissy and wished he knew how to make things better between them. He couldn't figure out what to do to breach the wall of silence that separated them since the other night. Because he really did want to be her friend.

But friendship with her was no easy thing. As soon as they got closer, he just wanted to be closer still.

And the whole point, as they'd agreed Saturday night, was to keep their distance. Not getting too cozy was the main job—and that job didn't lend itself to a lot of casual, friendly interaction.

Apparently, she felt the same—that it wasn't safe to try being good buddies.

Or maybe she was just fed up with him and had zero desire to speak to him at all.

Whatever was going through her mind, she was extra

quiet about it. So both of them ate dinner without saying much.

At least Arlen kept the conversation going. He praised the meal and discussed the new roof they would put on the barn as soon as all the materials he'd ordered arrived. Arlen had worked several years for a roofing contractor, so he knew his way around the job.

Every day now, Hayes thanked his lucky stars for Arlen. The man could work circles around most ranch hands, and he seemed to have a handle on just about every task Hayes threw at him. And if Arlen didn't know how to do something, he could usually figure it out.

No, Arlen wouldn't stay forever. He wanted his own land, and he was saving up, same as Hayes had, to make that happen. But until he decided it was time to move on, Hayes would be grateful for his skills, his willingness to work a long, hard day and his good humor that rarely flagged.

After dinner, Arlen suggested, "How 'bout a beer?"

"I'm in. Thanks."

They went out to the trailer, where they sat under the stars, sipping cans of Bud with Rayna at their feet.

"Want to talk about whatever's going on between you and that pretty woman back in the kitchen?" Arlen asked.

"No, I do not."

"Well, all right then. Just thought I'd make the offer."

"Thanks. No."

"So then, how's your dad doing?"

Not a question he was dying to tackle, either. But he did it anyway. "He's getting better very slowly. Which reminds me, I need to get over to Bronco for a visit."

"You really think he's doing okay?"

"I do. But I should check for myself. My mom says not to worry, that his recovery is just taking longer than usual,

but he is getting better. Knowing my dad, it's probably his attitude. He wants out of there and he's stewing about it, lying awake nights worrying over all the things he can't do anything about instead of getting some rest."

"Go tomorrow."

Hayes hesitated. "I hate to leave you here to manage everything on your own."

"How long will you be gone?"

"Half a day."

"It's not a problem. You know damn well there's nothing around here I can't handle."

Hayes grinned. "Now that you mention it, I've noticed that."

"So go. I'll hold down the fort here. If I run into a problem I can't solve, I'll give you a call."

"WELL, LOOK WHO'S HERE," said Lionel the next morning when Hayes entered his hospital room. The old man actually smiled. And he looked better, too, Hayes thought—thinner, both in the face and around the middle. His color had also improved.

The room had two hospital beds, one of which was empty. There was a curtain to pull for privacy when the other bed was occupied. Hayes noted the neatly made folding cot on his dad's side of the room. That must be where his mom slept. He asked, "Did Mom go home?"

Lionel nodded. "She left a half hour ago. You probably passed her on the highway. I think she and that ex-girlfriend of yours are in some kind of cooking competition."

That made Hayes smile. "Yep. Chrissy wants to do all the cooking to pay for her room at the house. Mom thinks the cooking is *her* job. I'll tell you this much, the deep freeze is filling up fast."

His dad actually laughed. "Sounds like a win-win to me."

Hayes put up both hands. "Hey, I try to stay out of it."

"Humph. Wise course of action." Lionel dipped his chin at the empty chair by the bed. "Sit down. Take a load off."

Hayes dropped into the chair. "So, Dad, how are you feeling?"

His dad heaved a long, weary sigh. "I keep telling the doctors to let me out of here. But they're still not ready to do what I say. I've got high levels of this and low levels of that. Who understands all the medical talk? Not me. I've lived my whole life taking care of business and suddenly a bunch of guys in white coats think it's their place to tell me what to do and how to do it. I should be up and seeing after things at home."

Hayes disagreed, but he didn't say so. So far, this conversation was going surprisingly well. He didn't want to set his dad off, so he kept his mouth shut.

Lionel wasn't fooled. The old man grunted. "Go ahead. Whatever you're thinking, spit it out."

Fair enough, then. "Look, Dad. You've come this far. Just stay here until the doctors release you. Get well. The ranch will still be there when you get back."

The old man drew a slow, measured breath. "You sure about that?"

"Yeah, Dad. I am."

Lionel got that stubborn look, teeth gritted, eyes narrowed. But he didn't say anything. Hayes tried to think of a suitably bland topic that would not in any way get his father stirred up.

As the seconds ticked by, he heard a sound at the small, narrow window. A blue jay sat on a leafy branch just beyond the glass. The bird gave the window a peck and then tipped his crested head from side to side, as though completely bumfuzzled at the invisible barrier between outside and in.

"That damn bird shows up at least once a day," grumbled Lionel. "Pecks the window every time, too. Like it's new to him all over again that he can't just come through to the other side."

Hayes tried not to stare outright at his dad. He wasn't sure exactly what was going on here. Had his father actually changed? Because overall, they were having a civil conversation. They hadn't had one of those since Hayes was thirteen years old.

"Tell me the truth," his father said.

"About what?"

"A few years back, Braden told me you went to college."

"I got a two-year online degree in ranch management from Casper College in Wyoming."

"You went to college on the internet?"

"Yeah, Dad. I did."

"Well. Ain't that a kick in the head." Lionel seemed impressed. And then he said so. "Good for you, son."

"Thanks, Dad."

"Your mother says your school friends from town came to work the place with you three or four days running, that they pulled things together."

"They did. I'm grateful."

"She says now you've hired a hand. A damn good one, too."

"Yeah. Arlen's the best there is."

"Your mother tells me you really do have everything under control."

"I don't know that I'd go that far. But I think we're keeping on top of it, overall."

Lionel nodded. And then he scowled. "Norma has also informed me that she's paying the bills with her freedom money and there's not a damn thing I can do to stop her."

"She does seem pretty determined about that." Hayes

made his voice carefully neutral. He watched the warring emotions battle it out on his father's road map of a face—love and pride, frustration and shame that his wife would be using her mother's dying gift to keep the ranch afloat.

"Well," said Lionel, "I'm just going to say this…"

Dread crept up Hayes's spine. Was this where the criticisms and demands started in?

"Son." His father's voice was thick and low. "I want you to know that I'm grateful." Was that the sheen of tears in the old man's eyes? "So damn grateful for all you're doing right now. I've spent years thinking I would never see your face again. And yet here you are, riding in just when things have gone from bad to worse to damn near impossible. I thank you for that. I truly do."

Hayes realized his mouth was hanging open. He shut it and swallowed. Hard. Was there hope for him and his father, after all? "Dad, I…"

Lionel stopped him by raising his hand, palm out. "Let me say my piece here?"

"Uh. Yeah, sure. Go ahead."

"It has occurred to me that I might have been too hard on you, and on your brothers, too—and you know what? Forget about might-have-been. I probably *was* too tough on you three. I mean, look at you. Gone at eighteen and staying gone for way too long. Now Braden's taken off, too, and I know I'm the main reason. As for Miles, he answered the call of duty, yeah. But he's still gone now, isn't he? Lying here in this bed, I've got all the time in the world to think about how I raised you boys and if I was in the wrong."

Hayes was starting to feel a bit misty-eyed. "Dad, I—"

That hand went up again. "Still not finished."

"Okay, Dad."

"Was I in the wrong? That's the question." Lionel paused and then announced, "The answer is no."

Hayes blinked. "No?"

"No." Lionel's lips twisted in a self-righteous sneer. "I was *not* too hard on you. Because life is tough, and a man needs to be tougher—and that's why I did what I had to do to make you boys ready to face all the crap this world is bound to throw at you. Because there is no free lunch, no big, fancy picnic and you boys needed to know that. You needed to understand that, to believe it way deep down in your bones and—"

"Dad, listen…"

Lionel leveled a furious glare on him. "Did I say I was finished? Because I'm not. I'm right about this and you need to realize how right I am. So as far as regrets go? Screw 'em. I raised you boys right, and I am not sorry about that. Not one bit, no, siree."

Disappointment. Hayes felt it like a hundred pounds of concrete pressing down on his shoulders. *Here we go again*, he thought. Just like old times, with Lionel ranting on, endlessly repeating his self-righteous reasons for being a jerk.

Hayes should probably leave it alone, let the old man rant. But by then he was just fed up enough to fight back. "Come on, Dad. A kid needs more than mean words and ultimatums, more than warnings and constant reminders of how he's doing everything wrong. A kid needs love and respect. Everybody does. You seemed to understand that with Rylee—or at least, you didn't ride her constantly about every little thing."

"It's different with girls."

"How?"

"If you don't know, I'm certainly not going to tell you."

"You're dodging the question."

"The point is, I did respect you, damn it. I respected you enough to teach you how to be strong. I taught you to keep going no matter what, to do it right and if you do get it wrong, to keep trying, to find a way to obliterate every obstacle in your path. I taught you never to give up! And, son, look at you now. Right here in front of me today when fifteen years ago you swore I would never see your face again.

"You showed up when it mattered. You've got the grit to do what needs doing to save the ranch. And I am proud to say that you've got what it takes because I raised you right. I made it my mission never to let you get away with one damn thing and that made you strong!"

"You're shouting, Dad."

"Damn right I am! I have plenty to say, and I mean to say it!"

The door swung open. A nurse bustled in. "What is going on in here?" She turned to Hayes. "Step aside, please." Hayes moved away from the bed as the nurse marched straight for it, her eyes on Lionel now. "Mr. Parker, you need to keep it down. This is a hospital, and many of our patients are trying to rest. I can hear you all the way to the nurses' station."

"Humph," Lionel replied.

"Beyond the disturbance you're creating," the nurse said more gently, "it's just not good for you to get all worked up like this. Your blood pressure is spiking. You need to calm down."

There was a stare-down. Lionel glared at the petite gray-haired nurse and she glared right back at him.

Hayes's dad was the one who broke. "Sorry," he muttered. Suddenly, he looked bone tired, the shadows under his eyes darker than before. "Fine. I'll keep it down."

"Thank you." The nurse smiled sweetly, patted him on the shoulder, and left.

As the door swung shut behind her, Lionel turned his glare on Hayes. "Well." He spoke quietly, but with an underpinning of steel despite the exhaustion on his haggard face. "I had something to say, and I said it." He folded his arms across his barrel chest.

Hayes managed to shut his mouth before a bitter response escaped. There was no win in starting the argument all over again.

His dad taunted. "You think you got something to say back to me, go for it."

"There's no point."

"Because you've got nothing. You know I'm right."

"That's not true. I just don't think you're listening, Dad."

"Say it."

Hayes drew his shoulders back. "All right. It's just that I do believe it's possible to teach a kid how to survive without constantly yelling at him, pointing out every error he makes and reminding him over and over again of all the ways he's messed up."

"You're wrong. Just wait. You'll understand when you have sons of your own."

"You drove me away, Dad. And Braden, too. Probably Miles. Is that really what you wanted?"

His dad only shook his head, sank back against the pillow and closed his eyes.

CHAPTER SEVEN

THAT EVENING, IT was just Chrissy and Hayes at the kitchen table for dinner. Arlen had gone into town to eat and most likely to visit the Grizzly.

Chrissy thought Hayes seemed thoughtful, and not really in a good way. Like he was stewing over something, trying to figure it out—and not getting anywhere. He'd mentioned at breakfast that he was driving over to Bronco to see his dad.

Had the visit gone wrong somehow? Probably. She wanted to ask Hayes about it. But the faraway look in his eyes discouraged conversation.

After the meal, he started to help her clean up. She shooed him away. "I've got this," she said, and took his dirty plate from him.

He gave her a half-hearted smile. "Have it your way." With Rayna close at his heels, he went out to take care of evening chores.

She cleaned up the kitchen, dusted the great room and then went upstairs to tweak a couple of menus for events in the coming weeks. It was almost dark when she finished but still too early to go to bed. Plus, she felt kind of edgy, like there was something she ought to be dealing with. She just didn't know what.

So she wandered back downstairs where all the rooms were empty. When she peeked through the window that looked out on the front porch, she saw Hayes sitting on

the steps and Rayna in her usual spot, sprawled out behind him. His back was to her. She couldn't see his face.

But there was something in the set of his shoulders that spoke of discouragement. He was definitely feeling down.

She wanted to comfort him, though offering comfort didn't exactly go hand-in-hand with keeping her distance. After Saturday night, she did need to watch her step or she could end up getting something started that would not end well.

It was only...

He just seemed so sad sitting there. She couldn't even see his face, but his body language spoke of burdens too heavy to bear. She couldn't stop thinking that he needed a friend, someone to talk to, someone to listen to whatever he had on his mind.

Before she could remind herself again of all the reasons to turn around and head back up the stairs, she was pulling the front door open.

Hayes glanced over his shoulder and saw her standing in the open doorway. "What's up?"

"Want some company?"

Time stretched out. They just looked at each other. Finally, he patted the empty space beside him.

Pulling the door shut behind her, she dipped to give Rayna a pat on the head, then stepped over the dog to join him. For several minutes, not a word was said. They stared up at the dark, starry sky.

"Nice night," she said.

"Yeah. Warm. Not too windy."

She tried again. "I noticed all that stuff for the barn roof arrived today."

He nodded. "Arlen says that the two of us together can get that job done in two days."

"That's great."

"Yeah. Eventually, I might even look into hiring professionals to paint the barn and the house. Maybe next month. Depending on the cost. If it's too much, at some point I'll just buy the paint and do it myself."

"Ah," she replied. "New paint would really spruce up the place."

"Yeah," he said glumly.

"Hayes…"

"Huh?"

She looked into his clear green eyes and asked, "You okay?"

He made a low, thoughtful sound. "I've been better."

She waited. After all these years, she could still read him. Right now, she knew he needed a moment to decide how much he wanted to say to her. Behind them, Rayna shifted, her tags rattling.

Finally he spoke again. "It's my dad."

"Yeah. I kind of figured."

"Today, I thought for half a minute or so that maybe we were getting somewhere, taking the first steps toward making peace with each other. But then it was just the same old crap from him all over again. How he was tough on me and my brothers because we needed him to be a mean SOB so we could learn how to survive in the world."

"You're right," she said with a sigh. "That's nothing new."

"Exactly."

"But tell me about that half a minute when you thought you were getting somewhere."

He looked down at the porch step beneath his boots and then back up at her. "He thanked me—for coming back, and for taking care of the ranch while he's laid up."

"Well, that really is progress."

"Yeah. Maybe…" He stared out at the night, his lean jaw set.

She knew she should avoid touching him. But come on, they were friends now, and she wanted to comfort him. She clasped his arm. "I'm glad to hear that he praised you a little. He *should* praise you for the way you've taken things in hand here at the ranch. Especially given that he disinherited you when you dared to strike out on your own fifteen years ago."

He let out a short laugh. "Yeah, about that…"

"What about it?"

He met her eyes again. She was still holding on to his arm. She should let go. But she didn't. They shared a long look. A hot, prickly shiver ran up the backs of her knees. His gaze shifted a fraction. He was looking at her mouth—and now her lips were tingling.

He said, "Turns out, my dad never did change his will. My mom told me last week. She said it was all talk, that my dad never would do a thing like that."

"Oh, Hayes." Her throat felt tight. She gave a little cough to clear it. "I'm so glad to hear that."

He touched her cheek. His finger came away wet. "If you're glad, then why are you crying?"

She sniffed. "It's only a few tears. And they are tears of happiness. Your dad *is* a good man. He shouldn't have threatened you with losing your part of the ranch, but at least he didn't go through with it."

"Yeah. Still, I'm not really over how he let me *think* for all these years that he'd cut me out."

"I hear you. And I'm not saying that you *should* be over it."

"Thanks," he muttered, staring at the low shadowed humps of the gray hills way out there in the far distance.

"It's heartbreaking, the way your dad tries to be so tough and only ends up pushing people away."

"Heartbreaking? To you, maybe. As for me, well, his attitude just plain pisses me off."

She nudged him with her elbow. "You might be a little bit heartbroken about it, too."

He scoffed. "Fine. Maybe a little."

"And at least today he gave you credit for coming back, for taking things in hand here when there really was no one else to do it. It's a step in the right direction."

He gave a half shrug. "Yeah. I'll try to look at it that way."

She knew she shouldn't reach for his hand—but she did it anyway. When he didn't pull back, she laced her fingers with his. "You're a good guy," she reminded him. "And your dad knows it. I do believe that eventually he'll come around completely. The two of you will end up working together. Just wait and see."

He chuckled. "There you go, looking on the bright side."

"Yep." She gave his fingers a squeeze. "I am a cockeyed optimist and proud of it."

His gaze shifted from her eyes to her lips and back to her eyes again. Were her cheeks flushed? They did feel kind of warm… "You sound like *your* dad now," he said.

That made her smile. "You're right. It's one of his favorite expressions. Whenever Mom gives him a bad time for not facing reality as she sees it, he just grins and says he's a cockeyed optimist and she ought to be used to that by now."

"I used to wish that my dad could be like yours," he said, "always thoughtful and understanding. Plus, your dad has an actual sense of humor." Now his eyes were focused solely on her mouth.

She felt that focus in her belly, which was suddenly full

of fluttery sensations. "Yeah," she said. "My dad's the best. Secretly, I think even my mom loves that he keeps things upbeat no matter what. She'd never admit it, though." Her voice sounded slightly breathless. Didn't it?

Because she certainly *felt* breathless. And those fluttery feelings in her belly? More so with every second that passed. He rubbed his rough thumb over the back of her hand. How could such a simple touch burn her all the way to the core?

Several seconds passed during which neither of them said a word.

By then, there was only his gaze holding hers, his thumb continuing its rough caress.

"Chrissy," he whispered, their faces so close now that their noses almost touched.

"Hmm?"

He moved then, leaning in that extra fraction of an inch, tipping his head just slightly so that their lips aligned.

"Hayes," she whispered as his mouth touched hers.

And then his strong arms were around her. She melted into him.

Now there was nothing but his mouth on hers, nothing but the taste of him, clean and sweet and so well remembered.

Her yearning had a pulse, and her heart was a wild thing, pounding away at the cage of her ribs.

When he pulled back, she almost slid her hands up over his chest, almost wrapped them around his neck, almost yanked him back down to her. Almost.

But not quite.

Instead, she drew a slow, careful breath and opened her eyes.

His were waiting. Slowly, as though afraid any sudden move might spook her, he touched her cheek. Catching a

loose curl of her hair, he guided it back behind her ear. "There I go." His voice was deeper than ever right then, dark as the shadows in his eyes. "Stepping over the line again..."

She laughed low. "It's not like I resisted or asked you to stop."

"Chrissy, we had an agreement."

"Yes, Hayes. I am aware."

"And now I've broken it."

"Oh, yes, you did."

"And you know what?"

She shook her head slowly. "Tell me."

"Now I just want to break it all over again."

"Do you see me stopping you?" She was whispering now.

"So, then...?"

She knew it was her move. And she made it. Surging up, she pressed her parted lips to his.

He gathered her in with a groan.

That kiss went on forever. It was so good, so sweet and so tender. So wild. Just what she needed right now—to be wanted as only Hayes had ever wanted her. To be swept away to that place where all the everyday stuff just didn't matter at all.

When she got lost in his kiss, there was only right now.

Too bad they couldn't just sit here on the front step and keep kissing forever.

She opened her eyes to find him watching her. When she pulled back enough to give him a wobbly smile, he released her. She faced the front walk again, but then his arm came around her. She settled against his side, resting her head on his shoulder.

His lips brushed her hair. She felt the warmth of his breath as he whispered, "So much for the friendship plan."

"Hey." She lifted a hand and patted his chest. "We're still friends. I promise."

"I'm glad." He sounded sincere. "Too bad I have so much trouble keeping my hands off of you."

"Same." She tipped her head up to him. His eyes were jewel-green now. She asked, "What are we going to do about this problem of ours?" When he frowned but failed to answer, she made herself offer, "If you want me to move out, just say so."

His arm tightened around her. "I don't. Uh-uh. Please don't move out, Chrissy."

"You're serious?"

"Oh, yeah. No way am I kicking you out. You carry your weight. And you're right there to listen to me gripe on endlessly about my dad. Having you here just makes everything better. You cheer me up, you really do."

Warmth spread through her at his praise. "Thank you."

"So then, stick with the plan. Stay until your condo's ready for you."

She drew a slow breath as she gathered her courage. "Hayes. We have to get real here. Promising to keep our distance isn't working."

"I know."

She made herself put it right out there. "I just have to say, if this goes where it feels like it's going and we end up in bed together, you should know it can only be for now. Because my life? It's kind of a mess. I'm not at a place where I can take on a relationship."

"I get it. I do. And as for your life being a mess, you're not the only one."

"Hayes, we can be friends. We can…consider adding benefits. But I'm not ready in any way for more than that. I'll say it again to drive the point home. It can only be for now."

He held her closer. "I can't believe you just said it out loud."

"That it's only for now?"

"No. The part about adding benefits."

She ordered the butterflies in her belly to settle down and answered him honestly. "Well, we can't just pretend that it's all buddy-buddy between us—and keep letting ourselves share the kind of kisses that could burn this house down."

"I hear you. And you don't have to worry. If it gets out of hand, we're agreed on where we stand about the future."

"Yeah." She swallowed hard. "There is no future for you and me."

He nodded. "You're not ready for more and I never will be."

She pulled away from the shelter of his arm, just enough to look him in the eye. "Never? Are you serious?"

"Yeah," he said in a gruff voice. "Losing you almost broke me. And then when Anna died… Well, it was bad. Really bad. We had so many plans, me and Anna. And all of them were wiped out by a patch of black ice on a cold December night. I can't do it again, Chrissy. I'm through with falling in love. I just don't have another damn heartbreak in me."

She wanted to argue—that he shouldn't completely give up on love. That someday he *would* be ready again. That love didn't always end in heartbreak.

But for him—and for her, too—it had. And she knew him well enough to know that he meant what he said. Plus, she was staring right into his eyes. She saw nothing but brutal honesty there. Steering clear of love was his choice and she needed to respect that.

"You have that look," he said with a crooked smile. "The one that says it's time to call it a night."

Her throat had clutched up again. "I just don't have the

words, that's all. I haven't had much luck with love, either. But still, for me, the way love has ended has always been a matter of choices—between you and me. And then between me and Sam. In both of those relationships, it ended with both of us still standing. It ended because it had become impossible to stay together.

"But you and Anna, you didn't get a choice and you didn't get all that long together, either. That just feels so completely wrong. I can understand why you don't want to go there ever again. I don't like it. And I'm sad for you. But I get it. I do." She stood.

He lifted his head to meet her eyes. "You're going in?"

"Yeah." She stepped over Rayna and went to the door. "Night, Chrissy."

"Night." She turned and left him there.

HAYES WATCHED THE door close behind her and had to actively resist the need to jump up and follow her, to catch hold of her hand, pull her close again, wrap his arms around her good and tight.

They really weren't going anywhere together. They'd been done for a long, long time.

He wanted her, yeah. He wanted her a lot. He wanted her for as long as it lasted. And he knew that couldn't be for very long.

But he didn't want to hurt her the way he'd hurt her in the past. They were on good terms now. Bringing sex into it could blow everything to hell all over again.

So he waited out there in the dark for another hour, long enough to be certain that when he went inside, she would be upstairs in her bedroom with the door firmly shut.

"GOOD MORNING!" CHRISSY announced way too brightly when Hayes and Arlen came in from the barn at seven a.m. the next day. "Ready for breakfast?" she chirped.

"I sure am!" Hayes ladled on the enthusiasm. To Chrissy, it sounded phony as hell. And that was just fine. The phonier the better. They would stomp out any promise of intimacy by faking friendliness for all they were worth.

They ate. Hayes told her that her biscuits and gravy rivaled his mom's.

She blasted him her brightest smile. "High praise! I'll take it!"

At dinner, he said her pork chops couldn't be beat. When he asked her about work, she beamed and announced it was, "Fine. Just fine!"

They spent a full five minutes on the weather—hot, with no chance of rain, just like every day in Tenacity, Montana, during the month of August. Then Hayes bragged about the progress he and Arlen had made toward getting the new roof on the barn. "Looks like we really will finish tomorrow."

"That's terrific!" she exclaimed.

Arlen hardly said a word through the meal. He watched Hayes and Chrissy as they alternately ate in painful silence and lobbed meaningless phrases at each other in ridiculously cheerful voices.

"Beer?" Arlen asked Hayes cautiously when dinner was finished.

"You're on," Hayes replied, grateful for a reason to get out of that kitchen and away from the woman he needed *not* to get close to.

They were sitting out under the sky by the trailer, Buds in hand, Rayna snoozing on the grass between them when Arlen said, "What the hell's going now between you and Chrissy?"

Had Hayes known that was coming? Pretty much. "Nothing," he lied through his teeth.

Arlen wasn't buying. "You guys were getting close—

and suddenly, you're making fake noises and wearing phony smiles."

"Who said we were getting close?"

Arlen enjoyed a long sip of beer. "If you're not going to answer my question, just say so."

Hayes said nothing for several long seconds. Arlen waited him out. Finally, Hayes explained, "Yeah. Me and Chrissy had a talk last night. Neither of us wants to get involved right now. So we're trying to keep things casual and no more than friendly, you know?"

"And you don't want to get involved, why?"

Hayes crushed his empty can and dug in the cooler for another. "She's not ready for anything serious and I'm never getting serious again. So it's better if we keep our distance."

Arlen frowned. "I don't get it. But hey. If you say so…"

"What's not to get? We're both just being careful not to start something we can't finish."

"So then, you got something sweet between you, but your plan is to pretend you don't."

"We're friends, okay? And we want to keep it that way."

Arlen put up a hand. "Enough. Do it like you need to do it."

"What does that mean?"

"It means that you want her, and she wants you and you're not hiding how you feel about each other with all those fake smiles you two keep dishing out."

Hayes said nothing for a long count of ten. Finally, he stretched his legs out in front of him and leaned back to stare up at the stars that were getting brighter as the night came on. "We're both just doing the best we can."

"I get that. On the other hand, why not just go with it, see how it shakes out?"

"Because the result could be a whole lot of heartbreak. I've had plenty of that—more than my share."

"You can't win the lottery if you never buy a ticket."

"Arlen."

"Yeah?"

"Just drink your beer."

His friend shook his head, but he did let it go.

The next morning as he helped Chrissy clear off the breakfast dishes, she said she would be having dinner at her parents' house. She went on, "But thanks to your mom, there's enough to feed an army in the freezer. Most of it's already packaged in serving-size portions. Pick out what you're in the mood for and stick it in the microwave."

Hayes watched her lips move as she talked and tried not to picture himself just grabbing her and slamming his mouth down on hers. "I think we can handle it."

"Great," she said glumly.

He knew that expression. "Your mom giving you grief again?"

"Not right this minute, no." She tipped her head down.

He resisted the need to put a finger under her chin and guide her head up so she would look at him some more. "But you have a feeling she will be when you see her to-night?"

Her answer was a tiny shrug.

He said, "She loves you and she means well."

She lifted her head then. Their eyes met again. Bam! Like a punch to the gut. "Yep." She forced a bright grin.

It took every ounce of will he possessed not to pull her close and kiss her.

Denial and bright smiles just weren't working.

He didn't know how long he could continue to resist the need to grab her close and hold on tight. He didn't really

even want to resist. He wanted to give in, just let it happen and hope for the best when the end came.

THAT DAY, HAYES and Arlen hit their goal. By the time they finished work that evening, the barn was looking a whole lot better due to the new roof.

Back at the house, Hayes didn't even bother to check the deep freeze. He decided to get out and go somewhere noisy where there was beer. Arlen said he was up for that, too. Hayes called his buddies. Austin was out of town, but Jake and Beck agreed to meet them at the Grizzly.

The bar was doing a brisk business for a Thursday night in their small, dusty town. They ordered some pitchers, played eight-ball and listened to ancient country on the equally antique jukebox.

A couple of women Hayes vaguely remembered from high school came in about eight. Jake must have seen the frown on his face as he tried to remember their names.

"Lana Colby and Kerry Fox," Jake said, leaning close to be heard over a Tammy Wynette song. "They were two years behind us at Tenacity High."

"Right. I remember now. They were best friends even back then, joined at the hip."

"Yep. Kerry's never tied the knot. But Lana got married right after high school. Her divorce was final last year, so she's a Colby again."

"Gotcha." It was more than Hayes really needed to know.

Lana and Kerry joined in taking their turns at eight-ball with the guys. Kerry was kind of shy. But Lana knew how to handle a pool cue. She was also a world-class flirt.

When Hayes squeaked out a win on her, she batted her eyelashes and grinned. "I think you owe me a beer, Hayes Parker."

Hayes frowned. "Wait a minute. Didn't I just win?"

"And so you buy me a beer. That's how it works." She sidled in close and nudged him with her elbow as she dished out a teasing smile.

He bought her a beer. She thanked him with way more enthusiasm than the gesture required. And after that, every time he looked up from the pool table, she was giving him the come-and-get-it eyes.

At one point, Arlen muttered out of the side of his mouth, "That girl has a goal and I do believe that you are it."

"Well, that's not going to happen."

Arlen clapped him on the shoulder and then bent to make a shot.

Hayes spent the rest of the evening avoiding eye contact with Lana Colby and trying really hard not to wonder how Chrissy was holding up at her mother's house.

"I HAVEN'T HEARD from Sam." Chrissy's mom cut a bite of herb-crusted lamb chop and then added glumly, "I suppose I didn't really expect to."

Chrissy nibbled at an asparagus spear. It hadn't surprised her in the least that Sam had sent her mom a chain of postcards. He'd always liked her mom. Patrice was very much like Sam's mother, a pretty woman who stayed home and took care of her family and had no desire to get out and mix it up in the workaday world. "Looks like Sam is moving on, Mom."

"Yes." Patrice sighed. "I suppose it's for the best."

"Probably."

"Do you miss him at all?"

Chrissy set down her fork and sipped her ice water. The person she missed was Hayes. They'd spent the past two

days speaking to each other in short sentences, trying to be cheerful and ending up just being weird.

It wasn't going well. Not for her, anyway. If he avoided her, she felt bereft. And when he was sweet and understanding—like this morning when he asked her if everything was okay with her mom and then listened to her answer with understanding in his eyes—it took monumental effort not to fling herself into his arms.

Maybe she really should move out now.

Too bad she couldn't bear the thought of that, though she knew very well that it was going to happen soon enough anyway.

No doubt about it. She was living in a fool's dream.

"Chrissy? I asked you a question."

"Hmm?"

"Honestly." Her mother pursed her lips in disapproval. "I'll ask again. Don't you miss Sam at all?"

"Miss him?"

"Well? Do you?"

Chrissy tried to answer honestly. "Mom, I loved Sam. It didn't work out. We got divorced. Yes, for a while I was sad, and I really did miss him then. But that feeling has faded. Now I only wish him well."

Her mom just looked at her, like she couldn't figure out what in the world to say to that.

Chrissy's dad came to the rescue. "I stopped in at your place today. They're making good progress on the repairs."

"Yes." Chrissy beamed him a grateful smile. "It's going well. I should be able to move back in sometime in the next month or so."

Her mom smiled then. "Your father says insurance is going to cover everything."

She nodded. "Yeah. It looks like it. And I'm so grateful for that." Which had her wondering, if she did decide

she really needed to put some distance between her and Hayes, how much of a housing reimbursement would she get? She should check into that.

"I'm just going to say it one more time." Her mom glanced down as she smoothed the napkin on her lap. "We would love to have you come stay with us until your place is ready."

"Thanks, Mom," she answered automatically. "I appreciate that."

"So then you'll think about it?"

She would definitely be checking into what her insurance would cover first. As for her mom's question, agreeing to *think about* staying here for a month would only have Patrice redoubling her efforts to get Chrissy to follow through. She just didn't want to do that if she could possibly avoid it.

"It's working out beautifully at the Parker ranch," she shamelessly lied. "So for now, I'm staying put."

"But you *will* think about it." Her mom wore her sweetest smile.

And Chrissy gave in enough to agree, "Of course."

When she got back to the ranch that night, Hayes's pickup was nowhere in sight and Rayna was waiting at the gate inside the fence that surrounded the yard.

"Hey, girl." She crouched to greet the big dog. "How's it going?"

Rayna panted with happiness as Chrissy gave her a good scratch along her back to her furry tail and also behind the ears. The dog followed her up to the porch. It was a warm, windless night, so Chrissy sat on the step the way she had with Hayes two nights before. With a big yawn, Rayna plopped down behind her.

Ten minutes later, Chrissy was still sitting there thinking that she would get up and go inside any minute now.

But she didn't. She stared out at the night for another half hour and tried not to wonder where Hayes had gone off to.

Tenacity was a very small town and there weren't that many options for nighttime entertainment. So yeah, probably the Grizzly. She propped her elbows on her knees and her chin on the heel of her hand and hated herself for picturing him picking up some pretty woman and letting her take him home.

"It would be better if he just went ahead and did that." She hadn't realized she'd said it out loud until Rayna gave a little whine.

"Sorry, girl." She reached back and stroked Rayna's head to reassure her that all was well with the world.

Even if it wasn't. Even if Chrissy felt like a hopeless fool.

After twenty more minutes had staggered by, she got up to go in. She would have taken Rayna with her, but the dog wouldn't cross the threshold.

"Okay, girl." Chrissy bent to give her a quick hug. "You go ahead and wait for him."

Inside, she went straight up the stairs to her room, changed into a big, soft sleep shirt and padded down the hall to brush her teeth. She'd just climbed into bed and turned off the lamp when she heard faint sounds outside.

And she knew.

He was home.

Downstairs, the front door opened and closed.

Not that she cared. She didn't. Not one bit.

With a huff of annoyance, she pulled the blankets up over her head like some scared little girl hiding from a bad dream in the middle of the night. She shut her eyes and breathed slow and deep and told herself she didn't care if he'd gone and brought some other woman home with him.

Hayes could do what he wanted to do.

They were not getting anything started between them, and if she ended up feeding breakfast to some buckle bunny tomorrow morning, well, wouldn't that just be for the best?

At least it would serve as a reminder that getting involved with Hayes Parker all over again would be the ultimate in unacceptable choices. And it might even give her the nudge she needed to talk to her insurance agent about her relocation allotment.

There were boots on the stairs, but she didn't hear voices.

So what? Voices or not, it didn't matter. She was never going to go there. Uh-uh. Hayes Parker was off-limits. The two of them were never, ever, ever going to happen again.

CHAPTER EIGHT

IN THE MORNING, it was just Hayes, Arlen and Chrissy at the breakfast table. If Hayes had brought home a woman, she'd left well before dawn.

Hayes kept looking at her funny. She mostly tried *not* to look at him. Once or twice, Arlen made the effort to start an actual conversation. Neither Chrissy nor Hayes responded.

She had no interest in chitchat right now. She wanted Hayes but she wasn't going to have him, so the best thing for her in this moment was to eat her food, clean up after the meal and get ready for work. No cheerful breakfast chatter. It would only have her letting down her guard, opening herself up to the temptation to put a move on the man sitting to her right at the table.

Hayes was equally silent that morning. He ate his biscuits and gravy and gave Arlen one-word replies whenever the other man asked him a direct question. It shouldn't have been that hard for Chrissy to completely ignore him.

Oh, but it was hard. Her gaze kept trying to stray his way.

When the two men finally went back out to work, she didn't know whether she felt relieved or deeply depressed.

At the inn, things went pretty well. She had two back-to-back luncheons to deal with but nothing any later in the day. She checked out at a little after four. There were no

events scheduled for Saturday or Sunday. The weekend stretched out ahead of her, feeling empty. Endless.

Hanging around at the ranch trying to avoid Hayes didn't sound like a whole lot of fun. Maybe she'd drive over to Bronco, do a little shopping, treat herself to an overnight stay at a nice hotel. That could be fun. Maybe.

At least in Bronco, she wouldn't have to lie in bed trying not to listen for the sounds of Hayes's pickup pulling in out front.

On the way home, she went to Tenacity Grocery and picked up a few things. From there, she drove to her condo, which still looked a million years from completion. But progress was being made. Eventually, she would have her home back.

By then it was a little after five. She decided to stop in and check with her insurance agent. Yes, he said, she could claim reimbursement for lodging until her condo was move-in ready. He gave her paperwork to submit when she found a place.

By the time she got back into her Blazer again, it was after six. Reluctantly, she returned to the ranch.

Hayes had left her a note on the kitchen table. Arlen was having dinner in town and Hayes had driven over to Bronco to visit his dad. Apparently, he'd taken Rayna with him. The dog was nowhere to be seen.

Chrissy heated up some leftovers and ate them standing at the sink, staring out the window toward the barn, feeling uncomfortable inside her own skin.

She needed to get out, move around. Upstairs, she changed into jeans, a T-shirt and sturdy boots and went for a walk on one of the dirt roads that crisscrossed the End of the Road Ranch.

She kept going until she came to a lone hackberry tree. Ducking in under the branches, she sat down with her back

against the trunk. A few yards away, beyond a barbwire fence, cattle grazed peacefully.

It did kind of clear her head a bit, just to sit here, alone in the shade of a tree, staring off past the grazing cattle toward the wide-open prairie rolling forever toward the distant hills. The feeling that she might just burst right out of her skin faded a bit. And her unreasonable anger with Hayes faded to a low hum beneath her breastbone. Really, she had no reason to be angry with him.

He didn't want to get anything started when he knew it would go nowhere. She could respect that. She *did* respect that. And from now on, whenever she had to deal with him, she would be civil and casually friendly.

It would all work out. And if it didn't, she would find herself another place to stay. There was no big emergency. She just needed to take things day-to-day.

The light was fading fast, the air cooling off as she rose and started toward the house. It was a long walk back, and by the time she let herself in the front gate, the sky was a star-thick indigo bowl overhead—and Hayes sat on the step as he had two nights before, with Rayna snoozing behind him.

She went in the gate, and he rose, six-foot-two of lean, hard cowboy, in faded jeans, his usual worn boots and T-shirt. He had on a black leather jacket, too. It looked vintage, like something a brooding fifties movie star might wear.

At the foot of the steps, she paused, feeling awkward and out of place, not knowing what to say, but not willing to be outright rude and simply dodge around him.

Forking his fingers through his unruly hair, he smiled down at her. "Hey."

She felt her own mouth tipping up in answer. "Hey."

"I got a little worried about you. Your Blazer was here and you weren't."

"I'm good. Just went for a walk."

"Ah."

"Yeah. I found a tree to sit under. I watched the cattle graze and stared at the mountains off in the distance. It was nice. Kind of soothing after a long day at the inn."

Okay, it was a lie. Her workday had been uneventful. She'd gone for a walk to try to clear her mind—of him. And why did he just stand there above her, looking down at her as though he was waiting for her to make some kind of move?

When she couldn't stand the silence for one more second, she said the first thing that popped into her mind. "Nice jacket."

"You like it?"

"I do. You've got kind of a James Dean thing going on wearing that."

He smirked. "Found it at a flea market in Boise ten or twelve years ago."

"Ah." And so much for the history of his flea-market jacket. She stuck her hands in her pockets. "Well, I guess I'll just go on in then."

He tipped his head and gave her a long, steady look. "Sit with me." Her hopeless heart skipped a beat and then started racing. She mentally ordered it to slow the heck down as she opened her mouth to say she really needed to go in.

He must have guessed what she was about to say from the look on her face because he coaxed, "Just for a little while."

"Why not?" She stared into those jade eyes of his and heard herself echo, "Just for a little while."

He scooted to the side and she took the empty space next to him. "I have news," he said.

Rayna gave a little whine of hello. Chrissy turned to her and patted her head. "Hey, girl…"

"My dad's coming home tomorrow."

"Wow. That's great news."

"Yeah. His test results are better. He's lost a lot of weight and things are looking pretty good. Now, if the two of us can just keep from killing each other…"

"Don't even start in with that. You'll work it out."

"Yeah, probably with our fists."

That didn't sound good. She sat up straighter. "What do you mean? He never used to hit you. Where is this coming from?"

His strong shoulders slumped. "No, he never hit me."

"So you were just being a smart-ass, then?"

"He and I don't get along, Chrissy. It's a fact."

She put her hand on his knee and then almost jerked it back. But she wanted to reassure him. So she gave that hard knee a squeeze and bumped his arm gently with her shoulder—and then she let go. "I'm thinking we should plan a low-key celebration of his return. Maybe a welcome-home barbecue on Sunday. We can invite Beck, Jake and Austin in thanks for how they helped you out. And Arlen. Rylee and Shep, of course. Just a small get-together, not a big deal."

"I don't know if that's a good idea. He's been really sick. I mean, he *is* better, but I don't think he's ready to party."

"If he gets tired, he can go to bed. Everyone will understand. But I think it's nice to make a little fuss, to make it clear how glad we are that he's pulling through."

"Yeah, but what if he acts up?"

"We can take it. We'll just keep on smiling. Besides, it

will be worth putting up with a little attitude from him for the chance to show him that we're glad to have him home."

He looked at her for the longest time.

Finally, she had to ask, "What are you staring at?"

"You."

"Why?"

"You get ideas. And then you get all excited about them. Remember prom? You were on the planning committee. The theme was Starry Night. Twinkle lights everywhere and a giant moon suspended from the blue velvet ceiling."

"I was proud of how those decorations turned out."

"You were obsessed."

"Fine. I was obsessed. And the grange hall was the best it's ever looked. It was absolutely stunning, as you well know."

"You were the stunning one. In that blue satin dress."

Her cheeks felt too warm, and her heart had found a faster rhythm. She reminded herself that she was no longer some giddy high school girl, getting all excited because Hayes Parker called her stunning. "Thank you. And please don't try to change the subject. Just say yes to the barbecue. You'll have to handle the grill, but I'll take care of everything else."

He scoffed, but in a playful way. "Don't kid yourself. My mom will be here, remember? She will never allow you to do everything on your own. She will pitch in no matter how many times you tell her to stop."

"I love your mom. I also realize there is no way in heaven to keep Norma Parker from pitching in—and making all the major decisions. So no worries, I'm good with that."

"How about you? Anyone you want to invite?"

"Hmm. Maybe Marisa Sanchez—you remember her?"

"Yeah. Invite Marisa."

"And there's Ruby McKinley. She works the front desk at the inn. She and I are getting close, becoming friends. She's a single mom with a little girl."

"Ask her to come—and her little girl, too."

"All right. I will."

"You should invite your mom and dad, too."

She blinked at him. "You're joking."

"No, I'm serious. Invite them."

"That could be a recipe for disaster," she warned—and then marveled at her own sudden lightheartedness. Somehow, all of her hurt and anger at him for ghosting her the past two days had vanished like fog in the light of the sun. She really needed to watch herself with him. He ran hot and cold. He would end up hurting her if she didn't keep her wits about her.

But it was hard to be wary when he looked at her with admiration, when he teased her about the good times back when they were together.

Maybe all she needed to do when it came to Hayes was to lighten up a little, kind of take things as they came.

"Come on," he teased. "Make the deal."

"There's a deal?"

"That's right. I'm all in on the barbecue as long as you ask your folks to come."

"I still don't get it. Why, exactly, do you want them here?"

"Why not include them? That's all I'm saying."

She had no comeback for that. Because he had a point. Back in high school, her parents had warned her off Hayes at first because of his reputation as a troublemaker. But he'd set out to charm them and he'd succeeded. Also, her parents had always been friendly with Hayes's mom and dad. Really, inviting her folks to join the welcome-home celebration would be a nice gesture.

"Shake on it." Hayes stuck out his hand.

She took it, but cautiously. His warm fingers closed around hers and a shiver of something dangerous skated up her arm. "Hayes?"

He didn't let go. "I've been thinking of only two things since the other night."

"What two things?" It came out sounding as wary as she felt.

He leaned close and whispered in her ear, "That I want to. But we shouldn't. But I want to. But we can't…"

Her heart melted, which thoroughly annoyed her. She pulled her hand from his. "You've been cold to me." The accusation came out on a husk of breath.

"I was trying to stay away."

"Oh, no kidding." Her tone was all sarcasm.

"I thought it would be better to back off, put some distance between us. But I can see now I just came off like a jerk."

"You're right. You did."

"I'm sorry."

She still wasn't ready to let it go. "Did you have fun at the Grizzly last night?"

He looked right in her eyes. "I had a couple of beers, played some pool and came home. Alone."

She believed him. Maybe she shouldn't. But she did. He took her hand again. She let him. "So what now?"

"Well, that's up to you. What do you think?"

"I think that look in your eye ought to be illegal."

"Chrissy." He said it low, with heat and clear intention.

If she said yes, it would be with no hope of forever. And she'd always been a forever kind of girl.

But maybe it was time to try something different, to go just a little bit wild.

She asked, "Just for now? That *is* what we're talking about here?"

His nod was slow and serious. "Yeah. Can you work with that?"

She was going to get hurt. She knew it like she knew every street and narrow sidewalk of the small, dusty town she'd grown up in. She was going to get hurt and that wasn't going to stop her from having him again.

"Just for now," she said firmly. "Yes. I can deal with that."

LIKE A PUNCH to the solar plexus, those words of hers hit him hard. *Yes. I can deal with that.*

He let go of her hand—but only to wrap his arm around her shoulders and pull her close against his body. "Chrissy…" Breathing in her scent, he nuzzled her hair. She smelled so good, dewy and sweet. She always had. Like a tropical flower magically blooming on dry, barren land.

He took her mouth. She sighed as she opened for him. He tasted her deeply, his mind full of tender memories.

Their first time, fumbling in his pickup under a tall cottonwood by the creek that meandered across a wide stretch of Parker land. The full moon shining down on them through the dust-covered windshield. Her eyes in the darkness of the cab, looking up at him with love and trust.

He'd broken that trust. And now he was setting them up to break it all over again.

But resisting his need for her? A man couldn't turn down clear, cool water in the desert. A thirst like his would not be denied.

She threaded her fingers into the hair at his nape, grabbing, pulling a little. He groaned.

And she giggled. He kissed that little laugh right off her lips, nudging her to open for him.

Kissing Chrissy.

Nothing like it ever in this big, hard world.

All the years apart and now here they were, hot and heavy as ever, holding on tight, letting the need between them have control.

"Upstairs," he said, catching her lower lip between his teeth, teasing it until she moaned.

"My room." She sighed. "It's got the bigger bed."

He saw no reason to argue. There were twin beds in the room where he slept. "Let's go." He got his legs under him and stood, pulling her right up with him.

Now they were on their feet but going nowhere. The moon, half full, hovered above them as he kissed her some more, long and deep and hungrily.

She pushed at his shoulders with another light, happy laugh. "Are we just going to stand here kissing all night?"

He caught her face between his hands. "The idea holds definite appeal."

She turned her head enough to press a soft kiss into the heart of his left hand. "A bed. Doesn't that sound wonderful?"

"Now that you mention it…" He scooped her up. She wrapped her arms around his neck as he cradled her against his chest. "Let's go."

He carried her to the door. She pushed it open. Rayna wiggled in ahead of them.

Inside, she shoved the door shut and engaged the lock. "Put me down. I can walk up the stairs."

"Uh-uh." He held her a little bit tighter. "I'm not letting go of you until I have you where I want you."

She touched his mouth. "You sound so determined."

"You have no idea." He started walking.

At the top of the stairs, he paused.

She laughed. "Out of breath?"

"No way. I'm tough."

"Right." Her dark eyes were softer now. "You are the toughest."

"But I need to make a little detour."

"To…?"

He was already moving again. "My room. For condoms." Yeah, she'd said that she and Sam couldn't have children. But the way he saw it, even if there was no chance of her getting pregnant tonight, they might as well just play it safe.

The door to his room was open. He set her down on the threshold. "Stay right there. Don't move."

"I wouldn't dare."

"Good." He got his duffel and took what he needed from an inside pocket. When he got back to the doorway, she was already turning to walk to her room at the end of the hall. "Oh, no, you don't." He picked her up.

She wrapped her arm around his neck again and whispered in his ear, "I wasn't trying to get away."

He turned his head and kissed her hard and quick. "Yeah, well, I'm taking no chances."

A minute later, he entered the bedroom at the end of the upstairs hall. By then, his heart was running riot inside his chest—and not because he'd just carried her up the stairs and down the hall.

It was Chrissy that had his heart going wild—having Chrissy in his arms again.

After all these years.

Carefully, he set her down on the rag rug by the double bed.

"Oh, Hayes…" She put her hands on his shoulders and

then slid them around his neck. "Hayes…" Lifting up, she touched her mouth to his.

That was all it took. He urged her to open and when she did, he kissed her hard and deep, gathering her into him, falling into the kiss, thinking that this couldn't be happening.

Oh, but it was.

Her hands were all over him, shoving his jacket off his shoulders, getting hold of his T-shirt. Her fingers skimmed along his sides. "Arms up." She kissed the words onto his mouth.

He did as she instructed, and the shirt went sailing back over her shoulder. She got to work on his belt buckle.

About then, he realized that she was still wearing all her clothes. He got down to business, tugging her T-shirt over her head, reaching around behind her and unhooking her lacy pink bra. The clasp fell away. He slid his hands up over the cool, silky skin of her back to hook his fingers under her bra straps.

A second later, that bra went flying toward the corner chair. She laughed and he kissed her. She tasted so good. Like all the beautiful things a man could lose forever— and then, by some miracle, find again.

For now, anyway. For now, he could hold her, touch her, kiss her. She was right here in his arms, and she was even more beautiful than all those years ago.

He cradled her pale, round breasts in his hands. "So pretty…" And he flicked the dusky nipples, his mind thrown back to their second time. In the bed of that old pickup he used to drive then.

"Remember, that night in the bed of your rusty old pickup?" she asked, as though she'd read his mind. "It was August, same as now, and hot. We parked under that giant cottonwood tree again, just miles from nowhere…"

Lost in her big brown eyes, he guided a long swatch of shining hair behind the shell of her ear. "I will never forget it."

"That was something, all those soft old quilts and comforters piled up in the pickup bed. We made love, and then we just hung out there, whispering together, staring up the moon through the leaves of that cottonwood."

"It was a good night."

"The *best* night." She laughed softly. "All that bedding, soft as a cloud. Heaven, that's what it was, just lying there together, you and me."

He smiled, remembering back to that summer so long ago. Recalling how, earlier that day, he'd waited until the house was empty. Then he'd run up to the attic. It had taken more than one frantic trip up and down the stairs to gather the old quilts and comforters his mom kept tucked in a couple of big trunks up there. He was so sure he'd be caught.

But he got lucky—twice. Because he also had to get all that bedding back where it came from before the next morning so no one would know what he and Chrissy had been up to out in the far pasture after dark.

Now he was smirking. Because the truth was, he'd gotten lucky more than twice if you counted him and Chrissy under the cottonwood that night.

"It was good—so good." She had his belt off and she was sliding his zipper down. Slipping her hand under the elastic of his briefs, she closed her fingers around him.

"It was perfect." He groaned against her parted lips as she stroked him. But then he caught her wrist. "Let's get everything off. Now."

She threw back her head, her dark waterfall of hair swaying as she laughed. "Good plan."

He took the condoms from his pocket and set them on the little table by the bed. Two minutes later their clothes

littered the floor, and they stood in the middle of the rug, naked, grinning at each other like a couple of naughty children.

"Well," she said, sounding breathless, her soft cheeks flushed, so beautiful it hurt just to look at her. "Here we are again."

He wasn't grinning now. "I missed you," he said, though he knew he shouldn't. Because they had an agreement. This was just for right now. Dangerous words should be scrupulously avoided.

But now those words had somehow gotten out of his mouth, and she looked stricken. "Please don't, Hayes."

He reached for her, took her hand, pulled her close and wrapped his arms around her good and tight. "Sorry." And oh, did she feel good, all soft and sleek and curvy, pressed right up against him. She made him ache for her.

She always had.

And then she tipped her head back, offering that beautiful mouth again. "Just kiss me. It's all right. We both want this and it's all right."

He did kiss her, a deep kiss that went on forever as he pulled her backward at the same time. They fell across the bed. Rolling her beneath him, he caught her wrists in either hand, pushing them out to the sides until her arms were stretched wide.

When he lifted his mouth, she said, "You know I can hardly move like this."

He nodded. "And that is exactly my plan." He kissed her some more. She sighed against his mouth as she tugged on her captured wrists—but not too hard, just enough to make them both smile.

In time, he moved lower. He scattered kisses over her pretty chin and down the satin skin of her throat.

Her breasts tempted him, so he lingered there, letting

her captured wrists go when she begged him to, feeling her arms twine around him as he took her nipple in his mouth. She cradled his head, holding him close as he moved to the other breast.

On down he went, biting her lightly right over her rib cage, pressing kisses to either side of her navel, and then moving lower still. He lifted her thighs and guided them over his shoulders.

She kept whispering his name. "Hayes…" All soft and sweet and hungry. "Hayes…"

His name from her lips brought back another flood of memories, the sweetest ones, of the two of them together, young and in love and so certain that nothing could ever break them apart.

They'd trusted each other. *Believed* in each other. She'd sworn never to leave him, and he'd promised the same…

Not that it mattered now. That was the past.

Right now, he had the feel of her, the taste of her, salty-sweet on his tongue. Impossible. And perfect. Right here.

In his arms again.

She caught his head between her hands. Urgently, she whispered his name as he kissed her deeply, using his fingers to bring her closer to the edge. She was so wet, so ready. He stroked her faster.

And then, with a sweet cry, she came. She tossed her head from side to side on the pillow, groaning out his name.

When she settled with a deep sigh, he moved back up her limp body, kissing as he went. Until he reached her lips again and covered them with his own.

She opened for him, kissing him back. And when he raised his head enough to look down at her flushed face and glassy eyes, she said, "I think I'll just lie here, limp and satisfied. Forever."

He smoothed her tangled hair back off her damp forehead. "You are a gorgeous woman. Did I ever tell you that?"

"Often." She grinned, cheeks red, eyes still closed. "You had me convinced I was the most beautiful creature on Earth."

"Because you were—you *are*."

She fake-punched him on the arm. "Or maybe you were just blinded by love."

"Maybe I was. But here we are years later. And you are even more beautiful than before. It's a simple fact. Live with it."

For that, he got a lazy, happy chuckle, one that ended when she reached down between them and took hold of him again. "Oh, my goodness," she whispered. "I mean, honestly…"

"Go ahead. Say it."

"Is this really happening?"

"You'd better believe it." He kissed her. She wrapped one arm around his neck as, below, she continued to drive him wild with that clever stroking hand of hers.

Too quickly, she had him hovering right on the edge. Any second now, he would lose it completely. When he groaned into her mouth, she stroked him faster.

"Hold on, slow down," he pleaded against her parted lips.

"Uh-uh, no way…" She nipped at his lower lip and kept right on driving him out of his mind.

So he took charge, fumbling out a hand for the bed table, getting hold of one of the condoms he'd tossed there.

With another groan, he lifted himself away from her.

"Get back here." She was laughing, a low, teasing sound, reaching for him as he got his knees braced on either side of her and rose up above her. Her eyes, warm amber now, gleamed up at him. "You are a bad, bad man,

Hayes Parker." She said it with a wicked little laugh as he rolled the condom down over his aching hardness.

"I do my best." He stared down at her. What a sight. She'd thrown her arms back over her head now. Her hair was spread out on the pillow, a dark, tangled halo around her unforgettable face.

If only he could bottle this moment, store it away, take it out and drink from it on the lonely nights when beauty and softness were nowhere to be found.

She grabbed his shoulders, urging him to cover her.

But he wrapped his arms around her and rolled them, so she was on top. She laughed at that, a joyful sound, and tossed her wild hair. "Really?"

"Really." He clasped the twin inward curves of her waist and lifted her. "Ride me."

"You got it, cowboy."

And then she was straddling him, reaching down, clasping him, guiding him into her soft, wet heat. They groaned in unison as she sank onto him.

"Perfect," he said on a growl. "Come down here," he commanded, reaching for her again to pull her close against his chest.

She resisted, her hair sliding over his throat, feathering along the skin over his collarbones, brushing his cheek as she held his gaze. "Not yet." And she arched her back, bracing her hands behind her on his thighs. She tipped her head to the ceiling. With a breathless little sigh, she started to move.

"Chrissy..." He reached up, cradled those pretty breasts of hers in his two rough hands, feeling the soft weight of them, loving the way her plump, hard nipples pressed into his palms.

"Yes!" she cried. "Oh, Hayes. Yes..." And she kept

moving, rocking back and forth on him, making soft, hungry sounds that sent him reeling toward the edge again.

He wanted to go on like this, the two of them, lost in this perfect moment of heat and need and unbearable pleasure. To be swept off forever, just him and Chrissy, connected in this most basic way, free of everyday concerns—about the ranch, about the future they didn't have together, about the tension and hostility his father might bring home with him tomorrow.

Now, in this moment, all the questions somehow seemed answered. He wanted this to last forever.

But then she was tipping her head down to him. He looked up into her dazed, night-dark eyes.

She said, "Now, Hayes. I…can't…"

"Wait," he commanded.

She laughed, the sound slowly morphing into a guttural moan. "Sorry. No can do…"

And then he felt her body closing around him, pulsing in rhythm with the rocking of her hips. She cried his name good and loud then.

He pulled her down to him. She collapsed onto his chest as the finish rolled through her.

That did it. The glorious contraction of her body around him was too much. He lost it.

His climax barreled through him, sweeping everything else into oblivion. There was only the moment, the two of them, together in a way he'd never let himself imagine would ever happen again.

CHAPTER NINE

TWO HOURS LATER, Chrissy reached over and turned off the light.

Snuggled close to Hayes in the after-midnight darkness, she traced a slow circle on the bare skin of his chest. "I have news."

"Tell me."

"Well, I had a talk with my insurance guy today."

He caught her hand and kissed her fingertips. "Is everything okay?"

Emotion clogged her throat. "Yeah. It's good news, I promise you."

He lowered her hand to his chest again and gently pressed it flat directly over his heart. She closed her eyes and breathed in carefully through her nose, banishing the tears that threatened to fall.

She was not going to cry. There was nothing to cry about. She and Hayes had just shared an amazing evening in her bed. They had an agreement that this magic between them was just for now.

But really, what was *now*, exactly? They should clarify that.

"So then," Hayes said, his voice a low rumble beneath her palm. "If there's no problem, what did you and your insurance guy talk about?"

"He told me that my insurance will pay for me to rent a room at the inn—or even to rent an apartment if I can find

one for just a month or so until my place is live-in ready again. Also, they'll pay your folks for me to stay here."

He frowned. "That's not necess—"

She cut him off with two fingers to his lips. "Don't you dare say it's not necessary. You came back to this town you once swore you'd never set foot in again in order to save this ranch, right? And money to help with that is a good thing, even though it will be a month or two before the check comes through."

He chuckled then. "There never was any arguing with you once you got an idea lodged in that brain of yours."

"I'm right and you know it. Admit it."

"Chrissy—"

"Admit it."

"Fine. You're right. Pay rent if you insist."

"I do insist." She chewed on her bottom lip for a moment. "That is, unless…"

He caught a curl of her hair and slowly wound it around his finger. "What now?"

"Well, I mean, you know…*this*."

"This, what?"

"You and me, Hayes, in bed together again."

He grinned. "Pretty damn spectacular if you ask me."

Those words filled her with giddy, foolish happiness. "You think so?"

"Yes, I do."

"Well, if you're sure…"

"I am."

Her doubts flooded in anyway. She slid her gaze away and asked carefully, "I mean, now that this has happened, maybe you're starting to feel a little…uncomfortable about having me around?"

"Hey."

"Hmm?"

He unraveled the curl of hair he'd wrapped around his finger—and then gave it tug. "Look at me."

She met his eyes. "What?"

"I like having you around."

"You sure? Because now I can afford to go someplace else if you'd rather I—"

"Shh." He cupped the back of her head and pulled her in until their lips could meet in a long kiss that was equal parts tender and playful.

When she lifted her head again, she whispered, "Think about it. Starting tomorrow, your parents will be here. They'll be sleeping in the room downstairs."

"So what? We're not kids anymore. We can sleep where we want to sleep—including with each other. There's a privacy lock on the door to this room and we'll use it." His grin would have made her panties melt right off if she hadn't already shucked them hours ago. "And I'll try not to make you scream too loud."

At that, she gave him a playful slap on the arm. "Rein in that ego, mister."

He cradled her head in his big hand and the look in his eyes turned from teasing to serious. "Stay, Chrissy. Let us have this time together, you and me, for the next few weeks until your place is ready."

No offer had ever sounded quite so tempting. At the same time, she couldn't help wondering how much harder it was going to be to leave him if they spent the next few weeks sharing a bed. "You're sure?"

"Absolutely." He kissed her again, hard and quick this time. "Stay."

Oh, she did want to. But how would she make herself walk away when it was over?

Somehow, she'd have to.

But not for a while yet. In the meantime, why not love

every moment for as long as it lasted. "Okay," she replied on a soft husk of breath. "Until my place is ready."

"That's what I wanted to hear." He kissed her again, a hungry kiss that sent heat sizzling through her.

And, well…

Okay, then. So be it. She wanted him and he wanted her and why shouldn't they have this time together?

No, it wouldn't last. He'd made that painfully clear—and so had she, for that matter.

But not everything lasted. Not their young love all those years ago. Not her marriage to Sam, nor his to poor Anna.

Chrissy was old enough now to see the value of living joyfully in the moment. She needed to stop worrying about the future. It would come soon enough. Nothing she could do would stop it.

As for now, though, she would love every minute and not let herself dwell on what would happen when it ended.

IN THE MORNING after breakfast, Chrissy called Marisa and then Ruby to invite them to Lionel's welcome-home barbecue on Sunday. Marisa was out of town, so she couldn't make it. Ruby said she and her four-year-old daughter, Emery, would be there.

Next, Chrissy called her mom. Patrice said yes immediately.

Chrissy wasn't surprised. Her mom had never been shy. Patrice liked to be in the thick of things. And an afternoon at the Parker place would include checking in with Hayes's parents and getting a good look at whatever might be going on between Chrissy and Hayes.

"Sweetheart, a party for Lionel," her mother cooed. "What a lovely idea. Of course we'll be there! What shall I bring?"

There was absolutely no need for her bring a single thing. But Chrissy knew better than to say that out loud. Arriving empty-handed would never fly with Patrice Hastings. "How about that broccoli salad you make?"

"Done. And a dessert, I think. I'll make my famous lemon lush."

"Perfect, Mom. See you around two."

As Chrissy ended the call, Hayes came up behind her and wrapped his arms around her. She indulged herself by leaning back against him. "My mom and dad are coming."

"Good." He kissed the word onto the side of her neck. "Austin, Beck and Jake are coming. My sister and Shep, too. I called my mom. She's planning the menu."

"Of course she is."

He dropped another kiss at the spot where her neck met her shoulder. "Arlen said yes, too."

She stiffened. Had she and Hayes just been putting on a show? "Where is he?"

"Relax. He left for the barn a few minutes ago."

She turned her head to look back at him. "We should keep a rein on the PDAs when other people are around."

"Whatever you say." He captured her lips then. It felt so good, his arms around her, his warm mouth moving on hers, his morning beard a little scratchy in a truly sexy way.

She turned in his embrace and slid her eager hands up to wrap around his neck as he caressed his way down her lower back, pulling her in nice and tight so she could feel how glad he was to have her in his arms.

"I should get going," he said softly against her parted lips. "We've got work that needs doing before my dad gets home."

"Okay." She tried to pull away.

He grabbed her tighter. "What I mean is, we're going to need to be quick."

She laughed as he took her hand and pulled her toward the stairs.

AT A LITTLE before one that afternoon, Norma's Suburban pulled to a stop by the front gate. Lionel was at the wheel.

Hayes had returned to the house a little while before, to be there for his dad's arrival. Chrissy went out the front door and down the walk with him to welcome his dad home and to help carry luggage into the house.

"Don't make a fuss," Lionel commanded when Hayes pulled open the driver's door. "I'm not a damn invalid. I'm feeling fine, and I drove us back from Bronco myself."

Hayes just smiled and clapped his dad on the shoulder. Because it was easy to smile. Didn't matter what raft of crap Lionel piled on his head, Hayes would be alone with Chrissy later and that made everything A-okay with him. "Welcome home, Dad."

"Humph." Lionel got out of the vehicle. "Well, I admit it's good to be out of the hospital and back where I belong." The old man's face softened. He aimed a smile over Hayes's shoulder. "Chrissy Hastings! I heard you've been helping out around the place."

"Lionel." Chrissy stepped around Hayes. "So good to see you."

Hayes's dad gave her a quick hug and then announced, "Let's get everything inside."

By then, Hayes's mom had come around the front of the car to join them. "Go on in," she said to Lionel.

"But I want—"

"We'll bring the stuff in. No problem."

Chrissy stepped up and took Lionel's arm. "This way."

Lionel huffed a little, but he let her lead him along the walk and up the front steps.

Hayes and his mom carried stuff in from the Suburban. When they went in the front door, Lionel was sitting in his recliner, remote in hand, watching *Air Disasters* on the Smithsonian Channel. Rayna sat on the floor beside him, watching him, looking hopeful. As Hayes watched, Lionel reached over and scratched the dog on the head. Rayna gave a happy little whine and braced her nose on the chair arm.

Lionel spotted Hayes. "Beautiful dog," he said. "Well-behaved, too."

Hayes nodded. "She was Anna's."

His dad blinked. "Anna. Your wife…"

"That's right."

"I…"

Hayes smiled, remembering. "Anna had a magic touch with dogs. Horses, too."

"Ah. Well. I'm…sorry, son. I regret that I never met her, and that you lost her." For Lionel, that was a major testimonial.

Hayes felt an ache under his breastbone. "I appreciate that, Dad."

His father clearly had no idea what the hell to say next. But then the door opened again, and his mom came in carrying a small bag in either hand.

"Stay put," she commanded before Lionel could push himself out of the chair. "Hayes and I are managing just fine."

"But I can—"

"Don't," she said sternly. And then, more gently, "Lionel. Relax. Your job right now is to take things nice and easy."

Reluctantly, Lionel settled back into his big chair and

returned his attention to the early-model flat screen above the mantel. Hayes carried the bags he'd brought in on through to the downstairs bedroom, and helped his mom put everything away.

"I need to go talk to Chrissy," Norma said once the bags were emptied.

Should he be alarmed? "About what?"

Norma reached up and patted his shoulder. "Shopping. There's lots to do to get ready for tomorrow."

"Right…" He needed to chill. His mom respected boundaries. No way would she be sticking her nose into what might or might not be going on between him and the woman he used to love all those years and years ago.

Norma trotted off to find Chrissy. A few minutes later, the two appeared in the great room together.

"Chrissy and I are headed for the market," his mom said. "There are just a few things we really can't do without for the barbecue tomorrow."

Hayes shut the front door behind the two women and turned back to the great room. His dad was fast asleep in the recliner, with Rayna snoozing on the floor by his chair. The dog didn't even look up when Hayes headed out to find Arlen.

HOUSED ON THE bottom floor of a century-old two-story brick building, Tenacity Grocery had rooms to rent on the top floor. Benches lined the wooden sidewalk in front of the store, providing seating for locals to gather and watch the world go by. Rough wooden signs dangled from the long second-floor balcony. The signs announced Beer! Ice! Wine!

Inside the store, the worn wooden floor was slightly uneven. The narrow aisles offered shelves tightly packed with canned goods and other staples. Glass-fronted re-

frigerators ranged along the back wall. There was a meat counter stuck in the rear corner and two old-fashioned cash registers up front.

Norma grabbed a cart. Chrissy pushed it while Norma loaded it with the items they needed. Walking side by side, they paused as they shopped, taking their time to smile and greet people they knew.

"What do you think?" asked Norma. "More beer, a six-pack of Pepsi and one of Mountain Dew—does your mom still drink Mountain Dew?"

"At a summer barbecue? Oh, you bet."

Norma slipped her arm in the crook of Chrissy's elbow and leaned in close. "I have to say," she whispered. "Just between us girls, it is wonderful to have you staying at the ranch. Reminds me of the old days when you spent almost as much time with us as you did at home. Sometimes lately I do have my fantasies that you and Hayes might—"

"Norma," Chrissy chided fondly. "I'm very grateful to Hayes for offering me a place to stay when I really needed one. That's all it is, though," she shamelessly lied. "Hayes is helping me out."

Hayes's mom clutched Chrissy's arm a little tighter. "Well, I can't help hoping it might turn into more."

You're not the only one, she couldn't stop herself from thinking. But somehow she managed to keep those dangerous words from slipping past her lips.

Really, what was happening to her?

She'd known from the first that Hayes was just being kind, letting her stay here when she needed a place. That they'd ended up in bed together, well, it was a bonus for certain. But it was never going to turn into love ever after. Hayes had made that way more than clear.

Too bad her hopeless heart wouldn't stop making other plans.

"I need my happy fantasies," Norma said with real conviction. "No matter how tough things get, I'll never change. I'm a shameless romantic at heart."

"Still reading those juicy romance novels?" Chrissy remembered that Norma had always loved a good love story.

"Of course. Love makes the world a better place. In real life *and* in my fantasies. Now come on. Let's get this stuff rung up and get home. We need to get cooking. Tomorrow will be here before we know it."

IT WAS ALMOST ten that night when Hayes tapped on her bedroom door.

Chrissy was feeling kind of contrary by then. Because she'd been lying there for half an hour pretending to read one of Norma's dog-eared paperback love stories, wishing he would come.

Was she pitiful? A lost cause? Oh, yeah.

If she had any sense, she would just stay right there in her bed and not make a peep. Eventually, he would give up and tiptoe back down the hall.

But then he tapped on the door again. And she threw back the covers, leapt from the bed and darted over there.

Pulling the door open a fraction of an inch, she asked, "Who is it?" in a whisper.

"Cute," he said darkly. "Sorry it took me so long. My dad wanted to talk about how I shouldn't have paid any of the overdue bills, hired Arlen or put a new roof on the barn."

She continued to peek through the crack in the door. "Be nice to your dad. He's still recovering. He's a proud man who hates to show any sign of weakness."

"I *am* nice. Let me in."

"Do you have the secret password?"

Through the crack, she could see him trying not to roll his eyes. "Yeah," he replied. "Let. Me. In."

"Hmm. I'm not sure that's the one."

He seemed unable to decide between smirking at her and scowling. "If you don't let me in, I won't be able to kiss you. Or take off that big shirt you're wearing. Or lay you down on the bed and—"

"Okay!" She pulled the door wide and grabbed his arm. "Password or not, you'd better get in here."

Once she had him over the threshold, she shut the door and turned the lock. Then she stepped in close to him, lifted her arms to rest them on his hard shoulders and got right up in his handsome face. "Get after it, cowboy."

"Yes, ma'am." His mouth swooped down to capture hers as he dipped enough to get those big, rough hands wrapped around the back of her thighs.

She jumped up and hitched her legs around his waist. He groaned against her lips, deepening their perfect kiss as he carried her to the bed.

When he laid her down, he caught the hem of her shirt and whipped it right off over her head. And then he was kissing her as she undid his belt, unzipped his zipper and pushed at his jeans and underwear.

He caught her hands in one of his and held them up over her head as he dug in a pocket and pulled out three condoms. He dropped two on the bed table.

The third, he ripped open. She wiggled her hands free of his grip and helped, pushing his jeans and briefs down far enough that he popped free, all ready to go. He rolled the condom on, eased a finger under the elastic of her panties just enough to get them out of his way.

And then he braced above her on one hand. She stared up into those beautiful eyes of his as he guided himself into her.

It was perfect. Urgent and needful. She cried out at the joy of it, of him, of the two of them, joined. Lifting her legs, hooking her ankles at the small of his back, she surged up until he filled her all the way.

After that, her mind was nothing but a spinning haze of light and wonder. Not caring who might hear her, she cried out his name.

His mouth came down to claim her lips. After that, she was quieter as they moved together, seeking that moment when the gathering heat burst wide open into the sweet, hot pulse of fulfillment.

HAYES WOKE CRADLING Chrissy in his arms. It was after five on Sunday morning.

"I'm late," he grumbled, nuzzling her hair.

She laughed, the sound sleepy and way too damn sexy. "Hey!" She tried to grab for him as he slid from the bed. "Where're you going? Get back here…"

"Can't. Arlen's got to be wondering what my problem is."

"Tell him it's all my fault." She propped her head on her hand. Grinning, she watched him as he ran around the room grabbing his clothes. And then she threw back the covers. Without a stitch on, she sashayed up close.

Wrapping those soft arms around his neck, she kissed him. Now he had his mouth on hers and his hands on her body.

Big mistake. Because he really didn't want to go. He deepened the kiss with a low groan.

And she chose that moment to get tough. Clucking her tongue, she pushed him away and pulled open the door. "Out you go."

"You are a heartless woman."

Standing there in front of him, wearing nothing but a

wicked grin, she swept out an arm toward the empty hall-way. "Move it."

Grabbing her close, he stole one more kiss before he made himself turn and head off down the hall.

In the barn, he found Arlen mucking out stalls.

Glancing up, Arlen muttered, "You're running a little late, lover boy." He braced his broom against the barn wall and clapped Hayes on the shoulder. "As you can see, I'm almost done with this dirty mess. It's your turn to gather the eggs."

Hayes didn't even argue. How could he? He should have been up an hour ago. Off he went to the chicken coop and those ornery hens with their tendency to peck.

Later, at breakfast, his mom and Chrissy chattered away about their preparations for the barbecue that afternoon as the men shoveled in their eggs and sausage. His dad was pretty quiet. Hayes had no idea what might be going on in Lionel's head. Overall, since his return home yes-terday, the old man had been mostly in good spirits. Even last night, when Lionel gave Hayes a hard time for put-ting his own money into keeping the ranch afloat, the old man hadn't blown up.

But Hayes still didn't trust him to keep his temper in check indefinitely. For way too many years, Lionel Parker had been a bomb looking for any excuse to detonate.

The day turned out to be cooler than usual, and cloudy, but with no rain in the forecast.

For the welcome-home party, Hayes's mom and Chrissy had decided to keep things simple—steaks and burgers with lots of sides. Everybody came who said they would, and they all brought something.

They gathered under a pair of sycamores out in back. Arlen and Hayes had brought out one of the long farm tables from the storage shed. Chrissy and his mom had

covered it and two picnic tables with bright checked table-cloths. There were the usual coolers full of beer and soda.

Lionel manned the grill. He wouldn't have it any other way.

Chrissy's mom and dad showed up early. Patrice had brought a big broccoli salad and a huge Tupperware container full of that addictive lemon shortbread and whipped cream dessert she used to serve now and then back when Hayes and Chrissy were a couple—lemon lush. That was the name of it. Hayes had loved that stuff.

Really, it was a great afternoon. Chrissy's friend from the inn, Ruby, had brought her little girl, Emery. The four-year-old was bright and curious.

She hung around by the grill for a bit, asking his dad an endless chain of questions. "Mr. Parker, you look kind of tired. Are you tired?"

"A little, maybe."

"Why don't you take a nap?"

"Well, young lady, I have these burgers to flip and these steaks to keep an eye on."

"Sometimes my mommy tells me a story to help me go to sleep. Do you like stories?"

"Emery, I love stories."

"Good. When you want to take a nap, I will tell you a story."

"Fair enough."

"Can I help you flip the burgers?"

Hayes's dad launched into an explanation of how flipping burgers was a one-man job. Really, Lionel seemed more than okay with fielding Emery's never-ending questions. But the old man had always been patient with little kids. It was when they got older and stood up to him that the trouble started.

Not that Hayes was bitter or anything…

Jake, Beck and Austin were gathered around the coolers, along with Arlen. Hayes wandered over there and shot the breeze for a bit. Then he sought out his sister and her fiancé, Shep. Rylee seemed so happy. She only looked worried when her gaze strayed toward their dad.

Leaning close to Hayes, she asked, "How's Dad doing?"

He glanced at the grill where Emery was still beaming up at Lionel, chattering away. "Better, I think. He's weak, physically, but he's improving."

"I'm so glad—I mean, that he really does seem to be getting better. It was touch and go there for a while."

"Yeah. He's still stubborn as ever, pushing to take on more than he's ready for. But he and I haven't come to blows yet. So, you know. It's all good."

When they sat down to eat a little while later, Hayes made sure he had Chrissy seated next to him. Wouldn't you know, Patrice and Mel Hastings ended up sitting directly across from them? Mel was his usual friendly, good-natured self.

Hayes braced for attitude from Chrissy's mom. Not that Patrice had ever been awful to him, exactly. She was much too polite for that. But back in the old days, the woman had been certain that her precious only child could do better than Tenacity's best-known bad boy—and she'd had her own subtle ways of making her opinion known. However, she'd softened toward him eventually. By the time he and Chrissy were in their junior year, Patrice had been downright friendly toward him.

But then he and Chrissy had broken up. He'd assumed that Patrice would not be a fan of his now.

Patrice surprised him. She chatted and smiled a lot. And when he finished his burger, broccoli salad, baked beans and fried pickles, she blasted him with a giant smile. "I hope you'll have some lemon lush, Hayes. As I recall you

used to love it. And I confess, I thought of you when I decided to make it for today."

He took a moment to come to grips with that. Patrice Hastings had made her famous lemon lush with him in mind? Pigs were flying and hell had clearly frozen right over. "I, uh…yeah, Mrs. Hastings. Of course I'm going to have a giant helping of your lemon lush. I've been looking forward to it since I saw you'd brought it."

"Excellent." Her eyes, the same color as Chrissy's, actually seemed to be twinkling. "And we're all adults now. Please. Call me Patrice."

"Yes. I will. Patrice…"

"Much better. Thank you."

Under the table, Chrissy's hand settled on his thigh, her fingers squeezing a little. He slanted her a warning glance. Because that squeeze had better be just for reassurance. The last thing he needed was Chrissy getting naughty under the table with her mom and dad sitting directly across from them.

Chrissy bumped his arm with her shoulder. He took the hint reluctantly and looked right at her. She gave him her sweetest, most innocent smile.

He wasn't fooled. Everyone considered her such a good girl, an excellent student, a hard worker, big-hearted, helpful and kind. Chrissy was all those things. And she also had a wild streak that he loved a whole hell of a lot. But not right now with Patrice beaming at them from the other side of the table.

Ten minutes later, Hayes's dad got up and made a little speech. "It's been a great day and I have all of you to thank for it," Lionel said in a voice weighted with equal parts fatigue and emotion. "I want you all to know how much I appreciate your coming over to wish me well. I would love to hang around out here till midnight with you. But I'm

feeling just a little tired now, so I think I'll head on back to the house." Raising his Solo cup of Diet Pepsi high, he toasted, "Here's to you—all of you!"

A chorus of, "To *you*, Lionel," went up from the group.

After the toast, Ruby McKinley's little daughter ran over to Lionel. He bent down and they shared a few words. The little girl lifted her arms. He bent even lower, and she gave him a hug before running back to sit with her mom.

Hayes stared at his father, thinking of all the years he'd spent on other ranches, chasing a life he could call his own.

And yet somehow, here he was. Back where he started, driven to save the home he'd been so sure he'd left behind forever.

He still felt some bitterness toward his father. But it wasn't the burning, angry kind. Not anymore. Now he watched his mother walk his father back to the house and thought that he still loved the old fool, and that it would hurt really bad to lose him.

But they wouldn't lose him. Not now. Not for a long time, not till years from now. Decades. Because Lionel was recovering and taking better care of himself. He would be fine.

Chrissy touched his arm. "You okay?" she whispered.

He looked down into those big brown eyes and never wanted to look anywhere else.

But he knew that was wishing for the moon.

She would go back to her condo, and he would go…

He wasn't sure where yet. But off to make a life of his own. Once he had everything in order here, once his dad was back on his feet and could run the ranch again, Hayes would be packing up and hitting the road.

Yeah, the money he was spending to keep the ranch going would put a big dent in his plans to buy his own place.

But he couldn't think about all that now—or about how,

without his continued hard work and backing, his dad and mom would have a hell of a time staying on top of things here.

It would all work out.

Somehow.

He just needed to keep his eyes on the prize here, keep doing everything he could to get the ranch back in the black. He needed *not* to think about walking away till the time for leaving came.

And even more than that, he needed not to think about losing Chrissy again—because after all, he didn't have her. Not really. What they shared was just for now.

And a man couldn't lose what he didn't have.

CHAPTER TEN

CHRISSY KIND OF hated to see the party end.

But the next day was a work day, so everyone called it a night around the time it got dark. Rylee and Shep headed back to Bronco. Ruby took her sleepy little daughter home to bed. Hayes's buddies stayed long enough to help put stuff away. Then they drove off, too.

Chrissy, Hayes, Arlen and Norma spent about an hour in the house, washing pots and serving dishes, just generally tidying up.

"What a perfect day," Norma said as she hung up the dishtowel. She circled the kitchen hugging Arlen, Hayes and then Chrissy. "Thank you," she said, "all three of you. Lionel can be tough to deal with, I know. But he loved every minute of the party today. Thank you for making it happen."

She wiped a tear from the corner of her eye and went off to join Lionel in the big downstairs bedroom. Arlen headed for his trailer a few minutes later.

That left Chrissy and Hayes in the kitchen. Just the two of them, alone.

He came up behind her as she went on tiptoe to put a stack of nesting bowls back in the upper cupboard next to the sink. When he grasped her waist with those strong hands of his, she almost dropped the bowls.

"Watch it," she warned, sliding the bowls onto the shelf, then shutting the cabinet door.

"I can't help myself," he whispered, so close now that she could feel the heat of him at her back. His hands glided upward and then inward to cradle her breasts over her shirt and bra. "You're just too damn beautiful to resist."

She laughed, the sound low and husky to her own ears. "No PDAs, remember?" she chided. He felt so good at her back, so strong and solid. His arousal pushed at her through the layers of their clothing. She couldn't wait to get upstairs, couldn't wait to have him naked in her bed.

He let go of one breast to brush her hair out of his way so he could press a line of kisses down the side of her throat. "It's just you and me here in this kitchen—and Rayna." The big dog had made herself comfortable under the table. At the sound of her name, she wagged her tail. It thumped against the wood floor. "Rayna doesn't judge." He scraped his teeth along the path his lips had made. It felt so good, like he'd struck a trail of hot sparks down the surface of her skin.

"Hayes…" Her breath had mysteriously fled her lungs. She sucked in a gasp. "Your mom could—"

"She won't. Relax."

"We should—"

"Shh. Kiss me." He caught her chin, guiding her face around so that he could take her mouth. His lips touched hers and she couldn't resist. She turned in his hold and slid her arms up his chest to twine around his neck.

The world spun away. Hayes filled all her senses. She breathed him in, surrendering completely to the spell only he could cast.

Right now, with her arms around him, her mouth fused to his and her body melting under his touch, she couldn't imagine any other life than one spent with him.

All these years she'd been telling herself that she'd moved on, she'd forgotten him. That he was just a boy

she'd loved when they were both too young to know what love really meant.

Wrong. She hadn't moved on. Not really. He was always there, in her heart. She had married Sam, known fresh heartbreak, got divorced and moved back home.

And all that time she'd believed her own lie that Hayes Parker was just a boy she'd loved in high school. It was a lie she could have gone on believing. Maybe for the rest of her life.

If only he hadn't come back. If only she hadn't taken him up on his offer to live here on the ranch with him.

If only she hadn't let him into her bed.

If only…

Too late. Here they were, holding on tight, kissing in the kitchen after dark on Sunday night.

She pulled away.

"Chrissy, wait…" He tried to pull her back to him.

She caught his hand. "Come on," she whispered. "Turn off the light. Let's go to bed."

He didn't argue after that. She led him up the stairs, Rayna following behind.

In her room, he took off all her clothes and then made short work of his. Outside, the clouds had cleared. The moon shone in the window, bathing their bodies in a silvery glow.

It was beautiful, just Chrissy and Hayes, holding each other in the moonlight. Whatever happened later, so be it.

Pushing all her thoughts of the future aside, she gave herself up to right now.

TUESDAY MORNING, RUBY suggested they get lunch together. "The barbecue Sunday was great," Ruby said, her smile bright and sunny as ever, her blond hair catching the light

from the lobby fixtures above. "But a little girls-only time never hurts. I'm free at noon if you can get away then?"

"I'm in. The Silver Spur Café?"

"That works."

At noon, they walked over to the café together and got a two-top by the window in front. Their server was quick. In no time, she bustled over with grilled cheese sandwiches and tall iced teas.

They dug right in.

"It's just what I needed," said Ruby. "Melted cheese and grilled bread. Sometimes you can't beat the classics."

Chrissy had her mouth full, but she nodded in enthusiastic agreement.

"So…" Ruby let the word trail off and pitched her voice low, just between the two of them. "You and Hayes Parker…?"

Chrissy swallowed too fast and almost choked. Carefully, she sipped her tea. "Is it that obvious?"

"Well, there's definitely a certain…vibe."

Chrissy laughed at that. "A vibe. There's a vibe…"

Ruby wasn't put off. "Just answer the question."

"Okay, okay. We had a thing, Hayes and me, way back in high school."

"Ah…"

"We were even prom king and queen our senior year, believe it or not."

"Oh, I can picture it now…"

Chrissy faked a giant sigh—one that turned out to be not quite as fake as she'd intended. "But sadly, it didn't work out with Hayes and me."

Ruby wasn't falling for Chrissy's act. She asked seriously, "Did Hayes Parker break your heart?"

Chrissy shrugged and quit trying to play it off. "He did, yeah. He broke my heart, and I broke his and we were fin-

ished. Or so I thought for the past fifteen years. Until he came back to town to save the family ranch and…well, stuff happened."

"I have to say," Ruby spoke gently, "judging only from what I saw Sunday, you two seem good together."

Chrissy just smiled. She liked Ruby a lot, but she didn't really want to get down in the weeds about where it was going—or not going—with Hayes. Because she had no idea how it would all turn out and she wasn't ready. Not to lose him. Not to step up and beg him to stay.

When the silence between her and Ruby had gone on too long, Chrissy spoke up, changing the subject. "Your little girl is such a sweetheart. She was adorable with Lionel on Sunday. He can be such a Grumpy Gus. Emery sweetened him right up, though."

Ruby's smile couldn't completely mask the sadness in her eyes. "Emery's my whole life. But sometimes…" She seemed not to know what to say next. Chrissy kept quiet, not interrupting, not pushing her either. Finally, Ruby continued, "Owen and I have been divorced for a year now. Sometimes it seems like forever."

"You miss him?"

"No!" Ruby looked horrified. "My marriage is truly over. I honestly don't want Owen back again. It's just that sometimes I feel guilty that Emery's an only child. That she won't have a little brother or sister, you know?"

Chrissy reached across the small table to run a hand down Ruby's arm. "Seeing you with her the other day, watching her make friends with Lionel, of all people… Ruby, it's obvious you're a great mom and that your daughter is happy. And even if I hadn't seen you with her, just the way you treat the guests at the inn, like each one of them is special, says a lot about who you are. It tells me

that you're kind and you care and that your little girl will grow up confident and ready to take on the world."

Ruby grinned. "So then, I take it you think I'm doing all right?"

"I know you are."

"Thank you." Ruby said that with feeling.

"It's only the truth." Chrissy sighed. "I want kids, too. So much. But who knows if that will ever happen."

Ruby was silent, her blue eyes full of understanding. Chrissy had mentioned in the past that her marriage hadn't worked out, so Ruby knew a little about Sam and about the divorce.

"Go ahead." Chrissy held Ruby's gaze. "Whatever you're thinking, Ruby, just say it."

"Well, I did hear that you'd struggled with infertility."

Chrissy sat back in her chair. "I'm not even going to ask who told you that. This is Tenacity, after all. Everybody knows way too much about everybody else."

Ruby's cheeks had turned bright red. "I shouldn't have said anything."

Chrissy touched her arm again. "It's okay. In fact, it's good." She tried to decide how much to say. "I mean, it's a small town. People talk. I consider you a friend and I would appreciate it if you would just tell me what people say about me."

"You're sure?"

"Absolutely."

"Well. Good, then." Ruby drew herself up straighter in the bentwood chair. "And I hope you'll do the same for me."

"It's a deal." Chrissy picked up her iced tea and offered a toast. "To honesty between friends."

"To honesty." Ruby tapped her glass to Chrissy's.

Now Chrissy felt a little guilty. They'd just toasted to

honesty, and yet she was only going to say so much. She gave her friend the short version of what she'd told Hayes two weeks before. "Sam's a good man, and a completely conventional sort of guy. He wanted a stay-at-home wife, and he wanted us to have children—as many as possible—together. When we found out that was not going to happen, Sam couldn't deal with it. He wouldn't even try. Our marriage was collateral damage. It was horrible, for me and for Sam. And it was so hard, walking away from our life together."

"Oh, Chrissy." Ruby shook her head. "I'm so sorry. And as far as walking away from your marriage, I know exactly what you mean."

They were quiet for a minute or two.

Then Chrissy said, "I'm so glad you have Emery—and that she has you."

"Yeah." Ruby's beautiful smile bloomed wide. "Me too."

A little while later, they walked back to the inn together. As they went in the side entrance, Chrissy's cell rang.

She checked the display. It was her mom. She didn't have time for a chat right then, so she sent it to voicemail.

On her afternoon break she called her mom back.

Patrice gushed. "We had such a good time Sunday, sweetheart. Thank you for inviting us."

"I'm glad you could come." Chrissy realized as she said the words that she meant them sincerely.

Her mom said, "I have to tell you…"

Chrissy braced herself. "What, Mom?"

"Well, everyone in town is talking about Hayes."

Chrissy stiffened. "What about him?"

"Sweetheart, please. Don't be defensive."

"Well, Mom. Since he came back to town Hayes has

been good to me, and I don't want to hear whatever mean things people are—"

"Wait! Stop. There are no mean things. I promise you, it's good! It's all good."

Surely she hadn't heard right. "Uh, it is?"

"Yes, yes. Everyone's saying what a beautiful thing he's doing, the way he's stepped right up to save the family ranch. Honest and truly, sweetheart, I will always be sad about poor Sam. But the truth is, Hayes has grown up into quite a man—a hero, you might even say."

Chrissy felt humbled. "Yeah. You're right. It's pretty great that he came back now. Lionel and Norma need him so much. And I'm sorry I jumped to conclusions when you said that people are talking about him."

"It's okay. I do understand. When people talk, they're not always saying nice things."

"You're right about that."

"And frankly, I have not always been Hayes Parker's biggest fan. But Hayes has grown into a fine man, sweetheart. And if you two did decide to rekindle that old flame—"

"Mom."

"Hmm?"

"That's not going to happen." It actually hurt to say those words. Partly because they were a lie. The whole rekindling thing had already happened. But the fire wasn't going to last. And she needed to remember that. She needed to keep firmly in mind that she and Hayes were not a forever kind of thing.

"Never say never," Patrice chirped on a happy little laugh.

"Mom…"

"I know, I know. You're at work and you have to go."

"I'll talk to you soon."

"Love you, sweetie."

"Love you, too, Mom."

Chrissy ended the call feeling simultaneously pleased that her mom could now appreciate Hayes, and sad that her time with Hayes couldn't last. It was really starting to get to her that they would lose each other all over again.

It wasn't supposed to be like this, with her pining for a future she just wasn't going to get. She and Hayes had agreed to share a special time. A time where they could enjoy each other and then say goodbye without either of them getting hurt because...

What had they said to each other? That she wasn't ready for love—and that he never would be.

He seemed to be sticking by what he'd said then, standing firm that love remained in the *never again* category as far as he was concerned.

For her, though, it just wasn't that simple. Maybe she still wasn't ready. But oh, sweet Lord, now she wanted to be.

Had she known this would happen?

Probably. But she'd gone ahead anyway. And she didn't regret that.

She would never regret this summer love affair with Hayes.

But the end wasn't that far away—it never had been. Soon, she would move out. They'd agreed they would be over when she returned to her condo. And then, once Lionel was back on his feet, Hayes would leave town. She would never have a future with him.

And for as long as this love affair lasted, she needed to keep a check on her feelings. She needed *not* to say more than he wanted to hear. It was what it was. She'd faced heartache before, and one way or another, she would survive it again.

That night, he tapped on her door at a little before nine. She set aside her sadness and went to let him in.

He hesitated on the threshold. "I have something I'm kind of needing to talk about," he said.

She took his hand and led him to the bed. They sat down side by side. She reminded herself not to hope that he might be about to say he didn't want to let her go when her condo was ready. "I'm listening."

He shut his eyes and drew in a slow breath. "It's just... Chrissy, I can't shake this feeling that here, on the ranch, is where I'm supposed to be."

Hope started to rise again. She shoved it down. This was not about the two of them and she knew that in her heart.

She asked, "So you're thinking about staying on, working with your dad?"

He winced. "You know, when you say it out loud like that, I can't see it happening, not in real life. We both know my dad."

"Hayes." She gave his fingers a reassuring squeeze. "He's better lately, not so quick to fly off the handle."

"He's not *better* enough—but yeah. I'm thinking about it anyway. I have money saved. And when Anna's dad died he left me a little something. I've already been helping out with the bills around here. But if I put in what I have to make things work here, if I go for it..." He drew a slow breath and let it out hard. "I don't know. I can't decide. For fifteen years I've told myself I could never come back home."

"And yet, here you are..."

"You're right." He gave a humorless laugh. "I said never. And yet I couldn't stay away when the old man really needed me. And right about now, I am completely confused."

"You don't have to decide right this minute. There's time."

"I just don't know."

"And that's okay. The right answer will come to you. Eventually."

"I hope so." He flopped back across the bed, tugging on her hand so that she came with him. For a moment, they were side by side staring up at the ceiling. Then he braced up on an elbow and leaned over her. Trailing his index finger up her arm, he paused to trace the words inked on her skin.

Be Bold. Be True. Be Free.

She should be more of all three of those things. But she wasn't.

And his brushing finger was moving on, his light touch gliding all the way to her shoulder and then under the fall of her hair.

When he cradled the back of her neck, she raised her mouth to him.

He kissed her.

All the questions faded away. She got gloriously lost in right now.

THAT NIGHT? IT was perfect. And so was the night after.

And the one after that.

Chrissy tried not to let herself feel blue that time was passing way too quickly. That she couldn't help wanting more than Hayes was willing to give. She tried to stay upbeat, to let herself be happy with each day—and night.

But it wasn't enough. She did want more. More than they'd agreed on, more than the magic they conjured between them at night in her bed.

Be Bold. Be True. Be Free.

Her own tattoo seemed to mock her.

And as each day passed, she felt like a bigger coward

than the day before. For not taking a chance. For not laying her heart on the line, not just telling Hayes how she felt, not asking him for what she really wanted.

Friday at the dinner table, Hayes said, "Arlen and I are thinking about heading over to the Grizzly tonight, having a beer or two, shooting some pool."

"Sounds like fun," Norma said.

Lionel huffed. "Don't go gettin' wasted, now. Morning comes damn good and early around here."

"Don't worry, Dad," Hayes said in that patient voice he used when Lionel got overbearing. "I'll keep a lid on it."

Arlen added, "And I'll be there to make sure he behaves himself."

"Hmph," said Lionel, and helped himself to more green beans.

Hayes scoffed. "Right. Arlen will keep an eye on me. Because I'm such a yahoo and all."

"Yeah." Arlen grinned. "A yahoo. That's you."

Chrissy felt hurt and despised herself for it. So he wanted to go out for a beer with his friend. He was in no way obligated to spend every night in her bed.

Even if their nights were numbered and counting down to zero fast.

"Chrissy…"

She glanced up to meet Hayes's green eyes—zap! Like a bolt of lightning straight to her heart, just from looking at the guy. Could she be any more pitiful?

"Come with us," he said, his slow smile just for her.

Happiness poured through her—and for what? Because he'd invited her to tag along?

Was she ridiculous?

Definitely.

Ridiculous and lying to herself and miserable—and totally and completely in love.

With Hayes.

All over again.

Her throat locked up with sheer misery. Because she'd gone and done it, admitted it to herself.

She loved Hayes.

And she wished with all her yearning heart that she didn't.

"Chrissy?" He was watching her. She could see the confusion on his face. He had no idea what was going on inside her.

Too bad. They had an agreement, and she was sticking with it. The last thing he ever needed to know was how she'd gone and fallen for him a second time.

And as for tagging along with them to the saloon? Forget it. The Grizzly was the last place she wanted to be right now. "Thanks for thinking of me. But I'm kind of tired. I'm just going to hang around here tonight."

Twin lines formed between his eyebrows. She read his expression. He could see that something was going on with her, but he didn't know what.

And he would never know. He'd made his position painfully clear. It would do neither of them one bit of good for her to go declaring her undying love to him.

She just needed a little time to herself tonight. She needed to start considering what her next move should be.

"You sure?" Hayes asked. He was watching her so intently.

Her heart did something painful inside her chest. For a moment, she just knew he must have read her mind.

But then she realized he was only asking about the visit to the Grizzly tonight.

"Yeah, Hayes. Really. I'm just going to stay here tonight."

He let it go at that and she was grateful. Twenty minutes later, he and Arlen headed for town.

Lionel helped clear the table and then, with Rayna at his heels, Hayes's dad wandered off to his big chair in the great room. Chrissy and Norma cleaned up the kitchen together.

"You're quiet tonight," Norma said as she put the last dish in the dishwasher and started it up.

"Just tired, that's all."

Hayes's mom gave her the strangest look, kind of tender. And also mysterious.

"What?" Chrissy demanded.

The older woman put her hand on Chrissy's shoulder, a warm touch. Reassuring, too. "I do love having you here. I keep hoping you'll stay. You and my son are good together. You always were good together."

Chrissy didn't know whether to argue that point or grab Norma in a tight hug. "Hayes isn't interested in anything serious."

"You sure about that?"

"He told me so. He was real clear on the subject."

"Come here." Norma clasped her other shoulder and pulled Chrissy close. It felt good hugging Hayes's mom. It gave Chrissy comfort, and she needed that right now. Then Norma took her by the arms and held her away. "If he lets you go again, well, I don't know what. That's just wrong and I don't mind saying so."

Chrissy couldn't help laughing—the kind of laugh that hovered on the verge of tears. "And here Hayes and I thought you and Lionel had no idea what was going on upstairs while you were sleeping."

Norma pressed her hand to Chrissy's cheek. "Oh, honey. We didn't get to be this old without learning to mind our own business at least some of the time."

Chrissy laughed again then, and Norma laughed right along with her.

"What's so funny in there?" Lionel called out from the other room.

"I almost dropped a serving bowl!" Norma hollered back.

"Be careful!"

"We will, we will!" Norma put her hand on Chrissy's shoulder again and lowered her voice. "If you haven't told him how you feel, think about it. Honesty really is the best policy."

"Not in this case. He doesn't want to know."

"But maybe *you* need to say it to him."

CHRISSY THOUGHT ABOUT Norma's words as she dried the last saucepan. She climbed the stairs thinking about them.

They ran through her mind as she washed her face and brushed her teeth.

Around nine, when she stood on the rag rug by the bed trying to decide whether to read a book or get a head start on the menus for the week after next, she was still thinking about it.

And still coming to the same conclusion.

Hayes didn't want to know, and she wasn't going to tell him.

Period. End of story.

She was just climbing into bed with a nice, fat novel about two women opening a bookstore at the beach in Malibu, California, when there was a tap on the door.

Her heart rate blasted into overdrive. She ordered it to settle down, reminding herself that it was way too early for Hayes to be home from the bar.

"Chrissy?" He called her name quietly.

Her heart raced even faster. And she couldn't breathe.

Yep. Ridiculous. No doubt about it.

Sucking in air, ordering her pulse to slow the heck

down, she dropped her book on the nightstand and went to let him in.

He stood on the threshold, hands stuffed in his pockets.

"You're back early." Her voice sounded bizarrely normal, though inside she was a riot of warring emotions—panic, dread, misery, excitement...

"I kept thinking about you," he said, "kept wondering what you were up to."

"Well, I'm up to no good, obviously." She tried to sound playful, but the effort fell flat. She was miserable and, at the same time, so glad to see him—like he'd been away forever when in fact he'd been gone, what? A couple of hours? It was just more proof that she'd somehow managed to lose her mind over the man. And for the second time, too. Really, she ought to know better.

He peered at her, frowning. "You feeling okay?"

"Uh. Yeah. Fine. Why?"

"Well, at dinnertime, you said you were tired, that you wanted to take it easy..."

"That's right, I did."

"So I was worried about you."

"Hayes, I told you. I'm fine. Stop worrying."

"It doesn't work that way. You seemed... I don't know, unhappy. Or maybe sick. Are you sure you aren't coming down with a bug?"

"I'm not sick. There's no bug. I keep telling you I'm fine." She hoped he would leave it at that. But he just went on frowning at her, so she added, "It's been a long work week, that's all. A long week with lots going on."

He just stood there and stared at her. Finally, he asked, "Chrissy?"

"Yeah?"

"Do I get to come in?"

She hesitated, yearning for him at the same time as she

wished he would just go away. "Uh. Sure. Of course." She stepped back and gestured him forward, shutting the door as soon as he was inside.

And then, all over again, they just stood there staring at each other.

It was excruciating.

And then he closed the short distance between them and took her face between his two hands. "Just tell me what's wrong." He looked a little freaked out. And apparently, he was. Because then he said, "You're scaring me."

She tipped her head back, groaned at the ceiling, and admitted to herself that Norma was right.

Too bad if he didn't want to hear it.

She needed to say it. "Look…"

"Yeah?" Gently, with slow care, he guided a few stray strands of hair away from her eyes.

That sweet touch undid her. She wanted to cry. "Oh, Hayes…"

"What? Tell me. Whatever it is. I'm here. I'm listening."

"I didn't mean for this to happen. I didn't expect it. Not in a hundred years…"

His mouth fell open—and then he seemed to pull himself together. He framed her face between his palms again and whispered, "I know you said there were…issues with Sam. That you never got pregnant. But just tell me. Are you somehow magically pregnant now?"

A weird, ragged laugh burst out of her. "No! Hayes, think about it. We've been careful. Not to mention we've been together that way for what, a week? Even if I was, I wouldn't know at this point."

He kept holding her face. And he looked at her so deeply. "So then, not pregnant?"

"Uh-uh. Not pregnant."

"Well, whatever it is, whatever you need, Chrissy, I'm

here for you. I promise you. I want to help with whatever is bothering you."

She caught his wrists and gently peeled his hands away from her face. "I just need for you *not* to be touching me when I tell you. Okay?"

"Uh, sure." He dropped his arms to his sides and fell back a step. "All right. Not touching you. Now what the hell is wrong?"

"I, uh…" Dear Lord, this was awful.

"Come on. You're killing me here."

"I'm sorry. It's just… Oh, Hayes. It's like this. I'm in love with you, okay? I'm in love with you all over again."

His face went blank. He actually fell back another step—like she'd pushed him. Or maybe like he really needed to get as far away from her as possible. "Chrissy, look…" He shook his head.

He actually shook his head.

She closed her eyes and drew a slow, careful breath. This was bad. She'd known it would be. And yet she'd gone and said those dangerous words anyway. "Tell you what, Hayes Parker. Just do it, okay? Just put me out of my misery."

He had the nerve to wince. "Chrissy, I really don't want to—"

"—hurt me?" It came out as an accusation. Because it was one. "You don't want to hurt me?"

He looked downright crushed. "You're right, I don't. I mean that."

She threw up both hands. "Well, too bad. Because you've gone and done it anyway."

He backed up yet another step and demanded in a near-whisper, "Why are you so angry?"

Because you don't love me back! Because you'll never

love me back! She wanted to scream at him, just run around the room in circles, screeching like her hair was on fire.

But she couldn't do that. She might be half out of her mind with the awfulness of laying her heart on the line and having him step back in horror and remind her that he didn't sign on for this. But so what? That was her problem. Her pain to deal with.

He *hadn't* asked for this.

In fact, he'd warned her upfront. He'd said it right out, made it perfectly clear that he wasn't going to be falling in love with her, or with anyone. Not ever again.

And she was totally in the wrong to keep torturing both of them this way.

"Chrissy, I—"

"No." Now she was the one putting up both hands and backing away. "You know what? This is my fault. This is me just…humiliating myself."

"No, that's not true. You're not. No way. You're being honest. And listen, I—"

"Stop. I mean it. Please just stop." Her stomach churned and her face felt hot enough to melt right off her bones. "I don't know what I was thinking to lay this on you. It was wrong and I apologize. And, well, that's pretty much it."

He gulped and glanced away as he forked his fingers through his unruly hair. "What are you saying?"

She wanted out. Now. "Well, Hayes, I just think that it's time for me to go."

He blinked at her. "You mean you've suddenly decided that you're moving out?"

She drew herself up. "Yeah. That is exactly what I mean."

"But why? It's not necessary. We can—"

"Hayes. No, we can't. Not unless you can look in my

eyes and tell me that you love me, too—or that at least, given time, you might be able to."

"Oh, Chrissy…" His tone, his sad eyes—they said it all. "Just don't leave, okay? There's no reason for you to leave."

She patted the air between them, as though the gesture could somehow ease the awfulness of what was happening here. "From my point of view, there is every reason for me to leave. I mean, maybe *you* could work it out with me so that you're okay with me and my feelings. But I can't. I am not okay with your feelings about me. I shouldn't have said anything, but I did. I can't call the words back. They're out. You know now. And I hate that. I can't deal with that and also have to see your face every day."

"But—"

"Stop. Listen. I don't want to live in the same house with you anymore. I'm finished here. I need to go, I really do. I'm going to call my dad first thing tomorrow and have him get over here with a truck. I'm hoping to be out before lunch."

There was a gaping hole of silence then. Finally, Hayes asked through gritted teeth, "That's it? You mean it? You're leaving just like that because I won't say I love you?"

"Finally. You're getting it. Yes, Hayes. I love you and you don't love me. It's awkward and it's painful. I want out and you should *want* me to go."

He shook his head. And then, with a slow breath, he faced her squarely. "You know what? Fine. You go ahead. Go." He turned for the door.

She knew she should stop him, that she should at least take a stab at smoothing things over with him. She didn't want it to end like this—as bad as the first time she lost him, in that crappy old trailer down in Wyoming.

But what could she say? There was no way to make it all better.

It was awful and she didn't know what to do about that. Right now, she had neither the will nor the heart to fix anything.

All she wanted was out.

So she did nothing. She stood there with her mouth firmly shut and watched him walk out the door.

CHAPTER ELEVEN

AT SIX THE next morning, Chrissy called her dad.

He answered on the first ring. When she told him what she wanted, he said, "I can be there at eight with a truck. Will that work?"

"Yes." By eight, she figured Hayes and Arlen would be done with breakfast and back out on the land. "Thank you, Dad. I love you so much."

"I love you, too, Sugar Bee. See you then."

She went down to help Norma with the morning meal. Hayes and Arlen came in at seven. Chrissy smiled a greeting at Arlen and tried not to look at Hayes because looking hurt too much. Lionel and Rayna wandered in from the downstairs bedroom five minutes later.

Somehow, Chrissy got through the meal, putting food in her mouth and chewing it, sipping coffee, trying to force her lips into a smile when anyone spoke to her.

Hayes and his dad got into an argument about when Lionel would be ready to get out and help with chores.

"For God's sake," grumbled Lionel. "It's not going to kill me to gather a few eggs."

Norma didn't want Lionel out working yet either. "Hayes and Arlen are managing just fine," she said, her eyes narrowed on her husband. "I want you to take it easy for at least another week before you try handling any chores."

"It's a walk, Norma. I walk out to the chicken pen, I walk around the coop collecting the eggs and then I walk

back here to the house. Walks are good for me. The doctor said so."

Norma shook her head. "You know there's more involved in egg gathering than just walking. I'm not going to argue with you anymore. One more week of taking it easy. That's all I'm asking. Then you and me can go visit the chicken coop together."

Lionel was not pleased. He got up in a huff and headed for his room with Rayna trailing in his wake. A few minutes later, Hayes and Arlen carried their plates to the sink and went back outside to work.

Chrissy's dad was due in about fifteen minutes. She got up and started grabbing stuff off the table to clear it.

Norma said, "All that will wait. Sit down and tell me what's going on."

Chrissy's eyes filled with tears. She blinked them away as she dropped back to her seat. "Oh, Norma…"

Norma slid over to the chair next to Chrissy's. Leaning close, she laid a soothing hand on Chrissy's back. "It's okay, honey…"

"No. No, it's really not."

"Now, now. Sometimes it's better just to let it all out."

"Is it? I don't know about that. I don't even know how much to say. Things just kind of blew up between Hayes and me, and now I need to get away. So I called my dad and he'll be here in a few minutes to move me out."

Norma's mouth formed a shocked O. "Hayes asked you to leave?"

"No. He wants me to stay. But I, um, told him I love him, and he turned me down and now I really need to go and stay somewhere else."

Norma pulled her closer. "Oh, honey. It's all my fault."

"No…"

"Yes. I talked you into telling him how you feel."

"Norma, no. No, you did not. You said maybe I needed to tell him. I thought about that. And I realized that I did want him to know. So I told him. I took my shot, and it didn't go well. That's what happened. It was my choice to open my big mouth, and this is the result."

"I'm still sorry. And I'm going to miss having you here, honey. I'm going to miss you so much."

"Oh, I'll miss you, too. I really will."

Norma pulled her closer. Chrissy let Hayes's mom hold her, just for a minute or two.

Then, with a sigh, she kissed Norma on the cheek. "Come on, now. Let's clean up this kitchen. And then I need to get started hauling all my stuff down the stairs."

By the time her dad arrived with one of the workers from the store, Chrissy's eyes were dry. With Norma's help they got everything downstairs and out to the truck.

After her dad drove off, Chrissy went in to say good-bye to Lionel.

Hayes's dad looked sad at her news. "You come to visit. Any time. You hear me?"

She thanked him and gave him a quick hug.

Before she got into her Blazer to go, she wrapped her arms around Norma again.

"Don't you dare be a stranger," Hayes's mom whispered.

"Oh, Norma, give me a little time to pull myself to-gether. I'll call you in a week or two. We can meet for cof-fee or something."

"Yes. Yes, let's do that." Norma hugged her even tighter before she finally let her go.

It was a few minutes after eleven when Chrissy turned into the driveway of her parents' house. Her mom came running out to greet her.

"Chrissy!" Patrice grabbed her in a hug—and then sur-prised her by not fussing any more than that. They all

got to work unloading the clothes and belongings Chrissy would need for the next few weeks. Everything else, her dad and his helper, Tim, took to store in the warehouse with the rest of her furniture and household goods.

The afternoon went by in a blur. She couldn't believe that she was really back in her old room in her parents' house again. She'd tried so hard not to let that happen.

And yet somehow, it had. At least her mom had cleared out all the fluffy pastel bedding and repainted her Pepto-Bismol–colored walls a nice, relaxing pale blue.

Her mom came in as Chrissy finished hanging up her clothes.

"So," Patrice said briskly. "What can I help you with?"

"Thanks, Mom." Chrissy dropped to the side of the bed. "But I've got it handled."

"You sure?"

"Yes—and I want you to know how much I appreciate that you're here for me to come home to."

Her mom walked toward her slowly. "Sweetheart. Are you okay? Is this about Hayes?"

She didn't even have the energy to lie about it. "Yeah."

"I'm so sorry." Her mom whispered the words.

Somehow, her mother's gentle approach had Chrissy reaching out a hand. "I can always use another hug."

"Oh, my baby…" Patrice dropped down beside her. Chrissy hugged her mom close. She breathed in Patrice's flowery scent and let herself be glad to have loving arms around her. "Don't you worry, sweetheart," her mom whispered. "Hayes Parker is a stubborn one. But he will come to his senses. You just need to give that man a lot of leeway and plenty of time to come around."

"Oh, Mom. I don't know about that."

"Well, I do. He's a good man," Patrice said softly as she stroked Chrissy's hair. "He can be difficult, I know. But

he does have a good head on his shoulders. And he really does love you, sweetheart. You two were always meant to be together."

Okay, now. That was just more than Chrissy could take without talking back.

She lifted her head off her mom's shoulder and said, "Please. What have you done with my real mother? Suddenly you're Team Hayes? What about Sam? I thought you were waiting for him to come back to me."

Patrice gave a small shrug. "Yes, well, I see things differently now. I'm older and wiser."

Chrissy blinked at that one. "Older and wiser than… last week?"

Patrice waved a hand. "Oh, sweetheart. You never did have the connection with Sam that you share with Hayes. I see that now. I see that Hayes is a good man, too—and of course, he's also a goner."

"A goner?"

"That's right. A goner for you. He's in love with you. It's so clear how he feels. He looks at you like you're the most important thing in the world. Are you trying to tell me that you don't know?"

"Mom. Yes. I'm telling you that I don't know because it isn't true. Hayes isn't—"

"Oh, yes. Yes, he is. It was so obvious last Sunday. That man can't take his eyes off of you. But as I said, he's also stubborn. And that means he needs a little time to come to grips with the fact that he doesn't want to live without you."

"Mom. Come on. I love you so much, but—"

"And I love you."

"But, Mom, sometimes you just don't know what you're talking about."

Patrice shook a finger at her. "Oh, yes, I do."

"He's not going to be coming after me."

"Oh, yes, he is—and if you're impatient for him to get over whatever's holding him back, there is another option."

Chrissy knew she shouldn't ask. "What option is that?"

"You could go to him to try to talk some sense into him—you know, be bold and true, like it says on your arm. And free, too." Patrice frowned. "Though in this case, maybe not so much free as just bold and true."

Chrissy laughed then. It felt good after all this misery she'd been stewing in since last night. "Oh, Mom…" Chrissy rested her head on her mom's soft shoulder again.

And she tried really hard not to hope that her mom actually knew what she was talking about. She tried not to let herself imagine that any day now Hayes would be knocking on the front door, begging to speak to her, ready to plead with her to give him one more chance to make it right.

ALL DAY SATURDAY, Hayes was deeply indignant that Chrissy had just packed her stuff and left. On top of his simmering fury at her, he also happened to be just plain miserable.

How in holy hell had it turned out like this—with him missing her as much as he had when they broke up the first time?

Not that her leaving this time constituted a breakup.

It didn't. How could they break up? They hadn't even been together this time—not really. This time they'd agreed it was a just-for-now, friends-with-benefits situation.

You couldn't break up when you weren't even a couple.

Or so he kept reminding his own sorry ass.

He missed her already and she'd only been gone since after breakfast—missed her like a *friend*. Because that's what she was—a friend with benefits. Spectacular benefits.

And it damn sure rankled that she hadn't even stuck around to talk this problem out with him. If she really didn't want him in her bed anymore, well, fair enough. He didn't like it, but he was bound to respect her wishes on that score.

Losing Chrissy as a friend, though. That cut him deep. He'd let himself get way too accustomed to their evenings on the porch, to letting himself imagine that the two of them would always be on each other's side from here on out.

As for her saying that she was in love with him all over again, well, what was he supposed to do with that? He'd told her he wasn't going there. She knew that.

Damn. He wanted to call her, call her and remind her that she was being completely unreasonable. They needed to work this problem out. Because he had no intention of losing her all over again. He wanted her in his life.

And if she *loved* him so much, well, why the hell did she leave?

That night at dinner, he announced that he was heading for the Grizzly again. "I feel like I missed out, coming home early last night. I need to make up for lost time."

Arlen said, "Have fun."

It wasn't the response Hayes had hoped for. "I will. And so will you. Because you know you're coming with me."

"No. Not me. I'm hanging out here tonight."

"Aw, come on. Come with me."

"No. Once a week at the Grizzly is way more than enough for me."

Hayes's dad chose that moment to throw in his two cents worth. "Arlen's right. Two nights in a row at that saloon is two nights more than any man needs."

"Stay out of it," Hayes snarled at his dad.

Lionel huffed out a breath. "I got a right to an opinion at my own kitchen table."

"Okay, then, Dad. You have shared your opinion and I have heard it. Now if you don't mind, this discussion is between Arlen and me."

Arlen rose. "This discussion is over, at least as far as I'm concerned. Norma, legendary meat loaf. Thank you, ma'am."

His mom gave Arlen her sweetest smile. "Arlen, hon, you have a nice night."

With a nod, Arlen picked up his plate and carried it to the sink.

Hayes debated taking another stab at getting his friend to ride over to the Grizzly with him—but never mind. When Arlen dug in his heels, there was no budging him.

So then. Fair enough. He'd go on his own. He needed the distraction. Maybe if he got drunk enough, he could stop being so mad at Chrissy for walking out on him like she had.

His dad was staring right at him. "Don't be a damn fool, son. You're in no condition to go out drinking tonight."

"Condition? I don't have any condition. I don't know what you're talking about."

"Yeah, you do. Don't think you're fooling anybody because you're not. You've got that wild-eyed, looking-for-trouble gleam in your eyes. The one you used to get just before you ended up doing something everyone was going to regret. I thought you'd grown out of that but look at you now. Bad as ever. If you leave this house tonight, you're just going to get yourself into trouble. I know it. Your mom knows it. Arlen knows it."

"I am perfectly fine."

"No, you're not. Stay home."

He opened his mouth to tell his father *again* to mind his own damn business.

But then before he got a word out, his mother piled on. "Stay home, Hayes. Your father's right. Whatever you're looking for tonight, you're not going to find it at the saloon. And the chances are much too high that you'll find trouble instead."

Grabbing his empty plate, he shoved back his chair. "I'm out of here." He carried the plate to the sink, took great effort to set it down quietly—and then headed for the door.

Rayna trailed after him. He turned on her. "Stay," he commanded.

With a worried whine, she dropped to her haunches just as his father called from inside the arch to the kitchen, "Don't be a damn fool!"

Hayes didn't answer. He was already out the door and pulling it shut behind him. In his truck, he gunned the engine and took off toward the gate.

It wasn't till he'd driven about halfway to town that he started feeling like the biggest jerk on the planet.

Probably because he'd been behaving like one.

He pulled over to the shoulder, turned off the engine and punched the dashboard twice. Not too hard, though. By then, he was already cooling off.

Fine then. Chrissy was gone and he needed to start getting used to that. It wasn't the first time. And her leaving was probably for the best. He'd been getting way too attached to her all over again, now hadn't he?

And getting attached wasn't good. Because now he felt like he'd lost her twice.

You'd think at some point, he'd learn his lesson. Getting too attached was a bad, bad idea.

As for the Grizzly, the more he thought about it, the

less he wanted to be there tonight. But to hell with turning around and heading straight back home.

He realized now that he didn't want to talk to anyone tonight. So when he started up the truck again, he just drove around, looking at the moon out the windshield, trying not to think at all.

It was well after midnight when he let himself back into the darkened ranch house. Rayna appeared, wagging her giant tail. He bent and lavished attention on her.

In the kitchen, he filled a glass with tap water and drank it down. And then he went up the stairs, Rayna right behind him. Somehow he resisted the temptation to wander on down to the end of the upstairs hall, to stand in the doorway of the bedroom there, staring at the empty space where Chrissy used to be.

In the morning, he was up at four. Arlen met him at the barn.

His friend looked him up and down. "I see you survived the night. Have a good time?"

"I've had better."

Arlen clapped him on the arm. "Come on. Let's get to work."

Work was exactly his plan. He figured it was smarter than drinking. From now on, he'd be up at four and getting stuff done, wearing himself out so when he dropped into bed at night, he'd go out like a light, dead to the world.

No spare down time to sit around and sulk about Chrissy. No opportunity to start wondering if he'd messed up big-time letting her get away. He had a plan.

And on Sunday, Monday and Tuesday, he executed it.

Too bad the plan was crap. He thought of her all the time, and he needed to stop that. He told himself it was merely a matter of focus, that he just had to keep working, pushing himself constantly, until the day came when

he didn't think of her at all, when he was too worn out to lie awake at night longing for the woman he couldn't let himself have.

Wednesday, after breakfast, Hayes and Arlen were headed out to the tractor shed to spend some time repairing machinery when a couple of heifers came wandering toward them down the dirt road that led off toward a far pasture. Wandering heifers pretty much always meant a fence was down, so they grabbed what they'd need to repair the damage, tacked up their horses and drove those heifers back to where they belonged. The whole process, including fence repair, took a few hours.

They got back to the barn around eleven, untacked the horses, put their tools away and were headed to the tractor shed when Hayes's mom came out the back door calling his dad's name. She spotted them and waved them over.

About then, his dad sat up in the tall, dry grass midway between his mom on the back porch and Hayes and Arlen on the way to the shed. "Over here!" Lionel hollered as Rayna, who'd been lying right beside him, stood up and wagged her tail.

Hayes, Arlen and Norma ran toward the old man. His dad shouted, "Settle down, settle down! Nobody died!"

The three converged on him. Lionel was sweating right through his shirt and his face was dead white except for two bright patches of red at his cheeks. Whining her concern, Rayna backed out of the way.

"Lionel!" cried his mom. "What in the world...?"

"I said, settle down," his dad grumbled. "I'm fine, just fine."

"Dad. You don't look fine."

Lionel held up a hand to Hayes. "Quit your yapping and give a man a boost."

"Slow down, Dad. Just rest for a moment more before you—"

"I don't need a rest. I need to get on my feet. Help me up, damn it!"

"Lionel," said his mom in a coaxing tone. That was as far as she got.

His dad snapped, "Norma, don't start!" as he kept right on groping for Hayes's hand.

Resigned, Hayes pulled him up. With a lot of groaning and huffing, Lionel got upright. "Come on," said Hayes. "Let's get you into the house." He wrapped his dad's arm across his shoulders.

Arlen stepped up on the old man's other side and Rayna herded them all from behind as Hayes's mom ran ahead to open the back gate and then the back door.

With Lionel grumbling and panting the whole way, they got him inside to his chair, which he immediately flipped into the reclining position. "Get back." He shooed them off. "Let a man breathe."

"What happened?" Hayes's mom cried.

"Norma, relax. A few chickens got loose. I just went out to get them back inside the pen. They were frisky and they tired me out, so I stretched out in the grass to rest a bit."

"You're sweating and your color's off."

"Leave me be. I'll be fine."

She had her phone in her hand. "I am calling Doctor Bristol." As Lionel kept on griping that he was fine and he was going nowhere, Norma got hold of Dr. Bristol's office in Bronco Heights and spoke to a nurse. As for Hayes and Arlen, they just stood there, waiting to find out if they were going to be loading Lionel into a vehicle and getting him off to Bronco Valley Hospital again.

"Okay, then. Thank you, Emily." Norma hung up and turned on Lionel. "Doctor Bristol's nurse has given strict

instructions that I'm to check your vitals and call her right back. If anything is out of whack, off we go to the hospital again."

"Humph. We'll see about that."

Norma turned to Hayes and Arlen. "You boys go pour yourselves some coffee. I just made some fresh. I'll check your father over and then we'll see what happens next."

Ten minutes later, Hayes and Arlen sat on the sofa sipping coffee as Norma called Dr. Bristol's office again and reported Lionel's temperature, pulse rate and blood pressure while the whole time Lionel kept insisting, "I'm fine, I'm fine. I'm not even sweating anymore. Just look at me!"

"All right then," Norma said into the phone after both the nurse and Lionel stopped talking. "Will do." She ended the call and then turned to Hayes's dad. "All right. You're to stay in the house and rest all day, and I will be monitoring you hourly."

"I only wanted to get the damn chickens back in the pen. It's not the end of the world, Norma," the old man insisted.

By then, Hayes had had about enough. He set his mug down hard enough that coffee sloshed out. "Knock it off, Dad. Can't you see she's trying to make sure you're all right?"

"And she could have just asked me, now couldn't she? I've been trying to tell the three of you that there is nothing wrong with me and nobody is listening to me. Pardon me if I've had about enough of all this fussing and fiddling and freaking out when there's nothing to be freaking out about."

"You had acute pancreatitis and you could have died, Dad. People are worried about you."

"And you can all damn well knock that off. I'll have you know I didn't die. And as for all of you hovering over me, I've had enough. You need to give a man some peace!"

Right then, in the middle of another pointless argument with his dad, Hayes thought of Chrissy—Chrissy packing up and leaving. He stood there with his mouth hanging open, realizing that he'd said all the wrong things and now she wanted nothing to do with him. He'd probably never see her again.

Somehow, he was going to have to accept that she was gone—gone again. And she wasn't coming back.

And just thinking that made something snap inside him.

He stared down at his mule-stubborn father and thought, *Lionel Parker, you can go straight to hell.*

Because Hayes couldn't keep on like this anymore. Yeah, he wanted to save the ranch. But he'd had about enough of his dad constantly taking stupid chances with his health and then bitching and moaning when someone tried to help him.

Lionel was still talking. "You hear me, Hayes? You understand what I'm saying to you?"

"Damn right I do!" Hayes was yelling now, too.

"Don't you shout at me, boy! By God, you'd better tone it down."

"Okay, Dad. Yeah. Good idea. I'll tone it down—while I'm walking out the door." He stepped sideways to escape from behind the coffee table and headed for the stairs.

"Hayes, you get back here!" his father shouted.

His mom wrung her hands. "Oh, Hayes. Come on, now. Settle down. Let's talk about this quietly."

Arlen said nothing. He knew better than to insert himself into the middle of a family fight.

In no time, Hayes was up the stairs and entering his childhood bedroom. It wasn't till he turned to slam the door behind him that he realized Rayna had followed him up there. The minute he spotted her, she dropped her butt

to the floor and looked up at him through sad, soulful eyes. A small whimper escaped her.

"Sorry, girl. We're out of here."

With an unhappy whine, she flopped to the floor and put her head on her paws.

Hayes couldn't stand to look at her—at those big brown eyes reproaching him. He spun around and made for the closet, where he grabbed three duffel bags and tossed them on the bed. Then he started pulling things from the bureau and stuffing them in the bags.

He kept thinking of Chrissy, which was pointless. And wrong. But still, he kept wishing...

What?

That things could have been different. That *he'd* been different when she said she loved him.

Because what the hell was wrong with him—to go turning her down? He should have been braver. Should have grabbed her and held on and said, yeah. Let's do this. Let's be together. Let's make the kind of life we used to dream about, you and me.

At the very least, he should have agreed to try.

Because turning her down to save himself from another heartbreak wasn't going so well. Somehow, his heart had gotten broken anyway—the worst kind of broken. The kind he'd caused by his own damn self.

He was stuffing a pile of underwear into one of the duffels when he heard a low, throat-clearing sound from behind him. "Son..."

He dropped the underwear on the bed and turned. "What now?"

"Son, I'm sorry." His dad stood on the threshold, looking worn out, regretful and very determined.

Hayes had to blink really hard—partly to clear the embarrassing moisture from his eyes. And partly because

he still couldn't believe what he was seeing. What he was hearing…

"I'm a foolish old man," Lionel said, his voice low, rough as a patch of bad road. "A foolish old man with way too much useless pride. I know it, I truly do. I know it, though it practically kills me to make myself admit it—especially right out loud. And even more so to you…"

"Dad." Hayes got the one word out. But he didn't know what he meant to say next.

Turned out that was okay, because his dad said, "It hurt my pride to have you see me laying out there in the grass, worn out from chasing a few ornery hens, just trying to scrape up enough energy to get back to the house. It hurt my pride, so I did what I always do, turned it back around on you—and on your mother, too. I have already said I'm sorry to her. And being the angel she is, she's accepted my apology right off, though I know I do not deserve that woman. I…well, son. I guess the hard truth is I don't deserve you, either. But I truly am so sorry—though, believe me, I know that being sorry is not enough. I know I've got to do better. But to start, let me just say what I should have said weeks ago, on the day you came home again.

"Hayes, thank you. Thank you for coming home—and please. Don't go. This land is yours as much as it ever was mine. Your mother said she told you that I never did disinherit you. She says you know now that that was a mean, ugly lie."

"Yeah, Dad. She told me the truth a while back."

Lionel hung his head. He was breathing heavy.

Hayes went to him. "You should sit down." His dad didn't even argue. He let Hayes lead him to the bedside chair and help down into it. Hayes hovered close. "You need anything?"

His dad looked up at him. "If you would sit, hear me out…?"

"Okay." Hayes went to the bed, shoved the duffels off on the far side, and sat down. "Okay, what? Talk."

Lionel drew a slow breath. "I, uh, I got a bad habit of saying things I shouldn't, things that make me a hard man to forgive. I got too much pride and not enough self-restraint. I'm going to work on that—and no, I don't expect you to believe me." He straightened his slumped shoulders and looked squarely at Hayes then. "But I do want to ask you, please, to stay. Let this time be different. This time don't allow me to drive you away. Because I need your help. I truly do. I need your help bad. Son, do you think that maybe you might see your way clear to sticking around, after all?"

Hayes studied his dad's roadmap of a face. "All right. I'll tell you the truth. I don't want to go. I've tried for years to convince myself that I've moved on. But it was a lie. The plain fact is, I love this ranch. I want to make this place everything we both know it could be."

"Hell, yes!" said Lionel. "I want that, too."

"But Dad. You really pissed me off just now."

Lionel let out a hard breath. His big shoulders slumped. "I get it. I was a jackass, worse even than usual. There was just something so embarrassing about those damn chickens running loose, pecking and clucking, moving too fast for me to catch."

Hayes nodded. "Yeah, I can see how that might get you riled up—and Dad, listen. I was no prince just now either. I lost my temper, too. And not just because you were out of line. For a few days now, I've been having this powerful urge…"

His dad asked gently, "What kind of urge?"

"The urge to run away from my own mistakes."

His father understood. "You mean Chrissy, don't you?" Seeing the understanding in his dad's eyes really got to him. Hayes glanced away. Lionel said, "I miss having her around, I truly do. And I've got to tell you, that one's a keeper."

Hayes hung his head. "Yeah. She is."

"Don't make the same mistake I did. Don't drive the ones you love away."

Hayes didn't know what to say. He muttered, "Too late, Dad. I already did. I messed it up with her. I messed it up bad."

"So fix it, son." His father got up. He took the few steps to the edge of the bed and clapped Hayes on the shoulder. "Fix it. And stay."

CHAPTER TWELVE

THAT NIGHT, IT was almost nine and nearly dark when Chrissy finally got back to her parents' house. Her workday at the inn had been endless, just one mini-disaster after another.

But somehow, she'd lived through it. Now she needed a long bath and maybe a good book to get lost in, something to keep her mind off Hayes and everything they could have had if only—

Her thoughts flew off in all directions. Because right there, in front of her mother's house, sat Hayes's big, black crew cab.

"What the…?" she whispered to no one in particular, slamming on the brakes a split second before she plowed right into the back of the dusty black truck that should not even be there.

But it was.

About then, she dared to turn her head and glance toward the house.

After blinking twice to make certain she wasn't seeing things, she finally believed that Hayes Parker was sitting in one of the Adirondack chairs on her parents' front porch wearing faded jeans and that black leather jacket of his, the glow from the porchlight picking up glints of gold in his brown hair. As she stared, he got up.

And she just sat there behind the wheel as he came

down the front walk, her pulse pounding so hard she thought she might be having a heart attack or something. He came around to the driver's side. Her window was open, and she hadn't summoned the presence of mind to shut it before he got there.

He leaned in. "Hey."

She closed her eyes, turned her head to stare out the windshield, and opened them again. He was way too close. His scent tempted her—leather, soap and man.

She couldn't make herself turn and look at him. Instead, she scowled at the dusty back end of his big pickup. "What's up?"

"Your mom said I could wait on the porch. She said you'd be home before seven. I was beginning to worry."

She glared hard straight ahead. "What do you want, Hayes?"

He didn't answer for the longest time. She was about to roll up the window, back up, drive around his truck and keep going until she was somewhere he wasn't when he finally spoke in a rough whisper. "Come for a ride with me, Chrissy."

No, Hayes. Never. Those words were right there on the tip of her tongue.

But for some unknown reason, she couldn't push them out of her mouth.

"Why?" she asked instead.

Silence. She wasn't surprised. Of course he had no answer to her simple, one-word question.

But then he said, "Because I screwed up. Again. Because if you give me one more chance, I promise that this time, I will finally get it right."

She turned her head toward him slowly. His eyes said it all. He was telling the truth.

"WHERE ARE WE GOING?" she asked five minutes later. She was sitting in the passenger seat of his crew cab by then.

He had the wheel. "A certain spot on the ranch, under a cottonwood on the banks of a creek."

She remembered. "Our first time…"

"That's right. And our second time, too."

They left the lights of town in the rearview. Soon, they were bumping along a dirt road on Parker land, the quarter moon leading them on. She spotted that cottonwood ahead and to the right. He kept going, finally turning the wheel, leaving the dusty road behind to bump along up a rise of land and stop under the branches of that old tree.

From where they sat, the land sloped down toward the creek below. The water shimmered in the light of the waning moon.

Reaching over the seat, he grabbed a blanket and tucked it under his arm. Then he shoved open his door, got out and came around to her side.

When he pulled open her door and held out his hand, she took it. He helped her down. Together, they spread the blanket under the tree.

"Take your shoes off. Have a seat," he said.

Out of nowhere, she felt awkward, in her work skirt, cotton shirt and short vest. But she did as he suggested, slipping off her practical pumps, setting them out of the way before dipping to sit and folding her legs to the side.

When he dropped down next to her, she tugged on her skirt to keep it from riding up her thighs. *Breathe*, she thought. *Just breathe and everything will be all right.* "Okay, Hayes. I'm listening."

He leaned in and whispered so tenderly, "I love you, Chrissy Hastings. I love you with all my heart." Her breath caught when he said those perfect words. And he wasn't finished. "One more chance," he said. "That's all I'm asking."

Yes! her heart cried. But she couldn't quite give him that. Not yet. She muttered, "Well, you're asking a lot."

"I know it. And I can't say I'd blame you if you turned me down flat. But still, I am asking for just one more chance, Chrissy. Please."

She met his eyes. Emotion rose inside her, making her throat clutch. "You hurt me. You really hurt me. Fifteen years ago. And last Saturday night, too."

He slowly nodded. "I know. I just hope you can forgive me. I had it in my head that I was done with love. But that was just fear talking. Looking back, I think I knew from that first day, when I walked into the inn and there you were, more beautiful even than I remembered, saying my name, reminding me of everything we had together, of all we lost because I was too proud, too scared and too messed up to wait for you when you asked me to. That first day at the inn, I thought I was smarter than I used to be, that I'd learned from my losses, that I wouldn't be screwing up in the same old ways all over again."

"But you did."

"Yes, I did. Can you forgive me?"

Really, there was only one answer to that question. She gave it. "Of course."

He blinked at her, stunned.

She took his hand and kept her eyes locked with his. "I forgive you, Hayes. Because I love you, too."

"Damn," he whispered prayerfully. "I didn't appreciate those words as much as I should have when you said them last Saturday night. Would you say them once more?"

"I love you, Hayes. I truly do."

He pulled her close. It was the sweetest moment. It meant the world to her, just having his arms around her again. They shared a long, sweet kiss.

When he lifted his head, he said, "I'm staying here in

Tenacity, Chrissy. My dad and I, we had a big blow up, but then we finally sat down and had a long talk. He wants me to stay and run the ranch. I'm going to do it."

She pressed her hand to the side of his face. "I'm so glad."

"We've got a lot of work ahead of us, my dad and me, but I believe we'll make it through."

"I *know* you will."

His eyes were shining. "Would you consider moving back into the ranch house, but this time on a permanent basis?"

"What are you asking me, Hayes?"

"I want you with me. I'm trying not to rush you, but now that I finally see what I want most of all, showing restraint on this subject is pretty damn difficult."

"You want me to live at the ranch with you?"

"I want you however I can get you. If you need to move back to your condo, we'll work it out. But what I really want is for you to share the room at the end of the upstairs hall with me for real. And not just for a few hours at night in secret. I want us together. I want that so much. Will you marry me, Chrissy?"

She gasped. And then her throat clutched up again. Her eyes blurred with tears.

"Hey," he whispered. "Hey…" And he took her face so gently between his two rough hands. "Am I pushing too fast?"

She shook her head. "No."

"Well, then, is this about kids? Are you worried because you can't have them? Because I swear to you, I really don't care if you can have my babies or not. Yeah, I want a family. But I'm more than willing to adopt or try some sort of artificial insemination…or not." He brushed a tear from her cheek with his thumb. Now he looked re-

ally worried. "I mean it, Chrissy. However it works out, kids or no kids, as long as it's you and me together, we can make it through."

That did it, a sob escaped her. And then she burst into tears.

"Aw, my darlin'." Again, he wrapped her in those strong arms and pressed a kiss into her hair. "It's okay. I promise you. It will be all right."

Sagging against him, she slowly got the tears under control. Swiping the moisture off her cheeks, she pulled away enough to meet his eyes. "Oh, Hayes. I wasn't hesitating, I promise you. I'm just so happy right now, and that made me cry."

He still looked way too concerned.

So she took his hand, pressed it to her heart and said, "It's like this, about the fertility thing. I'm always vague when I talk about what went wrong between Sam and me. People usually assume I must have been the one with the issue. And I let them assume that. My ex-husband is a proud man, and no way am I putting his secrets on the street. But after three years of trying to get pregnant the usual way, Sam and I finally went to a specialist. First thing, we were both tested. We found out then that Sam was sterile. And he couldn't handle that. He just didn't know how to deal with the fact that he would never physically father a child."

"So, you're saying…"

"I'm saying that all my tests indicated I'm perfectly capable of having a baby whenever we decide to get going on that."

"Wow." He nodded slowly. "Well, then. All right. So there's no problem, huh?"

"Oh, Hayes. There are always problems. Problems are part of life."

"But you're willing to face all those problems anyway, with me?"

"Yes," she whispered, and then she flung her arms around his neck and pulled him down onto the blanket.

They celebrated their reunion right then and there, at the spot where they'd first made love all those years and years ago. It was perfect, just the two of them, naked under that tree with the quarter moon watching over them from way up high in the night sky.

THAT FRIDAY IN the early afternoon, they drove to Bronco for a weekend getaway, just the two of them. They stayed at a nice hotel in Bronco Heights.

Saturday morning, after breakfast in bed, Hayes got down on one knee and held up a beautiful vintage diamond ring, a classic solitaire on a gold band. "Chrissy Hastings, you made me the happiest man in Montana when you said you would marry me. But there's a little something I left out of my proposal and it's time I made that right. Would you do me the honor of accepting this—"

Before he could finish that sentence, Chrissy leapt from the bed, sat on his bended knee and threw her arms around him. "Oh, Hayes… Yes! Absolutely. Yes." She peppered kisses all over his face.

He laughed. "You're sure about this now?"

"So sure. And never surer about anything in my whole life, ever, I promise you."

He kissed her lips, lightly. Tenderly. "This ring was my Grandma Tessa's. My mom gave it to me yesterday. But if you'd rather have something new, something that you get to choose—"

She clapped her hand over his mouth. "I love it. It's perfect. Nothing could possibly suit me better."

"Well, all right then." He slipped his grandmother's ring on her finger.

She held out her hand and admired the sparkling stone. "It's so beautiful. Oh, Hayes. I don't think I've ever been this happy."

He scooped her up against his chest and stood. "Let's celebrate."

And they did, right there in the wide, comfy bed.

Later, they walked up and down the streets near their hotel, holding hands, pausing to admire the displays in the shop windows. They'd wandered for a while when Chrissy spotted the big stone building on the corner.

She tugged on his hand. "Hayes…"

"What?"

"I have an idea."

"What kind of idea?"

"You'll see. Come with me." She led him to the end of the street and pointed at the three-story building across a thick, green stretch of lawn. "City Hall."

He seemed puzzled. "Should I be impressed?"

"No, Hayes." She took him by the shoulders, went on tiptoe and whispered in his ear, "You should marry me. Today."

He blinked down at her. "Are you serious?"

"Oh, yes, I am."

"But I thought you would want a big church wedding."

She shook her head. "What I want is forever with you starting right now. I want our marriage to begin today…" Suddenly, her confidence wavered. She added in a softer voice, "I mean, if you want that, too…"

He pulled her closer and kissed her. "Nothing would make me happier. Marry me, Chrissy. Marry me today."

"Yes!" she shouted loud enough that a couple of tall cowboys stopped right there on the street to stare. Chrissy

didn't care. She had her arms around her man, and she kissed him again, a long kiss, slow and deep.

When he lifted his head, he said, "We have to go back to the hotel first, though."

She frowned up at him, puzzled. "We do?"

He nodded. "My Grandma Tessa's wedding band. I left it in the room safe." She grabbed his hand. "Well, come on, then. Let's get that ring and make it happen."

An hour later, they were married. She had his grandmother's wedding band on her finger, with three sweet diamonds glittering along the band, a perfect match for the engagement ring he'd given her earlier.

"I can't believe we did it," she said. "We're married, you and me. After all these years, we're finally married…"

He nodded. "It's a good day, Chrissy Parker."

"The best," she agreed. Laughing, she grabbed his hand again and pulled him over to the town bulletin board on the wall near the double doors that led outside. "Let's see what's going on in Bronco." She studied the flyers announcing upcoming events. "Hmm. I see there are back-to-back picnics coming up in beautiful Bronco Park. And then there's the Golden Buckle Anniversary event, the Mistletoe Rodeo in November, and of course the Christmas tree lighting in December."

He pulled her close and kissed her. "We'll need to come back."

"Often," she added.

"It's a plan," he agreed.

She leaned closer to the board. "What's this? Oh, Hayes, it's a Missing Person poster about Winona Cobbs."

Hayes asked, "The famous psychic, right?"

"Yeah."

He was frowning. "It says here that she disappeared."

Chrissy nodded. "Yes, she did. She vanished on the day

before her wedding to Stanley Sanchez. Stanley's younger than Winona, only in his eighties—oh, Hayes. Nobody knows where she went. We all keep hoping she'll just show up again somehow. But she hasn't. And that can't be good. It's been a month now..."

"Hey." He pulled her closer. "I'm sure they'll find her."

"Oh, I hope so."

He kissed the tip of her nose. "She's Winona Cobbs. Never count her out."

"You're right. Winona is a force of nature. I'm sure she'll be back. She and Stanley will be reunited. Just wait and see."

"Yeah. Impossible things happen all the time. I mean, look at us, Mrs. Parker. After fifteen years and a whole raft of heartbreak, here we are, together forever. At last."

"At last," she echoed, holding up her ring finger, admiring the way the diamonds sparkled in the light.

"I love you, Chrissy." He tipped up her chin with a tender hand.

"And I love you, Hayes. So much."

And then, oblivious to the citizens of Bronco bustling in and out the double doors a few feet away, they shared another slow, sweet kiss.

* * * * *

Don't miss the stories in this mini series!

MONTANA MAVERICKS: THE TRAIL TO TENACITY

Welcome to Big Sky Country, home to the Montana Mavericks! Where free-spirited men and women discover love on the range.

Redeeming The Maverick
CHRISTINE RIMMER
July 2024

The Maverick Makes The Grade
STELLA BAGWELL
August 2024

That Maverick Of Mine
KATHY DOUGLASS
September 2024

MILLS & BOON

The Right Cowboy
Cheryl Harper

MILLS & BOON

Cheryl Harper discovered her love for books and words as a little girl, thanks to a mother who made countless library trips and an introduction to Laura Ingalls Wilder's Little House books. Whether the stories she reads are set in the prairie, the American West, Regency England or earth a hundred years in the future, Cheryl enjoys strong characters who make her laugh. Now Cheryl spends her days searching for the right words while she stares out the window and her dog, Jack, snoozes beside her. And she considers herself very lucky to do so.

For more information about Cheryl's books, visit her online at cherylharperbooks.com or follow her on Twitter @cherylharperbks.

Visit the Author Profile page
at millsandboon.com.au for more titles.

Dear Reader,

Life has a way of reordering our plans, doesn't it? Some people have everything mapped out, even when detours and dead ends mean plenty of recalculating. In *The Right Cowboy*, Grant Armstrong has had one goal his whole life: winning rodeo championships. Now that life has bucked him from that saddle, he's having a hard time dusting himself off. Coming home to Prospect is his only choice, until he finds his new direction.

On the other hand, some people go where the wind takes them, trusting that they'll end up in the right place at the right time. That's Mia Romero. And she's never been wrong. Prospect is definitely where she needs to be to track down the story that can redirect her plans—and Grant's—forever.

I'm so happy we're returning to Prospect, Colorado, together. I hope you enjoy visiting! To find out more about my books and what's coming next, visit me at cherylharperbooks.com.

Cheryl

CHAPTER ONE

GRANT ARMSTRONG GRABBED the handle over the window and swallowed an embarrassing yelp as he watched the highway's narrow shoulder disappear beneath the tires of his brother's speeding pickup. Matt always drove as if he could outrun consequences, unless there was a trailer attached to the hitch. His brother, the veterinarian, didn't take any chances with livestock, but humans had to brace themselves and hope.

"I thought saddle bronc riders were supposed to be brave," Matt said with a teasing grin. "Mama makes less noise when she rides shotgun. Betty doesn't even twitch an ear. You should be more like Betty."

Grant checked the hound dog that went almost everywhere with Matt. Betty had somehow stretched her forty-pound length to cover the entire backseat. Her floppy ears draped over her face. The only sign she was still alive was the whiffle of breath that flapped her loose lips. Betty had a clean conscience, and all was right with her world.

Matt was right. Grant would love to be more like Betty.

"Guess I'm a cat who's already eight lives in and holding on to number nine for all I'm worth," Grant muttered and forced his fingers to unclench. "What's the rush?"

"No rush." Matt waved one hand as if he was as relaxed as could be. "But we both know we need to be back to the Rocking A before dinner's on the table. These roads after dark are a real adventure."

Instead of ordering his brother to put both hands on the steering wheel or to slow down on the twisting two-lane highway through the Rocky Mountains, Grant stared straight ahead through the bug-spattered windshield. If he didn't look to his right, the specter of shooting over the edge like they were stuntmen in an action movie would recede.

And if he didn't look left at his brother, he would stop fantasizing about evicting Matt from the driver's seat and leaving him on the side of the road.

His mother would make him return to pick up her baby boy anyway.

"Thank you for going with me today." Matt finally took his foot off the gas to make a turn. "I wanted to see the course Macon had set up. The big splashy commercial I saw caught my attention, gave me ideas for something smaller in town. I'm determined to show your mother that I have a few exciting ideas up my sleeve for Western Days."

"*Our* mother would expect nothing less from her favorite," Grant replied.

Matt batted his eyelashes at Grant. "Aw, don't be jealous. It's a four-way tie for second place."

Grant grunted but it was difficult to blame Prue if Matt was her favorite. He was the easiest of the five of them to get along with.

"We couldn't waste a warm snap in February," Matt said. "Perfect weather to go for a ride."

The beautiful sunny day had presented a rare opportunity for a quick road trip, so when Matt had asked him to ride along to tour Horace Macon's Cowboy Games in Leadville, Grant had jumped at the chance. One quick look at the flashy website convinced Grant it was a bunch of activities for tourists who had seen some of Hollywood's glitziest Western movies and wanted the full experience from their

Rocky Mountain vacation. That wouldn't work in Prospect, but it was an interesting setup. Chaps-wearing employees had taught visitors how to lasso a cute little cow statue and then taken their souvenir pictures with it. There was target practice with a mock six-shooter, ax throwing and a train ride that featured a staged robbery, where the white-hatted town sheriff rode in to save the day.

Grant and his brothers had reenacted several different versions of that same show, only with a bank since they'd had no train. The old ghost town in the hills above the ranch had been irresistible for such scenes when they were kids, and they might have done it better. Grant had definitely enjoyed his role as the bad guy.

Matt had always preferred to "rest," so he was usually the banker, who could snooze in the shade, while the rest of the brothers were the good guys, with Wes in the white hat leading the charge to save the day.

If someone had convinced Grant to instead try on the white hat as a teenager, would he have made different choices as an adult? Instead of playing up a reckless side, he might have become the hero. Grant squeezed his eyes shut. No use in asking questions that had no answers.

Today's tour of Cowboy Games had confirmed his suspicions that the place was less cowboy and heavy on the games, but if he survived the ride home in one piece, it would be a pretty good day overall.

"We can do better, right?" Matt asked. "In my head, I was picturing something less glitzy and more real for Prospect, although I can't deny that the kids did seem to love tossing the lasso. Make a note that we need to include that somewhere in town."

Grant rolled his eyes. Matt had been trying the make-a-note thing all day as if he was employing a top-notch assistant or something.

"We definitely want one of a kind," Matt added, "but I'm not sure I see how to get there yet."

"Yeah, what we saw was an amusement park, not a real competition. Pretty sure everything there was presented as a backdrop for the most impressive vacation photos instead of a test of skill." Grant glanced over at him. "If you stage a real competition, with riding and shooting and all of that, Prospect's Western Days weekend will have to draw the cream of the cowboy crop or you'll never hear the end of it."

"*We'll* never hear the end of it." Matt smiled slowly. "You're going to help me. Mama said so."

Grant sighed. At some point, he and his brothers would learn to tell Prue Armstrong no, but Grant hadn't reached that blessed moment yet. Lately, he'd been ducking his mother every chance he got, because all the Armstrong men knew that once the calendar flipped over to a new year, planning the town's festival, known far and wide as Western Days, took over her life.

And she made sure to drag everyone she knew along for the ride.

They still had two whole months of increasing pressure to see out.

Matt had been late to a meeting months ago and been named the head person in charge this year. Grant was bored and available today. That was it. He didn't want any tasks or folks relying on him for this year's centennial anniversary weekend.

But frankly, none of the Armstrongs would escape the work ahead. Grant's only hope to avoid responsibility would be to lay low when Prue was on the hunt for volunteers. Since he was fully unemployed and also underemployed helping on the Rocking A, he would be at the top of his mother's list.

Ranching meant plenty of work, and all five Armstrong brothers loved the place, even when they were away from home. Prue and Walt had fostered them here before adopting them all, so the Rocking A was special.

For years, their father, Walt, and Wes had managed all of it. Then Travis had retired from the military to take up fostering another generation here. His brother jumped on every job around the place. Renovations on the ranch house had taken up the first couple of months after Grant's sudden return, but now having too much time on his hands was becoming noticeable. Luckily, many people wanted to give him unpaid jobs.

Being busy was good, but nothing excited him like rodeo. He missed the excitement of facing off against a wild bronco and the camaraderie of the rodeo circuit. He was supposed to be competing, not event planning.

"Problem is that we don't have a permanent setup for a riding course and marksmanship booth, like Macon does. The festival will take over all of the old town center, and whatever we build for shooting or riding competition will need to go up a week or two before and tear down quickly after the festival is over. We can put up tents, but we'll need a lot of open space." Grant tugged his hat lower on his head. He sounded confident even if he'd never done anything like this. Fortunately, he'd never met a horse he didn't like, and Macon had offered some names who might help design and judge shooting competition. His mother wanted something big and new for this special anniversary. Matt was on the right track.

She was also counting on Grant being a "celebrity" draw for competitors and visitors alike. Good thing he hadn't tossed all his gear in the trash when he had retired from the circuit and come home. He hadn't confessed how

that came about in the first place to his family, and he wasn't certain he had any star power left.

For years, Western Days had featured a large quilt show, other judged categories for crafts and baked goods, vendors lined up along the street through town, a parade, and plenty of opportunity to attract visitors to the town's businesses. Adding a cowboy games competition with riding and shooting would help Prospect's Western Days stand out from all the other festivals. Matt's idea was good, if they could pull it off.

That was the question that was nagging at him.

Could he pull it off?

When Matt swooped through a dip in the road at high speed, Grant clutched his stomach with one hand and realized that if they bucked right over the side of the mountain ledge, neither one of them had to worry much about the future anymore.

Even so, he said, "If you don't slow down, I'm going to tell Mama that you were being reckless, Matty. You don't want that. That's my job, not yours."

His brother's lips curled but he eased off the gas. "Imagine how much shine a riding competition will bring when we say it's being run by Grant Armstrong, saddle bronc champion for four years straight. Could it have been five? Yes, but he decided to come home and sleep in his old bunk bed instead."

Grant tightened his lips, determined to ignore Matt's prodding.

The sound of the road under the pickup's tires was too quiet to keep Matt under control for long.

"Why did he do that? Leave his successful career, the one he'd been dreaming of his whole life, to return to Prospect when he was rising straight to the top? When he was being approached for magazine cover stories and

small parts in made-for-TV movies?" Matt shrugged. "No one knows."

Grant returned to gripping the grab handle. The anger that boiled in his chest every time that he considered giving up the career he loved burned, but it was better for everyone if he kept the lid tightly shut. He was afraid of the fallout if all that emotion spilled over.

Matt sighed. "Well, technically one person knows, but he ain't talking. Why is that?"

Grant cut his brother a mean glare. "Do you really care? You got somebody to run your big idea. That should make you happy."

Matt's slow grin was irritating. "Oh, it does, believe me. Doesn't change the fact that fixing whatever is wrong with you during a one-day trip would convince the whole family I'm a hero. I'm used to being the best-looking brother, but I'd like to try for more. Give Travis a run for his money. Becoming a foster dad may have given him an unbeatable advantage there."

"Mama already thinks you hung the moon," Grant grumbled. To be fair, Prue Armstrong would have gone to war for any one of her boys...unless they were picking on Matt.

"Being the baby of the family has some perks." Matt took both hands off the wheel to shrug. Grant had to bite his lip not to snap about that.

Instead, he closed his eyes. That was his last defense.

The five Armstrong sons had been adopted through the foster system. Wes claimed the spot of "oldest" because he'd arrived first, but Wes, Clay, Travis and Grant were only months apart in age, and had all been in the same grade in school. Matt was a little younger, so he was the baby. He'd learned to accept the pestering older brothers and take full advantage of his mother's protective instincts.

"What about if I promise not to discuss whatever you tell me with anyone else? Not Wes, Clay or Travis. Not Mom or Dad. Not even if dessert is hanging in the balance and it happens to be banana pudding," Matt said. "You can trust me."

The concern in Matt's voice matched the expressions Grant had seen on his family's faces since he'd shown up at the Rocking A with a duffel, a box and a flimsy explanation that he'd grown tired of life on the circuit. For a few months, he'd faced pressure on all sides to spill the truth, but life and the ranch's beautiful neighbors on either side had taken some of the pressure off. His brothers were so busy falling in love that they'd had less time to poke at his bruises.

He and Matt were the last unattached ones left standing. Even his parents, who had divorced years ago and argued like grumpy badgers, had been struck by Cupid's arrow. Their bickering had turned to teasing with forays into flirting. Love seemed to be well on its way to conquering all of the Armstrong family.

But even if another interesting someone new did show up, if she happened to meet Matt first, she'd be hypnotized by his looks, so Grant wasn't too worried about getting tangled up with love. He needed a minute to get his life straightened out before he was ready for another knot.

Grant tried to loosen the tension in his shoulders. "I do. I trust all of you. I just…" He didn't want to tell them his whole career had been a lie. Not yet. The grift his best friends on the rodeo circuit were running wouldn't stay secret forever, but Grant wanted to be far away from that world when the news broke. He'd worked to build his bad-boy persona, taking risks others might not. Finding anyone to believe his side of the story seemed impossible.

Lying low in Prospect was his obvious choice. Eventu-

ally he'd figure out his next career and what happened to
the last one would matter less.

Nothing bad could touch an Armstrong in Prospect. His
family was here and he had known every person in town
for most of his life. The rest of the rodeo world would deal
with the shock of a cheating scandal when it came out, the
people he trusted most could try pointing fingers at him
and even succeed in turning Grant's fans against him, but
it might as well be happening on another planet as long as
he was in Prospect.

Since he'd come home, he'd convinced himself that he'd
ended that chapter. This after-rodeo life still fit him like
new chaps, pinched in the spots that hadn't been broken in
yet, but every day was easier. He'd stopped looking over
his shoulder and waiting for the mess to detonate.

If being betrayed by old friends still stung, Grant could
look around to see Matt, Clay, Travis and Wes and know
they were exactly who they said they were. Walt and Prue
Armstrong were salt-of-the-earth types who had taught
them all to live that way. Every single one of them would
choose to be a white hat in any scenario.

Days back at the Rocking A weren't a dream come true,
not like winning rodeo prizes and celebrating on the road,
but there were no surprises, either.

All he had to do now was find a way to be content with
life in a place where nothing ever changed much.

CHAPTER TWO

MIA ROMERO HAD always trusted the universe to put her in the right place at the right time, but she'd learned that sometimes the universe's sense of humor could be extremely inconvenient. On the one hand, being on the phone with her mother when her left front tire blew out along the deserted highway leading into Prospect, Colorado, could be considered good timing. Having someone on the line listening as she pulled over on the narrow shoulder meant that Mia wasn't alone in the growing shadows before sunset.

On the other hand, this was Mia's mother.

"What was that? Is someone shooting at you? If you'd stayed in Billings like I asked, this wouldn't happen," her mother squawked. "I'm calling 9-1-1 right now." It was easy to picture her mother snapping her fingers and pointing at an assistant to start punching numbers on the phone. Mia wasn't sure where her mother was calling from, but it was easiest to picture her behind the ornate desk in her office.

After Mia was safely off the road, she said, "It was a tire. That's all, Mother. I'm fine."

Was she fine? Not really. Changing a flat tire before dark would be a challenge for a person who had managed to change their own tire before. Mia assumed that to be true. She'd never even watched someone fix a flat on the

side of the road, so she expected it to be difficult, but there was no way she was admitting that to her mother. Not now.

Mia had learned when to tell her mother the truth. This was not one of those times.

Besides that, this would work out. Things always worked out in the end.

"I'll change it and get back on the road. No need to worry." Mia dug through her glove compartment to pull out the owner's manual. Quickly perusing the instructions on how to remove the tire seemed a logical first step.

"No, I'm calling roadside assistance. I knew this would happen. Have you been doing the proper maintenance, Mia?" her mother asked before answering, "Of course not, what am I thinking?"

Asking her mother exactly what that maintenance would entail would be satisfying, but it wouldn't do anything to end this conversation. Carla Romero let her driver handle all the automotive details.

"I can take care of this myself. You don't have to call anyone." Was she sometimes hit-and-miss about things like routine appointments? Yes, but there was no need to confirm her mother's suspicions now. The tire was flat. There was no way to go back in time to have these tires rotated and inspected now.

As her grandfather would have said, "That horse has left the barn, Mia mine." He'd been the one to teach her to drive. It was too bad she'd skipped the lesson on how to use a jack.

"I should never have let you talk me into this fluff story. Taking a trip up into the mountains in the winter, Mia? You should be at home. When I tell you it's time to finish your degree or learn the business side of the magazine or think about the future instead of 'living in the present,' this is what I'm trying to avoid—you stranded on the side

of the road." Her mother's tone was sharp, but that wasn't unusual. The magazine's advertising dollars were falling. All magazine advertising was falling, thanks to fewer subscribers, and her mother's glossy monthly dedicated to the American West was no exception to the rule. She'd sacrificed a lot to keep the magazine going, and she'd been telling Mia she needed a break. Repeatedly. "*The Way West* needs something big. Your little travel articles on local festivals are fine, but this one's still a month away."

Those "little travel articles" had been all her mother would allow Mia to contribute. Treating her education "like a hobby" by never actually graduating meant she was only ready for writing "like a hobby." A journalism degree might please her mother, but it wasn't necessary. Experience had been the teacher she needed most. Her small travel section had given that to Mia.

When her mother let go of the magazine's reins, Mia wanted to take off in a whole new direction, but they'd never agree about that, either. Her grandfather had built *The Way West*. Her mother wouldn't let anyone change it.

And when she'd told her mother that she'd "forgotten" to enroll for the spring semester, a semester that might have been her last if she'd managed to pass all the classes she needed, her mother had gotten angry and loud. Explaining that the classes were a boring math, science, and "health and wellness" hadn't improved her mother's understanding, but they had nothing to do with Mia's plans for her career.

Why waste that time in a classroom when she could be out working? For a piece of paper that said she could do what she was already doing?

If she could have taken only writing courses and walked out with a degree, Mia would have finished college on her first attempt right after high school. She had plenty of those class credits from the early years when her mother

was paying no attention to her grades or her plans. The first time around, only a business degree would satisfy her mother. Dropping out had been Mia's answer.

Going back to finish something had been her mother's price for continued employment with the magazine.

That employment paid Mia's bills, so keeping it had seemed prudent. They had negotiated a truce with an agreement that journalism would satisfy neither of them but equally, so it was a fair compromise.

If her mother had had a deadline for graduation, she should have been more specific.

And adult children over thirty should be exempt from most of this interference.

Mia swallowed a sigh. She had more immediate problems than convincing her mother that she was good at finding the stories the magazine needed. They'd spent years having that argument. Nothing would change in the time that it took to fix the tire and get back on the road.

"I'll call you as soon as I make it into Prospect. My weekend stay has probably stretched into a longer visit now, but I'll get good background for Western Days and be back home soon." Mia noticed headlights in her rear-view mirror and felt the leap of hope that she might not be changing this tire herself. That was followed almost instantly by the worry that she might not be meeting a Good Samaritan here in this deserted spot. Snippets of countless dark stories featuring innocent stranded women filtered through her brain before she got a handle on her wayward thoughts. There was no use in jumping straight to catastrophe. That was her mother's move, not Mia's.

"Actually, can you stay on the phone with me? Someone's driving up." Mia watched the truck pull up behind her vehicle.

"So I can identify your kidnapper by the sound of his

voice, I guess?" her mother snapped. "When you're home, it's time to discuss closing the magazine again. The worry is exhausting. Instead of going with the flow, you're going to need a plan for a real career."

Mia shook her head as she dug around in the backseat of her car. This wasn't the first time her mother had floated the idea of shutting down the magazine she'd inherited. Rodeo news once had a huge fan base of subscribers, but now the internet provided more results faster. *The Way West* had tried to pivot to lifestyle, but her mother's insistence that it was an extra instead of the feature meant they weren't ever all-in.

But back to the potential threat Mia was facing. She needed something... Any sort of defense she could scrounge up would be weak, but she wasn't naive. Even a flimsy weapon would be better than none if she needed one.

Unfortunately, the only thing at hand was a black golf umbrella branded with the magazine's distinct logo, a silver bucking bronc. Mia said, "Be quiet, okay? Just listen."

Her mother didn't answer, but the car's display showed the call was still connected, so Mia decided to take that as confirmation that her mother was following directions. It was also a sign that miracles still happened.

When two long, tall cowboys slid out of the truck on either side and ambled toward her slowly, Mia tightened her hold on the umbrella and rolled down the window. The cowboy on the driver's side tipped his hat back, and she immediately crossed her fingers, hoping that he was good with a jack. No one with a face like that should be a villain. He held his hands up as if he was trying to calm a skittish colt. "Car trouble, ma'am? I'm Matt. Prospect's vet." Everything about his posture and tone seemed intended to say "harmless."

Mia wrinkled her nose. "Flat tire. Could you help me change it? I was heading into Prospect for the night. If there's a garage, I'll see if they can repair it tomorrow."

His smile was nice. Open. Easy. Mia relaxed her posture. Then she opened the car door and slid out, noticing the second man had a hand braced against the back of the car. He was looking down.

"Pop the trunk." When he glanced up as if to make sure she'd heard him, Mia managed to maintain her composure, but it took every bit of brain power she had.

Her ability to follow his instruction froze when she realized she was meeting Grant Armstrong for the first time. Rodeo bad boy. Brooding, handsome and strangely absent from the biggest rodeo event of the year held every December.

Mia had a flat tire.

Grant Armstrong had pulled over to fix it.

Because lightning bolts like this coincidental meeting on the side of the road convinced her that the universe would work things out in Mia Romero's favor.

And so the secret idea popped into her mind. Mia had pitched several story ideas every issue for months and watched her mother take some of them and give them to more experienced writers. She'd heard the discussions of pursuing this loose thread of where Grant Armstrong had disappeared to, but no one was certain there was any kind of payoff to the story.

If this story was good, how many magazines could it sell? Enough to buy time to attract new advertisers?

And here he was. Right in front of her, one impatient eyebrow raised while he waited for her to raise the trunk so that he could get to the spare and the jack.

"Sorry," Mia blurted before she turned around to pull the trunk release. "I guess relief caused my brain to short

circuit." She waved the manual in her hand. "I was cramming for the test when you pulled up, but I'm not certain I'd pass."

Matt moved to the truck and opened the back door to let a rangy brown hound dog flow out onto the pavement. "This is Betty. She's a rotten guard dog, but she is an excellent character witness. Bring your pointy umbrella over to talk to her while you wait and we'll get you fixed up in no time."

This time, it was much simpler to follow instructions. Betty was still stretching when Mia bent to scratch behind her ears. "Hi, Betty, it's very nice to meet you." She dropped the umbrella on the pavement to free up both hands for important ear coverage.

The cowboys worked quickly to raise the car, remove the tire and put on the spare. After they had everything back in the trunk, Matt pointed. "We'll follow you the rest of the way. You'll see the Garage right inside the town limits, a big clearing over on your left. Not sure whether Lucky or Dante will still be there at this hour, so we'll make sure you get to where you're going."

The urge to reassure them that it wouldn't be necessary burned on the tip of her tongue, but she needed a minute to figure out how best to continue her acquaintance with Grant Armstrong without tipping her hand too soon.

The universe had presented her with an amazing opportunity. No way was she going to waste it.

Maybe he wanted his story to be splashed across the magazine's front cover, but the way he'd vanished from sight suggested he would be less than excited to meet a reporter from *The Way West*.

"That would be great, Matt. I appreciate it." Then she tossed the umbrella in the backseat, slipped into the driv-

er's seat, and drove slowly into Prospect. "You still on the line, Mother?"

"Yes, nervous as a cat, but I'm still here." Her mother huffed out a breath. "Can't see how this research is going to be worth such trouble, Mia."

The urge to tell her who had been her roadside hero burned, but Mia wasn't about to hype this might-be news story until she had something solid.

"I'll call you when I'm leaving town to let you know I'm headed home," Mia said and waited for her mother to end the call. She was relieved to see the town sign and the houses signaling civilization on the horizon. Traveling wide-open spaces was fun and the scenery was grand, but nearby food and restrooms were always a welcome change.

Matt's description was perfect. She pulled into the Garcia Auto Repair parking lot in minutes, but the dark windows and Closed sign answered the question about whether they were still open. She rolled down her window. "Is the garage open tomorrow?"

Matt nodded. "Yeah, they're open half days on Saturdays. If you're here first thing, they should be able to make a repair. If you need a new tire…" He tilted his head to the side as if he had bad news.

"I guess I'll be waiting until Monday for a delivery if they don't have the tire in stock." Mia shrugged. This could work out in her favor. She could use the extra time in Prospect to further her acquaintance with Grant Armstrong, somehow.

"Might even be Tuesday." Matt's beautiful smile softened the blow. "But this isn't a bad place to spend time. I didn't catch your name." He propped an elbow on the truck door as if shooting the breeze with a stranger was the easiest thing in the world.

"Mia. Mia Romero. I should have introduced myself."

She got out and offered him her hand to shake. "I'll be happy to buy you both a cup of coffee in thanks if you'll point me to a restaurant somewhere between here and Bell House."

She crossed in front of the truck. Shaking Grant's hand would be a step in the right direction. Since she couldn't figure out the next one, she better make the moment count. Mia was pretty comfortable with this part of the plan. She had a whole lifetime of experience watching and waiting for her next direction to appear.

Grant watched her closely. The fear that he had recognized her name made her pause, but she didn't let it stop her. It was doubtful a rodeo star like Grant was reading travel articles in his spare time. Besides that, she had a very valid reason to be here, and that made an excellent cover story for the scoop she wanted most.

"Hi, I'm Mia." She held out her hand. When he shook it, the shot of warmth caught her by surprise. His hand was strong, calloused, tan. And the power of his dark eyes convinced her he didn't miss anything. Mia had met people from all walks of life and shaken countless hands, but the instant connection between the two of them was brand new.

"Grant. Armstrong." He tilted his head back.

Was he waiting for her reaction?

She smiled and stepped back.

"Good thing you have a reservation at the B-and-B, Mia. February is not a big tourism month around here, but the craft store is running a popular retreat. You are going to be surrounded by sewing machines humming and usually a lot of laughter." Matt nodded. "That's a good Friday night, right there."

Mia bit her lip. If she'd learned the universe provided, she'd also come to understand that she could do a better

job of looking out for herself occasionally. "Think all the rooms are booked up?"

"No reservation," Grant muttered, but she couldn't detect much judgment there. He pulled out his cell phone and hit a button. When the call was answered, he said, "Could you ask Rose if her place is full up this weekend?"

They all waited. "Yes, ma'am, I know better than to start a conversation like that. I do, Mama. I'll make chitchat first next time, but we've got a visitor to town who needs a place to stay tonight, so I was in a hurry." He closed his eyes as if he already had regrets about his choices. Meanwhile, Mia's grin matched Matt's. "Thank you. I love you, too." He hung up the phone before shaking his head.

Mia sighed. "No. So…can you give me directions to the nearest place that will have rooms tonight? What else is close by?"

Grant made another call before Matt could answer.

This time when the call was answered, Grant said, "Hey, Jordan, how are you?"

He waited patiently for her to answer. "Those curtains sound really pretty." He shot a look at Matt before saying, "I was calling because we've got a visitor to town who needs a hotel room. Do you have one available?"

Grant yanked the phone away from his ear. Mia smiled at the squawking that even she could hear from where he was standing. "Yeah, we'll show her the way out there. Best room, yeah, I'll tell her. No restaurant yet but you're working on it. I'll make sure she knows that." Grant nodded. "Okay." Then he nodded again and repeated himself. "Okay." Finally he said, "Tell me the rest when we get there, Jordan." Then he hung up the phone and slapped it back in his pocket. "There's room out at the Majestic. It's a completely different atmosphere than Bell House, but it's close and comfortable."

And Grant was a friend of whoever ran the place, which suggested Mia could get some good background there.

"The Majestic is light on amenities like food, but we'll make sure you've got something to eat." Grant pointed at her car. "You okay to follow us?"

Mia nodded and hurried back to her car. She wasn't sure what might be coming next, thanks to the universe's always-on-time delivery, but all signs were pointing to Grant. This was the story that would change everything.

CHAPTER THREE

WHEN MATT PARKED the truck next to Mia's expensive luxury sedan in front of the Majestic Prospect Lodge, Grant was still trying to decide how to handle their visitor. There was no mistaking the logo on the umbrella she'd hoped would be an effective weapon in the worst-case scenario there on the side of the road. *The Way West* was one of the magazines that covered rodeo events. Maybe she was a fan who had won free swag in some kind of giveaway.

That didn't explain her lack of reaction on meeting Grant Armstrong in the middle of nowhere.

Was she here to dig up dirt on him?

"Okay, so the broody silence on the drive out from the Garage was broodier than usual." Matt pulled the key out of the ignition. "Why do I think it has to do with our rescued visitor and how do I know you aren't going to tell me why?"

Grant grunted. "Right on both accounts."

Matt was still shaking his head when they met Mia at the bridge that connected the Majestic's parking lot to the lodge on the opposite side of the stream that fed into Key Lake. Her doubts about the place were politely reflected on her face. The growing shadows hadn't done much to improve the curb appeal of the rundown exterior. Dry, weathered siding made a dull backdrop for empty landscaping around the lodge. When spring arrived, things would improve, but for now, the Majestic's outsides didn't match her insides.

Mia was the one who hadn't made a reservation ahead of time, so she was going to have to trust them.

"They're renovating. Inside to out." Grant bent and picked up her small suitcase, relieved to see that whatever her purpose was for coming to Prospect, she hadn't intended to stay long. He was ahead of them when Matt added, "And the rooms are ready for guests, I promise."

The pain in his jaw alerted Grant to the way he was gritting his teeth at Matt's charming tone.

Jordan Hearst stepped out of the lodge, with a brilliant smile on her face. "Welcome to the Majestic Prospect Lodge." Whatever perks the lodge might lack, the Hearst sisters did their best to make up for with warm welcomes.

While the women introduced themselves to each other and Matt flirted to keep all eyes on him, Grant stepped inside the lodge and set Mia's luggage down in front of the check-in desk. The place looked good. The Hearst sisters and every single one of the Armstrong clan, including Damon and Micah, the two boys fostering at the ranch, had been working hard to make sure of that.

Warm hardwood floors gleamed in the light from the rustic iron chandelier he'd nearly broken his neck installing in the center of the lobby's high ceiling. Wes didn't do heights, Travis didn't do electrical and Matt was absent as always, so Grant had been the one up the ladder. Pretending to be confident was second nature to him, but he was proud to see his work added a homeyness to the lobby. Jordan had insisted painting some of the wooden walls was the correct answer, and Sarah had finally given in once the third sister had voted yes over a video call from New York. All of the remaining wood beams and the panels flanking the large fireplace had been refinished. Instead of a rugged, old fishing lodge fit for crusty anglers, this

lobby had been transformed into a modern, comfortable space anyone would be comfortable in.

If Mia wasn't impressed, Grant would take her bag right back out to her car and give her directions to the highway.

"It's a work in progress, of course. We haven't done several of the big-ticket items yet. New furniture for the lobby, and we're still holding off on bathroom renovations, but I've got my best room ready for you." Jordan smiled at Mia as she moved behind the check-in desk. "We've had a computer system installed, so let me see if I know how to use it."

Grant leaned against the counter, his arms crossed over his chest as he listened to Mia give her address and phone number. Billings was home, and if he remembered correctly, that was where the magazine was based. Before he could spring the "ah-ha," like a detective solving a mystery in an old black-and-white movie, Mia sighed. Her eyes were locked on the large landscape of the Rocky Mountains hanging behind the desk. "This painting is amazing, Jordan. I know you've said this lodge has been a lot of work, but this space is a dream. I'm a travel writer, so I should know."

Grant pursed his lips as he considered that. "Travel writer for *The Way West*, I guess."

Mia's eyebrows shot up, and he shrugged. "The umbrella had a logo."

She smoothed a long piece of dark brown hair behind one ear. Was she nervous? Because he knew she was connected to the publication?

"Yeah, for the magazine. I wanted to do research on Prospect's Western Days festival. This year is a big anniversary. One hundred years of history should make for a pretty good story." Mia waved a hand around the lobby's great room. "And that was before I knew what was hap-

pening here at the lodge. It seems like the Majestic Prospect Lodge will need to be featured, too."

Jordan immediately clasped her hands to her chest and jumped up and down. Muffled squeals escaped before she closed her eyes and forced herself to breathe in through her nose and out through her mouth. "Oh, Mia, you don't know how thrilled I am."

Mia grinned. "I had planned to dig through the archives of *The Prospect Post*, pull up interesting information for background, and then return for photos and the finishing touches in April when the festival's happening, but I'm thinking I may need to stay a bit longer. I don't want to miss anything noteworthy now, do I?"

Her innocent expression as she met Grant's stare did not reassure him at all.

"Oh yes, you have come to the right place. Matt and Grant live next door at the Rocking A. Their parents, Prue and Walt, are the heartbeat of Prospect. If you ask them something and they don't know the answer, it's not worth knowing. They also have the five sons." Jordan leaned across the desk as if she was about to share confidential information. "Wes Armstrong and my sister and Travis and the new doctor in town are over-the-top in love. Clay is mine. But Matt and Grant are the single Armstrongs, so…"

Mia frowned at him, as if she couldn't make the connection as to why she needed that information, but he had no intention of acknowledging Jordan's boldness. If he argued with Jordan every time she tweaked him, he'd need to start taking vitamins to boost his stamina. The two of them were a lot alike, in that they enjoyed keeping people on their toes. He'd never wished for a sister, but getting one like Jordan seemed to be a very clever form of karma. When Wes, Clay and Travis managed to pop the impending question, his collection of sisters would be nearly complete.

Matt's open grin as Grant picked up Mia's bag convinced him he needed to spill at least part of the cheating story and fast.

What Jordan said was true. His family knew everything there was to know about Prospect, and his mother would make sure every door was thrown open for Mia to get the best story she could. Publicizing the town was his mother's pet project.

The fact that Jordan was laying a matchmaking trail was further proof that his family should be warned about Mia's potential danger.

"Bring Mia's suitcase down the hall, Grant." Jordan was already on the move. She never hesitated when it came to the lodge, and they'd all learned to follow orders when they were issued inside the Majestic. He ambled behind them to the last room in the hallway. This had been the first room tackled at each stage of the renovation, so it was the furthest along and the best the lodge had to offer.

"I love the artwork, Jordan." Mia had moved to stand in front of a landscape that showed Key Lake in fall colors. Right now, the lake was frozen in spots, even on a sunny day like today, but it was still a beautiful scene outside the window. The lake didn't have a bad season.

"Thank you. My father painted everything you'll see here. The big piece in the lobby, the mountains and this landscape. He teaches classes in town if you're interested in learning more about painting or him." Jordan clasped her hands together and fluttered her eyelashes. She was a hard-nosed businessperson with an eye out for capitalizing on all the opportunities a magazine feature could mean for Prospect. It was no wonder his mother loved Jordan as much as his brother, Clay, did.

Maybe more.

"I will make a note of that." Mia pointed at her bag. "Do you have Wi-Fi that I can connect to in the room?"

Jordan hissed as if someone had let out all of her air. "No internet connection yet, but I'll take you to the library in town, which has a good setup. We've got an installation scheduled, but it's a couple of weeks away."

Mia waved her hand. "No problem. I need to get to the library tomorrow anyway." Then she winced. "I forgot about the car repair and… Is the library open on Saturday? I could have planned this trip better."

Grant propped his hands on his hips as he considered that. It was true. If she wanted to see newspaper archives and spend time in the library, a weekday would have been smarter.

But if she was here to snoop around town to find out information on him, a busy Saturday in Prospect was a good bet.

"Yes, the library is open all day on Saturday. I'll take you myself after we drop your car off at the Garage in the morning. Tonight I'll leave you to get settled in. We don't have a restaurant yet, but sandwiches are free and available at all hours in the restaurant's refrigerator. I'll make us both some breakfast in the morning, and you can visit the Ace High for lunch or dinner. That's in town, and you'll need to make sure you rave over Faye's desserts. They're all based on Sadie Hearst recipes." Jordan waited patiently for some recognition.

The first sign that Mia might not be warmly received in Prospect was the fact that dropping Sadie's name brought about no reaction. Grant knew that would be a problem for the Hearst sisters, for sure.

"The Colorado Cookie Queen?" Jordan added. "She was my great-aunt. Left me the lodge." The change in

Jordan's voice, as enthusiasm for Mia faded, was impossible to miss.

Mia grimaced. "I don't cook much, Mia. I'm sorry, but I am definitely looking forward to tasting these desserts. I love cookies."

Jordan's smile was professional as she agreed. "Of course. We'll make sure you know who Sadie was before you leave Prospect." Then she stepped out in the hallway. "Please let me know if you need anything."

When Jordan was gone, Mia turned to face him. "I messed up. Seems like everyone should know who Sadie Hearst is, I guess."

Grant shrugged. "Don't worry too much. Plenty of people around to help bring you up to speed."

"What a relief." She huffed out a laugh. "Thank you for carrying in my suitcase. Actually, thank you for making sure I'm not still sitting on the side of the road trying to figure out how to put the jack under the car."

He nodded. "Instead of a cup of coffee, you could tell me the real reason you're in Prospect. Seems an odd time to be doing research on the festival when it's still two months away."

When she smoothed her hair behind her ears, he knew it was one of her tells. Mia was nervous, most likely because she was hiding something. He'd learned early on that people could bluff, try to tell him lies, but their body language usually dealt the truth.

"Believe it or not, I came to Prospect because I'm a dedicated travel writer for *The Way West* magazine. Meet me in the library and I'll pull up the website and show you the pieces I've written." Then she mirrored his stance, arms crossed over her chest, feet planted solidly. "But imagine my surprise at running into Grant Armstrong here. No

one on the rodeo circuit knows where he went for sure or why he disappeared."

Surprised by her honesty and impressed that she put her cards on the table without hesitation, Grant nodded. "Right. Exactly. My real question is what are you going to do about that?"

Mia bit her lip. "I'm going to write a story about Prospect, the festival and all the attractions."

Grant waited. There was more coming. He could see it in her eyes.

"And if I hear any other stories that need to be told, I'll find a place to tell them." Mia shrugged, as if she understood how the stark words might land, but she'd had no other choice but to say them. "I'll be happy to listen if there's something you want the world to know."

Since that was the furthest thing from what he wanted, revealing to the world the truth about his retirement, Grant dipped his head. "I'll keep all of that in mind, Mia. If nothing else, thank you for being so frank. Good or bad, that makes everything much easier."

She wrinkled her nose. "Does it? Even if it's something you don't like? You might be the only person I've ever met who would say that. I would have lied about my favorite Sadie Hearst recipes if I'd known how to. I want Jordan to like me, you understand?"

The urge to chuckle at the cute expression surprised him. Mia Romero could expose his story when he wanted it to stay buried. He shouldn't like her. Laughing with her could be a slippery slope, and a slide to the bottom would have serious consequences for a lot of people. Keeping his guard up was the right thing to do.

Why did repeating that over and over as he followed Matt to the truck feel like wasted effort?

CHAPTER FOUR

MIA'S FIRST NIGHT at the Majestic Prospect Lodge was more relaxing than she'd expected. Every one of Matt Armstrong's and Jordan Hearst's promises about the experience had been fulfilled. Mia stretched between the crisp, clean sheets, and noticed the early morning sunshine glowing along the edges of the curtains covering her room's window and realized she'd slept soundly through the night. There had been none of the usual turning and settling and adjusting that always accompanied her first night in a new bed.

Being the only guest at the lodge contributed to that peace, no doubt, but there was also something comfortable about the bare-bones room. Mia slipped out of bed and crossed the floor to tug the curtains open. The lake outside was surrounded by pines and shady banks with patches of snow. In the brilliant sunlight glittering across the surface, Mia could see ice crystals, but it was easy to imagine how the water would call to her on a summer day.

The Hearsts couldn't have chosen prettier scenery for their inherited lodge.

After a quick shower, Mia dried her hair and dressed quickly in jeans and an oversize purple sweatshirt. She slipped on the sneakers that her mother said made her look like a 1950s junior varsity basketball player and briefly considered whether she should have brought different clothes. She'd packed for doing research in the newspa-

per archives about the history of the Western Days festival and Prospect in general, which meant comfort above all else. If she'd known the high probability of meeting a handsome cowboy like Grant Armstrong, she might have chosen differently.

But breakfast was underway somewhere in the lodge, and she didn't want to miss it. The scent of something sweet filtered through and her stomach growled in response.

Mia heard a quiet tap on the door and opened it.

Jordan was standing in the hallway, her head cocked as if she was listening for movement inside. "Good morning. I hope I didn't wake you. I thought I heard the shower."

Mia nodded. "You did and this is excellent timing. Whatever you're cooking smells delicious. Is it pancakes? Waffles?" She loved both. Anything that could work as a maple syrup delivery mechanism was high on her list of preferred breakfast foods.

Jordan sniffed dramatically. "Hmm, sorry. I don't smell anything." Then she grimaced. "I obviously should have set lower expectations for the quality of the breakfast available here. I have toast. Scrambled eggs?" Her hopeful expression made Mia laugh.

"Also very good choices." Mia followed Jordan around the corner and stepped inside an apartment nestled at the back of the lodge. It was small but comfortable, with a large open kitchen area that joined with a cozy living room. Another woman was attempting to fry bacon on the stovetop when Jordan pointed Mia to one of the seats at the island.

"This is my sister, Sarah. As you can probably tell, neither one of us is a proper chef. Sadie did her best but we managed to forget everything she taught us." Jordan pointed to the oven mitt Sarah was wearing as she flipped the bacon. "It's a miracle we haven't burned the place

down. We don't make bacon under normal circumstances. Too much potential for disaster."

Sarah waved her oven-mitted hand. "Protective measures are required, but we wanted to step up our usual morning meal in your honor. I was at the Homestead Market last night when Jordan called to tell me we had a guest. I might have overestimated our abilities in this area, I was so excited to have a real-live visitor. But we do have coffee and orange juice to go with your toast, eggs and uh, burned bacon."

"Don't forget the company," Jordan said as she gestured at Mia. "That's one of a kind. You won't find better company anywhere."

Mia poured a large glass of pulpy orange juice and sipped before she nodded broadly. "And the finest juice I have tasted in… I can't even remember how long it's been since I've had orange juice this perfect."

Sarah's lips were twitching as she slid a plate of dark, shriveled bacon onto the island. "I believe she's humoring us."

"It's like she's known us forever," Jordan agreed.

Mia relaxed into the easy back and forth the sisters used as they dished up their plates and settled at the island. She had taken her second bite of toast when Jordan asked, "How is your room? Did you sleep well?"

Before she could answer, Sarah's phone rang. "Oh, it's Brooke. She's getting an early start." She answered the call and set the phone up against the juice carafe so they could see the screen. "The youngest Hearst sister. Lives in New York."

Mia nodded and spread strawberry jelly on her toast as Sarah said, "Brooke, meet our current guest. This is Mia. She's a travel writer." Her hushed tones suggested Mia

was important. Since that didn't happen very often, Mia appreciated it.

"Hi, Mia," Brooke said with a wave. "How has your stay been?"

"Very nice," Mia said, "and everything is so comfortable. Not fancy, but like…home?" She shrugged. "It's hard to put into a few words, but I travel enough to recognize that there's something special about how I can stretch out in the bed and, instead of immediately cataloging all the differences, my mind settles in to rest. That's unique."

Jordan immediately hopped up out of her chair and did a victory lap around the island while Sarah shook her head. "If you wanted a new best friend for life, you just got one, Mia. The shortest way to Jordan's heart is to recognize how special the Majestic is." Sarah sipped her coffee while Jordan settled herself at the bar. "Better now?"

"I was anxious to hear Mia's verdict. I am not surprised the feedback is good, but I am gratified." Jordan picked up her fork. "We've had a few people stay with us, Mia, but we're getting close to reopening officially, so it's nice to hear that all this hard work is paying off."

"Jordan has cleaned and cleaned and cleaned, painted, sanded floors, stained floors, repaired furniture and dug through years of storage to get right here to this place. If she does victory laps now and then, I can't blame her." Sarah bumped her sister's shoulder. "We've got a few hurdles still to clear, but I see success on the horizon."

Jordan sighed. "I need warmer weather to work on the exterior. And money." She grimaced.

"I'll call Howard again next week to find out about the dispersion of the funds." Sarah hugged Jordan tightly. "Sadie's LA house finally sold, so it should be anytime now that we'll get our share of the funds." She turned to Mia to explain. "Sadie left the three of us the lodge, but most

of her other assets were to be sold and distributed among the whole family, seventeen of us in total. Howard Fine is her lawyer and the executor of her estate. Sadie didn't leave us any hints on what to do with this place, sell or reopen it, so we've been moving slowly. Actually, Jordan has been moving quickly, but most of this she's managed to repair on her own…or with help from the neighbors." She raised her eyebrows. "Big improvements we can make are on hold until that money happens."

Brooke leaned closer to the screen "And they have this sister in New York who is struggling, so any extra funds have gone to her, and since her ex-husband is being a real—"

"We're trying to be smart about how we proceed, so it's wonderful to hear your feedback," Sarah said.

Mia picked up a piece of lightly charred bacon. "Well, I imagine you're anxious to get the renovations finished, but what you've got here will absolutely work."

Jordan propped her elbow on the counter. "Think the burned bacon will keep the guests coming back?"

Sarah frowned at her sister. "First of all, I will get better at making bacon, but secondly, no way am I cooking up breakfast for a lodge filled with guests. We'll have to find a solution for that quickly."

"No leads on a chef for the restaurant?" Brooke asked. "The sous chef I talked to at the diner next door heard the words *mountain* and *lodge* and evaporated into a mist like a vampire at sunrise. I don't believe he'll be leaving the city."

Jordan said, "I can do juice and pastries for a while, but we need to find a chef to run our kitchen. Mia was probably brokenhearted to expect pancakes or waffles and to get black bacon instead."

Mia laughed. "I happen to like my bacon cooked exactly like this. It's perfect. But I do also love pancakes. I

wouldn't have mentioned that except I smelled something sweet in the air, like you were making them for breakfast."

The furtive glance the sisters exchanged caught Mia's attention, but she wasn't sure how to ask about what they were communicating.

"Since you had a good night's sleep, I wonder…" Jordan bit her lip. "With all your traveling, do you have any experience in haunted hotels, Mia?"

Mia leaned back in her chair as she considered the question. Brooke's resigned expression convinced her that the topic wasn't as unexpected for the three sisters as it was for her. "Staying in them? No. I have mentioned them in passing, using other traveler's descriptions of the places, but I generally do my best to avoid the supernatural."

Jordan nodded slowly. "Yeah."

Sarah blinked and they shared more silent conversation.

"We don't know that we have a ghost." Sarah pursed her lips. "But we wouldn't be all that surprised if we did."

Mia crossed her arms, determined to wait for more explanation.

"Our Aunt Sadie…" Jordan stood and paced slowly back and forth in front of the island. "This was her apartment while she managed the lodge. She started a public-access cooking show from the restaurant here and places in Prospect before she moved to LA and her career exploded into the Cookie Queen Corporation." She tapped a stack of books on the counter. "These are all her cookbooks. All best sellers. All 100 percent Sadie through and through. Her own line of appliances and kitchenware. Ladies' Western wear. Television. Stars loved her. Audiences loved her more. She was a great cook but she was a huge personality, Mia."

Mia realized this was when a better understanding of Sadie Hearst, the Colorado Cookie Queen, would have

helped her. Jordan seemed to have forgiven her for not knowing Sadie the night before, but it was clear that the icon was a part of the fabric of this lodge.

Perhaps literally, if she was haunting the place.

"I don't believe in ghosts." Sarah pressed her hands to her chest. "We don't believe in ghosts."

Brooke interjected, "They didn't believe in ghosts before they met the Majestic."

"But…" Mia was certain that ghosts would not have been discussed unless their belief was being tested.

"Vanilla. Was it vanilla that you smelled this morning?" Jordan braced her arm on the island as if she was preparing herself for the answer.

Mia considered. "Wouldn't vanilla have been a pretty common ingredient for a cookie queen? Maybe it's part of the…walls?" Why didn't that almost reasonable explanation feel better than having a friendly ghost?

"Yes. Of course." Sarah agreed firmly. "The only issue is that we can't smell it all the time. It comes and goes. Some people and some places get vanilla and some don't."

All four of them were silent as they considered the implications of that.

"And she was the friendliest person you'd ever meet in real life. We wouldn't mind if she decided to hang around, but we also realize guests might not be as comfortable with that." Sarah sighed. "At least they have another choice for a place to stay in Prospect."

Mia realized Sarah and Jordan were both anxiously awaiting her verdict. If she didn't immediately pack up her suitcase and head for town, they could relax.

"Have you ever considered that Sadie's ghost could be a selling point? Fans might visit to have the chance to meet her, so to speak." Mia finished her juice. "I don't know how you work that into the advertising, but I'll be sure to

pass along any encounters of the spooky kind I experience while I'm here."

Jordan, clearly relieved, exhaled loudly. "If you'd seen the reaction we got when the bats flew out of the attic, my concern about Sadie's presence would make perfect sense. But I am happy to hear that we aren't looking at disaster of the ghostly variety."

Before Mia could ask for more information related to the bats and where exactly they'd left the building and when or if they might return, Sarah asked, "Brooke, did you call to catch up or did you need something?"

Brooke seemed unsettled. Mia would have called it forlorn and a little dramatic, but she only said, "I was missing you and I wanted to complain about my ex-husband, who refuses to pay his settlement, so I refuse to leave the apartment and he's being a real—"

Sarah smiled brightly. "Okay, you and I can talk about that. Mia, I guess you're ready to get to town."

"Oh, I already volunteered to show Mia the way to the library after we stop at the Garage. If you don't mind washing the dishes, Sarah, I'll take care of Mia's room when I get back. Love you, Brooke. Let us know if it's time for us to come get you." Jordan didn't give Sarah time to argue. She urged Mia out into the hallway. "You have to be fast to escape kitchen duty around here, Mia. Outmaneuvering my older sister isn't easy, but it is sweet every time it happens. I'll meet you around front." She pointed at a door and nodded.

Mia was grinning as she picked up her purse and laptop and headed for the lodge's parking lot. Breakfast was normally a solitary event in her life, whether she was on the road or home in her luxury apartment in Billings. Traveling regularly meant she'd gotten comfortable with her own company, but it had been nice to spend the time with

Jordan and Sarah. Mia was an only child. She had no experience with the kind of bickering the two sisters did as naturally as they breathed, but it was funny and sweet at the same time. They might argue now and then, but Mia could see that Sarah and Jordan were close.

She was still thinking about the mystery vanilla scent and the briefly mentioned bats when she slid behind the wheel of her car and waved as Jordan passed in front of her in a red SUV. On the way to town, Mia craned her neck to see the scenery. It looked different in the daylight. The night before, the growing shadows had made it difficult to spot the details, but the lodge's closest neighbor was the Rocking A and it looked like a cattle ranch. Then she realized it was Rocking A for Armstrong. Grant was nearby, once she figured out an angle on how to corner him for information.

There was a small house close to the road that might or might not be a part of the ranch, and then in the distance, there was a barn and another house, but beautiful scenery surrounded her on all sides. Winter still had a firm grip on the grass and trees, but every now and then, Mia could see the promise that spring wasn't so very far away.

Coming into Prospect again, this time from the opposite direction, inspired several different ideas on what she might feature in an article about the town...or the town's most famous bronc-riding champion. Prospect was idyllic, the postcard image of small-town life. How did the Bad Boy of Bronc Busting come from such a place?

Jordan led Mia back to Garcia Auto Repair and hopped out to escort Mia into the shop attached to the garage. "I'll introduce you to Lucky and Dante."

Before Jordan reached for the door, a handsome man stepped through it, his hand outstretched. "You must be Mia. Heard you have a flat."

"This is Dante." Jordan shook her head. "I haven't been here long, Mia, but I have learned that this is life in a small town. Everyone knows everything about you before you open your mouth."

Mia dropped the keys in Dante's hand. "I won't ask why or how. I'll say thank you and the tire's in the trunk."

He nodded and headed for her car.

"I'm guessing Matt called ahead to let you know we were coming," Jordan said to the beautiful woman behind the counter. Two little girls were playing in a toy-strewn corner of the office, penned in by a low mesh...fence?

Mia wasn't sure the right word was *fence*. She didn't know much about toddler security systems, but it was clear that the Garcias were interested in any help they could get corralling their daughters. The happy shouts that accompanied the clatter of a stack of blocks being demolished as one of the girls drove a large fire truck through the structure made the woman wince.

"Hi, Mia, we don't know if they have a brighter future in demolition or screaming, but they practice both regularly. I'm Lucky. Those two are Eliana and Selena."

Mia laughed and nodded. "Yes, they show a lot of promise in both."

Lucky smiled. "You have no idea."

"They're adorable." Mia knew it was the right thing to say, but it was also true. Both little girls had happy, confident grins...even as they were obviously plotting mayhem of some sort.

"It won't take Dante long to see if the tire can be patched. If we have to order tires for you, I'm afraid it will be Monday afternoon before we can get you fixed up." Lucky stood on her tiptoes to peer into the window that lined the wall between the office and the garage. She was wincing as she turned back.

"Bad news?" Jordan asked.

"He was shaking his head," Lucky said as Dante walked back in…still shaking his head.

"I can try patching it, but I wouldn't advise that, Mia. The placement of the puncture is bad. If it fails, it would be dangerous, especially on these roads. You have tread left on those tires, but the smart thing to do is replace this one. For safety and better handling, I'd recommend buying two. Otherwise, you'll have a noticeable difference in tread from one side to the other." Dante motioned over his shoulder. "Follow me and I'll show you what I'm talking about."

Mia held up her hands. "You could show me, but I wouldn't know much more than I know now, never having replaced a tire in my life. Can you recommend a good choice to replace two tires?" Mia followed Dante around the counter to the computer, where he pulled up a list of possible tires and launched into the pros and cons of each option. When his lecture wound down, he tapped the screen over the mid-priced option. "All in all, this is what I would put on Lucky's car if I were making the choice for my beloved wife and mother of my children."

His smile was contagious. Mia realized he was teasing her.

"That's the highest endorsement he can give anything," Lucky said from the seat she'd taken near the door. "Everyone around here knows that, according to Dante, Lucky deserves nothing but the best." She winked at her husband.

"Gross." Jordan rolled her eyes. "So much love and respect in the room." She pulled the neck of her sweater as if it was choking her. "It's a real epidemic of couples in love around this town."

"Says the woman who freaked out the Ace High when Clay Armstrong made an unexpected early arrival last

week." Lucky's eyebrows rose as she motioned toward Mia. "Shrieked louder than either of these two, ran to meet him at the door of the restaurant and jumped into his arms right there in front of his mama and everybody."

Mia knew her jaw had dropped as she turned to Jordan.

Her blush was confirmation that the whole story was nothing but the truth.

"He'd been gone for three weeks." Jordan held out her hands.

Dante cleared his throat. "Should I get these tires ordered, Mia? Driving on the spare should be okay if you're staying close, but I wouldn't go too far or too fast. We can give you a call when they come in."

Mia nodded. "Yes, I have some work to do in Prospect, so I'll stay until the car is ready for travel."

"What kind of work?" Lucky asked as she held open the door after Jordan slunk out in embarrassment.

"I'm writing a magazine article about Prospect's Western Days weekend, so I'm doing background. We're headed to the library next." Mia pointed at Jordan who was fanning her hot cheeks.

"Oh, what magazine?" Lucky asked.

"*The Way West*. If I can talk my mother into it, I might try for more than one story." And if she got any good details about Grant Armstrong and what he was doing here, laying low out of the spotlight, her mother would never say no.

Lucky crossed her arms over her chest. "Okay, we'll get you back on the road as quick as we can. Can't wait to see Prospect featured in a glossy magazine. I've missed having a newspaper in town. I do my best keeping up with events and posting them all over social media, but having a weekly roundup was special, you know?"

"I bet. It's tough to be in the newspaper business now."
Or magazine or print, Mia added but didn't say aloud.

"Yeah, I think about setting up an online version, with
the articles written by anyone who wants to submit a story.
We'd do some advertising to pay the bills, but…" Lucky's
daughters screamed, this time in a different, less happy
tone. "But then that happens, and I remember I also like
to sleep sometimes and I'd have to completely give that
up to do anything else." Lucky motioned her outside and
inhaled slowly in the silence of the parking lot. She was
waving as Mia slid behind the wheel of her car.

Jordan pointed toward the road and Mia nodded. She'd
lead the way to the library.

Once Jordan was occupied elsewhere, Mia would need
to return to Garcia Auto Repair to see if she could get in-
sider information on Grant Armstrong's sudden departure
from the rodeo.

Why did that fill her with dread? Lucky and Dante had
been welcoming.

Would they be as friendly with her when she started
hunting for answers?

And what about Sarah and Jordan? If Jordan was
wrapped up with one of Grant's brothers, how would they
react to a juicy story about Grant?

She was enjoying the life Prospect offered.

Perhaps it would be smart to maintain her distance.
Mia wasn't here to meet new friends; she was looking for
threads to pull to build her story. A smart reporter would
keep that in mind.

CHAPTER FIVE

GRANT RODE ON Jet behind his mother, who was on her dappled quarter horse, Lady. They ambled down through the pasture toward the barn. It was a quiet Saturday morning and Grant thought the perfect window to reveal what he'd been trying to hide ever since he came back to Prospect. Time was closing in on him rapidly. Mia seemed sharp as a tack, and as a journalist by trade, surely her instincts would ramp up anytime. As he'd walked out of the Majestic the night before, he'd promised himself that whatever happened after his confession, he would tell his family the truth. All of it.

Unfortunately, worrying over it all night hadn't led him to find the proper delivery.

That was his first problem.

Grant and his brothers had all been adopted by Walt and Prue Armstrong after fostering with them. The boys' beginnings were pretty similar, as far as the families and the situations they'd left behind, but Grant had still always been out of step with the others.

For a while, he'd measured up. His career had been solid. He'd been as successful in rodeo as everyone had always told him he would be.

Wes, the "oldest" because he'd arrived at the ranch first and because he couldn't keep himself from stepping up to lead, was the good brother who had come home to take over the ranch. He was also the town's only lawyer and

juggled a lot of responsibility. He could be counted on to do the right thing and know the correct answer. It was annoying, sure, but if Grant explained the tricky situation to Wes, his brother would immediately take over.

Having a lawyer on his side was good. It was. Wes would refuse to leave his brother to face any fallout all on his own.

So would Clay, the smartest of them all, the architect and builder who dropped everything if the family needed his expertise. Creating his own development company from the ground up had been a gamble, but Clay had made it pay off.

Travis, who was settling into foster parenthood as if the role was made for him, wanted to believe in the good in everyone, even after life had made that faith hard to hold onto. He'd served his country in the army, and now he was adding on to Walt and Prue's legacy with a new generation of fostered boys.

And Matt would love him, no matter what. His freakishly handsome face and ridiculous charm protected a soft heart that drew animals and people to him. The "baby" managed to skirt broken hearts by never letting that guard drop for long.

On paper, the Armstrongs were impressive.

In real life? Some people might call them intimidating.

Then, there was Grant, who'd never met a dare or a bit of trouble he could say no to.

And now all his "success" was about to disappear.

But right or wrong, Armstrongs stuck together, he told himself.

In the grand scheme of things, he was the one who usually brought the "wrong" to the table. The problem. The one in the family who kept things interesting. That was his role. Needling to get answers, pushing to make prog-

ress, pranks to keep his brothers humble… He'd taken his
job seriously.

Even after a lifetime of trouble and with zero explanation offered, his family had accepted him when he'd returned home.

Grant wouldn't say they'd rejoiced, since the space had
been pretty cramped when he'd landed at the ranch again.
For months, he'd fielded questions about why he'd come
back, with only vague answers about retirement. The fact
that none of them had given up on digging to the heart of
the matter was proof that the Armstrongs were steadfast.

Or cussed stubborn.

Grant wasn't convinced they'd believe his story. His
whole life had been about testing the rules, but cheating
to win had never crossed his mind. The Armstrongs would
rally around him and come to his defense, sure, but would
they trust that he was innocent here?

Did it matter? Grant knew the truth behind that scheme.

He'd never doubted his ability to ride horses better than
anyone…until now. That big question mark had shaken
him. If he wasn't that guy, the one who competed fairly
and won time and again, what did he have left?

Where did he go from here?

Spilling the whole story over the dinner table would
have been easier, now that a reporter had popped up in
Prospect. If any one of them had poked at him, pushing
for information on why he'd come home the way Matt
had on their drive back to town, Grant could have seized
the opening.

But his parents had eaten in town with Wes and Sarah,
Clay was in Denver overnight, so Jordan had been absent, and Travis and Keena had eyes only for each other.
He and Matt had outlined some ideas for Cowboy Games
at Western Days to present at the next planning meeting,

and everyone had scattered. Breakfast had been noisy and filled with lots of interrogation about the "double date" his divorced parents had been on. That would have been satisfying, but his parents' cagey answers had left Grant and his brothers with very few solid details.

"Whole lot of huffing going on back there," his mother called over her shoulder as she and Lady led the way down the cleared path turning back to the barn. "If I'd wanted a grumbly bear for company this morning, I would have made you wash the dishes instead of your daddy. I'm used to all his grumbles by now. I do love cooking in the farmhouse kitchen, now that he finally agreed to renovations, but heading back to my cozy, clean apartment and leaving the cleanup to you boys sure is sweet."

Grant tipped his head back to study the wide blue sky. He'd forgotten how startlingly clear the sky could get on cold winter days at the ranch. The blue was intense.

Just like his mother's stare as she waited for him to draw alongside. "Me and Lady not moving fast enough for your liking, son?"

"No, ma'am, just thinking too hard." Grant tugged his hat down to give his hand something to do. "Nice day to get Lady some exercise."

When his mother didn't move, Grant forced himself to meet her stare directly. "This dating thing you and Dad are up to... Is the divorce over? Can we expect an announcement soon?"

The corner of her mouth curled. "That's for us to know. I expect we'll be fighting again in no time, so don't go getting measured for a ring bearer's suit yet."

Grant smiled because that conjured up an image of him and Matt walking down the aisle, one tossing flower petals and the other carrying the wedding bands. He had no

doubt his mother would rope all of them in to any second wedding ceremony if she could find a way to do it.

"Speaking of brides, Matt mentioned your neighborly assistance yesterday, stopping to help a stranded visitor with a flat tire." She ran her hand down Lady's neck and watched him. "Does all this heavy sighing have anything to do with this beautiful woman or is this a general return to the black cloud you were under when you first came home? Really thought Damon and Micah had jollied you out of those doldrums, the way the three of you trash talk over your video games."

They had. She was right. Having the kids around was the perfect distraction. Fun uncle was the job he'd been training for his whole life.

"Was anyone talking about brides? I don't remember that." Grant urged his horse forward, hoping his mother would follow. If he was going to get into the whole mess, he needed more family present. Not for support, but because he didn't want to have to tell the story again. "I guess Matt said she was beautiful."

When his mother rode up beside him, her lips were curled smugly. "No, I added that part. Figured she had to be something to catch your attention like this."

Grant grunted. If he agreed that Mia Romero was beautiful, his mother's matchmaking would intensify. If he said she wasn't beautiful, his mother might shove him off the horse for being ungentlemanly. There was no way to win.

But starting off his confession with lying about Mia's attraction didn't appeal to him. "She was cute. That's what I'll say." Like the kind of woman who would match him step for step and still keep him on his toes.

His mother's grin grew. "*Cute* might be even better. *Beautiful* you can admire from afar, but cute will slip right through your defenses time and time again."

Grant huffed again. She was right. He didn't have to say that because she knew how correctly she'd summed up one of the issues with Mia. Even in the brief period they'd been together and knowing how dangerous she could be to his peace in Prospect, Grant's defenses had faltered. He couldn't let his mother catch a hint of that, though.

"It's time to talk about why I decided to retire, Mama." Grant watched her amusement transform into concern. "If we're gonna discuss Mia, we need the whole story out in the open."

She nodded as they passed the paddock. The barn door opened wide and Grant could see his father seated on the stack of feed that lined the interior wall. As if he was waiting patiently for their ride to end.

And he wasn't alone. Wes and Travis were cleaning stalls while Matt was checking the strained tendon on Travis's horse, Sonny. On his last trek to break ice on the pond for the cattle, Sonny had slipped, so he was getting some extra TLC.

He and his mother slid out of their saddles and moved their horses into their stalls. "You boys have been busy," his mother called. "Now, Lady, it looks like you have a full bucket of feed and all the water a pretty girl needs." Grant relaxed a bit as he removed Jet's saddle and listened to her murmur to Lady like a precious loved one. He and Jet locked eyes. The horse whiffled out a breath, and Grant nodded in agreement before running his hand down the horse's neck. His best friend understood him better than even his family. No words were necessary between them.

"Did I miss it? Am I too late?"

When Grant heard Clay hurry into the barn, his suspicion that this was an ambush, carefully planned and cleverly carried out, was confirmed.

"Just in time," his father said before sliding the door closed. "We're gettin' to the nitty-gritty part."

Grant stepped out of the stall and braced his shoulder against it. "Is this an intervention? Who's watching the boys?"

"Last I saw, Keena was playing that video game of yours. She was driving an ambulance through a car wash while Damon tried to coach her how to outrun the police and Micah was busting a gut, laughing." Matt climbed to sit on one of the stall slats. "Just as Keena intended, I'm guessing."

Wes, Clay and Travis found folding chairs and braced their elbows on their knees. After Lady was settled and curiously watching his family assemble in the aisle of the barn, his mother moved to sit on his father's lap.

When every head in the barn, even Lady's, swiveled to absorb that new development, Grant's hopes that this could be an easy conversation rose. He'd hit the highlights, smooth over as much as he could and warn all of them to be very careful around Mia Romero. They didn't need any exposés disrupting life in town.

"Do you think I'm beautiful or cute, Walt?" Prue asked as she settled his hat back on his head.

Walt was a man who understood the precarious nature of the question. After their divorce, Walt and Prue had argued and flirted in equal measure, confusing their sons and neighbors as to the will-they-or-won't-they nature of the relationship.

Walt was also a man who didn't want to lose any of the ground he'd recovered. "Yes," he nodded firmly. "Both on different days and depending on the weather."

Prue pursed her lips as she considered that answer, but she didn't show her cards. Whether or not the answer was

successful remained a mystery as she turned back to Grant and said, "Tell us about your retirement."

Grant was disappointed but not surprised when all of his brothers turned back toward him instead of following what was happening between their parents farther down the rabbit trail.

Wes clamped his shoulder. "All of it, Grant. You've been nursing this long enough."

"So…" Grant clasped his hands together and rubbed them as he considered where to start. No obvious answer came to mind and he wasn't good with words, like Wes, anyway. "Turns out, my whole career is a fabrication, a scheme run by the guy I thought was my best friend and the man I looked up to on the circuit. They've been pulling strings and conspiring with other riders to cheat, throw rides, to push me to the top."

Silence filled the barn. Even Lady had quietly stepped back into her stall. She didn't want any of the family drama. Smart horse.

"For what purpose?" his mother asked, confusion wrinkling her brow. It didn't surprise him that she couldn't see the upside of the grift immediately. None of the Armstrongs would lie to earn a dollar.

Grant rubbed a hand over his mouth. "Believe it was twofold. Betting on the outcome when you already know who will win is easy, sure profit, right?" That was bad enough, but it was the second piece that bothered him more. "And in Red's case, he could sell access to me, the price going up every time I won. He set me up against competition, controlled the standings. Since he also earned a piece of every prize pot, endorsement and boot commercial I taped, as my 'manager,' he was doing very well indeed. All he had to do was convince me to trust him."

When they were all silent, Grant crossed his arms over

his chest. Waiting for them to ask the question he dreaded wasn't easy.

"How did you find out about this? Why didn't you burn the whole operation to the ground before you left?" Travis asked before he yanked his hat off and smacked it against his thigh. "Of all the disgusting maneuvers, to take a man's trust and use it against him. I'll help you embarrass Red Williams so bad his mama won't claim him."

Clay leaned back and rested his head against the wall. "Can we ride out in the morning? I need a nap first."

Grant chuckled when no one else did. He appreciated the effort to dispel some of the tension. Hearing Travis, the quiet one, ready to exact payback had surprised him.

"So...you walked away?" Walt asked slowly. "From this career that you built, put all your heart into. You just quit and came home."

"I didn't know what else to do." Grant scuffed his boot in the scraps of hay on the floor. "If the story comes out, the fallout could be devastating."

"But you're not involved," his mother said. "How can that affect you?"

Grant shoved his hands in his pockets. He'd spent too many sleepless nights considering this. "Afraid proof of my innocence is going to be hard to come by, my word against Red's. But even if I can convince the Association I'm not involved, what if they strip me of my wins? Try to recoup prize money?" The whispers about a cheating Armstrong, the blow to his pride would be awful, and financially...any savings he'd managed to build had been rolled into the Rocking A and the purchase of land from the Hearsts. His whole family could pay consequences even if he was somehow cleared of any cheating himself.

"All of that and you didn't tell *us*, either." Wes frowned. "To me, that's the most puzzling part. Your family. All

around you. People ready to step up to settle this thing beside you got not a word about any of it until months later. Why?"

Wes was the lawyer in the family. He was good with words. Winning arguments against him was next to impossible. The tone in his voice suggested he was determined to get to the bottom of the issue immediately.

The last thing Grant wanted to admit was his shame. He should have known better, but Red had known his weakness: his own pride.

"Mia Romero works for *The Way West*. The magazine. It covers the rodeo circuit." Grant shoved his hands in his pockets. "I haven't heard any whispers about the cheating yet, but when they leak, wherever I am will turn into a circus for a bit. I can't tell if she knows something already or if she's a danger because she will probably start asking questions about me, but I'd rather not appear in any coverage about Western Days at all. And somehow I need help warning our neighbors about how much to tell her."

Everyone was silent as they absorbed the problem of Mia's arrival.

"So he doesn't tell us anything until he needs our help?" Matt said. "Is anyone surprised?"

He wanted to explain about protecting them and the Armstrong name, but Grant knew he deserved that arrow.

Wes pushed on. "What's the piece you aren't saying, Grant? Why didn't you talk to any of us about this before now?"

"I didn't…" Grant studied the faces of his family and realized this was the moment he'd been so afraid of all along. There was no way out of this except through it. "I've built this reputation of being the bad boy. Here at home. There on the circuit. The Bad Boy of Bronc Busting, right? That was Red's idea, too. A brand. It's a new age of rodeo, and

everyone needs a brand." Grant shook his head. He could remember the way Red had talked up the "brand" as if it was yesterday. Grant had eaten up every word, believing that his "personality" was exactly what rodeo needed. "I overheard Red and Trey discussing their next steps. Trey asked what would happen if they got caught. That answer was simple. Blame it all on me. Red explained that no one would bat an eyelash to find out this whole scheme was my idea all along. They might get some bruises, but I'd be the one to suffer the fall."

His father snorted. "And you believed that steaming pile of—"

"He expected all of us to believe it," his mother interrupted. "That's why he didn't tell us. He was afraid we'd believe Grant Armstrong was capable of such a thing. This boy we've known since he was fifteen and tame as a bobcat when he arrived here…" His mother stood and pointed her finger at him. "You better give me a minute here, son, because I am angry that you'd even entertain that thought for a second." Then she marched out of the barn.

They all watched her go. Walt's grimace when he turned back would be funny except it transitioned to pity immediately. "I believe the hole you dug for yourself is going to take some major work to climb out of, son."

"I expected you to wonder if I was telling the truth. What would stop me from agreeing to such a plan? I wanted to be at the top of the pile, and it was guaranteed to put me there. My best friend. My mentor. It makes so much sense." Grant propped his hands on his hips. "No one experienced a second of doubt that I would walk away because I wanted to do the right thing the right way?" How could that be true?

"My son doesn't trust his family." Walt shook his head slowly. "Now I believe that I'm almost as angry as your

mama." He left the barn at a mosey instead of a march, but it was easy enough to tell by the slump of his shoulders that his father was disappointed, too.

Grant flopped down on the hay bale and dropped his head in his hands. "Anybody else want to heap shame on?" The misery he'd experienced in the early days was nothing like this. The center of his chest burned and he had no idea how to put the fire out.

Clay clapped a hand on his shoulder. "Nah. I get it. It's still silly, to think the people who know you best would believe anything like that, but I'd wager the five of us understand where you're coming from."

Grant watched Travis open his mouth to say something and then snap it closed, twice. Of the five of them, he and Travis were the most alike. But while Travis had retreated when he'd first got to the ranch as a kid, Grant had planted his boots squarely and fought until all the rough edges had been filed down. They often butted heads, but he and Travis understood each other, too. In their own minds, neither one of them measured up to the other guys.

"Go on. Hit me with it." Grant waved him over. "I told you not to listen to your doubts when you were getting ready to start fostering. Lecture me. Yell at me. You were right not to put me in line to take over when you wanted to back out. I'm the problem. Always have been. Got us grounded for most of our junior year in high school by convincing you to come with me to the rodeo at the fairgrounds in Eagle after Dad told me I couldn't go. Then, there was the time I wrecked Dad's truck because I was trying to drive backwards down Main Street before school." He shook his head. "My birth mother's drinking, landing in foster care… I made sure more than one foster family washed their hands of me before I met Prue and Walt. The Armstrongs outlasted even my own anger, and

I thought I was coming to terms with that wildness, but I make bad choices. Always have. This time, I trusted the wrong people. That's all on me."

Travis tossed his hat down in disgust. "All this time, and all this emotional angst because you didn't even know us. It's a problem, Grant. You can try to pretend that it's a joke that you expected us to believe the worst of you, but it ain't." Instead of storming off, Travis inhaled and exhaled slowly. "You're lucky we know where that comes from, that fear that people will only believe the worst, me better than any of them."

Grant nodded. He was right. Travis had held so much of his past close to his chest until the doubts about his ability to be a good foster parent forced them out. None of them wanted him to carry all that old baggage around. How silly was it that he'd been doing his version of the same?

"I am lucky. I needed a reminder of how lucky, I guess." Grant cursed under his breath. "Now I gotta figure out how to make that right with Mom and Dad."

Matt whistled. "We are going to need more help with all of this, especially that part. Anyone know where Sarah, Jordan and Keena are?" Keena, Travis's girlfriend and the town doc, had proved herself to be an expert strategist when he'd accidentally messed everything up between them. "If we let them in on the planning, we improve our odds of smoothing things over here and containing Mia Romero's access around town to stories and gossip about Grant."

Wes stepped forward. He was their leader, so they all waited for him to study the problem from all angles and propose the best course of action. "Absolutely, we tell them. Let's get them some good information to work with first. They're Armstrongs in all but name…" He shot Matt a look to shut him down. The question about how

soon he, Clay and Travis would fix the name part hung in the air between them. "Not now, Matt. Let's work on the immediate problem first. Do you know how long Mia will be in Prospect?"

Grant shook his head.

"Okay, do you know where she is right now or should I call the lodge?" He pulled out his phone, prepared to call Sarah for intel.

"In town. She has to stop in at the Garage to check on repairing the tire, for sure." Grant ran his damp hands down his jeans, nervous at the thought of tracking Mia down. "We could send Matt to charm some information from her. She was as bedazzled by his face as every other woman he meets."

Wes looked as if he was taking this suggestion seriously. "Having an eye on her is important. We can rope in Faye at the diner. Until we know whether Mia has been tipped off about the cheating or not, it's hard to determine the proper plan." Then he smiled at Grant. "But not one of us will be as good at testing the waters as you." Grant wanted to object, but the idea had him speechless. "You have all the facts, you've been on the rodeo circuit, know all the players and even the magazine Mia works for. None of us have that. Haven't you heard the saying that offense is the best defense? Find out what she knows first. Then we'll move on to the next step."

CHAPTER SIX

SAM, THE RETIRED postal carrier who staffed the Prospect Library on Saturdays, put a cold bottle of water down on the table in front of Mia, and she realized she'd been poring over newspaper archives for so long that her shoulders had stiffened into an awkward hunch. The pop of her neck as she straightened up and stretched out her arms made Sam wince. "Shoulda forced you to take a break sooner, I reckon."

Mia removed the cap from the bottle of water. "I do that. I get so caught up in research that the time escapes me. When I resurface, everything hurts, but I can't believe how much time has passed." After a long sip, she added, "And that's my favorite kind of day, Sam. Can you believe it? Give me a library and a laptop over a hot sandy beach, please."

He straightened the pile of books on her table. "Well, now, they say variety is the spice of life, so I'll accept it even if I don't understand."

Delighted by his dry response, Mia laughed. She was exaggerating about her love of research but only a little.

She'd been traveling backward in time for hours, getting a clear picture of the way Prospect had changed in the past decade. In the beginning, she'd been disappointed by the lack of information about Grant Armstrong, but she'd started to identify different people in town, following their threads as if they were characters in a soap opera. When she stumbled across a photo that allowed her to put

a face to the character, the whole story grew more solid in her mind.

"You finding everything you need?" Sam asked. "If you come back on Monday, the librarian can give you better instruction on where to find what you're looking for. Lillian's got a whole card catalog stored in her brain."

Since most of Sam's suggestions had been to vaguely point her to the filing cabinets containing microfilm of the defunct Prospect newspaper, *The Prospect Post*, Mia was certain he was correct and she would definitely need more time in the library. "You've done a fine job, Sam. I appreciate your help." Mia braced her hands at the small of her back as she stood to walk around the square table in the center of the library. The bones of the church that had been built here made far more beautiful architecture than many of the blocky municipal buildings she'd visited. "This place is amazing. So pretty and so calming. How long have you worked here?"

Sam cleared his throat awkwardly. Was she making him uncomfortable? "I started volunteering a few months ago. Strictly part-time. The doc... Dr. Singh thought it might do me some good to get out of the house. Interact more with folks. Take my mind off of some of the worries that cropped up after my wife died." He turned in a slow circle as he surveyed the room. "Never was a big reader myself, but my wife made regular stops in here. Nice to be reminded of her. Retirement has not been everything I'd expected. I guess that's down to doing it alone when I'd assumed I'd have my best friend keeping me busy. My wife never ran out of activities for us."

Mia worried that she'd stumbled on to a difficult subject. "I sure am thankful you decided to add volunteering here, Sam. I bet your wife would love it that you're making your own activities now."

"Hadn't quite thought of it like that. Could be you're right." Sam motioned with his finger toward the door. "Closing up in about half an hour, miss. Might be a good idea to get to a stopping point for the day."

Ah, he was ready for quitting time. Mia had been there often enough, watching the clock, to understand the urge. She removed the film she'd finished scanning from the machine and replaced it in the box. "Do you know anything about the building's history?" When Jordan had led her to what appeared to be a church instead of a library, Mia had been confused. Then Jordan explained how all the historical structures in Prospect had been carefully maintained and many of them had taken on new lives, even while they kept the original facades, and Mia had been instantly charmed. A library inside of a church.

As a woman who loved the written word, she found the arrangement fitting. Simple stained glass windows lined both long walls and a larger window formed a beautiful frame for any preacher lucky enough to stand in front of a congregation here. More modern glass windows let in light along the sides of the church closest to the entrance, but mellow red-and-gold light floated down from above.

Spending time researching here could never be a hardship.

"Believe this building replaced one that burned around 1900, but the church itself was founded not too long after the town sprung up during the silver rush days. Had a couple of renovations to make the building safe. Library was moved out of the town hall annex in the seventies, if I recall correctly." He frowned as he considered that. "There's a plaque outside near the flagpole with the dates and information on the congregation if you'd like more specific facts for your story."

"I'll check that out." She wondered if he would recog-

nize the pun. Check out. In the library. But decided not to get distracted. "Are there any books about the town and its history?" If she had any extra time, Mia needed research into the background of the Colorado Cookie Queen, if only to make her conversations with Sarah and Jordan easier.

Sam tapped his chin and moved to his computer to type what she figured were a few key-word searches. "Well, I'll be. Nothing comes up. You'd think a place like this would inspire a history for sure. Some of the tall tales I've heard about the original silver miners who began all this sound like action movies." His confusion cleared. "Better check with the librarian on Monday, too, Mia. Can't say I believe there's not a single book dedicated to Prospect. Closest we'd have is Sadie Hearst's cookbooks. She does some storytellin' in them, about Prospect. We do have a complete collection of those. Would you like to apply for a library card? I can send you home with a few of those volumes."

The memory of books lining the counter in Sadie's old apartment at the Majestic flashed through her mind. She had a hunch that might make for a nice start on the Sadie Hearst cookbook library. She was surprised Jordan hadn't pressed the stack in her hands and told her not to skip a page of background.

"Not necessary this afternoon. Thanks, Sam, you've been a big help. I hope I'll have a chance to say goodbye before I leave town." Mia closed her laptop as it occurred to her that the retired mail carrier himself might be an excellent source of town news. Sam could have good information about Grant Armstrong if she knew how to access it. The clock was ticking on her time in Prospect, so Mia decided she had to take a shot. "I was surprised at how often the Armstrongs landed on the front page of the newspaper. Seems like their family is front and center in Prospect."

Sam sniffed as he considered that. "Guess Walt and

Prue and their boys do a lot for the town. The Mercantile's the unofficial community center, with lots of coming and going. Walt's family has been out at the Rocking A for generations. His dad and mine were fishing partners. Prue moved in after they got married, can't imagine her anywhere else, despite that silly divorce."

"How many sons do they have? Is it four or five?" she asked, even though she'd carefully jotted down the names and occupations of all five Armstrongs. She'd started scrolling through the newspaper archives hunting for stories about Western Days, but somewhere along the way, she'd gotten offtrack and widened her scope to any mention of Grant or his family.

Mia didn't have to think too hard to figure out where she'd gone wrong.

The front page color photo of Grant Armstrong leading the parade down Main Street as the grand marshal, tall and handsome on a shiny black horse, would be hard to forget. He'd been younger, in his twenties, and clearly hailed as a hometown hero.

"Five boys. All adopted after ending up in foster care."

Surprised, Mia spun to face Sam. That was a new detail. It seemed important to the story. "They were part of the foster care system?"

"Walt and Prue opened up the ranch to boys who needed a different kind of place. None of them were cowboys before they got here, but they sure found their way once they did. First met them all through Prospect's high school rodeo club. Used to meet out at my place, long time ago. The ranch made them feel safe, gave them confidence, Walt always said. These five became Armstrongs, too. Now they're doing the same for another generation. Travis has two boys on the ranch now who he's fostering. News around town is that the oldest is smart as a whip and the

youngest is…a real humdinger." Sam took the box of microfilm and returned it to the filing cabinet.

"A real humdinger?" Mia repeated slowly, amused and charmed at the description. It could mean anything from devil to angel, but either way, it seemed sweet. Old-fashioned, maybe, but also supportive somehow?

Sam held out his hands. "Librarian asked for backup for when the boy's class visits, based on the teacher's recommendation. Apparently he asks enough questions for a battalion of fifth graders."

Mia laughed. "That reminds me of the comment on my fifth-grade report card. 'Could learn more if she talked less.'"

Sam's rusty chuckle pleased her. She wanted to push for more details, but she was enjoying their conversation.

"As I recall, a couple of the original Armstrong boys were live wires, too. All good-hearted and smart, but Grant? That boy came into town wild. When our rodeo club met, he'd be first in the saddle and the first bucked off into the dirt. Never stopped him. It was like, once he found the horses and the barn and the thrill of rodeo, he had to make up for lost time. He was exciting to watch as a kid, but when he hit the circuit, every eye was locked on Grant Armstrong." Sam's eyes twinkled. "He eventually learned to stay in the saddle and win."

Mia could easily think of several photos of Grant holding prizes that had been featured in the magazine.

"Not sure how much time has knocked down the rough edges, but he'd help any neighbor in need. Wes came home after law school, helped run the ranch, while the rest of 'em went here and there. All them boys came home to help get the ranch ready for the fosters. Now they're pairing off with the Hearst sisters and the new doctor in town. 'Spect if we had a newspaper these days, the Armstrongs would

be newsworthy still." Sam tugged the chain on the desk lamp to turn off the light. "Wouldn't be surprised if there weren't wedding announcements in the near future, either."

Mia stored her laptop, tablet and pen in the bag she carried everywhere, before slipping the strap over her head to hang across her torso. Her time with Sam was drawing to a close, so she decided to press her luck. "Surely Grant Armstrong will be leaving town soon, though. He's still a big rodeo star, right?"

She was pleased at how innocent her query sounded. It flowed perfectly in with the conversation. Only someone who was suspicious of her in the first place would guess she was digging for information.

"Heard he retired." Sam shrugged as he pointed toward the front door. "I hope he don't come to regret that like I did in the early days. People don't know how much they need important work to do until they've got entirely too much time on their hands."

Disappointed that she'd hit a dead end, Mia bit her lip as she tried to find another angle. "Maybe he has a plan, a new business idea, or…" She let the thought trail off, hoping that Sam would take up the invitation to spread any tidbit of gossip.

"Guess we'll see. That boy knows horses better'n anybody around, so I imagine he'll land on his feet if staying in Prospect is his plan." Sam dipped his head. "And if a pretty lady catches his eye in the meantime, this place makes a good home."

Mia froze with her hand on the library's door handle. Was he implying that she might be such a pretty lady? As in she was pretty and also a lady or as in the pretty lady for Grant Armstrong?

Then she realized Sam believed she was fishing for information on Grant for a completely different reason than

her real impetus. He saw a woman hunting for information on a romantic interest.

Would he spread that news around town?

If so, it could help her. Most people loved love and wouldn't mind assisting her if that was her goal.

But if Grant Armstrong heard she had a crush on him, would he know it was her journalistic instinct prompting the questions or would he believe they were trapped in a movie-like rom-com?

"Let me get that door for you, ma'am," Sam said and carefully brushed her hand aside. "Time to lock up now and head for dinner."

Mia followed his very polite urging and stepped out on the landing where steps led down to the neat sidewalk, bemused at how easily library-volunteer Sam had ended her line of questioning. Had it been deliberate? Hard to say, but he was whistling as he locked the door behind them.

She hadn't realized she was still watching him when Sam straightened and pointed at a parked truck. "Well, now, speak of the devil."

Mia turned to see Grant leaning one arm out the driver's side window of a pickup. "You talking about me, Sam? You know how the rest of that saying goes. 'Speak of the devil and he shall appear.'" He patted the truck door. "At your service."

"Some things do not change, Grant Armstrong." Sam's rusty chuckle was a little less adorable this time, mainly because he was walking away.

Leaving her to face Grant all alone.

Grant's lips curled slowly. "Let me buy you dinner at the Ace High, Mia, and I'll answer any question you ask."

Mia's mouth was dry, but she tipped her chin up and nodded.

When his amusement spread into a full-blown grin,

Mia gulped and headed for her car. She'd follow him to the restaurant and use the time to lecture herself not to be taken in by a handsome man's smile. Grant Armstrong was no devil, but if she wasn't careful, he would become a temptation she couldn't refuse.

CHAPTER SEVEN

As GRANT SLID into the booth across from Mia at the Ace High, he regretted leaving the barn before he picked Wes's brain for a strategy. His orders had seemed straightforward: find out what Mia knew.

But as he'd driven into town, he'd realized that discovering the real reason Mia had arrived in Prospect without tipping her off that there was a story he was hoping to keep hidden would require careful moves.

Grant Armstrong didn't do caution all that well.

Never had.

He could do blunt.

Sometimes he might try for charming. It worked often enough that he always had plenty of company out on the rodeo circuit.

Diplomacy wasn't in his saddlebag.

It might be too late to learn at this point.

Mia smiled up at Faye as she put napkins and silverware on the table.

"Well, now, I wondered if I was going to have an Armstrong-less dinner service, but here comes Grant to keep my streak alive." Faye squeezed his shoulder and met his wince with a smile. "I'm Faye. How'd you get stuck with this rascal tonight?"

Faye had been as close as family, growing up as she had next door, so she was on the list of people he wanted keeping an eye on Mia as she moved through Prospect.

Running the Ace High meant that Faye always knew what was happening in town before everyone else. He wasn't sure anyone had had the chance to brief her yet.

"This is Mia Romero. She's writing a profile of Prospect and Western Days for *The Way West*." Grant watched Mia closely as she shook hands with Faye. It was impossible to find any warning signs in her open, friendly grin. He had no doubt she'd made an admirer of Sam, and Faye would be next.

His mother was right. Cute was dangerous. People didn't see her coming until it was too late. Mia was dressed casually, and her bright eyes gleamed with humor. He wouldn't mind sitting down to dinner across from her, but it would be better not to have this story he wanted to stay far away from standing between them.

"A profile! Well, now, I'm surprised Grant's mama isn't personally escorting you around town and rolling out our version of the red carpet. Prue will want to make sure you don't miss a single, solitary highlight. She loves this place." Faye thumped her pen on her notepad. "Tonight we've got roast beef or roasted chicken, honey-glazed carrots, scalloped potatoes, parmesan-crusted broccoli." She sighed. "That broccoli is a new recipe, so I'll be curious to get some feedback. Gran insists she's an artist and she needs freedom to explore ingredients. Whereas I believe we're business people and if it ain't broke, we don't fix the steamed broccoli and cheese sauce that even the Garcia twins will eat." Faye closed her eyes before shaking her head. "Never mind all that. Choice is simple tonight—beef or chicken. Which will it be?"

"You know me. Beef. Always beef." Grant tugged his hat off and set it down, interested in the way Mia studied his movements as he ruffled out the hat hair. Women had

complimented his hair often enough, but he enjoyed the boost of Mia's attention.

"I'll have the chicken. I like to buck a trend." Mia licked her lips before turning to face Faye. "And if you have a minute or two, I'd love to get some thoughts from you about Western Days and what it means to the town, to your family and business, a personal story. I want to cover the centennial for the magazine, so I'm working on the background now."

Faye slipped her pen behind her ear. "Oh, Western Days? Do I have stories. This one here—" Grant grunted as she thumped his shoulder hard "—when he was a reckless youth, managed to dump a full carafe of lemonade on my new dress, the one Gran made especially for me to wear on the float all the high school senior girls got to ride on that year. And it was before the parade, so yours truly looked like a drenched raccoon, just waving to beat the band. Once in a lifetime, and Grant had to splash me as he clip-clopped by on his fancy horse." Grant winced. "Don't know if it was because he was the only one of those Armstrong boys I never dated for two or three weeks before coming to my senses. Or if that helped me make my decision to avoid him. Most likely a chicken-and-egg situation, I'm guessing. What can I get you to drink, Grant?"

He coughed and eased out of her reach. "Iced tea, please."

"No lemonade? Hmm. His manners have improved over the years, Mia," Faye said sweetly. "Can I get you the same?"

When Mia nodded, Faye hurried away.

It left the two of them alone again and him with no good opening gambit.

"Does Faye hold a grudge? Beyond breaking your high school heart by never being your girlfriend? Are you wor-

ried about your food when you come in here?" Mia asked as she fiddled with her cutlery. Before he could answer, Faye slid a basket of rolls and cornbread onto the table, deposited their drinks and whizzed away.

"Good question. Obviously, yes, she holds a grudge. I'll never live that accident down. I was riding a new horse at the time, one that wasn't quite ready to be out in a crowd. He shied and by the time I got him back under control, I had scattered the crowd and bumped the carafe she was serving from. She brings it up at least once every time I come home to Prospect." Grant shook his head. "But no, I'm not worried about the food. Her grandmother runs the kitchen. Poisoning me would cause too much trouble."

"If you ruined Faye's dress, the one that Gran made special, she might not be a fan of you, either." Mia shrugged as she sipped her tea.

Grant pursed his lips. "Now that you mention it…" He waited for her to smile. "At this point, if it's poison, I'm probably immune. This is the only sit-down restaurant in town, so I've eaten here so often that they've been spoiled for choice in ways to get their revenge by now."

Mia nodded. "Sure. Unless they're biding their time, waiting for the right opportunity."

"You hoping for a murder while you're sitting in the front row?" he asked.

She shrugged. "I am a lucky woman, Grant. The universe drops unexpected gifts in my lap all the time. I've learned that if I'm open to fate, there's no limit to what might happen." She leaned forward. "Even revenge served cold at long last. My career needs a big story, one that will land me on the cover. Gran, Faye and I possibly converged at this point in time for that very reason." The teasing glint in her eyes was tempting, but Faye brought their dinners

before he could choose between flirting, or… What was the other option? Why couldn't he name one?

"Whoa, this is a plate of food," Mia said softly.

Grant watched her consider her options before he took a bite of his roast beef. It was perfection, as always. If Faye was playing the long game, waiting to bring him down, he was ready to take his chances.

"So, no repair. New tire." Grant eased back against the booth, determined to pretend he was making casual conversation. "No easy solution from the universe for your flat."

"Not beyond the timely arrival of two strong, helpful, handsome cowboys in my moment of need." Mia popped a bit of broccoli in her mouth, chewed and nodded her approval. "New tires will be here Monday afternoon at the earliest. Dante and Lucky and their twins are great, though. I was happy to have the introduction. And then there's you, turning up like a lucky penny every time I turn around. All things considered, my faith in the universe is unshaken." She closed her eyes as she sampled the scalloped potatoes. "Oh my."

Grant's attempt at amusement came out as a choked grunt. Her face as she learned why no one complained too much about the missing menu options at the Ace High was unforgettable. The chef's way with potatoes was miraculous. Mia blinked slowly and laughed. "I wasn't expecting heaven on a plate."

Grant had to force himself to return his attention to his own dinner when she grinned at him. The warm glow that grew his chest by her happiness surprised him. It was too much.

"Everyone in town has been lovely. The Hearsts. The Garcias. And Sam? Over at the library? He was a big help

with the newspaper archives. It's sad that the newspaper closed." Mia sipped her drink.

"Yeah, small towns can't support them, I guess." Grant turned his fork in his hand absentmindedly. Here was another opening but he wasn't sure how to capitalize on it. He needed Wes's lawyer brain right about now.

"Print is expensive. Distribution costs. Writers and photographers. If there's not enough advertising, these newspaper owners have to make hard decisions." She sighed. "Magazine owners, too, for that matter. My mother harps on falling advertising revenue and the need for bigger and bigger stories often enough that even the travel writer has it memorized."

Grant put his fork down. "Your mother? Does she work for the magazine, too?"

Mia huffed out a breath. "Interesting question. She… owns it and runs it, but her work is less hands on and more…making phone calls to tell other people to get their hands-on or else. My grandfather knew how to do every single job, even down to answering the front desk phone. My mother prefers a less direct approach." Her lopsided grimace was adorable. "I used to think she was only holding on long enough to drop everything in my lap and head for a resort somewhere, but she has proven resistant to that solution."

Her grimace was almost adorable enough to distract him from the fact that she was more than a reporter. Mia was not just an employee, but had a family stake in getting important stories for *The Way West*.

"I needed to get some space from Billings, so this little weekend visit was my solution."

He wished he'd spent more time preparing for this dinner conversation, because the next remark…

"So you see why, if I could write a story about the real

reason Grant Armstrong left the rodeo circuit behind, I'd get all kinds of coverage for Prospect, Western Days and anything else I wanted. Scooping every reporter that follows the sport would be huge." Mia pinched a chunk off the cornbread muffin, applied a dab of butter and popped it in her mouth. She sighed happily, and Grant realized she wasn't acting out her pleasure for effect. The food at the Ace demanded a pause for enjoyment every now and then.

"Instead of listening to my mother's threats about closing down the magazine," Mia said as she buttered another bite, "I could make my own decisions." Her serious expression convinced him that, whatever she did or didn't know about his situation, this was the truth. Mia wanted a story that would prove her capability to her mother.

Since he'd been tormenting himself with worries about how his own family viewed him and his traits, Grant understood where she was coming from.

"My family needed me here. That's the truth. We were all involved in this renovation so that we could take in fosters. The Rocking A ranch house was too small, cramped and out-of-date. Since all five of us needed the ranch when we were kids, we all wanted to help Travis. And it was a good time to leave. Smart people go out when they're on top. Sliding back to the middle or worse is a sad way to be remembered." Not as gut-punching as being remembered as a cheater who never deserved the prizes he'd won, but that was the part of the story he wanted to knock down or at least keep away from.

Grant rested his elbow on the table and waited to see where she took the conversation next. This was the story he'd given his family in the beginning, when he'd been desperate to deflect their anxious concern. They hadn't believed it, but they knew him too well.

Mia's eyes were warm as she mirrored his pose, one

elbow on the table as if they were having an easy discussion. "Sure. What else could chase you out of the limelight? You seem to be lying pretty low here in the shadows. That surprises me. Sam mentioned how hard filling his time in retirement has been. Are you finding the same issue? No other projects on the horizon?"

Grant tipped his chin up. "Lying low? This whole town knows my every movement, and if anyone from that old life wanted to track me down, seems like it would be easy enough to guess home might be a good place to look." He held his arms out to show he had nothing to hide.

"Okay. Your friends could track you down, but I guess they know the whole story about why you left anyway. I'm trying to remember if I've seen any heartwarming background pieces about the rodeo star who was adopted or even any background on where you grew up." Mia took a bite of her chicken as she seemed to be considering her next question, and Grant wished he had a good distraction. Telling her that it didn't fit with his "image" would make him feel twice as foolish as admitting it to his family.

Mia didn't let the topic go. "I'm not sure anyone started asking questions until you failed to show up for Nationals in December. That was weird. Before you disappeared, the odds were good that you might even take the lead this year as one of the league's richest overall purse winners. You've been on such an amazing ride. Even I heard about it from the travel desk."

That was true, even if the "ride" had been carefully orchestrated by Red Williams. He'd never been in it for money, but he'd eaten up all the attention.

"Well, you know how it is, one cowboy leaves, another one takes his place." Grant pinched the brim of his hat resting on the table. Should he drop names? But if she were the one to mention Red Williams or Trey McClintock here,

Grant could take that as solid proof that Mia knew more than she was admitting. Trey was the most likely candidate to step up to keep the scheme alive.

They were quiet as he considered conversational tactics and discarded each one and Mia methodically finished every morsel on her plate.

Instead, she flopped back against the booth and covered her stomach with both hands. "I can see how you would be drawn back to Prospect if the appeal of your family is half as powerful as Faye's food. In fact, I'm surprised you ever left. I'd love to know more about that, how you hit the circuit in the first place, but you haven't answered my question about your plans or any projects. What comes next for Grant Armstrong?"

Her question was valid. He needed the answer himself. "I'm organizing a new competition for Western Days. That's been keeping me busy." If she bothered to really consider that, she'd quickly determine that last part was false. A change in subject would be good. Why couldn't he find one?

If this had been a normal conversation, like a date, where getting to know him was an important step, Grant would have been happy to tell her wild tales of life on the road. Fans loved those stories. Most of the women he met were fans in one way or another.

He couldn't tell if this was a simple change in topic or a subtle probe for another way into his story.

"Are we talking on the record or off?" he asked, reminding himself as much as her that any conversation between them was dangerous.

She propped her chin on her hand. "Well, now, what an interesting way to pose that question. You have something you'd like to share that would need to be off-the-record, Grant? I am a very good listener."

He realized that he'd stumbled badly. He should have kept to his original story about the renovations and leaving on top. Mia was smart enough to realize that he'd let on more than he should have.

Grant didn't have time to attempt a recovery, because his mother stepped into the dining room, her eyes scanning the crowd. There was no doubt in his mind that she was a heat-seeking missile aimed right for them.

Relief settled over him. She would have been the first call his brothers made to rally the troops.

Prue Armstrong might be disappointed that he didn't share everything that was happening because he'd been afraid his family would believe the stories were true, but there was no way she'd abandon him in the midst of battle. She was their chief strategist, and she was going to save the day here.

"There's my boy," she trilled theatrically as she crossed the dining room, waving here and there as if she were a star acknowledging her fans. "I heard you came into town for a good meal."

When she wrapped her arms around his neck in a warm hug, Grant patted her back awkwardly, very aware that his mother had captured every bit of attention in the room and it was all now centered on their table.

His mother stepped back and turned toward to Mia. "And who is this? Introduce me to your friend, Grant."

The way her voice carried through the Ace convinced Grant that this was part of an escape plan. Retellings of this meeting would sweep through town overnight, with extra color commentary added that would influence how his neighbors welcomed Mia after.

So he cleared his throat and announced, "This is Mia Romero. She's working on a story for *The Way West* all about Western Days." He didn't glance around to make

sure everyone heard him. He'd have to rely on the power of the story to carry it where it needed to go.

"Oh my goodness." His mother clapped her hands together. "Publicity for our little festival! How wonderful. I know everyone will have a good story to tell you about our famous weekend. You know, we all take part in it. The whole thing depends on volunteers."

Grant would have laughed at her obvious campaign to recruit helping hands, if he wasn't aware of the accompanying message she was sending: tell the nice reporter visiting town only the glowing stories about Western Days.

To solidify her pitch, his mother turned to survey the room. "We'll be holding an informal meeting about the festival tomorrow afternoon at the Mercantile to discuss committees and next steps. Everyone's invited. I'll be serving Sadie Hearst's famous Palomino Peanut Butter Cookies to everyone who drops by…just to hear the plans." She held her hands up as if to show she had no ulterior motives and there was nothing up her sleeves. He was pretty certain everyone listening was already wise to her ways.

Except Mia Romero.

"You should join us, Mia." His mother tapped the table. "Get a solid start on your article that way."

Mia nodded. "What an excellent idea and such great timing." How she held his stare made Grant wonder if Mia was an expert at reading between the lines. Did it matter if she knew exactly what they were hoping to accomplish with this scene? "Grant tells me he's been working hard on this year's festival. Sounds like there must be big things brewing."

His mother glanced down at him. He could see the calculations in her eyes. What could she volunteer him to do right now that he wouldn't be able to escape, thanks to Mia's presence?

"Can I get you a plate?" Faye asked when it became clear that his mother hadn't written an exit line into her script.

"Oh no, Faye, I've got a fridge full of leftovers I need to run out to the ranch before they go bad as it is," his mother said. "It's been too long since I saw this rascal." She nodded at him, and neither one of them acknowledged that it had been less than three hours since she'd swept out of the barn with an epic cold shoulder.

"Well, the timing is excellent." Mia pointed at Faye. "If you'll give me the bill for this meal, I will be able to repay at least one of the Armstrongs for helping me with a flat tire." She craned her neck to make sure the rest of the diners were listening. The resemblance to his mother's delivery was uncanny.

Faye ripped off the top page from her order pad and passed it over. "Holly can ring you up at the front there. If I somehow miss this planning meeting tomorrow," Faye said without looking at his mother, "I hope you'll come back in for another meal or two before you go, Mia. I have many stories to pass along of Grant Armstrong's misbegotten youth. Not for the article. Just because."

Mia grinned at Grant before nodding. "Definitely. I wouldn't miss my chance to try more from the Ace High's kitchen."

After she slid out of the booth, Mia touched his hand briefly. "I will definitely see you again, Grant." Then she offered his mother her hand. "And Prue, I spent the afternoon reading front-page stories about you and your family. It's nice to meet you in person. Can't wait to find out what you have in store for me…and the town's big celebration."

His mother took Mia's vacated seat, but Grant watched Mia slide through the tables toward the cashier and the exit. Before she left, she glanced over her shoulder at him,

one corner of her mouth curled in amusement. They might have successfully spread the word throughout town about what the official story should be if Mia showed up on any doorstep, but he wasn't convinced she didn't see right through their tactics.

"No one told me she was adorable." His mother tangled her fingers together on the table.

"Does it matter?" Grant asked, fidgeting as he was caught dead center in her sights. He had the urge to defend himself and remind her that he'd definitely called Mia "cute," but he had a feeling that was his mother's ultimate goal: to get Grant to admit he was attracted to Mia Romero. Why? Grant had no idea. His mother always had an end goal for her sons: happy marriages and settling back down in Prospect. If Mia was the one to tempt Grant into staying, his mother would change sides in the middle of battle.

If one of his brothers had been here, Grant could have created a diversion by starting an argument.

"It might matter, Grant." The gleam in his mother's eyes wasn't reassuring.

It commonly accompanied her matchmaking efforts.

He needed a distraction pretty darn quick. "My gut says she knows something is up, but I'm not getting any hints that she has a line on the story yet. I do think she saw straight through your acting."

His mother waved a hand. "I wasn't acting. We'll have a preplanning meeting. I want to make sure Matt has all the help he needs. I also believe it's important that we make Prospect look good in this story. If that's what she saw, mission accomplished."

Grant rolled up the straw wrapper as he considered that. She was right. "You gonna be mad at me forever?" He had tried to prepare himself for that, to be on the outside of the circle because he was the one who couldn't avoid

trouble. That's where the guilt had come from. Prue and Walt had done their best, but there was something in him that let them down.

Losing his career hurt.

He would never recover if he couldn't get everything between him and his parents straightened out.

The way she rolled her eyes immediately reassured him. "The only thing I'm gonna do forever is love you, Grant Armstrong, and you know it."

He gripped her hands to hold her attention. "I'm sorry. This time I messed up and had no idea it was even happening."

Prue frowned. "You didn't do a thing wrong except carry too much of this yourself, son. Consider how you'd explain such foolishness if it was one of your brothers acting so silly." Her lips curled. "Pretty sure you get that from your dad."

She touched his cheek.

Overcome with her easy acceptance and the love that was clear in her eyes, Grant said, "Thank you."

She patted his hands and slid out of the booth before he could apologize again. "Don't you miss this meeting at the Mercantile, you hear me? I love you, but I will volunteer you for more work if you aren't there to defend yourself."

She marched away to make small talk with one of the teachers from the high school before he could agree or disagree.

"Seems like Prue has rallied the troops. Not much to worry about, right?" Faye asked as she cleared the dishes from the table in front of him.

"Hope so. Nothing to do but hold on for the ride." Grant shook his head. He wasn't a worrier like Travis or Clay. His whole life, he did the best he could. Put him on a bucking horse and he'd hold on until he couldn't anymore. Trans-

plant him from the home he knew to a ranch in the mountains, and he'd strap in until the ride smoothed out. Even putting an end to the career he'd built had been a simple decision. All it had taken was pointing his truck toward home and never looking back.

Mia's arrival had given him that nervous knot in his stomach, which made him think that even if the story that would change everything never came out, something big was still about to happen and he wasn't prepared.

CHAPTER EIGHT

MIA'S HUNCH THAT something changed on Saturday, after the theatrical encounter with Prue Armstrong in the Ace High, was confirmed by the second breakfast at the Majestic Prospect Lodge. Instead of a family occasion where the Hearsts bantered and bickered while they all ate toast, Sarah tapped on the door as soon as Mia stepped out of the shower. She was holding a tray with a covered plate and a small carafe.

"Good morning. Jordan discovered these trays and plate covers when she was rummaging through Sadie's storage closet. Apparently your stay here is a 'golden opportunity' to test our room service items." Sarah's smile was warm but it didn't make it all the way to her eyes.

Mia hated the sinking feeling that came from being shut out of the Hearsts' easy company, but she took the tray with a smile. Whatever happened between her and Grant, Sarah and Jordan had been excellent hosts. "I'm happy to be the test subject. It looks like another beautiful day outside." The curtains were open because she'd wanted more of the bright sunshine.

"Better get out and explore while we have it. I have my fingers crossed we've seen the last of the messy winter storms, but the forecast does include flurries and cold for the rest of the week. The lake is pretty all four seasons, and if you want to walk, there's a marina down the hill. It's still closed but we've got it on the list of things to work on,

too." Sarah awkwardly glanced over her shoulder. "We're getting an early start today, headed over to the Rocking A for a family...meal. I hope you won't mind having some time to yourself." She wrinkled her nose. Mia wasn't certain she was reading it correctly but she would label it regret. "Prue mentioned that you're planning to come to the meeting at the Mercantile. It's in the center of Prospect, across from the Ace High. Do you remember seeing it?" She rocked from one foot to the other. Was she nervous around Mia now?

"I do. What time should I be there?" Mia asked.

"Three. Prue said it will be a short check-in." Sarah licked her lips. "But don't miss the cookies."

"A famous Sadie recipe, I heard." Mia picked up the covering to see scrambled eggs and toast.

"I skipped burning the bacon this morning." There was an apology in Sarah's voice, so Mia laughed.

"Hey, before you go, I asked if there were any books about Prospect at the library. Sam said no, but he suggested I check out Sadie's cookbooks to find out more about the town through her stories." Mia shoved her hands in her pockets, aware that nerves had kicked in while she was talking with Sarah. She hated the awkwardness between them. "It seems like Sadie might have been one of the best sources to understand this place."

Sarah tilted her head to the side. "Hmm."

Mia waited. It was a strange answer, not confused but... considering.

"A book about Prospect." Sarah huffed out a breath. "I can't believe Sadie didn't think of that herself. You would not believe some of the photos we found in Sadie's old files." She marched away without explaining.

"Okay." Mia turned toward the table where her breakfast waited but instead headed out into the hallway and

walked to Sadie's apartment. If Jordan was still there, she'd make a direct request to borrow the cookbooks. When she stuck her head around the corner, Jordan was seated at the island, scrolling through something on her phone. Mia tapped lightly on the doorjamb, interested to see Jordan jerk guiltily in her chair.

"Hey, Mia," Jordan said brightly and loudly. "Finished breakfast already?"

Mia fought to keep her face pleasantly bland. She was desperate to know what the conversation was about her presence in town, and what Grant Armstrong was working to keep her from discovering, but she understood that the family had chosen his side.

She liked them better for it.

"Could I borrow some of Sadie's cookbooks?" She pointed to the stack on the counter. "I'm still building a background on the town, and I hear she was a good storyteller. Without Wi-Fi, I'd be stuck squinting at my phone for internet searches." The way Jordan had just been squinting.

Jordan seemed ready to try some excuse, but Sarah breezed into the apartment, a cardboard box in her hands. "A book, Jordan. That's another project we can add to our list. We have so much material, this box, all the others we moved into the kitchen to sort through. Sadie loved this place. Can you imagine how awesome it would be to have a book for sale in the museum?"

Jordan's eyebrows shot up. "Who is writing a book? I am not writing any book. I will learn to retile all the bathrooms, but there is no way you are going to chain me to a laptop to write a book, Sarah." She scooped up the stack of cookbooks and handed them to Mia. "Where did this idea come from?"

Sarah wrapped her arm around Mia's shoulders. "Neither of us will write it, but we can hire someone to do that.

This is so much easier than renovating this lodge, Jordan."
Sarah bit her lip. "I wonder if Brooke could write it…"

Jordan was wildly shaking her head when Sarah disappeared down a hall that must lead to the bedrooms.

"I was thinking about *reading* a book, not suggesting
anyone write one." Mia shifted the books in her arms. "So
I'll go do that. With my breakfast. See you later."

"Okay, when you're finished you can set the tray in
the hallway or return it to the restaurant's kitchen. We've
been going through all the serving dishes, pots and pans
that were in storage." Jordan rubbed a hand on her forehead. "One million things still to do around here before
the Majestic is ready for guests and Sarah also wants us
to do a book."

Jordan seemed exhausted as she stood there, so Mia
froze in place, worried that she wasn't well.

Sarah breezed back in. "When my sister has inspiration,
it's a grand thing. When I do it, Jordan shuts down. With
the deadline to reopen the lodge looming and the museum
in town, we're both overwhelmed with the items on the
to-do list." She patted her sister on the back. "No worries,
little sister, this can be done later. Okay? No panicking
today. I believe Michael might even be able to handle this
through the corporation." She turned to Mia. "Michael's
the cousin who was named CEO of Sadie's company. He's
been pretty supportive of all these projects we're rolling
out in Prospect. I came up with a way to get him to pay
for the siding refresh last night, so when Jordan returns
to the land of the living, I will share it with her. That will
give her a shot of energy like nothing else." Sarah tapped
her temple. "Jordan's the brawn. I'm the brains."

"I can hear you. I'm standing right here," Jordan mumbled.

"Go put on your shoes. We're going to be late for…"

Sarah turned back to Mia with a fake, polite smile. "Our family breakfast."

Ignoring the urge to comfort Sarah by explaining that she understood their "family breakfast" was intended to discuss "family business" that might be centered on what to say around her, Mia nodded. "Enjoy. Tell all the Armstrongs I said hello."

Back in her room, Mia ate the breakfast off the Majestic's room service tray and stared out the window as she considered how her welcome had cooled.

Prue's theatrical speech at the Ace High.

Sarah and Jordan backing away.

Even Grant's surprise invitation to dinner.

The Armstrongs were doing their best to keep an eye on her movements in town. Why they would go to the trouble to alert their neighbors to her presence and the approved line of questioning was difficult to misunderstand.

"What don't they want me to find out?" Mia picked up her phone and wished the lodge had already undergone the Wi-Fi installation, but the small screen would work for a quick search. When entering Grant's name didn't turn up any recent news items, she slipped the phone into her pocket.

Mia turned pages in the cookbooks without reading, aware of the faint vanilla scent wafting in the air. There was a clear explanation this morning. When she landed on a spread with Sadie Hearst grinning from the pages, Sarah studied her face for any resemblance to Jordan and Sarah. She couldn't explain which features were familiar, but the sparkle in her eyes leaped off the page. Sadie's grin was contagious and she looked perfectly at home behind the stainless steel bowl of a large mixer. The recipe

on the page was for Lemon Drops, a sort of twirled cookie made of two doughs that had to taste absolutely delicious.

Mia didn't cook, but there was something about Sadie's encouraging smile and the need to have one of those cookies that blossomed immediately. It made her wonder if Sarah and Jordan would let her test her skills against the Cookie Queen's recipes as long as she cleaned up whatever mess she made.

When she realized how far she'd wandered from her original plan for the morning, Mia slumped back against her chair. She'd gotten no helpful information from Sarah or Jordan or her halfhearted phone search.

Asking around the magazine's newsroom to see if anyone had heard any new whispers about Grant was an option, but it was the final, last-ditch choice. If there was a story to tell here about Grant, she wanted to be the one to get it. Bringing it to her mother to publish would be proof that she could deliver big wins for *The Way West*.

She pulled up the results of the Nationals competition from December to see who had benefited from Grant's retirement. She didn't follow the circuit standings closely but none of the names seemed unusual. *The Way West*'s summary featured a large action photo of Trey McClintock bent low over the back of a bucking horse. She scanned the article, but there was no whisper of a question about Grant's absence. Then she noticed the photo credit.

"Well, Casey Donaldson has made it to the show," Mia muttered to herself, uncertain how she felt knowing that the guy who'd been one of her least favorite photographers to work with had realized his goal of getting more than fried-food-and-craft-show assignments. Mia could remember long days of complaints when she'd worked with Casey. "But he did get good photos."

Did she still have his number? She scrolled through her contacts. His name didn't come up but there was an entry for Do Not Answer Photographer.

She considered her options. "Should I open this door, or…"

How important was getting this story? Did it matter enough to put herself back on Casey's radar?

A picture of her mother's shocked face as she read the story that Mia scooped right out from under her experienced news writers flashed through Mia's mind, so she punched the number before she could talk herself out of it.

"Please don't answer. Please don't answer. Please don't answer," she whispered as the phone rang.

On the third ring, just as she was composing her cheery voice mail in her head, Casey said, "Mia Romero, I was thinking about you and here you are. What are the chances?"

Mia wasn't good with math calculations like that, but she hoped he was lying.

"No way. That must be what made me pick up the phone this morning. Where are you in the world today?" She stuck her tongue out, grossed out at her perky delivery.

"Got downtime before I head to Utah next weekend. Should I swing through Billings on the way? We could grab dinner." He made some weird humming noise. "Catch up."

"Actually, I'm in Colorado, working on a story. I was doing some research and saw the amazing photo you took of Trey McClintock at the Nationals. I couldn't let it go without passing along my congratulations. You have come a long way." Mia didn't want to overdo her praise, but she had a feeling Casey would accept this as his due.

"Yeah, years of kids showing off their fat goats and grandmas with their prizewinning pies was good training,

I guess. So, dinner? I'm in Denver now. This was truly meant to be," he said.

Mia cringed, disaster looming. "Wow, I wish I'd called sooner. I'll be on my way back home on Monday, and I'm buried in research on Western Days until then." She glanced around the empty hotel room. Nothing was burying her here.

The pause that followed convinced Mia that he was regrouping. Better she should try to redirect, so she asked, "What was the unofficial story at Nationals? Anything exciting happen?"

The longer pause that followed her question made her wince. Had she shown too much of her hand?

"Well, there was a whole thing about one of the barrel racers hitting on a married judge, but that was more of a laugh than real news." He sighed. "Seems like everyone wanted to talk about Grant Armstrong missing the competition but no one knew anything about what had gone on with him, so it never went very far."

Thinking fast, Mia said, "I read about the newest phenomenon. What was her name?" If he was on the trail of her real reason for calling, this might throw him off the scent.

"Annie Mercado. Yeah, she's one to watch, for sure. You doing feature stories, Mia? That's new. We should definitely reconnect if you're going to need shots for whatever you're working on."

"Me? Writing news?" Mia chuckled loudly, hoping to keep him distracted from her mission. "You know how much I enjoy the craft show and parade circuit I'm on. Plenty of characters out here, but I'm sure there's a story in the works about her. I thought there might be some travel connection I could work in." She realized she was pacing tight circles in front of the sunny window and forced herself to stop. This phone call was almost over.

"I might be able to swing it if—"

"Oh no, someone's at my door, Casey. Gotta run, but I appreciate the dinner invite. We'll definitely catch up soon." Mia ended the call and set her phone down on the table. Did it feel good to poke for information from someone who didn't know her true intention? No. It would serve her right if she was ducking Casey for months. Mia pressed her forehead against the cool window and stared out at the lake. She was the one who needed a distraction from the dread that conversation had inspired.

"Without accomplishing a single thing," she muttered as she yanked on her coat and shoved her feet in her sneakers. Getting out of the lodge room was her only hope. Since she hadn't had an opportunity to explore the Majestic, she might as well take advantage of her solo time. Mia shoved her phone and her car keys in her pocket and picked up the tray. It was a new experience to be the only guest in a hotel, but that meant she had plenty of time to make note of the details. She'd learned that the lodge had been closed for many years before the Hearsts came back to town. The wood floors and trim were no doubt original, but the place had obviously been cared for. Everything had a timeless quality to it, as if the place was outside the normal world. As she paused in the lobby, the sweet scent of freshly baked cookies filled the air.

"Ha, Sadie, I guess I'm not completely alone, am I?" Mia studied the large painting of the Rockies as she decided how she felt about ghosts. "If they are real, one that smells this delicious is okay with me." She continued through the restaurant, where it was clear the Hearsts had been making plans. Tables were neatly arranged with chairs turned over on top to make sweeping and mopping the room easier, but the place was spotless. If they

found a chef today, they could start serving meals in the room tomorrow.

"And the place would be packed. Look at that view." Wide windows lined the front of the dining room, letting warm sunlight filter through the trees. The lake was perfectly framed, glittering in the distance. Determined to get a closer look, Mia hurried into the kitchen. A magnet stuck to the dishwasher said Dirty, so she rinsed her plate and silverware and slipped it all inside. Several different ceramic pieces lined the countertop. There were three pie keepers, one blueberry, one cherry and one apple. A large cookie jar shaped like a cowboy hat with a red-and-white gingham band was lined up next to a canister set rimmed with the same gingham. Mia picked up one of the canisters to see that it had been made by the Cookie Queen Corporation. "Sadie, you were the real deal, weren't you? A celebrity chef. I had no idea."

There were cardboard boxes stacked next to the counter and more were arranged neatly beside. At a quick glance, Mia could see notes about a TV schedule, doodles of funny horses and cows along the margins, file folders that were labeled with recipe names, and a few photos of completed cookies. The open box on top contained more paperwork, old calendars, and Mia realized she was looking at a bunch of Sadie's papers. When she pulled out the first recipe folder, the top sheet showed a handwritten recipe and contained Sadie's notes as she tested it. There were minor adjustments made to ingredients here and there and comments for each change. If she was reading the notes correctly, Sadie had tested this recipe for No-Bake Bear Paws four times, and she hadn't been satisfied until she'd added pumpkin spice at the last step. The last bit of writing said "Scrumptious."

Sarah and Jordan had so much of Sadie's materials to work with, not just for redoing the lodge but for a book.

Even her work files were scattered with drops of Sadie's enthusiasm and personality.

Whoever worked on a biography of Sadie Hearst was going to enjoy every minute.

What would it have been like to work for Sadie? In her mind, the headquarters for the Cookie Queen Corporation was filled with people wearing overalls and straw hats or aprons and chef hats, for some reason, and everyone was very happy.

That couldn't be right. A job was a job, but there had to be a special Sadie touch to the place.

She pulled her phone out of her pocket to make a note to contact Michael Hearst, CEO of the Cookie Queen Corporation. Mia realized his input on Western Days would be negligible, but if the magazine needed new advertisers, this story could be the beginning of a beautiful relationship. Her mother would never believe Mia had pulled it off, but it would be a big win.

Then she made a note to find out why neither of the town's celebrities had any signage or historical markers or even a tourist trap making money by selling souvenirs. Why wasn't there a Home of Sadie Hearst sign as people rolled into Prospect? Or a statue of Grant Armstrong mastering a bucking bronco that visitors could pose in front of?

Cold, clear air hit Mia as soon as she stepped outside. There was something different about the atmosphere in the mountains, and she'd learned to appreciate how the light landed particularly at the high altitudes, even if her heart beat a little faster and her breathing was quicker, too. It was an effortless walk down to the water's edge. Snow was still covering spots here and there, but it was easy to believe that spring would be coming soon. Mia followed the bank for a bit until she saw the closed marina in the distance. When the Hearsts reopened, this place was set

up for success. The lake was crystal clear. Every single piece was in place for Jordan and Sarah. How could anyone walk away from a location like this?

Even if she failed to get the story on Grant Armstrong, she would look back on her short stay in Prospect fondly.

Since Mia had plenty of time before the Western Days meeting, after she explored the lakeshore, she opted to window-shop along Main Street. She hadn't seen much of the town, and discovering some of its history had increased her curiosity. The drive into Prospect took only a short while and parking next to the Mercantile made perfect sense, since that was her final destination. Mia hesitated as she scanned the storefronts from the sidewalk.

"Mia, it's a round trip. Either direction, just go." She was glad there were no crowds just then. No one had overheard her talking to herself. The invisible line that marked the end of the oldest section of town was easy to see, so she decided to check out the businesses surrounding the Homestead Market. The store had been built into the facade of the old livery stable.

Across the street, she saw a newer portion of architecture, storefronts with large plate-glass windows and charming red brick that were neat as a pin and made her think of mid-century modern homes. The largest was empty, but the faint gold lettering on the glass said The Prospect Post. The newspaper hadn't been a large operation when it was open for business, but it had covered the heartbeat of the town: what mattered to the people there. There were a few desks inside, but nothing much else to investigate. Imagining settling in to work there was easy, though. Telling the stories of her neighbors, a real community, would have been satisfying, Mia thought.

She shook her head to clear the daydream and continued on to the heart of town: the Mercantile, the Ace High restau-

rant and the bed-and-breakfast, Bell House, a beautiful old Victorian building. As she walked, it was simple to see why the people who had stayed in Prospect must love the place. There was so much history at every turn.

The line of storefronts leading to the theater was missing the obvious markings of the livery stable and the saloon, but there was a small plaque that described the Fashion Row of Prospect's heyday, during the silver rush. These buildings, where there had once been an exclusive milliner, a cobbler and boot maker, a tailor who created fine men's suits, and three competing seamstresses, was empty, but there was a sign in one window.

Future Home of the Colorado Cookie Queen Museum and Gift Shop, Mia read as she moved closer to peek around the edges. In the shadowy interior, it was hard to see anything clearly, but the shapes suggested wood crates and possibly displays being built.

That answered one of her questions about why there was no sign for Sadie Hearst.

Prospect had been waiting for Jordan and Sarah to come to town.

When she stopped to check her phone for the time, anxious to be there on the dot for the Western Days planning meeting, a woman stepped out of the historic theater, the Prospect Picture Show, with a box under her arm.

"Oh, hi, I almost bumped into you, Mia. Sorry about that." The woman turned a key in the door and the loud thunk of a sturdy lock proved it was secure.

Mia was sure her surprise showed on her face when the woman smiled. "Sorry. We haven't met. News of your arrival has preceded you, obviously. I'm Amanda. I bet we're both headed to Prue's completely voluntary, and in no way mandatory, meeting for Western Days." She tapped the box she was carrying. "I'm delivering some of the Sadie

Hearst memorabilia we've had stored here at the theater to Sarah. There's no need for me to attend, per se, Prue has already given me an assignment, but I do like cookies."

Mia laughed. "I did receive a lovely, public invitation, so yes, that's my next stop."

Amanda matched her pace, the box resting on one hip. "I've been here so long that I've forgotten how weird it can be when someone you've never seen before calls you by name. The town's busier, in the summer months. I wouldn't have assumed then you were the magazine reporter I'd heard about."

"A Prospect transplant? It's nice to meet you. I had begun to think everyone here was hatched from the Mercantile," Mia said as they paused on a corner to check for nonexistent traffic.

Amanda chuckled. "I can see how that could happen, but no, my husband wanted us to live here, and then I never moved away, even after he was gone. It's a good place to call home. I have lived here long enough to have raised an adult daughter who is out conquering the world, though, so you might as well think of me as one of the old-timers."

Mia liked her easy personality. Come to think of it, she hadn't met a single person in Prospect who treated her with actual suspicion.

"Your theater is lovely. Plays the classic Westerns." Mia motioned over her shoulder at the marquee. "Too bad I'll miss next weekend's show. *Along Came Jones* is one of my favorites. I was half in love with Gary Cooper when I was ten, thanks to my grandfather's collection of movies."

"That role was different from the strong, silent, solid hero he usually played. Lighter. Your grandfather had good taste. So did young Mia." Amanda patted Mia's shoulder. "My first crush was a dancer in a toothpaste commercial. The silver lining is that I had very few cavities."

Amanda wrinkled her nose as Mia laughed.

"Before I married a man who inherited a historic movie theater that shows only Westerns, I didn't know much about those old silver-screen cowboys. Now? I have them memorized and I couldn't pick a favorite out of the lineup. Favorite villain? That one's much, much easier. Jack Palance. At every age, he made an excellent villain. I'll have to remember to set up a Gary Cooper double feature for when you come back into town." Amanda shrugged. "That's one of the benefits of owning your own movie house. I can take requests at any time. We'll get *Along Came Jones* back up on the big screen for you."

"That would be a perk," Mia agreed. "Will the new museum be opening soon?"

"During Western Days. If all goes according to plan." Amanda waved her free hand broadly. "This whole town will be buzzing with fresh attractions. I have a lot of faith in Sarah and Jordan, but they have filled their plates, for sure. Sadie Hearst was a dreamer, but she also worked those dreams until they became her reality. Must be part of the Hearst family tradition to shoot for the moon."

They reached the Mercantile, and Mia opened the door for Amanda.

Mia wasn't sure what to think when she stepped into a short hallway. A display of pamphlets for local attractions was the only piece inside; there were two doors, one on either side. Amanda paused. "The Mercantile used to be one large open store, like what you expected when you stepped in, but when Prue and Walt divorced, she demanded to have her own space carved out. This was the solution. Hardware on one side, and her store, Handmade, on the other side." She frowned. "As a woman who moved to town and got carried away by her husband's career and family, I get Prue's need. Now that they seem to be reassessing their di-

vorce, I wonder about what happens to this space. It was weird when they built it, but it'll be weird if they take it down, you know?"

Mia followed Amanda into Prue Armstrong's shop. She didn't realize how her head was swiveling from side to side as she trailed Amanda to the staircase, but she knew she'd have to find time to come explore Handmade before leaving town, if only to touch all the fabrics.

Then, before Mia was completely prepared, she was in the center of an extended open space where everyone turned to stare at her. Some of the faces were unfamiliar, but there was no question they knew her name, her job and her stated purpose in town.

Grant was slouched against the wall near the podium at the front of the room. The way their eyes locked was reassuring. As Mia settled into the back row near Lucky, she pulled out her tablet, to jot notes about the meeting, and considered a creative way to get Grant Armstrong alone.

So she could ask him questions.

Without an audience.

That was the only reason to plot private time with Grant.

Mia was especially glad no one could hear her thoughts this time. She didn't even believe what she was telling herself.

CHAPTER NINE

ON SUNDAY AFTERNOON, Grant was relieved when Mia stepped inside his mom's large room on the second floor of the Mercantile. He'd also been happy to see a decent turnout. The two things were related. Mia's appearance wouldn't have meant much without the rest of the crowd and vice versa. Since it was impromptu and his mother hadn't had time to compel as many folks to report for duty, he'd been concerned that attendance would be too low to convince Mia that this was a real planning meeting.

He should have known his mother would never waste an opportunity to prepare for the town's most important weekend of the year.

Matt had been thoroughly coached, because he was doing a credible job of taking the lead. The first order of business had been to announce Mia's presence in the room. She'd introduced herself by outlining her Western Days article and giving her email address in case anyone had a story they wanted to share with her about it. As she'd settled into her spot in the back row of the folding chairs he and his brothers had set up that morning, Mia met his stare and their instant connection snapped into place like a magnetic field existed between them. It was hard to fight.

His mother had named him head of the Cowboy Games Committee, an "exciting addition to the festival's lineup," before he knew that was the next order of business. Since every single one of his brothers had been placed in charge

of a committee of his own, it was impossible to argue his way out of what seemed inevitable anyway.

"Grant, you want to tell everyone about what we've done so far to plan for the Cowboy Games?" Matt asked, his eyebrows raised.

Had he missed his first cue? Grant realized he was watching Mia again, so he cleared his throat and stood. "My plan is to set up a timed riding course. We're going to hire some help with this because we need experts making sure this is challenging but safe, and it will be an all-around skill competition with riding, roping and a shooting category. Every event will be scored, with a grand prize and then first, second, third places in each." Grant was speaking off-the-cuff, since he and Matt hadn't made it quite this far, but if they were hoping to attract talent, it made sense to pattern pieces after other official rodeo competitions. "Gonna need to offer monetary prizes along with trophies. I nominate someone else to be responsible for finding sponsors." He went to sit down but Matt gave him a small shake of his head, so he quickly reversed course. "In the park back here—" he motioned vaguely behind the Mercantile to the city park that was used for every town celebration, large and small, and everyone in the room knew exactly what he meant, except perhaps Mia "—we'll set up a minicourse for kids. I'm thinking we'll have a lasso station, maybe archery... We'll need to do more thinking on that, but if anybody has suggestions, I'll take them. I expect this will be prime real estate to set up photo opportunities for families, as well, so we'll need props."

It was clear Matt expected him to do more, but Grant hadn't intended to give a multimedia presentation or anything. He crossed his hands in front of him. "Any questions?"

"The park is the perfect size for the children's course,

but have you two thought about where we'll hold the adult competition? I don't think we've got room in town." His mother bit her lip. "There's always the ranch, I suppose, but…" Grant knew very well his father and all of his brothers were loudly disagreeing with that option, even if none of them said a word. The disruption to their cattle business caused by a crowd of that size would be wrong and bad, and immediately shot down if anybody other than his mother had tossed it out.

"It's too bad the ghost town isn't accessible," Sarah Hearst said from her spot next to Wes. "That would be an excellent backdrop."

"It's also not safe. Those buildings need to be examined properly before we could let people loose up there." Jordan turned to Clay and smiled. "Right, Clay?"

Grant was certain they were communicating on a deeper level than the rest of them could hear when his brother wrapped his arm tightly around Jordan and murmured, "Jordan is right."

"What about Sam's hay field across from the high school?" Reginald McCall stood to make his case. "It's a real good space. Since the Prospect Rodeo Club shut down, no one's using that land or the barn."

Grant turned to Wes for confirmation that the rodeo club was no more. Coming to Prospect had been tough but finding that club and a group of kids who loved the competition in the ring as much as he did had put him on the path to the professional rodeo circuit. He was sad to hear it had closed.

Low chatter filled the room as everyone debated the merits of his suggestion until Matt raised his voice. "That seems to be a solid contender, Reg. Thank you. Grant can talk to Sam. The next time we meet, we'll have more de-

tails to discuss, with an outline of the course and a budget. You can do that in a week, right?"

Grant had no idea whether he could or not. Budgeting wasn't exactly in his wheelhouse, but he had a lifetime of bluffing his way through questions he didn't know the answer to. "You bet."

Matt's lips were twitching as he nodded.

Almost as if he was aware how little Grant knew and how that had never stopped him from agreeing to a request. "Include tents for the competitors while they're waiting. Any construction we'll need for the course and targets. A fair price for using Sam's land for a month or so and any setup, teardown and repairs necessary." Matt offered him a pen. "Should you be jotting this down?"

Grant grunted. "Of course not. It's a budget. I got it." Then he sat down.

Wes leaned over. "I know my way around a spreadsheet. I'll be happy to help."

On the other side, Clay tapped his chest. "Construction. I got you."

Grant nodded and forced himself to relax. Somehow, in his mind, this megasized event was in the distance, too far away to be a big concern.

Having a plan and a budget in a week? That prompted a cold sweat, but he could count on his brothers to get him across the finish line.

He tried to relax, but then he noticed his mother's frown.

"Are we ready to move along?" Matt asked her uncertainly.

She nodded but it was not convincing. "I just..." She waved her hands vaguely. "I want to make sure our event is unique. Right? Have we got that piece yet?" She pointed at Grant. "I mean, we'll have our own rodeo star on hand,

so that definitely helps, but lots of other places do riding and shooting competitions." She sighed. "Let's all consider if there's another way to do this, to make us stand out."

Grant exchanged a what-are-you-going-to-do-about-this? look with Matt, but he wasn't sure which one of them was the person responsible for the "doing."

"Moving on for now. It looks like Lucky has a long list of food vendors committed for the weekend." Matt held up a printed list and tapped it. "If everyone could be like Lucky, I would appreciate that. I love a good list and if you can turn it in early?" Matt fanned his face with the paper. "If she wasn't married already, I'd propose."

Laughter bubbled through the room. Grant turned to see what Dante thought about that, but he was sidetracked because Mia was seated next to Lucky. Her face as she and Lucky exchanged a look was captivating.

As soon as the thought filtered through his brain, Grant wanted to bury his face in his cowboy hat. *Captivating?* That wasn't a word he used, but it was the only one that fit. Mia's expression was so open. Her eyes gleamed and those lips curved… When she locked eyes with him again, he knew he wasn't the only one feeling the attraction.

"I got her first and it's a good thing. The whole town needs Lucky right where she is. She keeps the business running, so I'd have to fight you for her." Dante pressed a kiss to Lucky's lips. Grant wondered if Mia experienced the same pang of envy he did at the way Dante and Lucky were behaving.

"Fine, fine, enough of the personal affection, please." Matt flipped through the giant binder his mother had handed off when she'd volun-told him to run the festival this year. "How is the quilt show coming, Mom?"

"Right on track! We've gotten in a few entries for this year's juried competition. The deadline is in mid-March,

so the early entries are a good sign." His mother smiled. "You're doing a fabulous job, Matty. Once we get everything ironed out, this will be the best festival yet."

Matt cleared his throat as if stalling for time to think. "Thanks, Mom. That means a lot." He tugged on the neck of his shirt before asking. "Is there anything we need to discuss before we break for refreshments?"

"What about an update on the status of the Majestic?" Walt called out. "We gonna have rooms available for rent? I got a phone call at the hardware store asking for recommendations since Bell House is all booked up already."

"I'd like to know that, too. I can pass the information along to callers. I've already got a waiting list for any cancellations." Rose Bell was seated in her usual spot, right next to his mother, but she'd removed her usual Broncos jersey and hat, so it was hard to recognize her.

The fact that she was holding hands with Patrick Hearst, Sarah and Jordan's father, was something he was going to need to discuss with someone later at great length.

"Our only holdup is the restaurant," Jordan said, "but our most recent guest, experienced travel writer Mia Romero, gave us her stamp of approval, so I'd say we'll be open for business in time for the festival. Let's get it booked up." She inhaled slowly, held that breath and then released it. "Looks like we'll be hiring, too?" Her voice squeaked on the end, as if the nerves had taken over.

Sarah squeezed her sister's hand. "We were working up a plan of our own to get some interest going in the restaurant, a cooking competition that will be broadcast live on the Cookie Queen website."

Jordan ducked her head. "We are? You're moving forward with that?" She started fanning her face. "This, the lodge, a book, Sarah?"

Sarah wrapped her arm around Jordan's shoulder and

squeezed her hard. "It's fine. I've overloaded Jordan with too many ideas all at once, but Michael's working with an LA chef to get us two competitors for a cook-off. We're going to shoot it at the lodge for one week next month. People were drawn to the Cookie Queen website to see Sadie's weekly recipe videos, so this will provide some new content. In exchange, Michael is supplying a location fee that should cover most of the siding repairs. By the time Western Days rolls around, the Majestic is going to shine." She waved her hands. "More on that to come, but I'm hoping that one of those cooks will jump at the chance to build their own kitchen at the Majestic."

Everyone in the room watched as Jordan inhaled deep breaths, held them and exhaled slowly. Eventually her face returned to its normal color.

"If the new chef's not ready to open by Western Days weekend, we'll offer breakfast pastries, coffee and juice and send everyone into town for everything else. Lucky's food vendors will offer plenty of variety." Jordan crossed her arms over her chest. "The Majestic is open for business."

Applause filtered through the room. It had been a long time coming and everyone understood what it meant to Prospect to have the lodge attracting visitors, even beyond Western Days weekend.

Grant was pleased that the meeting was going so well.

Until Jordan turned to face him. She smiled brightly. "I have the best idea for a business venture for Grant, one that will add some real shine to the Majestic's experience."

That didn't reassure him at all. He'd forgotten this part of being in Prospect. He ended up being involved in projects before he knew a thing about them, somehow.

Matt shrugged. "Any other updates?"

"What about the museum?" his mother asked. "Sounds like you might be overextended, Sarah."

Sarah rubbed her forehead. "You aren't saying anything I haven't been thinking. We've got all the displays installed, so now all I have to do is…set it up. Order items and stock a gift shop, while I also work with Michael on the displays at Cookie Queen headquarters, plan this cooking competition, negotiate sponsorship and prize money out of my cousin for these Cowboy Games, because everyone in this room knows that Cookie Queen should be an official sponsor, and help out at the lodge." Sarah huffed out a breath. "Every Hearst and Armstrong in the room and anyone else I can rope in will be involved, but it's all important to me and it will all happen before Western Days weekend."

Her expression was grimly determined.

"Let me worry about the gift shop," Prue said. "You and I can decide what to order, but I can handle the merchandising. I do well enough in my own shop. And Faye will run the cooking competition." Her delivery was so matter-of-fact, as if there was no doubt that it was the correct answer.

"Faye, who isn't here right now?" Walt drawled slowly from his spot at her side. "The Faye who is always in the Ace High because the place would fold without her?"

Prue snorted. "Looks like it's time to find a solution to that little problem, too." She nodded firmly as if it was all settled.

Grant could see that Mia's head was down as she made her notes. There was a lot happening in Prospect. Surely she'd have the story she needed without involving him in any way.

"The to-do list is long enough for now. We'll meet again next week with status updates." Matt held up the binder

and banged it on the table in front him, like a makeshift gavel. "Let's have cookies."

Grant waited for the feeding frenzy to die down before he eased over to the counter of the small kitchen. For as long as he could remember, the second floor of the Mercantile had served as the unofficial community center for the town. It was used for potlucks, planning meetings, occasional dance rehearsals and choir practices, and soon monthly Sip and Paint nights organized by his mother and Patrick Hearst, the man responsible for the large landscape over the check-in desk at the Majestic and the soft smile on Rose Bell's face. Prospect was a small place, so the crowd that showed up for the different events never changed a whole lot, but it felt different today.

That had to be because he was so aware of Mia and her location in the room.

She'd already chosen a cookie and had retreated over by the windows.

It was a testament to his mother's acting skills and the success of her veiled messages that Mia was standing alone. Why did that seem so wrong?

The answer had something to do with how Sarah and Jordan were trying not to stare at her with worried expressions. Then he noticed Lucky doing the same, and headed for Mia. The urge to warmly enfold their visitor would overpower their caution soon, so Grant had to step in. For the town's good, obviously.

"Get enough to start your article?" he asked, leaning one shoulder casually against the wall. That was his intention. Misjudging the distance, so he landed awkwardly, meant he lost some cool points, but he couldn't acknowledge that now.

She nodded. "And these cookies are incredible. I wondered what made them palomino peanut butter. It never

would have occurred to me to add white chocolate to peanut butter." Mia smiled up at him. "I guess that's why she was the Colorado Cookie Queen and I am not."

He returned her smile before he knew it was happening. "Do you enjoy baking?" Why did his voice sound like that? It was cracking as if he was a sophomore trying to ask a senior to dance.

Mia frowned. "I don't think so?" She shrugged. "I don't spend enough time in my tiny kitchen at home to practice, but these results are impossible to argue with. This morning I was paging through Sadie's cookbooks and fell in love with a lemon-drop cookie, so if I'm in town beyond tomorrow night, I may have to borrow the lodge's kitchen to give them a try."

"Good thing you'll be on your way home by Tuesday morning. The last thing you need is a cookie addiction, right?" Grant surveyed the room, well aware that he had more attention than he liked. Technically, no one was watching them, but every antenna in the room was tuned to his frequency.

When his mother popped up at his elbow, Grant did his best not to jump.

"You should take Mia over to the storage building, Grant." His mother pointed vaguely over her shoulder. "If you want to see pieces of the town's history, there's a nice collection in one place, Mia. And Grant needs to go through the various backdrops we've got stored. I know some will work for his sweet idea for the kids' photo opportunities." Then she clasped her hands together. "Oh my, I bet you've seen awesome setups in your travels. Please, you have to help us." Her firm grip on his arm convinced him his mother wasn't acting this time. She'd been struck with inspiration. "We need to pick her brain before she gets out of here."

Before he could answer, Reg McCall stepped up. "If you'd like to see this field and barn setup, I have a key. As the last remaining active sponsor of the defunct rodeo club, Sam told me to hold onto it. We made a few improvements after you left town, Grant. With some polish, it could be perfect for some kind of activity."

His mother's enthusiastic nods were easy to read.

Grant turned to Mia, but he had zero hope that she'd rescue either of them from this idea.

Mia smiled. "Do you think we can work both visits in this afternoon? I wanted to spend tomorrow morning at the library before I get my car fixed up."

Before he could answer, his mother said, "There's no time like the present. Grant, the two of you come by my apartment later. I'll make dinner." The way his mother blinked innocently while she waited for his agreement worried him. Was she moving Mia from opponent to possible matchmaking target in so obvious a manner? She touched his cheek. "Retirement has made you so helpful. Mia, I definitely want to discuss the history of Western Days with you."

Mia smoothed hair behind her ear. "Dinner sounds like a great time to do that, if you're sure you don't mind."

His mother's wry smile made him nervous.

"I love to cook for others. Ask anyone. We won't be disturbed and I have so many photos to show you." His mother turned on her heel before Mia could accept. "I'll see you at six!"

"I understand it takes a minute to catch up when my mother starts planning your life," Grant said as he touched Mia's shoulder. She was still staring at the spot his mother had already vacated. "She's always in motion."

Mia laughed. "Yeah, I get that."

"You two want to ride with me or follow behind?" Reg asked and shook the keys again.

"My truck's downstairs. Want to ride shotgun?" he asked Mia. Why was he so nervous as he watched her weigh her options and relieved when she nodded?

Before he realized what he was doing, he'd unlocked the passenger door and held it open while Mia climbed inside.

Like this was a date or they were a couple or something romantic was in the air. After he shut the door behind her, he reminded himself that this was part of the plan to keep an eye on Mia.

Nothing more.

Why was he struggling to remember that?

CHAPTER TEN

MIA KNEW THE afternoon had taken an unexpected turn because Grant seemed deep in thought as they followed Reg out of town. It was a short distance, but wide pastures immediately lined both sides of the road and Prospect's school campus, first grade through twelfth, was the only development as far as she could see.

"'Prospect School District, Home of the Wildcats.'" She read the large sign that arched over the entrance. "I wasn't sure what the mascot would be. Were you a proud Wildcat once upon a time? Football? Basketball? Math team?" She grinned at him.

"None of the above. I was always all about rodeo and horses and riding and getting out of high school so I could move on with my life." Grant pointed at the large structure a little farther down the road. It was more modern than Mia expected in Prospect, with red and white metal siding. "This is where I spent all my spare time."

"Ah, the rodeo club." Mia frowned as she tried to pull up anything she knew about high school rodeo clubs. It was a sparse pool. "That's where you learned everything you needed to be a winner?"

He glanced over at her before he parked. "A lot, yes, but it was really what kept me here in Prospect until Walt and Prue could domesticate me a little." The corner of his mouth curled as he made the joke about himself. "It was

pretty helpful to be a little wild and lack the ability to think things through when I was learning to stick in the saddle."

He slid out of the truck and Mia hurried to hop down to join him and Reg near the barn doors. She didn't want to lose this thread of the conversation.

"Reg, how did you get involved with the rodeo club?" Mia asked as she regretted not bringing her recorder. She pulled her phone out and waved it. "Okay for me to record our conversation?"

Reg's enthusiastic "Sure thing" interrupted Grant's more restrained shrug, so she started the recording even though she had no idea why.

"Grant and I were in high school together." Reg clapped Grant on the back before stepping inside to flip on the overhead lights. The wide open space lit in a wave, and Mia was impressed with the shape of the barn and the amenities. "I was never as fearless as he was, which is why I run the doctor's office and he rides on the circuit." His good natured grin was accompanied by a wink, so Mia got the impression that Reg was happy with how his life turned out.

It was clear who her best source was going to be, so Mia moved closer to Reg. "What kind of things did you do in the club?"

He waved his hands. "Pretty much what you'd imagine. We had some guys that would come in and work with us to improve techniques, we learned how to take the best care of our livestock, we trained for state competition. There were fundraisers and exhibitions. We always rode in the Western Days parade. It almost kept us all out of trouble." He raised his eyebrows at Grant and Mia wanted to know so much more about the trouble.

"After Grant graduated and started winning, he made some sizeable donations to help us improve the amenities. Better lighting, stuff like that." Reg pointed at a large sign

leaning against a line of empty stalls. "Amanda Gipson's daughter, Carly, painted this for us before she graduated. Did you know Carly?"

Grant shook his head.

"I couldn't get that girl on a horse for love nor money, but she was the best organizer I ever had. Good thing she was in love with my top team-roper, I guess." Reg sighed. "I miss the club these days."

"Why did it disband?" Mia asked as she watched Grant pace slowly down the aisle between the stalls.

"Our original sponsors are a little," Reg coughed, "gray now. Sam retired and dropped out. Walt had some health issues so he had to take a break. One or two of the guys from our years might be interested, but I haven't found the right spark to get it back up and running yet."

Mia met Reg's stare and could read the message he was broadcasting silently but so loudly there was no way to miss it. She glanced over her shoulder.

"A spark, you say?" Mia said. "Like what?"

Her lips twitched as Reg ducked his head in thanks. "If we had a big rodeo star move home and agree to help get this club back in business, I am certain I could find more help and the kids would jump at the chance."

Grant slowly shook his head as if to say he wasn't falling for it, and Mia was amused all over again at how he might put up a fight, as he had wanted to with his mother, but even she could see this writing plainly on the wall.

His involvement in the reborn rodeo club was only a matter of time.

Reg wasn't quite finished with his pitch. "Grant and I both know Travis wasn't much for competition, but I've heard through the grapevine that his foster sons, Damon and Micah, are already comfortable in the saddle. If I

could get two or even three of the Armstrongs to agree to step in, we'd be set."

Grant tipped his head back to stare up at the ceiling. Mia followed him and was impressed again with how well kept the barn was. "I think this might be the cleanest barn I've spent any time in."

"When you have kids to keep busy, you come up with plenty of chores." Reg pretended to pick up a whistle and blow it. "I coach flag football, too. You should see how nice the practice field is."

Satisfied that he'd completed his outline for the new and improved Prospect Rodeo Club, Reg motioned them out and turned off the light. After he locked up, he said, "I know Sam will be amenable to renting out the spot for your Cowboy Games. If you need to check out anything else to make your plans, you can let me know." Reg held out his hand and waited for Grant to shake, which he did. "Sorry for the ambush, but that club meant a lot to me."

"Yeah, me too." Grant ran his hand over his nape.

Mia leaned in. "When I met Sam yesterday, I got the impression he was a man who would be interested in renewing the club." It was easy to remember his happy face when he'd talked about his doctor encouraging him to get out to work some.

"Yeah, he has regular chats with Dr. Singh." Reg shrugged. "I can believe he would love to have the club to talk about again."

Grant held his hands up in surrender. "I will think about the club. That's all I can promise right now."

Reg clapped loudly in satisfaction. "You always were a smart one, Grant. I know you'll see the benefits to the kids of this town."

Mia bit her lip as she watched Grant struggle in the face of such enthusiasm. He had his concerns, but the size of the

wave was eventually going to wash them away. She hadn't known him long, but every interaction she'd had with him convinced her that he had a hard time letting people down.

"Thank you for showing me the barn. You're right." He motioned with his hand toward the pens and the large, fenced paddock next to them. "This is the right space for whatever we come up with."

"So, no actual livestock roping or herding," Mia said as she stared out over Sam's property. It wasn't impressive in the spring, but it was spacious. They'd have room to park trucks and horse trailers, set up tents for competitors and rope off an area for spectators, in addition to any course they set up.

"No, we aren't prepared to launch a rodeo," Grant turned to grin at her over his shoulder, "and please don't even hint to my mother that we have that ability. We don't. I don't."

Reg hurried back to his truck, whistling loudly.

Mia tilted her head to the side. She didn't recognize the tune.

"'You Can't Hurry Love.'" Grant rubbed his forehead. "That's the song he's whistling."

"Thank you," Mia exclaimed, "that would have bothered me for days, until I woke up in the middle of the night with the song name in my head."

His smile was attractive, as always, but she could tell he had a lot on his mind as they slid into the truck. This time he let her get her own door, which was the smartest choice, but she missed that old fashioned sign of respect.

One of those sweet things a cowboy might do for the woman he was courting.

Courting? When Mia realized she'd stepped back in time to pull that word up, her eyebrows shot up. Luckily,

Grant was still deep in thought over everything Reg had laid out about the high school club.

She cleared her throat in the silence as they went back into Prospect. "How long will it take you to get comfortable with this idea of leading the rodeo club for Prospect's next generation?" When his hands tightened on the steering wheel, she swallowed the smile that bloomed. He could see it was inevitable, too. When had she learned to read him so clearly?

After he parked next to the Mercantile, he turned to face her. "Think you've got a read on me, don't you?"

"I've met your family, traveled your hometown, understand your career, and seen firsthand how you treat me, an adversary who might discover something you don't want to see the light of day." Mia shrugged. "I can't complain about your treatment. Changing my tire, finding me a place to stay, saving me from being the awkward wallflower standing all alone. A club that meant so much to you? One you can rebuild by doing things you love?" She squeezed his arm and let him take her hand instead of pulling away. "This is an equation anyone could solve."

"There's a variable you're still missing," Grant said as he slid out of the truck. Mia followed him to a building across the street from the Mercantile and waited as he unlocked the door.

"I can't believe you've got me making math analogies," he muttered.

Mia grinned as he opened the door. When they stepped inside, she could see what appeared to have been an office space at one point. He motioned at another door. "This is the bank vault. My mother has a storage system for all the quilts that have won the Western Days quilt show over the years, stored in sealed plastic containers and labeled with the winner's name, the quilt name, and the year. She ro-

tates the quilts on display at the festival each year and the records rival a Fortune 500 company's accounting system." One corner of his mouth tilted up. "You do not have security clearance for that room."

Mia knew she was getting closer to hearing his whole story and considered her options to find that missing variable. Her only solid choice was the direct one.

"If you'd tell me whatever it is that you don't want me to find out, whatever it is that is important enough to involve the whole town to keep quiet, I'd be able to write a much better feature on Western Days." Mia's eyes held a challenge.

If this terrible, secret thing was no longer between them, what would change? Mia wasn't sure, but there was something about him that made the answer important.

And if she was reading Grant's face correctly, he was seriously considering…something. She couldn't say for sure that he was weighing his options in laying out the truth about…whatever it was he was hiding, because his dark eyes were hard to read, but he wanted to trust her with something. She followed him to the jumbled back wall of the large open room.

Grant pulled his hat off and set it down on a table there. Did he do that hair-ruffling thing to confuse her on purpose? If so, he was diabolical, and if not, he was too powerful for his own good.

"How much did you know about my background before you rolled into town, Mia?" He studied her face. As much as she was testing the waters between them, so was he.

"Not much. I knew the name and I had seen photos of you, but I don't follow the standings closely. The magazine's staff is pretty small. We rely a lot on freelance writers and photographers, but I overhear phone calls, meetings, things like that. I never put Grant Armstrong

in Prospect, Colorado, until we met on the side of the road." Mia paused as she considered what that meant to her news-tracking skills. If she was a real reporter, would that connection have been immediate? "While I was thumbing through the most recent copy of *The Way West*, on newsstands this week, I noticed the advertisement for Western Days." She held her hands out to demonstrate that it was a splashy two-page ad. "The centennial festival, back and bigger than ever. I needed a story for the May issue. It seemed like the universe was sending me a road sign. I pay attention to those gifts, right?" She turned on her imaginary blinker as if she was exiting the highway.

"Plus, I was supposed to finish my college degree this semester, but I forgot to register. My mother was vocally unhappy about that and I'm honestly tired of having the conversation, so it seemed a perfect time to hit the road to do research."

He frowned. "You forgot to register."

"I don't need a degree for the job I'm already doing. My mother views it as a way to prove I can run the magazine. An exciting story could do exactly the same thing and boost advertising dollars at the same time." She shrugged, certain he was picking up on her hints.

"You want to write. You don't want to go to school." Grant took a step forward. "I get that. My whole life improved once my high school diploma was behind me and I could live life instead of studying."

"I actually like the studying part," Mia confessed, and giggled when he frowned at her as if she'd switched languages suddenly.

He started pulling dust sheets off so they could see what was underneath. "Do you want to run a magazine?"

Mia watched the muscles in his back work as he moved

down the long line. Of all the Western Days work assignments, this one had some perks.

Then he turned to stare at her and she realized she had dropped the conversational ball. "Maybe not, but what else can I do? Let the magazine my grandfather built and loved just…disappear?" Understanding lit his eyes. That made it harder to face him. She inhaled slowly. "I'll pay bills and file taxes and paperwork and so many millions of tiny, similar, annoying paper cuts to keep it going."

To avoid showing Grant more of her own soft spots, Mia stood and wandered over to the closest stack of large wooden pieces. It was a horse with what had once been a flowing mane attached. "If you have a wig around, this would be a cute backdrop for your kids." She flipped through the smaller pieces until she uncovered the final one. It was big, maybe six feet tall at the highest point.

"Is this a schoolhouse?" It was painted to suggest a log cabin, but there was also a large bell at the top. In the dusty recesses of her brain, she remembered some kind of TV show or movie where the teacher tugged on a rope to ring a bell and call the kids to school.

"Yeah. It's big enough that it could work for something." Grant moved closer to hold his hands out to get an idea of the width. "We'll have to brace it to get it to stand tall, but it might be perfect."

Mia gazed down the length of the storage room. "I bet there are other gems in here. Want to keep going, or do you want to bare your soul and your secrets to me?" The side-eye he shot her was so unexpected that she chuckled aloud.

It felt good.

"Fine. We'll keep going." Mia wasn't sure exactly when she lost focus on slipping under Grant's skin, but a couple of hours later, they had created stacks of pieces that might be reused. There were multiple horses in different styles, but

Grant suggested repainting them all to try to use every one. In addition to the school house, they found a large covered-wagon backdrop, and a jail with a forlorn prisoner peeking through the bars in the windows.

"Western Days was darker than I remembered, I guess." Grant shook his head as he tapped the miserable face. "Probably a cattle rustler. Nobody likes a thief."

Mia was laughing along with him, but she was also watching him closely enough to see the emotions flit across his face. Amusement was replaced by... The closest guess she could come up with was worry.

Their conversation had been easy. As if they were old friends.

"I've been in the magazine a few times, here and there." Grant gripped the jail cutout and moved it to their "use" stack. "You're pretty sharp. I'm having a hard time convincing myself meeting you on the side of the road was a happy accident."

"If you're about to accuse me of flattening my own tire to lure you into my web, please join me in the real world, Grant." Mia sighed. "I've always been luckier than I deserve. I've confessed being a college dropout, my general lack of ambition and hard-hitting reporting ability. Does it help to know it's the second time I've quit a degree close to the end? I'm only on the fringes of the news department. She protects the magazine and me, mainly by keeping us separated." She leaned forward. "But for the life of me, I can't remember seeing a single feature on Grant Armstrong or his close-knit family of adopted brothers living in Prospect, home of an exciting local festival."

Mia wrinkled her nose. "What you don't know is that whatever it is that you don't want told... There's not much chance my mother would let me be the one to write about it anyway."

That caught his attention. "Even if you uncovered it? Why is that?"

"A lifetime of never hitting the mark?" Mia knew that telling him this was another roll of the dice. If she wanted to be the reporter he trusted to tell his story, impressing him with her skills and experience would have been a smarter route. "I don't know if a successful, championship rodeo star can understand this, but my mother had high expectations for her only daughter. Instead, she ended up with one who can't change her own flat tire or get a college degree."

"I can only do one of those things myself." Grant grunted. "I'm guessing that's more common than not. Your mother good with a jack, is she?"

Mia shook her head. "No, but she finished the degrees her father asked her to do and she stepped up to learn the business side of the magazine right after. She would tell you that success requires sacrifice, doing things you don't like to earn rewards later."

He brushed a smudge of dust off her cheek. "Yeah, seems I've heard that sentiment around here a time or two."

"Of course you have. Reading a decade of newspaper articles has shown me the Armstrongs understand that." And it wasn't that Mia wouldn't make sacrifices for the things that mattered to her, but she wanted those decisions to make sense to her. A college degree she didn't need would show obedience but how would it change Mia's life? The magazine was her past and her future, no matter what happened this semester in health and wellness.

Mia leaned forward to touch his arm, certain she was going too far. "Stay with me. I know she loves me, right? She will tell me she did all that hard, boring work because she loves the magazine and her father and me. Even though

she doesn't understand me, I believe that my mother loves me. Sometimes I can't understand why."

Mia knew she'd jumped right into the oversharing deep end. There was no way she was coming out of this conversation with his trust, but then he clasped her hand and held on tight. Since she knew clinging to this bucking ride would turn into real attraction if she wasn't careful, Mia almost pulled her hand free.

But it was nice to have his warm, reassuring hand wrapped around hers.

"Out of all the things you could have said, I don't know how you picked the single collection of words to cut right through all my defenses. You know your mother loves you, but you aren't sure why." He traced his thumb over the back of her hand absentmindedly while Mia did her best to ignore the effect his light touch had on her nerves. She was comforted and energized at the same time. "I could say that about my whole family sometimes. Worse than that, it's my own fault. I've spent a lifetime being a burr under their saddles, agitating when things got too quiet around here. How do I have the right to ask if they trust me now?"

He narrowed his eyes at her. "We may need to go back to that 'off-the-record' status if I start to cry into my hat, confessing my innermost wounds."

Mia couldn't stop the blooming smile. "As long as you swear not to tell my secret, I won't tell yours. We have made these messes, haven't we? We'll have to muddle through on our own, but it's nice to have company on the journey."

He stared down at her hand, tracing one finger back and forth. "When you're building a brand as a bad boy, heartwarming stories of the amazing couple who adopted you from the foster care system and the impressive brothers who round out the rest of the family don't fit the tale."

Mia wasn't sure why, but she believed this was a piece of the puzzle she was trying to assemble. She needed more pieces to fill out the border. "Who decided being the bad boy was the right way to go?"

Grant tipped his head back. "Which time?" His wry grin landed somewhere in her chest with a warm splash. He was nearly irresistible like this.

"When I first showed up at the Rocking A, Wes and Clay were settled. They were solid, you know? Smart. Conscientious. Good in school. Travis and I arrived not too far apart, but he was mostly an alley cat at that point, roaming around on his lonesome…unless I prodded and made him square off against me. I wanted him to be my… What's the right word?"

"Friend?" Mia asked and laughed at how he grunted in response.

"You didn't want to do this all alone. I get that. You and Travis could tackle it together and have each other to lean on." Mia moved closer and tangled her fingers through his, intent on keeping Grant talking.

"I couldn't be all open with my emotions and ask him to be my friend because I was lonely and worried about this new place. As a teenage boy who'd grown up where being seen was dangerous and no one ever complained or cried about it or they were sorry." Grant rolled his eyes, inviting her to laugh with him, but Mia couldn't. It might be something he could poke fun at now, but it was so easy to imagine how scared she might be in the same spot. "So I picked at Travis until the older boys decided to 'teach' us or 'guide' us, which meant being disgustingly good examples of all that is right in the world, and then Travis joined me—the two of us against the model boys." Grant covered his heart with his hand. "Fortunately, I was very good at provoking reactions. Always have been, most likely always

will be. Never met a dare I wouldn't take or an argument I wouldn't fight or a horse I couldn't ride."

Mia wasn't sure what reaction he expected, but his stillness told her he was waiting for something.

"And you took all that from Prospect to the rodeo and you started winning." Mia tilted her head back. "Why would you change it then, since it was working?"

He pointed at her. "Exactly. That wise-cowboy philosophy says 'if it ain't broke, don't fix it.'"

Mia pursed her lips. "Did a cowboy come up with that?"

Grant wagged his head. "If it wasn't a cowboy who started it, we definitely perfected it. So, when Red Williams started working with me, training me on how to talk to interviewers and when to make a statement by way of a splashy spectacle to keep everyone's attention, I listened. I was good at being bad, so the bad boy character was the right way to go." He grimaced. "Guess it's not a character, now is it? Genetic, most likely."

She had no idea where this trail was leading but they were getting close.

Mia knew that because his muscles were tense as she held on to his hand.

"Could be," Mia said slowly. "But I keep telling myself that I'm in charge of where the road takes me. Someday, I might need that college degree. There's nothing that has convinced me yet that I can't get it if I need it. Figuring out my job and my mother… That problem's harder, but it doesn't mean I should change who I am to please her." She realized she was getting offtrack and shook her head. "But I don't know that a bad boy would be digging through dusty storage to find pieces that could be reused for a kids' photo op and a competition that he's been forced to organize to help his hometown." Her lips twitched as he frowned at her.

"Even that cattle rustler in the jail had a hometown, Mia. Not sure that's a solid character witness."

Mia giggled in relief. Things had gotten so serious between them that it felt good to return to solid footing. "My stomach is telling me it's time for dinner. Do we have enough backdrops here to please Prue?"

When he nodded, she turned to head out to the sidewalk and waited for him to lock the door behind them. The fact that he never let go of her hand meant something, but Mia was too afraid to consider what it might be.

CHAPTER ELEVEN

GRANT HAD NEVER expected to spend so much time with Mia after the planning meeting at the Mercantile, but as he walked with her toward his mother's apartment, he realized how much he'd enjoyed her company. Dancing around the story between them was getting harder.

Because he wanted to share the whole truth with her.

The way Prospect's old town took on a romantic rosy tinge as the sun set didn't help that. Shadows lined the street and it was so quiet. They might be the only two people in the world. Since her fingers were tangled with his, that thought filled him with... Peace. It was the only name for the emotion that Grant could find. Had he ever experienced peace like this?

Mia brushed her free hand down the front of her over-sized sweatshirt. "At times like this, I regret not packing for a longer trip. Luckily, I brought every baggy sweatshirt that I own, in order to make a sloppy first impression. My mother would be proud of that, too."

The way she blew out a raspberry and held out her arm made him think she was making a joke at her own expense. "You're dressed exactly right for the job you're doing. We were just digging through a century of dust back there."

She brushed bangs off her forehead. "When I come back for Western Days, I'll bring my good jeans. The whole town will be impressed then."

"I like this Mia." He squeezed her shoulder. "But you

can count on me to say that about whichever Mia you show me next, too."

She froze as she watched his face. Then she exhaled so loudly her bangs ruffled. "Grant Armstrong, cover-model cowboy, likes my sweatshirt? This is some kind of tactic, right? You're trying to throw me off the trail of whatever it is you're hiding." She tapped his chest with one finger. "I'm on to you."

He wrapped his hand around the poking finger. "I was about to accuse you of sneaking under my guard by being all cute and soft and aggressive with that pointer finger, so now where do we go?"

They were both smiling when she stepped back.

Mia opened her mouth to say something but must have thought better of it. He immediately wanted to know what question she'd reconsidered. "You can ask it, whatever it is. I might not answer it, but asking won't offend me." He wanted to tell her about himself. It was a weird urge and it could get him into trouble if he wasn't careful.

"Prospect is special. Do you have other family elsewhere?" Mia asked and then wrapped her arm around his. "I'm sorry. You don't have to answer. I don't know much about the foster care system."

He questioned whether this was something he wanted Mia to understand. Since his family's reaction to his secret was top of mind still, he said, "I do have an older brother, but we were separated when my mother was sent to jail for her third driving-under-the-influence charge. He was already eighteen, so he didn't go into the system. I did, and I made sure to make three different families regret my stays, mainly by running away. When I got caught, I got a fresh start. And the only time I didn't run was at the Rocking A. Most of that was Travis's fault." He shook his

head at her muffled laugh. "It's like once I met the kid, I forgot how to be wild all on my own."

"Sounds like you owe him. A lot." Mia squeezed his arm.

"I do." Grant owed them all so much. "It's the kind of debt you never repay."

She stared into his eyes and he wondered if she would pursue that unintended bit of honesty or do them both a favor and let it go.

"Family who will not stop supporting us or loving us. How did we get so lucky?" Mia asked.

It was a good question, one he didn't have an answer for, so he returned to the business at hand. "Cowboy Games. Some kind of riding course, target practice. What do you think?"

Mia chuckled. "Your mother likes to aim for the stars, I know. It seems like that place is perfect for a competition. If you had a rodeo club in place, they could help you run it, too."

Grant groaned. "Relentless."

Mia bumped his shoulder with his. "Just saying."

He sighed and produced his phone to tap out notes. "Cowboy Games first, rodeo club later. Maybe. I need to get Sam's buy-in first, then talk to the school administrators." He rubbed his forehead. "Oh, and can't forget the budget spreadsheet."

Mia was quiet as she strolled slowly along the fence line. He could tell by the way her face changed swiftly that she was deep in thought.

"An obstacle course with target shooting, using the backdrops we salvaged, may save you a bit of extra construction." She bit her lip as she faced him.

"Doesn't sound very impressive, does it? I'm not sure how we're going to attract a crowd of stars like my mother hopes, especially in two months."

She nodded but didn't explain whatever it was that caused her eyes to momentarily light up before she shook her head.

Grant was surprised to discover that he didn't like that, being shut out of whatever inspired thought lit her eyes like that. He wanted Mia to trust him with those sparks.

To get there, he'd have to tell her everything. Grant forced himself to let go of her hand as he raised his own to knock on his mother's front door. Whatever came next between him and Mia would be decided by his own choice to trust her with the story that had been keeping him awake at night for months.

So much of where he went from here depended on the answer to one question.

How much faith did he have in Mia Romero?

MIA WAS STILL staring at her empty hand when Prue Armstrong yanked the door open. The wreath covered in pink-and-red hearts swung wildly before Prue caught it. "All right, Valentine's decorations. Settle down." Then she waved them both inside. "Come in, come in. You kids ever wonder why we have mistletoe for Christmas but nothing for kissing around Valentine's Day? That's a missed opportunity right there."

She hurried back to her small corner kitchen and picked up a ladle. "Been craving a nice beef stew for a week or so, and this morning I gave in. Dumped everything in my slow cooker first thing so I'd be sure to have a hearty dinner. Might not be fancy enough for guests but it's right for family."

Family? Mia raised her eyebrows at Grant but he only shook his head in resignation.

Prue pointed at two seats across the counter from her. "Only got seats for two, but that's fine. Perfect for roman-

tic rendezvous when I need 'em, and tonight I'll hop up on the counter."

As Mia slid into the chair, she noticed Grant's hand was loosely clenched, like hers.

Mia missed the warmth of his palm next to hers. Was he experiencing the same sensation? As if they'd both discovered something new and neither wanted to return to being empty.

"How many romantic dinners for two are you having, Mama?" Grant drawled. Mia hid her smile by picking up the digital frame that was scrolling old family photos. He took his job as the troublemaker seriously.

"Stay out of my business, Grant. Did y'all accomplish a lot in the storage room?" his mother asked as she dished up dinner and plopped a hank of crusty bread on each of their saucers.

Grant started naming an inventory of the pieces they found to use and the trip they'd made to the high school. As he answered his mother's rapid-fire questions, Mia studied the photos. Intrigued by a group shot of four teenage boys, she pulled it closer. Each of them was lanky, long arms and legs, as if they'd sprouted up quickly and the rest of their bodies had to catch up. If she looked closely enough, it was easy to pick Grant out from the quartet. Clay and Wes had wider grins, Travis stood apart from the group and Grant had his arm wrapped around his shoulders as if he was anchoring him in place. They were heartbreakingly young in the photo and had already been through so much. The desire to ask a million different questions about his childhood surprised her.

Before she was ready, the photo advanced. She lost track of whatever it was that Prue and Grant discussed as she watched ranch photos morph into school pictures and candids of each boy. Matt eventually joined the fam-

ily, and Prue and Walt were scattered throughout. It was a slideshow of the Armstrong family through the years, and Mia was charmed.

Whatever story she'd told herself about them based on the newspaper clippings and her brief encounters was fully illustrated as one frame followed another. Small-town neighbors. Prospect leaders. Good kids who became successful men. A loving couple who changed the lives of their sons for the better.

The most recent photos were from Christmas. Sarah and Jordan appeared here and there, along with a beautiful redhead she had yet to meet. Then a picture of Grant shuffled up. There were two younger boys, each one hanging over Grant's shoulders as he propped a T-shirt over his chest. Funcle was in bold letters with The Fun Uncle underneath. The kids were proud of their gift, and the broad grin on Grant's face changed his appeal from brooding and handsome to too much.

Way too much handsome.

There was no cowboy hat or serious expression. His happiness was on full display, right there in that moment.

She loved this photo because she knew there was probably not another one like it.

"When the renovations commenced at the ranch, my boys took down a lifetime of photos. I had them lining the hallway in my house. In my husband's house? My ex-husband left them up after I moved out?" Prue shook her head uncertainly and dipped her spoon back into the bowl. At some point, she'd settled herself next to the sink and seemed comfortable there. "Anyway, they gave me that rotating picture frame, most likely to keep me from hanging all those photos up somewhere else that would contribute to the scarring they still carry from their awkward phases."

"I was wondering which of the brothers was the fun-

cle. I would not have picked Grant." Mia wrinkled her nose at him.

"That is because you have not seen my gaming system." He pointed at the frame. "As soon as I can wrestle it away from Damon and Micah, I will show it to you."

Mia reluctantly set the frame back down and picked up her spoon. Then she noticed that Grant had finished eating. Had she been looking at the photos for that long? "I'm sorry. I missed some of the conversation." Her first bite of the stew landed with a swell of pleasure. "Whoa. I should have been paying closer attention to the food."

Prue laughed. "No harm done. Besides, I'm proud of my boys. Warms my heart to show them off. That little smile on your face as you watched the slideshow was the kind of reaction I need."

"Even from the dangerous reporter in town?" Mia ate two bites before she could add, "Travel writer. I'm not a reporter. Yet." But I could be, she tacked on mentally. If she got the chance, she could do something great.

She managed to tear her attention away from dinner long enough to find Prue watching her closely.

"Mia has some inspiration for our Cowboy Games, Mom," Grant said as he hooked his arm over the back of her chair. "Don't know what it is, but I can't wait to hear it."

She'd intended to keep her ideas to herself. After too many story pitches that had been shot down or co-opted, she'd learned to pick and choose her opportunities.

But the way both Prue and Grant were waiting convinced her to go for it.

"Fine. Have you ever thought about building a 'Western competition unlike any other'?" She waved her arms grandly to punctuate her idea.

Grant tipped his head to the side. "I wouldn't know how to go about building one of those, so no, I haven't."

Prue leaned forward. "I am intrigued. Go on."

"Cowboys expect horse riding and shooting." Mia raised her eyebrows. "What if you gave them something else entirely? Wild-card events? I was trying to think what might make Prospect's Western Days stand out from all the other small towns scattered across the West, who have parades and craft competitions and livestock shows. Like you could have a relay race scattering hay bales. On foot. Or you could do a Dutch-oven cooking contest, best meal and cup of coffee wins so many points. Western life wasn't only about cutting herds and sitting on a horse." She shrugged. "Western life had a whole list of hard work that is ripe for competition."

Grant studied her face as he thought about her suggestion.

"Repairing a fence. Mucking out a stall. Breaking ice in the pond. Chopping wood for the fire. Washing clothes in a tub and hanging them on the line in the shortest time. Best cowboy serenades around the campfire." She counted items off on her fingers as she named them. "Instead of professional cowboys who ride the rodeo circuit, you could recruit real men and women who work cattle and award good prize money. Coed teams, even. The judges could be stars instead."

"Turn our idea on its head," Grant murmured.

The Armstrongs' long pause triggered the uncertainty again. Mia scraped the bottom of her bowl with her spoon and wished she hadn't eaten quite so quickly. Now she had no reason to pretend not to be paying attention.

When Mia's nervous swallow made an obnoxiously loud gulp, she wanted to disappear in a cloud of embarrassed smoke.

"Or not. Just spit balling. That's a thing I do, throw out ideas that no one asked for. People don't generally appre-

ciate it, either." Mia shrugged. "Don't worry about telling me all the whys and hows this won't work. Not necessary."

"That's the thing… I think it will. It might even be genius. No one in Prospect wants to do things the same way other places do if we can help it." Prue's beautiful grin convinced Mia her idea might be the winner all three of them wanted.

Grant squeezed her shoulder and the instant shot of heat filled Mia with a jittery, excited awareness.

The admiration on his face was overwhelming. He murmured, "I might be coming around to your way of thinking about how this universe works if you let it."

Her eyebrows shot up. "No way! Not practical Grant Armstrong?"

"I can't deny your timing is suspicious," he said as stared into her eyes, "but you are proving to be the kind of gift I had no idea I needed, Mia Romero."

The flush that immediately covered her cheeks was embarrassing, especially when she glanced over at Prue to see Grant's mother watching her closely.

"Seems like the travel writer had some good input. I love it." Prue leaned back to cross her arms over her chest. "Might have changed my opinion on Mia Romero, too."

Mia straightened in her chair. "In a good way?" She wasn't as experienced with someone accepting one of her ideas and giving her credit for it at the same time.

Prue laughed and winked at her. "Only one little thing stood between me and you being the best of friends, honey." She motioned with her head toward Grant. "Overcoming that was never gonna be easy, but I underestimated you."

Mia grinned at Grant. It sounded like his mother was ready to pick Mia over her son. It was unclear how one good idea could accomplish that, but while she was sitting

in Prue's kitchen and contemplating asking for a second bowl of stew, Mia wasn't going to ask difficult questions.

"In fact, I think you should tell her everything, Grant." Prue opened a large container from the shelf near her elbow. "About why you left the circuit."

Grant hesitated. Was he about to argue?

His jaw clenched and his mother added, "Give her a chance. Let's see what she says."

Then he raised his eyebrows.

Prue held up her hands. "Me? Part of the wallpaper. You won't even know I'm here."

Mia worried about making too big a reaction and scaring the moment away, so she shifted slowly in her seat to face Grant directly. "Give me a shot. I'm listening."

She reached for his hand and forced herself to wait patiently.

The loud clatter of the plastic container on the counter didn't interrupt their moment, but Grant's lips twitched as they shared some amusement at their "invisible" audience.

"The Bad Boy of Bronc Busting." Grant scratched his chin. "All thanks to Red Williams. He taught me which bars to skip, which women to avoid, which questions to answer and how, and at every step, his advice paid off." Grant cleared his throat but he didn't let go of her hand. "Rodeo's kinda like one big, dysfunctional family, right? You're all traveling from one stop to the next, but the faces don't change that much. You get to know each other. Trust each other." He huffed out a breath. "And I was as successful as I always knew I would be. Growing up, I'd have told you I was going to win whatever event I entered."

Mia wasn't sure where he was going with this, but the pain on his face worried her. "And you were right, but you decided to leave because…"

"I left because I recently heard my mentor, my man-

ager, the man whose steps I followed almost like my own father… I overheard him and my best friend discussing this scheme they had been running to get me to the top by convincing other riders to…falter. Lose just enough time on their rides that Red and Trey could also bet on my first-place finish and come out with a nice payday all around. I don't know how many people were involved, but Trey was worried it was about to come out. Red reassured him that it would be easy enough to convince the world the scheme was all my idea. That's what a bad boy would do, right? Cheat to win?"

Mia laughed because she expected there to be more to the story. When he remained silent, Mia said, "And you were thrown out or threatened with possible charges because you punched him in his lying mouth. That's the end of the story?"

Grant shook his head slowly. "It's like the boy who cried wolf. I've done a bunch of silly stunts. I'm convinced they're right. People would accept their version over mine."

"He thought his family would believe that he was involved with such a grift," Prue said, scoffing from her spot at the counter. She'd moved closer to lean her elbows and rest her chin on her hand. "Didn't tell us what was going on until this suspect travel writer rolled into town. We needed to know if you were here snooping for proof for that story while also handing you a barrel of Chamber of Commerce advertising for the town and Western Days."

Mia closed her eyes as she realized the universe was pulling strings again to land her in exactly the right place at the right time. "I only came to research Western Days. Then all your espionage and public theatrical displays tipped me to the existence of something else."

Prue plopped the plastic container now filled with stew on the counter. "This is for you. Take it out to the Majestic

and have another bowl with Sarah and Jordan. I'll wrap up the bread to go with it."

Mia watched as Grant rolled his head on his shoulders to try to relax.

"What next?" Mia asked.

"What do you suggest?" both Armstrongs asked at the same time.

Grant frowned at his mother and she held up her hands in surrender.

Mia bit her lip as she reviewed their options. "Do nothing, because the story will come out or it won't, but then you'll have the threat of discovery, and an investigation always looming and what would happen to your wins and your record. You're innocent, so there's no proof of your involvement, no matter what story Red might spin. If you don't expose Red, he may still be running the scheme, keeping other good riders from winning fair and square. You Armstrongs strike me as men and women who dislike cheaters like that." She watched the photos slide by in the frame as she thought some more. "Or you can strike first. Tell the story to someone who will publish it in one of the industry's most respected magazines for rodeo news. Investigating might take time, but you could have your truth out there in the next issue of *The Way West*."

Mia watched how his frown changed from worried to dissatisfied to concerned… It was a lot of movement for one frown. "You wanted a third option, I'm guessing."

"I came up with those two on my own." His disgruntled mutter was punctuated by a squeeze of her hand and his mother's snort.

"Now that I know the background, there might be a third," Mia said. "If the right person investigated the story, you might be able to avoid being connected to it at all. I hear the next big competition is in Utah." She bit her lip

as she wondered what kind of excuse she could invent for nosing around behind the scenes.

Then she considered how much trouble it would be to dodge Casey Donaldson the whole time she was hunting for sources.

"Too bad you can't hang around, Mia. I love your idea for the games. I bet the two of us could put up some real big shenanigans by April. People would talk about Western Days in all fifty states, Canada and Mexico." Prue put the leftovers in a tote bag displaying the name of her shop, Handmade. "Come into the store before you go. I want to say goodbye, 'mkay?"

Mia nodded and accepted Prue's hug.

"This was lovely, Prue. Thank you for giving me a chance to win you over." Mia hated to leave, but she was so relieved that she and Grant and every Armstrong and Hearst by association had cleared the suspicion they had about her. She was also sad that she would be leaving town so soon.

In the back of her mind, she was churning through ideas to convince her mother that she needed to go to Utah instead of returning home and how she would wriggle her way into Red Williams's inner circle from the travel desk. The universe would have some heavy lifting to do to make this story come together quickly.

As they slowly walked back toward the Mercantile, where they'd both parked before the meeting, Mia and Grant were silent.

"I'll follow you to the lodge." Grant nodded as she started shaking her head. "I live next door, Mia. This is not out of my way. Even if it was, I want to make sure you're safe."

Mia sighed. "Fine. Thank you. I do tend to trust things

to work out. Sometimes it would be nice to have someone watching over me to make sure they do."

"I know what you mean." Grant stepped forward until they were close enough to touch. "Thank you for listening."

Mia smiled at him. "All off-the-record, of course."

"I hope you mean that." His lips curved before he pressed a gentle kiss to her lips. When she wrapped her arms around him, he kissed her again, deeper. It was a new kind of kiss for Mia, one that she wanted more of, one that spoke to his steadfast character and meeting her where she was. They fit.

"What a kiss. And from a man who doesn't fully trust me," Mia said softly. That little wrinkle should absolutely bother her, but she trusted him, so her own lips were ready to go.

If she wasn't careful, her heart would follow.

He urged her into the car. "Right behind you."

She was dazed as she started the ignition. There was no denying the new feeling of trusting Grant Armstrong to keep her safe.

Mia wished she had time to get used to it. When they reached the lodge, he pulled up next to her and rolled the window down. "Have a good night, Mia. Thank you for everything you did today."

She wanted to get out and kiss him. It wouldn't be too hard. She'd have to stretch, but it was possible. Or she could go around and hop into his front seat and kiss him there.

"We both have plenty to think about tonight," Grant said softly before one corner of his mouth curled up. He wasn't a big talker, but the more minutes she spent with him, the easier it was to read his eyes. He was thinking about kissing, too.

And they both understood why it wasn't a good idea.

She'd be headed out of Prospect the next day…or she could stretch it another twenty-four hours? Thirty-two?

Jordan was framed in the lodge's doorway. Her audience convinced Mia to slide out of her car. "Good night, Grant. Let's talk tomorrow."

He nodded, and she went inside.

"Is that Prue's beef stew?" Jordan asked as she took the tote bag. "And I smell bread."

Sarah poked her head through the opening to the restaurant. "We have bowls."

Mia laughed as Jordan towed her toward the restaurant's kitchen, where they heated up the stew, divided it and the bread evenly, and then moved to one of the tables with the best view of the lake. Moonlight gleamed across the dark water. "Even the night view is spectacular," Mia murmured.

Both sisters agreed, but they didn't take a break from eating until spoons were scraping the bottoms of the bowls. Then Sarah propped her elbow on the table. "Grant told you everything, right?"

Mia blinked as she tried to figure out how Sarah could possibly know that. "Did Prue call you while I was on the way home?"

Jordan grinned. "Home. I like that." She patted Mia's hand. "No, Sarah tried to convince the family that you would be a help in this situation, while we were arguing over breakfast at the Rocking A. She generally believes the best about people."

Mia leaned back. "But you had your doubts?"

Jordan pursed her lips. "Not doubts, exactly, but I'm careful about who I trust with my family. I wanted my sister to be right, if that counts for anything."

Mia finished her bread as she considered that. "Okay. I'll accept that."

"Sure am glad I don't have to keep my distance from you anymore. It's been a struggle." Jordan wiped her brow dramatically.

"It was one meal, Jordan. What an epic battle," her sister drawled.

"Thank you." Jordan pretended to bow.

"I didn't enjoy it, either. I almost called my mother." Mia stared up at the ceiling and pondered the horror that might have unleashed. Calling Casey had been bad enough.

They all giggled at Mia's tone.

"I wish I had better options." The urge to share how much she wanted to be the hero for Grant and the Armstrongs surprised her. She hadn't known Jordan or Sarah for long, but she believed they might support her slowly evolving plan to head for Utah, wait for the universe to unravel the cheating scandal while she was there, and write up the most amazing expose that reignited the magazine's readership, exonerated Grant clearly from any part in the scheme, and made it possible for her to kiss Grant without either one of them having to navigate any trust issues.

It was a lot to ask from a travel writer, but the part of Mia that expected things to work out was almost sure it would happen exactly that way.

Mia picked her bowl up and followed Jordan and Sarah into the kitchen. The vanilla scent that accompanied her trip this time didn't bother her. In fact, it was building her faith in the existence of the Majestic's ghost.

After the dishes were loaded in the dishwasher, Jordan wiped her hands on a dishcloth. "Tonight let's brainstorm a way to keep Mia in town. I don't want you to leave."

Mia loved the warmth that filtered through her to hear Jordan say such a thing. It was sweet to be so welcome. Her mother would say Mia should be in Billings, but they didn't spend much more time together when that happened.

They had made it through the lobby when Sarah said, "Oh, I already know the answer to that one."

Mia stopped in her tracks. "You do?"

Sarah grinned. "Yeah. All it'll take is one hardheaded cowboy."

It was impossible to misunderstand what she meant.

"I can't leave the magazine. To hear my mother tell it, she's only keeping the magazine open for me, to pass it along. And I like *The Way West*. I was meant to write." Mia believed that completely.

"I don't have an answer for the magazine, but you can write anywhere, especially if there's a cowboy next door who keeps you coming back. What if the universe is already working that out, Mia?" Sarah wrapped her arm around Mia's shoulder. "If Sadie were here, I would suspect her of leading us all to this spot. I can't figure out how she's doing it now, but I'm also not putting it past her."

Jordan chuckled under her breath. "Sadie always was two steps ahead of us, but managing this would be impossible even for her." Then she stopped. "It would be, wouldn't it?"

Mia shrugged. "We'll wait patiently for more information from whoever is pulling the strings."

Sarah smiled. "Waiting. It's a nice concept, Mia, but I've never met a Hearst who excelled at it."

CHAPTER TWELVE

GRANT WAS STILL thinking about his conversation with Mia from the night before on Monday morning. The day had dawned crisp and cold; it was a relief to give up on pretending to sleep. The old bottom bunk he'd claimed when he'd returned home was never comfortable, but going back and forth in his mind about trusting Mia had battled with the memory of her kiss until he was worn out.

He'd expected everyone to accept the worst about him, and it turned out no one did. Apart from himself. At some point, he was going to have to come to terms with that fact.

But that was a long-term project.

Unfortunately, that didn't mean there would be no consequences if the story broke. Unless he proved his innocence completely, his history would always cast a shadow. Some people would probably always wonder if he'd been a part of the cheating scandal since he'd benefited from it.

That shadow would attach itself to the Armstrong name, too. That was unacceptable.

His sleepless night had picked up a third item on the list of things to worry over. First, his career.

Second, Mia, who'd separated herself from the problem of keeping Red's scheme under wraps to rightly stand on her own two feet and asked a different kind of question. He had a strange, empty spot in his chest, brought on by telling her good night the evening before instead of kissing her again.

And now, third, he was considering all the things he could do to help kids through the Prospect Rodeo Club if it was resurrected.

He wanted to give that a shot because it had meant so much to him as a youngster. That club had given him a place to shine, build confidence and helped make him who he was.

But it was easy to imagine it crashing in flames if his star was tarnished by cheating.

To find a distraction, he offered to drive Micah and Damon to school. The way Travis and Wes had stared at him, with their dropped jaws, from their spots at the breakfast table, still rankled.

After seeing the boys on their way and avoiding most of the other parents, it struck him that he had another stop to make. "I'm helpful. I volunteer to do nice things," he muttered to himself as he opened the door to the Mercantile.

Grant tapped his hand against his thigh as he made the short journey into his mom's store. As always, it took him a minute to adjust to the collection of color and texture that surrounded a person upon arrival. When they were growing up, Grant and his brothers were taught the basics of needlework by Prue, but beyond reattaching a loose button, he had missed out on the sewing gene.

That didn't mean he missed how much work and skill every piece in her shop took. He paused to scan the walls. There were two new quilts and an embroidered sampler with Bless This Mess in the center. Prue Armstrong was a one-of-a-kind who enjoyed collecting unique patterns.

"I hoped I'd see you today. Tell me what happened after you left the apartment." She didn't stop talking as she wrapped her arms around him and held him in place for a comfortable minute. That was one thing he had immediately loved about Prue. Before he landed in her care,

hugs had been scarce in his life. His father had left when Grant was a toddler. There were a few pictures, but Grant couldn't remember anything about the man clearly. Once Grant had gone into the foster care system, he lost track of his mother, too. Prue and Walt had given him everything and he hadn't missed one day at home without a hug since.

"I followed Mia out to the Majestic and I drove home." He met her stare and did his best to leave it all there. "The end."

"Not even the last chapter, my boy. When are you two getting together so Mia can start writing up something for the magazine? Don't tell me you're still not sure? I can't believe you've managed to sit on the truth this long. She'll do a good job."

Grant motioned to a poster advertising Western Days. "She's already got a story, remember? She may decide to stick with that." He recalled how she spoke about finding the one big story that could change the way her mother treated her and knew that Mia was committed to doing both as well as she knew how.

His mother peered at him over the rims of her reading glasses. "You'll never get that whopper past me. You're wasting time. Sounds like you have a perfectly valid reason to be tracking down that pretty magazine writer." She shooed him toward the door. "Don't let me keep you."

Grant laughed. "Don't you want to lay groundwork for wooing the 'pretty magazine writer' to stay in Prospect, marry your black-sheep son and contribute to the growing Armstrong-ization of this town?"

Prue smiled slowly. "Well, now, that hadn't even occurred to me. I ought to let you tell on yourself more often." She braced her hands on the table in front of her. "Thinking of long-term possibilities, are you? Perhaps you should start with a kiss first. See where it goes." The tense silence

between them stretched out until her eyebrows shot up and she exclaimed, "Oh, my heavens, you kissed her!"

Her volume registered, and she clapped her hand over her mouth.

The door swung open wildly and Walt stepped inside. "What's all the noise? Surely he's kissed someone before?"

Grant was prepared to stonewall both of his parents on his kissing history and then his phone rang. "Saved by the bell," he muttered as he saw Matt's name on the display.

"Where are you?" Matt asked.

"I'm at the Mercantile. What do you need?" Grant moved to the window to see his brother's truck parked in front of the storefront he'd been using as a veterinary office in town.

"I've been volunteering with this animal rescue group, and they have a case of animal neglect, a horse over near Leadville. I agreed to evaluate the horse and foster it at our ranch, but I'm not sure how easy it will be to get the horse home. Can you help?"

"Of course. I'll meet you at the barn to pick up the horse trailer." Grant hung up immediately. Matt would be anxious to leave right away. "Matt needs me to assist with a horse, a rescue. Are we rescuing horses now?"

His dad shrugged. "Different kind of fostering, but it seems to fit in pretty well. Can't see anybody having a problem with that."

Prue blew him a kiss. "Imagine if you weren't here, Grant. Who would lend Matt a hand?"

Grant shook his head. "There's a list of at least twenty people I could name who would help your baby."

She shrugged. "Not a one of them would be as helpful as you."

Grant squeezed her close and then clapped his father on the shoulder before he trotted out to the truck.

Matt blew past him on the way out of town, so Grant pressed the gas pedal a little harder and managed to hop out of his truck as Matt was backing up to the trailer hitch.

He took over while Matt hurried into the barn to grab rope and gloves, whatever he thought they might need to put the horse in the trailer.

"Ready?" Matt asked as he trotted back out.

"Yeah." Grant jumped into the passenger seat and they were on the way, Matt driving as assertively as usual.

"What's the story about the horse?" Grant asked.

Matt shook his head. "Apparently, his owner died and the family hasn't done anything to take over the horse's care. Probably too old to bring much for sale but starving him to death…" Matt bit off the rest of his sentence.

Grant didn't need to have the blanks filled in. Every single one of them had been raised to care for animals, but Matt had been born with the sensitive soul to feel their pain.

"How did you hear about the horse?" Grant asked.

"I've been working with an animal rescue organization. They focus on abuse and neglect cases, especially hard-to-place rescues like this one." Matt shrugged. "I started while I was still in vet school."

Grant gripped the dash as they rattled around a curve. "How come you don't toot your horn over the breakfast table?" Was he trying to keep his charity work secret?

"Nothing to brag about. It's part of my job." Matt grinned at him. "But now and again, I need help. That's where you come in."

Grant considered that as he watched his brother maneuver the road's curves. He was happy to help, of course, but it bothered him that this was the first he'd heard of Matt's extracurricular activities. They all gave him grief over his handsome face and the attention it got him.

All this time, he could have been annoying Matt by poking at his heroic work to help animals. It was wasted hours that Grant resolved to recapture as soon as he had his family all gathered around the kitchen table. Surely he could work in Dr. Dolittle somehow. "I wanted to tell you this great suggestion for the games." He gave Matt the shortest version of Mia's idea and was gratified that Matt was as impressed as their mother had been.

"I love it. If we have to, we can field enough teams from Prospect alone, no need for outside competitors, although that would certainly help spread the word for next year." Matt sped up as they came out of a curve. "Smart and beautiful. It's a miracle she's still single."

Grant swallowed the immediate response that rose up because he knew when he was being baited. That didn't mean he was smart enough to avoid the trap completely. Matt interpreted the silence correctly and chuckled. "Maybe she's not exactly single anymore. Does she know that?"

"There's a whole lot of world between her job and her place in Billings and mine here." Grant yanked his hat up before resettling it. He wasn't going to ask this, was he? "Got any advice on tackling that problem?"

Matt scratched his chin. "I believe one of our happily matched brothers might be more help, but..." He glanced briefly at Grant. "The two of you have proven you can come up with solid ideas when you work together. Try that again. Talk to her. It's okay if she's the smart one in the couple. That was bound to happen anyway."

Matt's evil grin surprised a chuckle out of Grant.

"Have you decided how to handle telling the world about Red?" Matt asked.

Grant sighed. "I want to get the story out. It's the right thing to do for everyone riding on the rodeo circuit. If I

can't make my case well enough, there might be some gossip about me, about us, that I can't shake." He wouldn't have to explain how much that bothered him to one of his brothers. They understood.

"In your boots, I'd want the same thing, a little bit of justice," Matt responded. "Maybe you can't get even, but you can get a lot of satisfaction by telling the truth."

"I should have yelled loud and long as soon as I overheard Red and Trey talking, saved us all a lot of angst," Grant muttered.

"Yep." Matt's easy agreement landed on top of the ache in his chest that had replaced the hot burn of anger. "If you were a real bad boy, like your 'brand,' you probably would have punched first and ironed out the consequences later."

Instead, he'd been afraid and a little ashamed. He might even have believed he deserved whatever happened next.

Matt glanced over. "I'm glad you're here to help with this, Grant. I'm glad you came home, no matter what sent you to us. We missed you."

Unexpected real, raw emotion between him and his brothers always made them awkward, so Matt cleared his throat.

"How glad? Are you glad enough to, say…" Grant inhaled as he considered what came next. As soon as he put the words out into the world, they would take on a life of their own. "Would you be interested in a role as advisor for the new and improved Prospect Rodeo Club? If Reg and I can get it up and going?"

Matt tilted his head to the side as he considered that. "On one condition." He held out his hand to shake.

Grant waited. It was never a good idea to agree to an Armstrong bargain until all the details were known.

"We wait until Western Days is all wrapped up before we start recruiting members." Matt offered his hand again.

Grant immediately clasped it. "And the club will be ready to serve for next year's festival."

Matt groaned. "Do you think I'm now stuck with doing this for the rest of my life?"

They both immediately nodded and Grant chuckled.

He was surrounded by people, smart ones, who were telling him to stand up and fight.

Dealing with the fallout after the story went into print and was out there for the whole wide world would be hard, but he could work through any concerns his neighbors had.

And Mia...

Well, they'd have to collaborate on the story first and figure the rest out later.

CHAPTER THIRTEEN

RESEARCHING SADIE HEARST had been Mia's first order of business when she'd settled at the table in the center of the church-turned-library. Thanks to fast internet and remarkably few interruptions, given it was a Monday morning, she'd jotted down notes about Sadie's first public-access cooking show and the almost magical way she'd parlayed that regional popularity into the early days of celebrity chefs with their own television programs. Mia knew all the basics: the year she was born; number of siblings; date of her death; broad descriptions of how she'd left her modest empire to her nephews and their children, a large, varied group spread out all over the United States, including the Hearst sisters.

As she surfed through all these web pages, Mia couldn't shake the notion that Sadie was impatiently waiting nearby for lightning to strike, for Mia to find something important. As if it was waiting for her, Mia, when she should be focusing on Grant's story or Western Days' lore.

Getting sidetracked by more and more ideas was a hazard Mia faced often enough that she wasn't surprised, but the undercurrent of excitement that fueled her work now was different.

Then she found a news story about Sadie's first cookbook, an international best seller filled with cookie recipes that she'd learned from her own mother, her neighbors and the people who'd made her who she was. The reviewer

was both confused and charmed by the simplicity of the collection and parlayed it to a description of the personality driving the book's success.

The writer's theory was that Sadie herself was a secret ingredient that no other chef could match. All of the bits and pieces of Sadie's background had created something that was one of a kind.

Mia glanced up at the beautiful sunlight pouring in through the multicolored glass windows as she realized she'd found it, the project she was meant to tackle next.

A book about Sadie Hearst's life started to outline itself in her head.

Those first recipes had seemed to follow along with the places Sadie visited, the events in her early life and dreams she chased. The reviewer quoted one interview, where a talk show host asked Sadie if she knew how lucky she was to make it from her little hometown to the national stage, so Mia hunted up the video clip.

The male late-night talk show host seemed to imply that Sadie might be overwhelmed or outclassed in the kitchens of New York City or in front of Hollywood cameras. Mia was offended on Sadie's behalf, but Sadie was gracious and beautiful as she demonstrated the proper way to divide chilled dough into a dozen balls. Her laugh had been so light and genuine in response to his question. "Luck, you say? My daddy used to tell me 'luck ain't nothing but hard work and good timin'' and he was never wrong. The timin' is in somebody else's hands, of course, but I don't mind working at what I love while I wait for luck to show up."

Then she'd frowned at the man. "If you want cookies to eat anytime soon, you're going to have to give work a try, pardner. Spread these out evenly on the cookie sheet." Her can-you-believe-this guy? shake of her head at the crowd got laughter and applause.

Her warm eyes as she nodded at the camera and said, "Timing *and* hard work. Remember I said that, you hear?" caught Mia.

There was something so familiar about Sadie, pieces she recognized from Sarah and Jordan and their father, Patrick, but Mia knew in her heart that Sadie would have agreed wholeheartedly that someone or something put Mia where she needed to be. She and Sadie had that in common. Mia wanted to keep digging to get to know this incredible lady.

"I can't believe there isn't a whole collection of philosophy books or humor books to join Sadie's best-selling cookbooks," Mia murmured as she stretched the knotted muscles in her lower back.

"Well, now, that would have been a moneymaking idea, to be sure." The petite redhead, Lillian Schultz, had introduced herself as the official librarian when Mia walked in, but she'd been occupied with rearranging her desk and going through book requests that had arrived over the weekend while Mia worked. "Sadie was a true original. You couldn't help but love her."

Now that Mia turned to face her, she could see that Lillian had transformed the bare-bones desk Sam had sat behind into a display of… "Are those crocheted dolls?" Mia bent closer to study a couple that were posed front and center. The period attire and the embroidered features on the man's haughty face added up to one simple guess. "Is this Darcy and Elizabeth? In crochet? I had no idea that could be done!" She leaned closer to see a tiny letter-sized envelope clutched in the woman's hand.

Mia wasn't sure how it could be accomplished but there was no denying the talent or Lillian's delight that Mia had identified the correct fictional characters. "I'm inspired by my favorite books, of course. Can you guess any of the others?"

Mia moved down the line, half bent to catch all the details. "Overalls. Straw hat. Mischief on his face. Huckleberry Finn?"

Lillian nodded. "I would have also accepted Tom Sawyer. I have a raft to put him on, but Sam hates all the clutter, so I take all the dolls down on Friday afternoons and put them up when I come in on Mondays. Recently, I've cut back on my desk decor."

This was cutting back?

"Is this a seersucker suit?" Mia asked. Lillian nodded. "Glasses, seersucker… It's not a lot to go on but this reminds me of Atticus Finch in the movie." Lillian clapped. The next one was harder. The figure was wearing a dilapidated cowboy hat and boots, a dusty overcoat and a stoic expression. "I'm going to need a hint for this cowboy."

Lillian tsked. "My goodness, he's the one who started it all for me. Famous book by Larry McMurtry?"

Mia only knew one. *Lonesome Dove*. She'd seen parts of the TV adaptation, but it had been years.

"Exactly. That's retired Texas Ranger Woodrow Call. I wanted something to get my patrons asking about this Pulitzer Prize-winning Western. I knew they'd love it, and I am a fan of the book, the series, the adaptation, both Woodrow and Gus, and the actors who played them." Lillian fanned her cheeks with one hand.

Mia grinned as she proceeded past Harry Potter with a tiny wand, Dorothy Gale from Kansas and her little dog, and Sherlock Holmes complete with a signature deerstalker. At the end, she said, "This is quite the collection. Who's next?"

Lillian bit her lip. "I'm having trouble deciding. Which one would you choose—Holly Golightly for a very fashionable addition from *Breakfast at Tiffany's* or Brienne of Tarth? I've been wracking my brain for a good fantasy

character. I could put her in a suit of armor which seems like a fun challenge." Lillian bent and studied her collection.

"They're both great characters." Mia had her doubts about the "fun" part of crocheting armor, but it was a wonderful hobby. "How long does it take to make one?"

Lillian jerked upright as if she was shocked. "Oh, now you sound like my husband, Mia. Don't ask those kinds of questions. If I think about the time I spend on these for too long, I begin to worry about all my choices, you see? My husband is pondering his retirement, and I'm encouraging him to put it off. I don't need him hanging around under my feet while I design my pieces." Her warm smile convinced Mia that she was teasing.

"What does your husband do?" Mia had spent idle minutes considering what kinds of jobs were available in Prospect.

For no particular reason.

Definitely not because the idea of leaving town was filling her with dread.

"He manages the sporting goods store in Fairplay. Makes the thirty-minute drive every day, so I do understand his readiness to stay closer to home. I asked Sam to write down a good list of reasons to keep working." Lillian grinned. "Just in case my husband happens to ask."

Mia nodded. "Sam was a big help on Saturday. I asked about books available on the town history. None?"

Lillian pursed her lips. "No, none in this collection. We do have a copy of a paper Clay Armstrong wrote when he was a college student about the architectural methods used in building the old ghost town, Sullivan's Post, up above the lodge. I'd be happy to show that to you. It does have some good history, thanks in part to Sadie's contri-

butions. It's like she's the thread that runs through every part of this town."

Mia agreed as Lillian summed up the point she'd been coming around to during all of her research. "She certainly does. I wonder why she never came back home."

Lillian fiddled with Huckleberry Finn's hat. "I imagine she loved her life, no matter where she lived, whether here or Los Angeles or even New York City. I didn't know her well, but that's the impression she gave me. Happiness isn't in a place but a person. Sadie probably chose happiness no matter where she hung her hat."

Just then, a biography of Sadie Hearst became Mia's new goal in life. A goal she wanted to accomplish, a goal that meant something to *her*. If she could capture that personality on the page, she would have accomplished something worthwhile.

But first, she had other projects to finish. Grant's story had been percolating in the back of her mind all morning, too.

When her cell vibrated to indicate that she'd received a text, Mia picked up her phone.

Tires are in!

"Oh, good, it looks like I can head over to the Garage. It'll be good to have real tires instead of that spare." Mia put her laptop away. "When I come back to town, could I check out Clay's paper? It will be a few weeks till then." She wasn't sure what the paper would tell her, but she was interested in finding everything she could about Prospect, especially if it had Sadie Hearst's fingerprints on it.

"Yes, ma'am. I'd also suggest talking Clay into taking you on an official tour around here and up at the old ghost town. He's got a big, successful business right now, build-

ing houses, but he's an expert on the town's architectural history. Do you ride?" Lillian asked.

"I do. I'm no superstar like Grant Armstrong, but I do enjoy time in the saddle." Mia finished packing her bag and waited to see if Lillian would take the prompt.

One way or another, Grant's story had to be told.

"I'll never forget the first time Grant came home to be the grand marshal for the parade, riding on his glossy black horse." Lillian pointed to the Texas Ranger in her lineup of desk characters. "There's the beat-up-saddle-tramp version of the cowboy, right? Grant Armstrong is the other archetype. Powerful. Movie-star handsome. So wild you know you'll probably never tame him, but you can't help but try." Lillian smiled warmly. "Grant was my husband's favorite rodeo cowboy—the hometown boy, of course, but he's more of a bull-riding fan. I don't get the obsession." Lillian shrugged, a blank look on her face. Mia wondered if Lillian's husband had the same expression when he talked about Lillian's dolls.

Amused and grateful at how generous Lillian had been with her time, Mia said, "I'll stop in next time I'm in town. Thank you for all your help today."

Lillian returned her wave as Mia headed for the door. She was sorry to leave the quaint library and its helpful staff. Telling herself that she could always come back helped a bit.

Before she got in her car to drive to the garage, she stopped at the historical marker that Sam had mentioned, outlined in bronze. As she pulled out her phone to take a photo of the dates on it and the building, it rang.

"Hey, Mom, I'm still in Prospect." She tugged her wool coat closer to her neck. The breeze was sharp.

"Casey Donaldson called to ask if we needed him to

swing through Prospect while you were there. He was close, so I told him to do it," her mother explained.

Mia pressed her hand to forehead. This was not what she wanted, especially now that she knew the story. "Why? What is he going to shoot? There's nothing ready for Western Days yet."

Her mother sighed. "Casey had an angle I wish you had suggested. Grant Armstrong. His family is right there in Prospect. We can ask the question about what happened to him, even if we can't find him. If you had pitched that, along with your travel idea, we could have run with it. Casey wondered if I might want to do a background story that calls out the mystery of the cowboy's sudden departure from the circuit, Armstrong's rise to the top and theories about why he left. Even if we can't dig up the man himself, we can ask the question and then do a couple of paragraphs about his hometown and his history and call it out on the cover. You could have written it and gotten a news byline, but you were focused on the festival. This is why I can't let go of the reins here, Mia. You see that, right?"

The unfairness of the accusation landed first.

Was it true? If Mia had pitched that story, would her mother have allowed her to write it?

Or would she have taken the idea and given it to a trusted, professional investigative reporter?

Mia moved over to her car, ready to get out of this muddle. "That's pretty shady 'news,' Mother. Even a woman a semester short of a finished journalism degree understands that. You don't have any real facts, but you're capitalizing on this to sell magazines. Is that the way we do business?"

With heat blasting from the vents, Mia stared through the windshield at the church-turned-library and waited, disappointment weighing her down.

"If you had finished the business degree you started at

eighteen, you would see that selling magazines is the first goal here at *The Way West*. That means we can pay employees who do those very important stories. Every time I fork over the rent on this office space I wonder how much longer I'll be able to do that. That's the kind of thing that makes it hard to sleep, Mia." Her mother huffed a breath. "A story like this can pay the bills for one more month at least. Meet Casey and show him some spots in town to support this cover story. Then leave in the morning. Make him a reservation in town. He'll be there overnight."

Mia evaluated her arguments and discarded each option. If he was on his way, there was little hope that she could persuade her mother to change the plan. All she could do was support the Armstrongs in their strategy of closing ranks around Grant until he was ready to face the mess himself. "Okay, I'll do that."

"Good. I told Casey you'd meet him at Bell House around four." Her mother sounded suspicious, as if Mia had given in too easily.

"If you could get the story on Grant's reasons for leaving, who would you assign that story to?" Mia asked quietly. "What kind of writer do you want me to be?"

There was silence over the line. "Never mind writing, Mia, I want you to be a leader. Jesse Martinez. Now that's the writer you're looking for. A good managing editor would have him out on these news pieces, with Casey to get the shots, and then find a nice young college student or recent graduate to send in pieces about fun weekend festivals. Invest in the important stuff, Mia, and be here to manage all the moving parts. That's what I want from you. For you."

When Grant told his version of the cheating scam, he needed Jesse Martinez to write it up. That was helpful to know.

She'd also gotten the clarity she wanted.

The struggle to prove herself to her mother would never end, not while Mia was at *The Way West*. She'd loved every minute she'd spent with her grandfather, her hero and the one she'd based her understanding of cowboys and Western life on. That didn't mean she was the right person to keep his magazine alive, not if it made her miserable doing it.

Sadie's beautiful smile flashed in her mind, as if she agreed.

"We can talk about my future with the magazine when I'm home. Meanwhile, I'll get Casey set up in town." And make sure everyone in Prospect knew he was the intruder they'd been waiting for all along.

Her mind was racing as she worked through different approaches and punched the number for Jesse Martinez, a grizzled reporter who had spent his entire career watching rodeo change. His reputation would add credibility to Grant's story if she could convince Jesse to keep an open mind. That would be the most important piece of the puzzle that she needed to fit before she left Prospect.

At first, she thought the phone had malfunctioned because the first ring was answered with a loud screech.

"Hello?" Mia said uncertainly before checking the phone display. Still connected.

"Give me that, you little polecat," someone muttered before Jesse said, "Mia? Everything okay?"

She understood the reason for the question. Her only phone calls to Jesse had been to deliver orders from her mother, ones she didn't want to handle herself. "Yeah, hey, have you got a minute?"

The screech was muffled this time, but Mia heard it. Whatever the source was, it seemed to be running away.

"Can I call you back? I'm babysitting for my daughter

right now and my grandson is—" A loud crash covered whatever it was Jesse intended to say.

"Is there any way I can have five minutes?" Mia drummed her fingers on her steering wheel, determined to do something to help Grant.

"Okay, one sec." He must have covered the phone somehow, because his voice was muffled, but Mia heard him yell, "Babe, I need to take a work call. Ten minutes." Then there was the loud snap of a door closing. Firmly.

He sighed with relief as he returned to the phone. Mia pictured the bushy mustache that covered most of the bottom of his face and how on a windy day it would blow in the breeze. "Don't know how she could hear me over all the racket, but the house will most likely still be standing in ten minutes. What have you got?"

Mia bit her lip. "Have you ever heard any whispers about cheating on the circuit?"

"Oh yeah, every now and then, some disgruntled young'un gets upset because he can't shoot straight to the top, so the story kicks up that someone's messing around, but there's never any fire behind the smoke." He paused. "Why? You have a source?" He paused again. "Where are you right now?"

If she answered and he followed that string, it wouldn't take long for Jesse to untangle the answer she wasn't quite ready for him to have yet.

"If you could name anybody whose success seemed too good to be true…" Mia shook her head. That was the wrong tactic. She needed him to find the story first, with actual proof. Grant could be Jesse's confirmation, but no one would believe the story if he was the only source.

"Spit it out, Mia. Something may be burning in the kitchen at this point. The smoke detector is going off."

Mia hoped that was a joke. There was amusement in

his voice, but he was so crusty it was hard to tell. "How well do you know Red Williams?"

Jesse hummed. "Professionally, well enough. I've interviewed him once or twice. He likes to take kids coming up under his wing, sort of mold them." The silence stretched over the line as he considered the conversation. "Cheating. Fast-rising stars. Red Williams. What's the connection?"

Relieved, Mia relaxed in her seat. "Exactly."

Jesse grunted. "That's for you to know and me to find out, I'm guessing."

Mia smiled. "Yes, but the payoff? If you can find that story, I have a connection to answer one of the hottest questions on the circuit right now. I'll hand that over and you'll have the kind of story that will go far beyond *The Way West*. The only problem is that it's gotta happen quickly. Casey Donaldson is going to be awfully close to the source of the story, hunting for angles. If he manages to find the right one, we'll be scooped." And she knew Jesse and Grant together could tell the story better than anyone else.

She wasn't sure how many fans would still be listening if they weren't the first to speak.

"My wife is going to be airin' her lungs when I tell her I'm headed out to Utah." Mia would have worried, but he sounded more excited than concerned about his wife's emotional state.

"Call me as soon as you think you have something you can use," Mia said. "Or if you run into a dead end. We'll come at this from a different direction, okay?" She bit back the urge to tell the professional how to do his job.

"Why don't you meet me there? I have a phone interview set-up with this new hot-shot saddle bronc rider. I'll call and tell her I decided to come in person and bring you along for…a woman's perspective on her story," Jesse suggested. "Something about what you're saying makes this

feel personal. We could tell everyone you're…" He paused as he weighed the options. "You're gathering hometown stories on rodeo's rising stars. That'll get a lot of doors open. Then we both step through 'em and poke around."

Mia bit her lip and mulled over the proposition. How long it would take to drive to Ogden, Utah, and what she could accomplish while she was there. The quick turn-around to get back to Billings to file the story.

All of that after riding herd on Casey while he was in town.

Letting Jesse go alone would be faster.

But he was absolutely correct. This was personal. And she wanted to make sure it was done right.

"If I won't slow you down," Mia said and waited.

"Text me when you get to town. We'll plot out our moves over a burger and see what we dig up. See you to-morrow." Jesse had ended the call before she was fully convinced she should agree.

Then she dropped her phone on the passenger seat and covered her face with her hands. Her easy, straightforward plans had just been scattered.

That was how the universe worked, though.

Being in the right place at the right time, over and over, was proving itself to be the key to her luck. Mia was cer-tain this was the right track for her, for the magazine and for Grant.

But the clock was ticking.

At the Garage, she warned Dante and Lucky about the photographer coming to town while she built towers of blocks for Eliana and Selena. The twins clapped with ex-treme pleasure every time the slender stacks grew too tall and crumbled down. Lucky nodded her understanding while she rang up the total for the repairs. As Mia took her credit card back, she wondered if she should use it to catch

up on the maintenance and any other repairs now…while her mother was still covering the credit card payments.

When she returned to Billings, everything would change.

Then she realized this might have been the "lack of adult survival skills" her mother had lectured her about.

Dante was swarmed by the twins when he came back into the office. "They are stern supervisors. You can't stop with the blocks until they are done and they are never done. Run away while you can, Mia."

Mia laughed. "They're adorable, but you have to stop feeding them whatever it is that is giving them this energy and then pass me the recipe because I could use a boost."

"You are welcome to return to babysit at any time. The pay is not great, and neither is getting up off of the floor after hours of entertaining these two," Dante said as he held the door open for Mia, "but you will have our eternal gratitude. We only offer that deal to special family members."

Mia waved, but she was touched by his words. They had taken good care of her. What if being "safe" as her mother wanted had more to do with the people she surrounded herself with than a guaranteed paycheck?

"Why not both?" Mia mumbled as she started the car and drove over to the Ace High. Her plan to get the word out was based heavily on the first informational campaign she'd witnessed in town. There was no need to do a dramatic reading in the center of the dining room, since she'd seen Faye herself in action. The woman who knew and saw everything that happened in Prospect would be enough for this task.

Especially since she was standing behind the host station as soon as Mia entered. A petite older woman was shaking her head angrily as she walked away when Faye

said, "Hey, sit anywhere you like. May take a minute to get your food because the chef is in a mood." Faye held both hands out. "She's always in a mood lately. Evidently, she can't work like this. She needs freedom." When she realized she was saying too much, Faye's mouth snapped close. "But there are no bad menu choices. Trust me on that."

Mia checked the time. Casey was supposed to arrive at Bell House in less than two hours and she had to get to Prue Armstrong. "If it's okay, I'll swing back through during the dinner rush. I'll have someone with me."

"Grant again?" Faye winked. "Is he still underfoot?"

"Yeah," Mia said as her lips twitched, "he's been sticking pretty close."

Faye's grin bloomed slowly. "Well, around here, the next step is love." She sighed and leaned closer. "Between you and me, there's not a bad Armstrong in the bunch, even if Grant is probably the orneriest one of the five. I take my job as honorary Armstrong seriously, and I've done my best to keep him humble. He's always been a star, you know."

Mia said, "It's working. Grant understands your power, especially with control of his favorite restaurant." She was amused to see the twinkle in Faye's eyes. As an only child, she'd never experienced sibling rivalry, but it seemed that the Armstrongs treated everyone like family and Faye had assumed her role with gusto.

Faye shook her head slowly, as if the burden was heavy. "I sure am glad I'm getting some help lately. Sarah and Jordan have been valued reinforcements in my battle to keep the Armstrong boys in check. Thank you for sharing. I will make sure to needle Grant until he confesses his devotion. It's part of my job as honorary little sister, you understand."

Mia nodded. "But my guest tonight isn't Grant. It'll be

Casey Donaldson, a photographer who works the rodeo circuit. He's hunting for a story, so…"

Faye pursed her lips. "And there is no story. At all. And that will last until Grant changes it."

Relieved that Faye had understood as easily as Lucky, Mia said, "Exactly."

"Fine. Come in for dinner. We'll take care of you." Faye pointed over her shoulder toward the kitchen. "Gotta smooth some feathers."

Mia trotted across the street to the Mercantile, conscious of the time.

She hadn't checked on a reservation at Bell House yet, but there was no way she was installing Casey Donaldson in the lodge room next door to hers. There had to be a room available at the bed-and-breakfast in town on a Monday night in February.

She was in a hurry as she hustled into Handmade and slid to a stop at the sight of Prue and Walt Armstrong kissing.

There, in the middle of the afternoon.

Just kissing as if it was the thing to do.

Stammering and excusing herself was what she wanted to do most, but she froze.

"Hmm, looks like we got a crowd started," Walt murmured as he stepped back and tilted his hat back down. "Hello there, Mia. What's got your tail on fire?"

Prue half smiled, half scoffed. "He's not smooth, is he? But he will always offer to help. When you get an Armstrong man, they fall on a scale like that. Romance on one end, utility on the other. We can nudge them toward the middle."

"Um…" Mia cleared her throat. "Today I could use some assistance." She wasn't sure how much Walt knew about the dinner she and Grant had had with Prue. Then she remembered the kiss and guessed there weren't many

secrets between the couple. "There's a photographer headed to town—" she checked the time again "—and if he's early, he might be in front of Bell House any minute. I talked with Lucky and Faye, but if you could do your thing—" Mia waved her hand at Prue "—to let everyone know that this is the person hunting for a story, the one you originally were warning them about, it would be good. It's my fault he's here, so I have to do whatever I can to try to fix this."

She shoved her phone back in her pocket and shuffled her feet as she waited for Prue to agree.

"Your fault?" Prue asked, her intent to find out exactly how Mia had caused this evident on her face.

"I'll explain it all eventually, but I won't have another chance to get the word out before he's here." Mia clenched both hands. "Let's take care of this first."

"Why didn't you set him up at the lodge?" Walt asked. "All of us would be watching him then."

Her automatic grimace made him whistle loudly. "That was a thousand words right there. I'm guessing he's not your bestie?"

"Casey's fine, just not my cup of tea," Mia replied. "He can be pretty dogged about things when he wants to be."

Prue's narrowed eyes convinced Mia that she was reading between the lines. "Well, Rose will be glad to host. There isn't much she can't handle." She punched a button on her phone. "Rose, we've got an undesirable headed into town. Can you make sure he's comfortable but ready to leave tomorrow as the sun comes up?"

Mia crossed her arms over her chest, amused at the opportunity to watch an expert at work behind the curtain.

"Jordan still complains about the bells that kept her up all night when she stayed there. Was that Silver, or…?" Prue covered the phone to say, "All the rooms are themed and all

the doors have wreaths to match the theme. There's one that jingles with teeny, tiny…" Prue nodded. "All right. That sounds perfect. And the Christmas decorations will add to the experience. Not a word about an Armstrong, okay?"

When the phone call was over, Prue put her phone on the counter next to the cash register. "Handled. Nobody on earth is better than Rose Bell at resolving a tricky problem. We've been friends for four decades. Never seen her rattled except when Patrick Hearst asked her to the Picture Show the first time." Prue shook her head. "As if the whole town couldn't see they were meant to be together."

Mia bit her lip and decided not to mention how many different people had said the same to her about Walt and Prue…who had just been caught making out during work hours.

"You talk to Grant today?" Walt asked.

"Not yet, but I have a new strategy, the third option we needed. I hope Grant likes it. I'll show Casey around town for photos, escort him into the Ace High and run interference. Casey's a good photographer, so everyone should definitely be friendly. Just careful." Mia was hoping to avoid tipping off Casey the way she'd been alerted that there was a story under the surface. "And I'll leave town same time as Casey, bright and early, so as long as Rose's performance is successful, he'll be none the wiser. It would be best if Grant stays close to home. I guess I won't be able to say goodbye in person."

"Close to home puts him right next door," Walt drawled. "You could drop in anytime you wish."

Mia appreciated that open invitation. Leaving without a proper goodbye wouldn't be the end of the world. This wasn't her last visit to Prospect.

Seeing him again would make leaving that much more

difficult and there was no other option right now. She was driving out of Prospect bright and early in the morning.

"Let me give you my number. If anything comes up tonight, call me." Mia took Prue's contact info and entered it into her phone. "You can also get in touch with me through the magazine and I have email there." Desperate was how she sounded. She didn't want to leave and she wanted to see Grant now and tomorrow and the day after.

"I'll be back for Western Days no matter what happens." She knew Prue thought it was a promise to get the town the coverage she wanted most, but Mia heard it as an attempt to comfort herself.

This visit wouldn't be her last chance to kiss Grant Armstrong.

CHAPTER FOURTEEN

GRANT PROPPED HIS boots up on the old coffee table in the center of the lodge's lobby. Jordan had uncovered the worn gem in the Majestic's magical storage room while she'd been applying every bit of elbow grease she had to clean up the lodge. The furniture in the lobby wasn't stylish, but it had obviously been built of real wood, hand tools and enough time to make it sturdy.

That was a good thing. He was frustrated that he hadn't had a chance to speak to Mia all day long. That made sitting still in one place difficult.

It had taken most of the day to get the skittish rescue horse loaded into the trailer and settled back at the Rocking A. The caution required to approach the old gelding had paid off as soon as he and Matt unloaded him in the barn. Grant would swear he'd seen relief replace flat distrust in the horse's eyes as soon as he'd stepped inside the empty stall.

Grant figured he'd had the same expression the same night he'd come back home. He'd been so hurt and angry that his best friends in the world had betrayed him but stepping into the comfort of the Rocking A and his family had been a relief. He'd had a long way to go then, and his future was still hazy, but having a safe place had convinced him recovery was possible.

Rodeo had been his first chapter; he'd find his way through the next one here in Prospect.

He and Matt were a good team, and it was eye-opening to see his brother at work like that. Together, they'd managed to get the horse fed and watered, and the last he'd seen Matt, his brother was carrying on a one-sided conversation as he brushed and examined his newest patient.

When Faye called to tell him that Mia had made it as far as the Ace High with *The Way West*'s photographer, he'd decided that missing Mia wouldn't do. He needed to see her, so camping out in the Majestic's lobby had been his only option.

Every Armstrong he talked to that day made it clear that he should avoid Prospect until Mia called the all-clear.

He was doing his best to trust that there was a logical reason for this photographer to appear now. Had she arranged the photographer to get shots for Western Days?

That didn't make any sense.

Had Mia called for help with her investigation? The one she'd sworn was never a thing as recently as the night before.

Maybe.

He understood Mia was trying to contain the exposure for now. Why? If she wanted the story bad enough to call in the photographer and Grant was ready to talk, what was the plan here?

Then his mother had mentioned that Mia had confessed the photographer's arrival was her fault and she was trying to control the damage by any means necessary, including activating Rose Bell's unique people-handling skills.

It all added up to a confusing picture. He wanted to trust Mia, but he needed answers.

Unfortunately, the sturdy furniture was not conducive to waiting comfortably or quietly.

"I said you could wait in the lobby, even though those were not the instructions you received from Mia," Jordan

said as she skidded to a stop in front of the check-in desk, "but I never once agreed to you putting those boots on the furniture or huffing your displeasure like the wolf trying to blow down a straw house." Then she smacked a hand to her forehead. "Have I been possessed by Sadie Hearst? I swear that was her voice, not mine." Then she pointed. "Boots on the floor."

Grant sighed *again* but it was clear this would be a losing battle so he straightened on the hard seat and saluted. "Yes, ma'am."

Jordan walked over to sit in one of the rocking chairs. "These aren't too bad. That couch? I think it was made before cushions were invented."

Grant grunted his agreement. "What project are you working on tonight?"

"My office. Would you like to see it as a distraction from impatiently waiting for Mia to come home?" Jordan said as she nodded wildly and held out her hand. She'd popped up out of the chair before he could convince her otherwise.

As she towed him into the restaurant, he said halfheartedly, "I don't want to miss Mia if she's leaving first thing in the morning."

Jordan froze in her tracks so suddenly that Grant stumbled while trying to keep from running over her.

"And why is that?" Jordan asked slyly.

Grant coughed into his hand. That was an excellent question. "I want to be clear on her plan. For the story."

Jordan narrowed her eyes and scanned his face. If she'd been shocked to hear Sadie's voice earlier, what would her reaction be if he told her he'd seen the same suspicious expression on her great-aunt's face many times?

Most often after he'd been caught doing something

around the lodge that was off-limits, out-of-bounds, and that he'd definitely been ordered more than once to stop.

Having the lodge next door growing up hadn't meant a lot to him, but the ghost town that sat up in the hills above the lodge? He'd trespassed there plenty. He and his brothers had all spent more time climbing around those buildings than anyone should have. The weathered structures there drew him in.

When the weather was right and the walls of the house crowded in on him, he still took every opportunity he could to ride up there.

"Sadie will probably let us know when Mia comes in. If she doesn't, I bet it won't take Mia long to come looking for me." Jordan motioned him to follow. When he wasn't right on her heels, she said, "What? We're friends. People like me."

Grant chuckled as he obeyed her orders and trailed through the doorway of the restaurant and took a slight left to the corner behind the host station. "Did you find a completely new room hidden inside the storage room? This place keeps on giving," he drawled.

Jordan rolled her eyes and flipped on the light. "Turns out, when you remove all the carefully stored inventory and return it to where it belongs, there is actually a room inside the storage room." She held her arms out to show him…the empty storage room. The washer and dryer remained, but all the furniture pieces, bedding, and odd bits and pieces that had been neatly arranged inside had been removed to make way for a perfectly acceptable office.

"If and when we get the funds from Sadie's estate, and if and when there's any left after the repairs we have to make to get the lodge restored, and if and when we can make another door into the closet to join it to the back of the kitchen—" Jordan pointed vaguely at the wall that

must separate them from that space "—I'm going to sweet talk Clay into moving these appliances out, but for now, I have a desk, electricity, soon there will be high-speed internet, and a laptop. Ta-da! The Majestic has a business office that is not the kitchen island in Sadie's apartment."

Grant spun in a slow circle. With the yellowed paint, dusty shelves and scratched wood floors, it wasn't an impressive space, but it made a lot of sense. He studied the washer and dryer. "Might be easier to put up a wall here—" he toed a line with his boot to show her where he meant "—to build a laundry room." He tapped the opposite wall. "Then cut a door right here. To the back hall. Laundry in and out without interrupting restaurant service. If you wanted, you could use that door for entry to your office, too."

Jordan shoved a paint brush at him as she paced off the space to envision it. "You could put up a wall, couldn't you, Grant? No need for Clay to leave his construction company in Colorado Springs to come here for that." She clutched her hands in front of her face and gave him puppy dog eyes. "For your favorite sister-in-law." Then she held up both hands. "Someday."

"Someday you'll be my favorite?" His lips twitched as he pointed the paint brush at her.

"Someday I'll be your sister-in-law." Then she patted his shoulder. "You and I know that I will always be your favorite. Thank you for helping me paint this room." She tapped the paint can and scooted to sit on the desk. "I think Sadie would have loved this color." The lid came off, and Grant could see Jordan was going with a sunny pastel yellow for the Majestic's new business office. If Sadie Hearst had been a paint color, he figured it would look exactly like that.

"I will help you paint, not because you roped me into

it, but because I find myself with too much time on my hands. I'll load up Damon and Micah this weekend and get it all knocked out." He handed her back the paint brush. "We might be able to do something about this floor, too." They'd refinished the floors in most of the lodge because both boys loved power tools and the floor sander had been popular.

"What about the wall? And the new door? And can you put a keyed lock on both entrances, one with a code that you enter?" Jordan asked as she imagined the possibilities. "Someday, there will be a night manager, maybe even an assistant manager, too, so we'll need access codes. Things like that."

Grant blinked as he tried to trace the winding journey from relaxing in the lobby to figuring out high-tech security systems for the Majestic's corporate offices, but it didn't make sense to waste a lot of energy asking himself how he'd gotten there. It happened so often around the Hearsts that he'd acclimated by now.

"Let's work on the construction piece. We may need expert advice for anything else." Grant picked up a binder from the solid desk. It reminded him of his mother's organization system for Western Days, the large black binder that she'd handed unceremoniously to Matt when she'd chosen him to lead it this year. "What's this?"

Jordan shrugged. "Right now, I have more ideas than time or money, but that doesn't mean they won't work someday, so I put notes or advertisements in there to jog my memory." She flipped through the pages and tapped one. "In the summer, we should have a band playing on Friday nights. Old country, the kind that will have people two-steppin' on the deck outside. We'll also need to expand the deck."

Grant knew his eyebrows shot up, but she wasn't pay-

ing any mind. Something had caught her attention and now she had a goal in mind. Jordan flipped steadily until she said, "Here it is. This is the business opportunity that I wanted to talk to you about." She held up the binder so he could see a hand-drawn flier for a trail ride. The artist rendering of a horse was memorable. There had to be a thousand glossier ads to choose from, ones with photos of real, beautiful horses, so he studied her choice to guess why this one made it into the binder. Then he saw the reference to a "special Halloween ghost ride."

He met her stare. "Jordan, please tell me you aren't planning to lead city slickers into the mountains on the hunt for Bigfoot or things that go bump in the night." Her fear of horses in general was well-known among all the Armstrongs, and that would seem confirmation that he was on the wrong track, but with Jordan and her inventive ideas, he wasn't sure.

"Not me. You." She gripped his arm as he straightened, prepared to march outside to wait for Mia in his cold truck. "Not ghosts or paranormal, but the ghost town. Trail rides to Sullivan's Post. Along with riding lessons. Kids. Adults. You know you enjoy working with horses and their riders." Jordan smiled encouragingly. "Imagine having a job where you ride up to the ghost town and help people learn to love horses."

Grant propped his hands on his hips as he considered that.

What did it mean that it was so easy to imagine?

"You could work as much or as little as you like, bring in money for the ranch, train the horses as needed." Jordan held her hands out as if it was so simple. "As long as you can pretend to be a people person for as long as the trail ride takes, I don't see how you can lose."

Grant grunted his amusement at that. "I'll have you

know I was pretty popular on the circuit. Men, women and children loved me."

She patted his arm as if to say, "Of course you were, sweetie."

"Does anyone ever tell you no?" Grant asked, unwilling to jump on board immediately. He had a reputation to uphold as the troublemaker. Was her suggestion actually brilliant? Sure, in a world filled with only round holes, Jordan had managed to build her own spot, one perfect for a square peg. She and her sister kept generating these ideas that were so right for the town that it was tempting to wonder why they had taken so long to conjure.

Prospect had needed the Hearsts to roll into town with no other option except to make room for them. The town was going to be better for it, too.

Grant was the agitator. He kept people from getting too comfortable. In a battle of personalities, he wasn't sure he would win against Jordan Hearst.

"Sounds okay, but what if I had something else in mind for my golden years besides free labor spent on this lodge and escorting tourists on amusement park trail rides?"

"You like to argue. I also enjoy arguing, but it is late. If you had plans for your retirement, you'd be doing them already. No one makes it to the top of the standings in the rodeo circuit without putting in lots of hard work." She held up a hand. "Don't try to deflect this truth by trotting out the cheating thing. You've been the first one to volunteer for every job around this place, big or small. You might have fooled your family with skillful misdirection, but I have been playing that game for decades. Get real with me. You need something to do. You're amazed and impressed with my judgment and foresight. After Western Days, you'll be ready for something challenging. You can count on me and the Majestic for help."

Jordan held her hand out to shake.

"As long as it leaves plenty of time to rebuild the Prospect Rodeo Club, I'm in." Grant hadn't realized he'd made up his mind to give it a shot until that very second. But after working with Matt and getting his promise to help, and spending time thinking of Mia and his family and what life would look like after this cheating scandal was resolved… In his mind, it was easy to picture introducing kids to the rodeo he loved, teaching them to give it their all and win the right way.

He so needed Mia here, because he didn't want to wait any longer for the story to finish.

And selfishly, he'd missed her company all day.

"I don't know what a rodeo club does," Jordan said, "but I have no doubt the Armstrongs can build the best one in the West. We will all make time for that, Grant."

Grant had returned the handshake when Jordan added, "I know you're waiting here for Mia to show up because you need to see her before she leaves. Right?" She held on tightly when he tried to pull away. "You like her. Are you going to tell her?"

When he realized that Jordan might not be as strong but she was twice as determined to hold on, Grant stopped trying to free himself. "Is this grade school? Should I hand her a note and ask her to be my girlfriend? Do adults do that?"

"I had high hopes that you were the Armstrong brother with all the romantic grand gestures, but if a note's all you've got, do it. You'll be sorry if you let Mia go without telling her how you feel." She held her hands out to indicate the dingy storage room with a bright future. "While we wait, you can paint and rehearse everything you'd like to say. I can give you feedback."

"Or I can head home. Will you please ask your lodger to

call me when she returns from Prospect?" Grant pointed over his shoulder. "Should I leave a note at the front desk?"

Jordan tapped her temple. "Nope. I have it committed to memory."

In the lobby, Grant inhaled slowly, determined to shed some of his restlessness before sliding behind the wheel. "That's a sign of new maturity, Armstrong," he muttered to himself. Almost every ridiculous stunt that caught up with him had been the result of shooting off half-cocked. The way sweet vanilla filled his nose surprised him. Should it? No. He'd heard plenty of people talking about the Majestic's delicious-smelling ghost but he'd yet to experience the phenomenon himself.

Until tonight.

"All right, Sadie, if you were here, you'd be filling my ear about something I'm doing wrong or about to mess up." Grant scrubbed his hands over his face, tired and confused about how his life had ended up with him talking to his imaginary neighbor. "She's leaving. And that's for the best. Once we have published this story…" Then what? That was the question. How did he want to complete that sentence?

He stared around the lobby. Some kind of visible manifestation might be nice. Then he remembered the way Sadie Hearst's eyes had gleamed with fire when she got angry.

The vanilla stayed with him as he moved through the lobby and arrived back at his truck. The urge to ignore his mother's delivered message about staying at the ranch was strong. If he went into town, he could track Mia down easily.

Then he could say his piece and get on with his life.

But it was hard to forget that everyone in Prospect, including Mia, had done their best to protect him from be-

coming the gossip of the rodeo circuit while he figured out how he wanted to proceed.

So he turned toward the Rocking A instead of storming into town. Light blazed from every window along the front of the ranch house, and trucks lined the yard. That meant most of the Armstrongs were inside. There were enough of them now to make a crowd wherever they went.

Instead of going inside to face the chaos and noise, the usual scene when the whole family was gathered, Grant decided to spend time in the barn. On a cold night like this, it was a good idea to check to make sure all the horses had feed and water.

Whenever he needed to get his head on straight, horses never let him down.

CHAPTER FIFTEEN

MIA WAS RELIEVED when Casey trotted up the steps to Bell House without giving her an argument. That meant her tightrope walk was coming to an end. Heading back to the inn was also the first suggestion she'd made since he'd slid out of his SUV earlier that afternoon that he agreed with. There was no "playing devil's advocate" or "it would be smarter to…" or even "let's try this instead." Every idea had to be Casey's, no matter whose thought it might have been originally. She hadn't forgotten that part of the challenge of working with him, but she'd either gotten softer from working with more reasonable photographers lately or he was determined to show off his skills.

She was exhausted by running interference and advocating for the shots she would definitely want for her piece on Western Days. They'd taken a few exterior shots before the sun set, and then moved inside to get some "local color." They had managed to get nice photos of the Mercantile and the pretty park behind it, Bell House, the Prospect Picture Show and Homestead Market. These were "the landmarks" as Casey called them.

Not because he thought they were particularly noteworthy, but because they were what Prospect had to offer.

The urge to snap at him about the beauty of the Majestic Prospect Lodge burned, but her careful plan to keep Casey separated from Grant was stronger. Instead, she took him on the side trip to see the future spot of Prospect's Cow-

boy Games across from the high school. He had brightened momentarily at the way golden light filtered through the breaks in the line of mountains to scatter across Sam's field as the sun set, so Mia was satisfied that he wasn't completely immune to the charms of the town.

Casey had also shown true excitement for the dishes coming out of the Ace High kitchen. And when Faye had deposited a slice of chocolate pie with a toasted meringue that rose all the way to heaven, she and Casey had both been speechless.

That might have been the straw that broke his bad mood because Casey was rubbing his stomach in an I'm-so-full-but-I-regret-nothing sort of way. In this, they were on the same side.

"You want to come in?" Casey asked. "We haven't had much of a chance to catch up. Seems like you had a story to tell about every single citizen of Prospect."

She had.

Except anyone named Armstrong. She'd stayed carefully away from the danger zone.

It had been an exhausting few hours. "It's been a long day. You did good work. I expect we'll have plenty of shots to use when it's time to cover Western Days."

Mia forced her feet to remain planted.

"See if you can get me assigned to that story when you come back for the festival. We work well together." Casey reached out to touch her arm. "Unless… Are you seeing someone, Mia?" He exhaled in a gust. "Of course you are. Why didn't you say so? Is it a secret?" His teasing grin flashed as he bent to stare into her eyes.

"It is. That's it, Casey. It's great that we've had this time to catch up, though." She cleared her throat nervously because he was too close to the truth…all of it.

"Are you involved with someone here in Prospect?" His

eyebrows rose and he waggled them as if they were plotting something. "The only way I see you needing to keep that a secret is if it's an Armstrong."

Mia managed not to react as he tossed out the name between them, but it was likely he could add up the pieces now. She had to trust that Jesse Martinez would make good use of his connections and that together they were up for the challenge of beating whoever Casey might call with the tip. He'd been working with the busiest freelance writers covering the circuit for a while now. Casey would know exactly who to contact to get the story out there.

"No answer to that," Casey murmured as he looked as if he had the answer anyway. "I guess we know where Grant Armstrong is hiding. Want to share why?" He shook his head. "I guess I'll have to be content with understanding why you reached out to me in the first place, huh, Mia? Trolling for information. Interesting. I didn't know you had the sneaky reporter's side to you."

Mia hated that he called her behavior out. She had used him for connections.

"Thanks for stopping by to grab these shots. I know my mother will love that sunset photo. Be sure you submit it to her." She had to get out of here before Casey started reading more secrets from her face. "This will probably be our last assignment together. I wouldn't want to drag you away from the action for craft shows and fried foods." Mia raised her hand to wave over her shoulder as she walked back down the sidewalk, willing him to get the hint to stop pushing for more info. "Safe travels on your way to Nevada."

She knew it was Utah.

Mia also heard him correct her, but she waved cheerfully in the dark night, got into her car and pulled away from the B-and-B after saying a quick prayer that Rose

Bell was as good at quelling overly interested visitors as Prue promised.

Rose Bell was their only hope of sending Casey on his way, and Mia had stacked the deck against her. He knew there was something brewing here and he even had a good idea of what. Heading out of town in the morning might help lead him away, but the clock was ticking on Grant's story and the discovery of his whereabouts.

She jerked in her seat as the phone rang.

"Is that nerves or a guilty conscience, Mia?" she muttered as she punched the button to answer.

"Hey, Jordan, I'm leaving town now. I think we limited any potential exposure." She hoped. Now wasn't the time to launch into the evening's saga.

"Good, good, I'm calling to deliver a message." Jordan paused so Mia frowned at the display.

"Okay? What is it?" Mia asked, her patience running out.

"There's been a cowboy sprawled in my lobby tonight. Waiting."

Mia hadn't known Jordan all that long, but it was easy enough to imagine mischief on her face to match her tone. "Didn't he get the message that I had this situation under control?" Yes, her control was slipping, but no one needed to know that at this point.

"I believe he received multiple messages, but the caution is wearing thin. I've finally shooed him home, but Grant requests a conversation with you at your earliest convenience." Jordan cleared her throat. "Like now? I promised I'd pass along the message."

"Okay. I'll call him and explain…everything I've done this afternoon. If he's got concerns or wants to change direction on his story, I'll take care of it." Mia clenched the steering wheel. How would she stop what she'd set in mo-

tion? Jesse Martinez was good at his job and had been for a long time. There was no telling how far he'd made it with her tip without stepping foot in Utah.

And Casey had gotten a late start, but he'd make up for lost time.

"Hmm," Jordan said, "you should stop in at the Rocking A now. Face-to-face conversations are so much more pleasant." Then she ended the call.

Mia cursed under her breath. Jordan was up to something. Then she remembered Walt and his standing invitation for her to visit the Rocking A. Had they traded notes at some point in the afternoon to put Mia and Grant in the same physical location?

This whole town was always up to something.

How did people who lived here deal with the constant "something" going on?

Instead of calling her back, Mia slowed down as she neared the turn to the Rocking A. Then she realized this was an excellent excuse to satisfy her curiosity about the place Grant called home.

"Unless they're having a party because..." Mia slowed down to park next to a long line of trucks. She turned off the ignition as she asked herself if she was brave enough to crash a house full of Armstrongs and pulled out her key.

Then she noticed the shaft of light spilling from the partially open barn door.

Instinct whispered that if she had to track Grant, there was a good chance the trail started with a horse.

CHAPTER SIXTEEN

GRANT DUMPED THE last pitchfork of dirty hay on top of the pile in the wheelbarrow and brushed his shoulder across his jaw to scratch the itch that never failed to appear when he was mucking stalls. Travis would lecture him tomorrow for tackling Sonny's stall instead of leaving it for him, but it was always easier to brood when he had something to occupy his hands.

"Therapy by mucking out stalls, Jet. Can you imagine?" he asked and ran a hand over Jet's muzzle before he dumped the wheelbarrow outside the barn. If he didn't offer Jet and all his buddies a treat after all the hard work they had done, standing around and watching the silly cowboy shovel hay, they might cause a ruckus. He stopped by the office on the way back to grab the apples Travis kept on hand for special occasions. When his pockets were full, he guided the wheelbarrow back toward the empty stalls. When Sonny's stall passed inspection, he refilled Sonny's water bucket and then led Travis's horse back inside his usual spot for the night. "Please leave a tip if the service is satisfactory, sir."

Sonny butted his hand, asking for a scratch behind the ears, so Grant obliged.

"The service here is nice. If you want to apply for a housekeeping job at the Majestic, I'll happily give you a reference." Mia had climbed the bottom rung of the stall

to hang her arms over the top. "I don't know how good the tips are, but I am sure you could learn to make a bed."

Grant pulled off his work gloves. "I had given up on hearing from you."

Mia said, "Jordan told me you wanted to talk, but then she suggested I come in person rather than use the phone."

Grant crossed his arms. "I hear you've been busy. Not working on our story with someone else, are you?" He wondered how hard he'd have to push to get Mia to explain how this whole thing with the photographer had happened. He studied her face. Mia was a beautiful woman, but he could tell the day had been long and exhausting. There were fine lines around her eyes and mouth, and more than anything, Mia looked like she needed rest.

"About that…" Mia motioned between them. "Can you come out of the stall or should I come in?"

Grant eased out of the stall and closed the gate. "Sonny's a gentleman, so either would have been fine. You like horses, right?"

She nodded and reached inside his pocket to pull out an apple. "I do, but I learned to be careful until I know them. My grandfather came out one morning to find me all cuddled up with a foal and explained loudly that I had to be careful because even pets can be unpredictable sometimes."

Grant watched her twist the stem off the apple and grip it firmly. As she pushed and rolled her hands, the apple cracked into two perfect halves.

"Very handy trick for someone who spends a lot of time with horses."

"My grandfather taught me how to do that, too." She stepped over to their new rescue's stall. "Will I lose a finger if I offer it to this distinguished gent? My grandfa-

ther rode a chestnut American Paint like this one. What's his name?"

Concerned that the horse might require folks to be more cautious around him now that he'd been fed and had some rest, Grant stepped closer. "This guy might be as unpredictable as your grandfather warned. Matt and I went to pick him up today. Looks like he's been hungry and hobbled for way too long, but he's getting some high-quality care here." Grant took the half she offered and reached through the slats to give it to the horse. "Don't know whether Matt has thought of a name for him yet, but he's pretty sure this old guy will be our horse now. Not too many people looking to adopt geriatric riding horses."

Mia leaned in to stare into the horse's eyes. "All you need is a little love, right?" When she glanced up at Grant, he wasn't sure whether she was including him in that statement.

But he was ready to agree.

A little love was all he wanted, too.

"I think you should name him Stretch." Her lips curled as she waited for his answer.

Grant sighed loudly enough that the Paint's ears twitched. The fact that the horse didn't retreat gave Grant hope he was settling in. "Stretch Armstrong. Do you know how many times my brothers and I have been called that?"

"What's one more?" Mia asked as she spun away, the other half of the apple in her hand. Grant grinned as he followed behind her.

"I didn't know you were the kind of man who rescued animals. That's…cute."

Grant frowned. "Cute?"

"Who is this?" Mia asked as she held out the apple to Lady.

"This is Lady. My mother's horse. She's almost 100 per-

cent human at this point. You only need to worry about losing a finger if you try to walk out of the barn without giving her a treat, too."

Mia chuckled. "Rude. I don't believe a word he says, Lady. His mother mentioned Armstrong men struggle with romance and I'm starting to believe it. It's a good thing they're so cute."

After the horse delicately accepted both the treat and a rub on the nose, Mia turned to face him. "I'm glad you helped Matt today."

"I was happy to be there." Grant braced his hand on the stall next to Mia's shoulder. "I parlayed my assistance today into a promise from Matt that he'd help me with Prospect's new rodeo club."

She wrapped her hands around his biceps and squeezed. "I knew you couldn't say no!"

He wasn't certain what her faith in him was founded on because he hadn't been sure himself until he'd roped Matt into the task, but he liked it that Mia had believed it was inevitable.

"I wasn't sure what you would do when you heard about the magazine's photographer skulking around." Her smile grew wide. "Would an angry Bad Boy of Bronc Busting storm into town and demand answers about why I had invited him to Prospect before I had run it past him first?"

"Storming isn't my style," he said before he coughed into his hand.

She raised an eyebrow as if she was skeptical about his truthfulness.

"What was your other guess?" he asked because he was curious. "Mucking out stalls in the barn?"

"No, but now I can see that was shortsighted of me. I'm realizing that time with a horse is your answer to a lot of different emotions. Anger. Sadness. Happiness?"

Grant pursed his lips as he considered that. "You're reading me like an open book. One filled with mostly pictures."

Her smile eased something inside of him.

"The photographer is here because of me, but I didn't invite him and he didn't have any information to go on." Mia ran her hand over his sleeve, brushing off bits of hay. When she would have stepped back, he clasped her hand tightly. "Casey and I had worked together in the past. When I was using my best detective skills to find out what the good people of Prospect might be hiding, I saw a photo from Nationals that Casey had taken. I called to test the waters, to see if there were any hints about what might be going on in the rodeo world." She wrinkled her nose. "Gross, right? Trying to use my connection without explaining what was going on?"

Grant tangled their fingers together and led her over to the next stall. "This is Jet. He's mine."

She sighed. "Oh, he's so handsome." Jet had heard similar comments his whole life and knew how to work a crowd, so the horse hung his head over the top rung and stared into Mia's soul. If hearts made a sound when they tumbled into love, it would match Mia's murmur of pleasure.

His horse always was better at flirting than Grant, but it burned to see it in action with a woman he wanted to impress.

"And from that, he followed you here?" Grant said. "The photographer?" He wasn't sure she cared to continue her story, but eventually she blinked.

Grant hoped that some day, they'd have plenty of time to stand next to each other in the barn and stare into each other's eyes.

"Yeah, he called my mother to find out what kind of

assignment I was on, and whether the magazine was look-ing for photos, because he had time before he needed to be in Utah on the weekend. She called me to give me or-ders to show him around and I…did a kind of Paul Revere move, running through town to warn the neighbors that the enemy was coming. I messed up. I'm sorry. I'm start-ing to realize that I don't have either the variable ethical standards or the sleight of hand needed to be a great re-porter." Mia grimaced. "And now my mother understands the same thing."

Grant studied her eyes as he tried to decipher exactly what she was telling him. "So *The Way West* won't be able to publish the story about the cheating scandal, even if we can find proof to support my story."

Mia immediately shook her head. "Oh no. *The Way West* will print it. We just have to get it first."

Since that had been the plan all along, Grant wasn't un-derstanding what had changed.

"And when my mother was asking me why I hadn't pitched a shady what-happened-to-Grant-Armstrong story when I headed for Prospect, I realized that my reputation isn't going to give your story the weight it needs."

Grant settled on the bag of feed and pulled her down next to him. It wasn't romantic, but it was warm and he was grateful to have Mia's hand in his. She settled into his side.

"What about your big break? The one that would change her mind and convince her to give you control of the mag-azine?" Grant asked.

Mia shrugged. "Your best bet to protect your name or your brand is to have a pro doing the reporting. I gave Jesse Martinez a couple of targeted hints. I'm meeting him in Ogden. Together we'll find the proof that we need to build this out without you or I'll pass him your name and number to get in touch." She straightened her shoulders.

"When I get back to Billings, I will convince my mother to hold off on the original idea, because the scoop she's been dreaming of is coming in, one way or another. I'll get her to promise to run that story and the one on Western Days, and then we'll..." She stopped. "We'll figure out what to do about the magazine from there. She wants to step down, but the more time I spend in Prospect, the better I understand that I don't want to step up. I want to tell stories. I don't want to stare at spreadsheets all day and worry about the cost of office space. I keep hoping for a lightning bolt of an answer, but the universe is being very quiet so far."

Grant wrapped his arm around her shoulders to pull her closer. He hated how worried she was about her own future, something that she hadn't even considered before he and Matt had pulled over to change her tire. Surely she wasn't giving up on the universe?

When she eased back, he glanced down at her face. Her eyes were narrowed suspiciously. "You thought I had sold you out to Casey to get your story, didn't you? Like Red and Trey?"

Grant shook his head. "I can honestly say that... I was confused but I wasn't angry. I wanted to talk to you, not hear cryptic directions from various sources, but..." He paused as he tried to replay the long afternoon in his head. "I don't think I ever once believed you had turned on me, and I gotta say, that is something. Walking away from you never occurred to me."

Her slow smile filled him with warmth. "Really?"

"I'm as surprised as you are. I'm learning something in my old age," Grant drawled. "Or maybe it would take a lot to shake my faith in you."

She pressed her forehead against his. "We haven't known each other for long. My mother, who has known

me my whole life, will give you a list of my faults. I'm flaky, Grant."

"Not sure that's true, but even if it is, what does that have to do with trusting your heart?" he asked.

When she leaned back to blink up at him, he couldn't read her face, but the kiss she pressed against his lips was much easier to understand. He wasn't sure exactly where he was headed with Mia, but as long as he considered each step instead of reacting immediately and regretting the fallout, he was making progress.

"But you're still leaving in the morning," he whispered against her ear after she wrapped her arms around his neck. "I want to take you out for a ride. I can show you the ghost town, one of my favorite places in the world, and we can discuss Jordan's wild plan to have me running trail rides up there for the lodge's valued guests." He pressed a kiss against her jaw. "And then you can help me recruit teams for these Cowboy Games and find cheap wigs to create beautiful manes for old wooden horses, and at least a thousand other things that my mother will cook up as we go."

"I can't believe how fun all of that sounds." Mia grinned at him as he chuckled.

"Fun? Okay, no, but wouldn't we be good at it together?" he asked.

"We would." She nodded. "We will. I have a plan."

He checked her expression. "A plan. You have a plan?" That didn't fit with the free spirit who counted on the universe to direct her steps.

"Yes, I am familiar with the word, Grant, even if I don't always carefully plot out each journey." She held out her hand to count off the points. The thumb went first. "Get Grant's story tied up and ready for print. That's number one. Then figure out what to do with the magazine." She unfolded the third finger. "Figure out how to write for a

new editor, maybe even a book editor, but one who doesn't have the same last name or pay my credit card bill."

Grant unfolded her ring finger. "Make it back to town before Western Days weekend."

She nodded and then wiggled her pinky. "What's number five?"

Grant grew serious as he stared into her eyes. "Figure out what we do about us?"

Her eyebrows rose but she considered it and smiled. "Reasonable. What are we if we aren't on opposing sides of your big secret?"

He leaned closer. "That's already been answered." He pressed a kiss to her lips. "What we need to know is what comes next."

"And when I leave, when there's distance between us, our heads could clear and we'll realize that what we had was some kind of weird chemistry caused by this one moment in time. Breathing room will fix that and then we can be good friends." She grimaced. "And don't worry if it happens. You won't be the first man to break my heart by realizing what a great friend I am."

Her eyes didn't match the sunny grin.

"You don't really believe that will happen, do you?" Grant asked.

"Are you certain you don't want to head back out on the circuit? No matter what, there will be some fallout from the story, but you could return to the competition, dispel any doubts by winning." She tipped his hat back. "You want to stay in Prospect. Whatever happens with the story, you want to stay on this path instead of going back." Mia brushed her hand over his shoulders.

"I do. It's weird. I get it. But since you got here, I feel more at home than I ever have anywhere else." Grant covered his face with his hands. "I can't believe you've got me

emoting like this. If you were one of my brothers, I'd knock your hat in the dirt to get a fight started right about now."

"That must be a sign of growth." Mia's lips were twitching. "I don't know if you'll have other reporters hanging around town, but let your friends and neighbors tell other Armstrong stories to their hearts' content." Mia stood and frowned. "Even Faye was singing your praises this afternoon. I think her tough shell might be covering a gooey center."

Grant stood to follow her back to her car. "I'm going to be waiting for you to call me, Mia."

"I'll let you know how the story is going," she said with a smile.

"Tell me about the magazine and your mother and your travel and...whatever." Grant nodded. "I just want to hear your voice."

Her teasing grin faded. "Why am I nervous about leaving Prospect? I drove all over these United States on my own, with hardly a thought, before I had a flat tire outside of town and met this cowboy who wanted to keep me safe." She squeezed his hand. "I'm happier here than I ever have been. I can't explain it, but it's hard to give up."

"If you need me, I'll be there as fast as I can." Grant bent his head. "No matter what happens when you get to question number five."

Mia blinked rapidly and he was almost certain it was because of tears, but she stood on her tiptoes and pressed a kiss to his lips before trotting out to her car and driving away.

He was still staring down the lane when Travis bumped his shoulder. "You coming inside? You're bound to freeze solid out here."

Grant turned to his brother. "You ever wonder why I needled you so much when we were growing up?"

Travis reared back. "No! Why? Why would I need to know that? That's entirely a you problem."

Grant chuckled, relieved that he could laugh even though he was already missing Mia fiercely. "Okay. I was going to apologize, but never mind."

Travis slung his arm over Grant's shoulders and urged him toward the house. "Quit being weird. You're creeping me out. I knew you were the closest thing I had to a friend then, even if you were ornery. You still are."

"Which one? Ornery or a friend?" Grant asked as they climbed the steps up to the porch.

"Oh, both." Travis rolled his eyes. "You are most definitely still both, but no one can argue what a good brother you are. Damon and Micah are waiting to spend some time with their favorite uncle."

"And you and Keena are ready to cuddle up on the couch, huh?" Grant asked, relieved that life went on inside the Rocking A, same as it ever had.

Mia had changed his world, but he still recognized the most important parts.

And when she came back, they'd figure out how to assemble all the new pieces.

CHAPTER SEVENTEEN

MIA FOLLOWED JESSE MARTINEZ into the lobby of the hotel outside of Ogden, Utah, after a long day of driving and then tagging along with the experienced reporter through the event center while he shook hands and made chitchat. They had met for lunch to discuss how they might pursue a story about cheating without pointing any fingers to their possible source. Mia's part of the investigation was to ask friendly questions about their hometowns that she could use to build into theoretical stories some day.

"I have no idea how you do this," she muttered to Jesse as he pointed to the quiet bar where they were supposed to find Annie Mercado. "I want a nap and different shoes. I don't even care which order they come in."

Jesse grunted. "Years of conditioning. There'll be time to rest after you file the story, Mia."

She nodded. If the man who had to be considering retirement could do this, she would force herself to keep up. "I'm just going to wash my face. Maybe that will kick-start my brain."

He hitched the strap of his laptop bag over his shoulder. "I'll make sure no one's waiting for us, grab a quiet table near the back."

"Order me something with caffeine in it?" Mia requested before trudging toward the restroom. The aggressive fluorescent lighting hit her first, but she realized she wasn't alone before she cursed out loud.

Annie Mercado was washing her hands at the sink. "This place oughta hand out sunglasses at the door, right?"

Mia inhaled slowly and sent a grateful thank you toward the universe. Her faith had been shaken lately, but she was almost certain that the lightning bolt was about to strike.

"Since I've been on the road half the day, I definitely needed a wake-up call." Mia set her bag and notebook down before running her hands under the cold water and pressing them to her face. "I'm Mia Romero. I came with Jesse Martinez. I'd shake your hand, but…" She waved her dripping hands ruefully before repeating the process. Her brain needed to be alert and ready right now.

"Yeah? Where are you coming from?" Annie fluffed the limp curl of her bangs as she stared into the mirror.

"Prospect. Colorado." Mia did her best to study Annie's face without letting her know she was under observation.

A slight frown wrinkled the young woman's forehead. "Why do I know that name?"

The sizzle of electricity didn't surprise Mia this time. She was in the right place at the right time.

"Could be the Western Days festival they have," Mia said as she yanked paper towels from the dispenser, "or it's the hometown of Grant Armstrong. Do you know him?"

Annie crossed her arms over her chest. The hem of her shirt rose enough to reveal a red and white gingham belt.

Mia instantly recognized Sadie Hearst's distinctive plaid. Annie Mercado was wearing part of Sadie Hearst's line of women's Western wear.

There was no hint of vanilla in the air, but it was impossible not to feel Sadie's presence.

"Sure. We've met. He's kind of a hero of mine, you know, because he's pretty fearless in the saddle." Annie's demeanor suddenly shifted. "Why do I get the feeling that you also know Grant Armstrong?"

Mia tried to control the grin on her face and play it cool. "Oh, I do. I was just talking with him about these Cowboy Games he's organizing for Prospect's upcoming Western Days and his plans to put together a new Prospect Rodeo Club for the kids in town." Digging in her purse for a brush seemed a casual way to divert some suspicion. How could she be digging for information while she was trying to fix her hair?

"I guess the story of his retirement is true? It doesn't make much sense. He was on top." Annie's eyes narrowed. "Did something run him off?" Her lips were a tight line. "Or someone?"

Mia desperately hoped the racing of her heart wasn't clearly audible in the restroom as she bit her lip. "If I said yes, would you have a guess what or who might be involved?"

She wanted to channel Jesse's cagey expression and ask the perfect leading questions, but the closer she got to what she wanted, the harder it was to be patient.

"Red Williams is a shady character if I ever saw one, so he'd be my first guess as to what might convince a man to take all his prizes and head home," Annie said with a sniff. "I tell every newcomer to the circuit not to give him the time of day."

Mia nodded. "Why is that?" Before Annie could answer, she held out her hand to stop her. "Before you go any further, you should consider what you tell me and whether you want to be named in a published news story or not." She desperately wanted this to be the break they needed, but not if it came at the expense of another innocent person's career.

"How about this? I'll tell you what I know. We can compare notes to see if we're on the same page." Annie picked up the white hat from the countertop and Mia saw the dis-

tinctive Cookie Queen gingham band. "About the fourth or fifth competition, the first time I placed in the winner's circle, Red approached me with an offer to be my manager. He had a tried-and-true method to get me to the top, he promised. I fell for that for a hot minute, but it quickly became evident that his plan didn't involve coaching, helping me improve, or anything other than helping himself to a piece of my winnings and making phone calls that he could never explain to me." She pursed her lips. "Where I'm from, we don't do business that way. I even reached out to the Association to make a complaint, something official that might cause them to look into his dealings with new riders, but I only had one tiny piece of evidence to go on."

Mia clenched her hands together. "What was that?"

"Red accidentally copied me on a text where he congratulated another rider on their winning time." Annie shook her head. "Before we rode."

Mia knew her mouth was hanging open but she was too excited to speak.

"Yeah, Red said it was a joke, something he might say to psych out the competition." Annie rolled her eyes. "To me, that was more smoke, even if I wouldn't touch that fire."

Mia pressed her clenched hands to her mouth.

Annie patted her shoulder. "You okay, hon?"

After nodding wildly for a moment, Mia gathered herself. "I am. We are on the same page. If you trust me, trust Jesse, I want this story for *The Way West*. We will put so much smoke out there that the Association will have to take this seriously."

Annie moved over to open the door, and Mia met her own eyes in the mirror. "I did it. I got the story."

"Yes, you did," Annie said with a smile.

Before she could second-guess herself, Mia decided to press her luck. "And I'd love to tell you more about

Prospect. It's the home of Sadie Hearst. The Colorado Cookie Queen."

Annie pointed excitedly. "That's where I recognize the name. I loved watching her on TV, and I always wear a little bit of her clothing line. I'm such a fan."

Mia's smile could not be contained. "You have to come to Prospect then. There's a lodge. The ghost of Sadie might even be hanging out there. A museum. Big, fun Cowboy Games coming up. Lots of kids there to get interested in rodeo." She squeezed Annie's arm. "If you decide to make a visit to Prospect, they will treat you like family. I promise."

Annie looked a little overwhelmed, so Mia decided to wait until after the story was finished to press her luck and ask for a special Western Days visit from rising star Annie Mercado.

But she wasn't going to waste a single minute of this opportunity the universe had given her.

ON FRIDAY, MIA opened the doors to *The Way West*'s corporate suite. She was tired but energized and ready to get on to the next battle: the conversation about what to do with the magazine. She'd driven all day to pull into her condominium's parking deck after sunset and then spent a long night tossing and turning as she tried to get comfortable in her own bed again. Instead of marching in bright and early, she was dodging lunchtime traffic in downtown Billings and already anticipating a difficult conversation.

Stepping inside the magazine's offices always boosted her confidence. She could remember coming down on the weekends to "help" her grandfather read the stories in each issue before he approved the magazine to be printed. Most of her help had consisted of stapling things, removing those staples, spinning in his office chair and asking for change for the vending machine on the bottom floor

of the historic old Sunrise Building. It had been built in 1914, and for as long as Mia could remember, it had housed the magazine. During the magazine's heyday, employees had spread out across all three floors, but now the staff had been condensed to one suite with a few cubicles and a larger open area that held desks for anyone who might need a temporary work space.

As she wound between the desks, she saw that Jesse's cube was dark. The computer was showing the lock screen. He'd sent her the final version of Grant's story for approval that morning.

Her mother should have read it by now, complete with Mia's name following Jesse's on the byline.

The executive assistant was on the phone when Mia stepped up to the counter, but she waved Mia into her mother's office. It had been updated once or twice from when her grandfather's heavy desk had filled the room, but there was still a wall of windows that showed the sidewalk below and beautiful old trees that were ready for spring.

"Well, I guess it's technically still morning for a minute or two," her mother said as she stood to hug Mia. The scent of her expensive perfume was comforting, even as it illustrated the differences between them. She tugged the edge of Mia's oversize sweater down. "Jesse says he couldn't have gotten this story without you." She motioned at the cushy chair across the desk. "Tell me about Prospect and Grant Armstrong and why you forgot to mention you knew him better than you let on when we were discussing what kind of story would or would not be appropriate for me to run about him."

"Jesse is being too kind." Mia fiddled with the hangnail that had been bothering her since somewhere near Idaho Falls.

"Is he?" Her mother held out her hands. "It was a re-

lief to find out what was behind his sudden jaunt to Salt Lake City. Especially after I got a phone call from Casey."

"I knew he was going to be hot on the trail of this story, too, after he showed up in Prospect like that." Mia shrugged. "Jesse and I had to beat him to it. If we get it in this month's edition, *The Way West* will have the first story and the best story out about Grant and a cheating scandal involving some of the biggest names in the sport right now."

"After all the story ideas you've pitched and all our arguments over giving you a chance to write something big, you passed it over to Jesse." Her mother's slow smile was beautiful. "A proud mother would view that as a sign of growth, and the first step to managing a magazine. This story is exactly what we needed, Mia."

"What did you tell Casey?" Mia asked to buy time. The next part of their discussion was going to be hard, especially now that her mother was beaming with pride over Mia's work. She hated to see that fade too quickly.

"I told him the magazine was already put to bed, ready to print. That I couldn't possibly change that on the basis of such a vague inquiry. Then I distracted him by making an offer on a full dozen of the shots he took in Prospect." She sighed. "Are any of these pictures I bought from Casey going to work or have I wasted money the magazine desperately needs?"

Mia rubbed her forehead as she considered how much to tell her. "You are going to pull the magazine back and put this story in, aren't you?"

Her mother's inelegant snort surprised Mia. Carla Romero did not often do anything as normal as snort. "Of course I am. This is big. Huge. I've already got the art department laying out new pages. Jesse is hoping to get a quote from the Association before we print, but the clock

is ticking. We'll go on without it and have a follow-up next month." Her mother smiled. "In the Prospect Western Days issue, for which I have a nice collection of photos already. Sure hope there's enough going on in Prospect to make all that space worthwhile."

"There is. So much." Mia thought about all the work Sarah and Jordan Hearst were doing. There were going to be plenty of new stories about Prospect to come.

Her mother didn't say anything, and Mia wanted to squirm in her seat. She'd always been much better at the waiting than Mia was. Nine times out of ten, Mia would confess immediately to whatever it was she suspected her of when she did this patient, watchful routine.

Mia would confess things her parent hadn't even discovered yet.

It was a powerful tactic, but today her mother gave in before it worked. "You know, I've been going back and forth between being angry that you didn't bring this story to me immediately and hurt that you didn't trust me to discuss this idea at all." She shook her head. "But I understand that I bear some of the responsibility for both of those issues."

Mia knew her shock showed on her face but she immediately tried to cover it. She wanted to say the right words, but she had no idea what they might be.

"When I took over from my father, I was so concerned about doing things his way." Her mother held her arms out to indicate the office. "I mean, staying here, in this space, in this exact office, in this location, it's indulgent at this point because there are smaller spaces with lower rents that would have eased some of the burden over the years."

Mia crossed her hands over her stomach. "The memories of the time I spent here, trailing behind Grandad, are always close by when I'm working in the office."

Her mother smiled. "Me too. I have my memories of scribbling stories on one side of the desk while he worked on the other, and then I can see you banging on the stapler while he bit his tongue and tried to ignore the scratches on his expensive furniture. If I had done the same? He would have explained to me about the finishes of antique desks, but 'Mia-mine' could do whatever made her happy."

The message behind her words sank in. "Writing for the magazine makes me happy. It does. But managing this business won't."

She nodded. "I get that. So, even though I was extremely shocked and proud and excited that you took control of this Grant Armstrong story the way you did, I agree that it's time to figure out the next phase for *The Way West*."

Mia bit her lip. "I always want the best for the magazine. Being the kind of news reporter you wanted was my goal for a long time, but this story showed me that it's not what I was meant to do. I was lucky to meet Grant and Annie. I'm thankful that a conversation with you helped me see that Jesse was the reporter this story needed. And watching him work…" She put her hand over her heart. "I don't have the instincts he has as a reporter or the business savvy you have to run the magazine. And I know that I'll never be happy or really successful in either role. I like small towns and craft fairs and funny characters and telling those stories. I like following the universe's direction to the next interesting project. I think I need to be in Prospect to be happy."

Her mother's slow smile instantly relieved some of the emotional stress building in Mia's abdomen. "I can't say that I support your theory about the universe gifting you with these moments, but…" She held up her hand as if she thought Mia might argue. There was no reason to fight about that. Mia knew what she knew, and one of those

things was that her mother would never trust someone or something else to make plans for her life.

And that was okay.

"But you're my daughter." Her mother reached across the desk to grasp Mia's hand. "If you aren't working for me, how are you going to pay the bills?"

"I guess I'll do whatever other writers do, the ones who were born to parents who didn't inherit a magazine." Mia realized she was going to have to get serious about quickly figuring out exactly what that might be.

"Struggle. That's what they do. I don't want that for you," her mother said softly. "I want you to be safe and happy. Always have and always will."

Mia rubbed the ache in her chest at her mother's words. She believed them. She and her mom might not agree on the plan for Mia's life, but there was no doubt that her mother wanted good things for her. "I can only do one of those things here. I can be safe, but to be happy, I need something more."

Her mother sighed. "Determination. I hear it in your voice."

"Yeah, that runs in the family, I guess." Mia smiled as her mother laughed.

"I have to admit that I definitely admire how well you know yourself, Mia. That is a gift that I want." Her mother stared out the window. In a month or so, the trees would leaf out and the view would transform from historic Billings architecture to a natural green screen. Both were beautiful. "The question that keeps popping up in my mind since I got serious about closing down the magazine is what in the world I would do with myself and my free time without this keeping me busy." She wrinkled her nose. "I hate to say it, but the fear of the unknown has been an incentive to keep grinding away here."

This was another place she and her mother were completely different. Mia never experienced this fear. The unknown might bring some jitters, a nervous energy, but she'd never been afraid.

"What if you hired a managing editor instead of closing the magazine?" Mia asked. As long as she was out of the equation, Mia would be happy to brainstorm solutions until the sun set. "You could take on a part-time role, oversee the finances and figure out what you wanted to do next?"

Her mother paused and gave the notion some thought before replying.

"Moving out of this space, switching to a fully remote working setup and running any required in-person work through a much smaller office would lower the overhead." Then Mia remembered her inspiration—the Cookie Queen Corporation possibly becoming their newest advertiser. "And I have a line on a new advertising partner. I plan to make a very personal pitch to the CEO of the Cookie Queen Corporation soon." Mia wanted to get on a plane bound for LA immediately, in fact, but she was going to make sure Grant's story got every bit of the magazine space it deserved first. She couldn't drop everything to run after her next exciting idea. Not when Grant's predicament and future was so important.

"You have a personal pitch to make to a corporate CEO?" Her mother's gaze drifted down Mia's outfit, but Mia decided to call it progress that none of her opinion was expressed verbally.

"I do. If I have the assistance of an experienced magazine executive to polish my proposals, I know we'll be bringing in new advertising dollars before next month to help cover an editor's salary." Mia was certain this pitch was going to work, no matter how she was dressed. Sometimes it was difficult to see how the universe could pull

all the threads together, but this time, everything was clear to Mia.

"Would we only be prolonging the inevitable if we do that, bring on a managing editor and patch the leak in advertising? Is this magazine fading into history?" her mother asked. It was hard to decide whether it was sadness in her eyes at that idea or if it was resignation. "It might be unwise to believe it was meant to last forever. Rodeo has changed. The West has definitely changed since my father started the magazine."

This had been the heart of Mia's pitch to add the travel articles about interesting locations.

"Could you sell the magazine, Mom?" Mia inched forward to sit on the edge of her chair. "If you could do that, you could take whatever comes from selling the subscriber list and the advertisers and whatever photography and assets the magazine holds, and create something new. A digital property, one that leaves you all kinds of freedom to change as you wish. It could be a new you and a new focus on the West."

Her mother's grimace was an instant judgment and Mia respected that. "Online, Mia?" She blinked for a moment before she stood to stare out the window at the street below. "What would that even look like?"

Mia laughed. "That part is up to you. That's what I was getting at, see? There are no rules, but you have the opportunity to create something only you would make, not Grandad and certainly not your weird daughter. Lots of people try this, but they don't have your experience or your taste. I believe it could be great."

Her mother glanced over her shoulder. "And where would my 'weird daughter' fall in all of this?"

Mia followed her over to the window. "Not fully clear

at this point, but I believe she's going to be in Prospect, Colorado, working on a project for the foreseeable future."

"So…" Her mother narrowed her eyes as she considered the possibilities. "For more than a sweet story about one hundred years of Western Days."

Mia nodded. That much she knew.

"And does the handsome cowboy who happens to be lying low there play a part in that foreseeable future?" her mother asked.

"I would definitely not be surprised if he becomes the only permanent piece of my future planning." That much was becoming clearer. The number of times she had almost called him on the way home was embarrassing and only the uncertainty between them had stopped her from phoning to discuss the story, her plans for the future, his trail ride business, the funny roadside signs and why there was always a line for the women's restroom no matter which gas station she chose.

Her mother blinked but seemed ready to accept that.

"If you were to decide that you needed a change of venue," Mia said as she slowly worked through the jumble of thoughts in her head, "there's this adorable place right outside the historic district of Prospect. The town newspaper used to be there, but it closed years ago. It might be a wonderful place to get a feel for small-town life in the modern West, where rodeo is a piece but not the heart of the story."

Her mother's slow smile convinced Mia to wrap her arm around her shoulder. "All you need is an internet connection, Mom."

"You've been saying that for years." She slipped her arms around Mia's waist and pulled her close.

"I've been right for years, too," Mia responded.

They were laughing when they stepped apart. "Let's

see what the new pages for this month look like and make sure Jesse's story has all the room it needs. Will you help me with that? We can also hunt up some photos while you tell me about Grant Armstrong." Her mother pointed at the desk. "It's not Grandad's, but we can still both work there."

Mia nodded and pulled her chair around to watch as her mother paged through the magazine layout. The future was still unclear, but there was no doubt in her mind that she was in the right place at the right time.

CHAPTER EIGHTEEN

TWO WEEKS AFTER Mia left town, Grant had reached the end of his patience with staring at the same four walls of the ranch house's living room. His brothers were ready to lock him in the barn for everyone's safety. There had been zero reports of strangers around town asking probing questions about Grant, but he had done his best to lay low. The cabin fever was getting to him.

When the bitter cold receded and warm sunshine called him to come outside, he marched into the kitchen and said, "Who's up for a ride to the ghost town today? I gotta get Jet out of the barn, stretch his legs some." And clear my mind, Grant thought.

"I want to go!" Micah said immediately. He never missed an opportunity to ride out with Grant. The kid hadn't met a horse before he got to the Rocking A, but his enthusiasm was making up for lost time. "Can I go?" He turned to Travis immediately to wait for permission.

Grant knew how far Travis and the boys had come from the early days when Micah had mistrusted almost everyone except Damon, the older boy who had become Micah's truest brother.

And he'd always been pretty comfortable with Funcle Grant, too. He took some pride in that.

"Still pretty cold. The ground's going to be slippery in places." Travis tipped his head back. "Damon, what do you think? Should we all go?"

Damon shoved a whole slice of bacon in his mouth as he nodded. As long as no one took the kid's plate away before he was ready, Damon was up for almost anything. Since he'd grown at least two inches since November, it was a constant struggle to keep the kid filled up. "I'll bring a biscuit or two. Just in case." He reached over to wrap two in a napkin and shoved a third in his mouth.

Travis turned to Grant with raised eyebrows but shook his head. "As long as you can guarantee that we will return before Damon gets hungry enough to pick one of us to eat, we're all in."

Grant chuckled. "Good. I gotta get some fresh air." Wes walked in. "You up for a ride?"

Wes immediately nodded. "Always."

After they had all the horses saddled, Grant lifted Micah up to sit in front of him after some brief negotiation. They were working on his riding skills and the kid was going to be an awesome cowboy, but with the higher degree of difficulty, thanks to the snowy patches and terrain, everyone felt better if he rode with Grant. Even Micah.

They were quiet as they rode across the pasture and through the gate onto the Majestic's land. Sadie Hearst had been the Rocking A's neighbor for a long time, and they'd always had permission to journey across and up to Sullivan's Post.

"As long as they can act right," Sadie would always tack on when they were kids.

It was as if she knew that, most of the time, they were ready to act all wrong when they were out of sight of Walt and the barn. Now that Jordan and Sarah had taken over the Majestic, the gate between the two properties got regular use and no one was surprised when Sarah stepped outside to wave at them.

Wes immediately peeled off from the group to go over

for a hello kiss, but she sent him back with a wave, and they continued the steep climb up the hills.

"Think this is too challenging for beginners?" he asked Travis and Wes. The idea of running trail rides had grown on him. Jordan had been right, but he was delaying telling her that, because she didn't need any extra confidence in ordering people around. He smiled inwardly at the thought.

Travis motioned with his head toward Damon, who was in the lead. The older boy was guiding the horse, but most of the time, his head was swiveling left and right as he took in the landscape. "I'd say on the right horses, you should be fine. Damon's had you teaching him for a while, so he might be ahead of the casual visitor, but he's not worried at all. And with enough experience on the trail, the horses will do most of the heavy lifting all by themselves."

Wes joined them. "You may want to consider a minimum age for your riders, and be sure to put that in the advertising. Micah could do this, but it seems risky to let kids you don't know loose up here."

Grant frowned. "You mean I have to bring kids up here, too?"

"Hey," Micah said in outrage from his spot in front of Grant. "Kids love this stuff."

Grant chuckled. "You aren't a kid, Micah. You're middle management in a kid's body."

"Uncle Grant loves kids," Travis said and squeezed Grant's shoulder. "So much that he's going to run a club for them, teach them all about rodeo."

Micah craned his head back to stare up at Grant. "Can I join the club?"

Grant bent his head so they were staring at each other upside down. "You're number one on the list, but I need you to do me a favor."

Micah tried to nod enthusiastically and started to tilt

so Grant steadied him. "Talk Travis and Wes into helping out, would you?"

The kid's wicked grin convinced him he had his best man on the job.

Wes gave him a stern side-eye but Grant wasn't worried. His brothers would probably have agreed if he'd made a simple request, but Micah could be relentless when he had a mission.

His brother rubbed his forehead, looking slightly worried. Most likely with his usual consternation over Grant's impulses to shake things up. "With the age limit, a solid contract, and your stern lecture about safety for the horse and the rider, Grant, you could do trail rides up here. If you want. If not, there's work around the ranch that will keep us all busy."

"But you have to be the one to tell Jordan you aren't going to add this amenity to the Majestic's lineup." Travis's grimace matched the twist in Grant's gut at the thought of Jordan's disappointment.

They made it to the ghost town. Snow was still gathered in drifts in the shadows but the wide main street was clear. The old settlement was in rough shape, many of the roofs missing, but the history was there. It would make a great attraction for visitors to Prospect if they could ensure everyone's safety.

"You guys ever wish we had sisters?" Grant asked out of curiosity. It was hard to imagine life without Sarah and Jordan keeping them busy, but they'd managed happily enough before the Hearsts had rolled into town.

"Faye was trouble enough." Travis shook his head firmly.

Wes laughed. "Me, neither, but it's hard to complain, now that we have them. They have made things exciting around here."

"Grant, let me down. I want to check on whatever it is that Damon's looking at." Micah slid out of the saddle as he hurried over to where Damon was kneeling on the ground. Travis followed and moved to stand by them.

"Looks like…a bear track?" he said uncertainly as he turned to look over his shoulder at Wes. "Come here."

They were both headed over when Grant's cell phone rang. He'd expected to be out of range, but the clear skies had improved reception.

Then he saw Jesse Martinez's name on the display. "Hey, Jesse," he said as he turned away from the group studying the print in the snow. "What's up?" They had spoken off and on in the rush to get the story in under the magazine's printer deadline, but that was done.

"If you somehow missed the disturbance in the force, March's issue is out today. Your face is front and center wherever *The Way West* is on newsstands and will be landing in mailboxes in the next day or two." Jesse cleared his throat. "I sent a copy to Annie Mercado and Red Williams. I heard back from Red before sunrise this morning. He's unhappy with his image in the article. The angle of the story was misrepresented to him by me in order to sell magazines and he's exploring his options with legal redress." Jesse hummed. "Yeah, that's what I wrote. 'Redress.' To me, that does sound like he's got a lawyer feeding him lines, so in case that blows up, I wanted you to have fair warning. I wouldn't be surprised if Red's worried about losing everything. The whispers I've heard include a lifetime ban from the sport as well as legal or civil penalties he might face."

"What about the Association? Any word on their investigation or outcome?" Grant kicked his boot against the icy edge of the closest snow drift as he waited to see if panic or fear surfaced.

"I've already talked with Carla Romero, and she had a legal review to make sure there's no case against us. That doesn't mean Red won't try it. As far as sanctions by the Association for not reporting the scheme when you first learned of it..." Jesse let the sentence trail off.

"Okay, we can weather some bad press if that's what it boils down to, but please let me know if you hear anything more from the Association or their lawyers." If there were penalties of some sort...

Then he noticed that Wes had turned back to listen to his side of the call. "My oldest brother is a lawyer. If it comes to a battle in court, we'll be ready." The idea of a drawn-out legal or financial fight involving his family made his head hurt but he knew they had his back. Together his family would figure it out.

At that moment, Grant realized he'd accepted that standing up to Red to defend himself was the right thing to do, no matter the consequences. He hadn't done anything wrong except trust the wrong person.

And the only way to make that right was to ensure no one else made the same mistake if he could help it.

"Good. My hope is Red's mainly rattling his cage at this point. We have the evidence, and I can't imagine Annie Mercado being afraid of anything."

Grant wished he'd had a chance to meet the young woman who had taken over all the space his disappearance had created. The few times he'd wandered into rodeo territory on the internet, she'd been front and center. And she was smart enough to do it without Red Williams.

"You still up for any interview requests that might come in? Wouldn't be surprised if there's a TV appearance, and everyone would be relieved if I offered your pretty face instead of my mug." Grant heard a screech in

the background. "Oh boy, he's up already. You have kids yet, Grant?"

He laughed as he watched Micah sneak up on Damon to slip snow down his collar. "Nope, just an uncle so far."

"You better get started. I wish I was a younger man, now that I know how challenging grandkids are. If I hear anything else, I'll text or call."

"Okay, sounds good." Before Jesse could hang up, Grant asked, "Hey, how's Mia?"

The silence on the other end of the line was loud because all noise stopped around Grant. He turned to check on his family and saw that every single eye was locked on him.

Eventually Jesse said, "Well, now, I did not expect this." He chuckled. "She's a firecracker, but I believe you are fully aware of that. She has stirred up some conversation around the office. Appears there's a plan to shut down production of the magazine. Every time I've seen her in the past week, she has been moving at high speed."

Grant raised his eyebrows at Travis and Wes, but they shrugged in response.

"Oh," Grant said and wished he had something more interesting to add, but no, nothing was coming.

"Wonder where she might have got the idea to move out of Billings and change her career path, cowboy," Jesse drawled. "It ain't like she's ever been one of those career-driven journalism types, like yours truly, but it did seem like my job would last as long as I wanted it to. Now Carla Romero's finally made some decisions about her future and the magazine's, and so I'm a man faced with retirement myself. You got any good tips for me?"

"Uh, no. For me, leaving rodeo just means a new job, new pursuits, not retirement." Grant was stuck on what

it meant that Mia was moving out of Billings, away from her mother and career.

And he wished he'd heard the news from Mia herself.

Jesse laughed again and the tension seemed to evaporate. "Carla and I have worked well together for decades now, and I never saw such a smile on her face as I did when she made her announcement about stopping production."

Grant propped his hand on his hip, anxious to pace as a hundred different questions arose, but Jesse said, "Mia left town yesterday, so I'm not certain how she is at this moment, but it seems that things are moving at a fair pace here in the office. Most of the staff are planning a nice long vacation with a piece of the generous severance package Carla is offering."

Grant sighed. "To be honest, all I needed you to say was 'fine' or 'good,' something to convince me not to call Mia and ask her how soon she was coming back."

"It's like that, is it? You've got it bad." Jesse chuckled. "I bet you'll hear her coming from a mile away. She's got some plans. We talked 'em over a bit and I expect she's ready to shake things up."

Grant liked the sound of that. "I don't doubt it, Jesse. Thanks for the heads up about Red. We'll be ready and if you need to pass any phone calls along to me to field, I'll be happy to take them. Working with you has been a pleasure."

"Yeah, I'm thinking I might pack up the family and bring them down to see these Cowboy Games. Mia tells me there ain't another competition like it. Got a grandson that would sure like to have his picture taken with you. What would you say to that?"

Grant rolled his shoulders as more of the tension eased. Surely if his reputation was going to take a beating, Jesse would know and he'd keep his grandson far, far away.

"We're going to have the perfect photo opportunity set up just for that. I'll be happy to meet you all there." The loud screech that interrupted him made him second-guess the "happy" part, but he wasn't going to take it back. Jesse's T-rex soundalike grandson was a problem for another day.

After he hung up, he saw that Travis and Wes were both watching him, arms crossed across their chests, as if they were patiently waiting for him to come to his senses.

"What?" he asked.

Damon stepped between them. "You aren't trying to play it cool, are you, Uncle Grant? Girls hate that."

It was satisfying to watch Wes and Travis turn puzzled stares at the teenager, but it was impossible to argue with his certainty.

Still, Grant had a long history of arguing. "How would you know? Did your girlfriend tell you that?"

He tipped his head to the side, anxious to hear the answer.

Damon sniffed. "No, but Keena has been giving me hints on how to talk to girls that I like. Poking them is a bad idea, but asking them about their favorite song on the radio and then remembering some of the words is a good tip. I tried it and Trina Smith responded favorably."

All three of the adults exchanged a glance. The evidence was strong. It should work.

"What was her favorite song?" Travis asked.

"It changes, but she started singing 'Love Story.'" Damon shrugged. "That Taylor Swift song? I figured that was a good place to start, so the next day at lunch, I mentioned hearing the song, something about Romeo and Juliet." Damon rocked back and forth in his boots. "She's been sitting at my lunch table ever since. Keena would probably help you if you asked her nicely, Uncle Grant."

His wicked grin as he watched Grant come to terms

with his own need for dating help made Grant laugh. And it wasn't a chuckle, it was one of those laughs that he couldn't stop, not even if he was worried that the people watching would think he'd lost grip on reality. Luckily, Wes and Travis were laughing along. Micah had joined the conversation, but his confusion made it clear he wasn't quite ready for Keena's flirting advice.

Before Grant could second-guess himself, he pulled out his phone and dialed Mia's number. When she instantly answered, his worry melted away.

"Hey, I had my phone out, staring at the screen, wondering what you were up to and whether I would bother you if I called you," Mia said before asking, "Can we make this a video call? I've missed your face."

Grant mimed a celebratory high five to Damon, Travis and Wes before he switched the call. "You've missed my face. That might be the nicest thing anyone has ever said to me. I've missed your voice, your face and the weird way my heart stutters when you're around."

The low whistle Travis let out made Grant scowl over his shoulder, but considering all the grief he'd given Travis over his courtship with Keena, he deserved it.

"Do we have an audience?" Mia asked as she moved closer to the screen, as if she could stick her head through to peer around.

"No one important, my brothers and my nephews." Grant waved a hand to shoo them away. They ignored him.

"And you're being sweet in front of them?" Mia silently said "wow," her eyes big in surprise. "Grant Armstrong is a romantic gentleman. I love to see that."

He shifted his shoulders, aware that he was losing this argument and then decided it didn't matter. "Jesse called to tell me the magazine's out. Are you happy with it?"

Her pleasure filled him with that fizzy, happy glow

that he was still coming to terms with. "I am. It's good work and my name is on it, too. Now that my mother and I finally see eye to eye, it's not quite as important to me anymore. I still appreciate it, though." Then she rolled her eyes. "But if she tells me one more time how I'm using all the business and journalism classes I've taken, I'll have to run away from home forever. Do I have the degree? No, but I never once complained about taking the classes. I like the classes, I just didn't want to waste my life on things I didn't love." She inhaled slowly. "Sorry. She and I are coming around to understanding each other. Slowly."

Grant would have listened to her theories on education and the universe for as long as she wanted to share them. He was so happy to see her. Then he realized she was walking as she talked. He could hear garbled noises, too.

"Where are you?" he asked.

"Baggage claim at LAX. This place is a nightmare. A horror movie. A nightmare that takes place inside a horror movie." Mia disappeared for a second before her face popped back up on the screen. "Remind me to carry on the next time I need to fly to Los Angeles."

"What are you doing there?" Grant asked. Whatever he'd expected her to do next, this was not on the list.

"I want to explore this idea I had for what I'll do once the magazine is finished." She slung a bag over her shoulder. "I've got a meeting tomorrow with Michael Hearst at the Cookie Queen Corporation and then I'm back to Billings. After that, I'm going to drive back down to Prospect to stay until Western Days. I'm looking forward to being within kissing distance again."

Grant wanted more information on this trip to LA and the career she was planning there, but he forced a smile on his face. "Kissing distance is the right distance."

Her sweet smile reassured him. "Gotta find a rental

car in this maze. I'll call you when I get back to Billings, okay? And be on the lookout for photographers and reporters who want to have their own follow-up to your story. I don't want you or your family caught off guard."

Grant nodded. "I hope your meeting goes well."

"Oh, it will. I have no doubt about that. I miss you, but I'll see you soon." She waited for him to say goodbye before ending the call, but before he hung up, he asked, "Hey, what's your favorite song?"

Her eyebrows shot up.

"You know, that they play on the radio?" Grant ignored the way Travis and Wes grinned.

Mia pursed her lips. "Interesting question. When I was driving back to Billings, I heard Miranda Lambert's 'If I Was a Cowboy.' Since I'm part tumbleweed myself, I've always liked that." Then she moved her face closer to the screen. "But if I was there with you and we didn't have such an audience watching us, I'd go with The Chicks and sing 'Cowboy, Take Me Away.'" When she leaned back, he could tell she was pleased with herself.

He had to admit that he liked her answers. A lot. But the reminder of their audience was helpful. "Good to know. I definitely want to discuss this again. Soon. Within kissing distance. Call me when you can."

After he hung up, Damon came over and patted his shoulder. "It wasn't smooth but it was effective. I could tell she liked the effort."

Grant wasn't sure why his teenage nephew's approval made him feel so much better, but at this point, he was prepared to count that as a win.

And when Mia returned to town, working her song into conversation would be his best idea yet.

CHAPTER NINETEEN

MIA WAS ON the phone with her mother when she pulled into a visitor parking spot in front of the headquarters of the Cookie Queen Corporation.

"I told you the traffic in LA would be horrible. Why not take a taxi or a ride share?" her mother asked.

Mia didn't even consider answering the question, because she knew her mother would be on to something else in a matter of seconds. Even if they were getting along better, her mother might never be a calm voice of reason when Mia was traveling away from home. Is that how all mothers were?

"It was a wrong turn, Mom. Everyone makes a wrong turn now and then." Had she made a poor decision by turning the wrong way into a one-way entrance into the parking lot? Yes, but no one else knew that and she had done her best to calmly get the rental car headed in the correct direction to begin with. "I'm still early for this appointment, so there's no reason to be so anxious."

Her mother sighed. "You're right. I worry about you, but you've done much harder things on your own. This is a meeting. That's all, and we both know you're the right person for this project."

Mia studied her reflection in the mirror before giving herself a firm nod. "I absolutely am. Thank you for helping me get my presentation in order. We made a good team on this pitch."

"We did, and I'm glad." Her mother's voice had lost some of the boss tone.

"Are you thinking about what happens after the last issue?" They'd agreed that the last issue would be the one following the Western Days spread. Mia was certain that was the best decision. "I want you to consider a visit to Prospect. The pictures are beautiful, but there's something about the place that you have to experience to understand."

"It's not some magic destination where your future is revealed." Her mother laughed. "But I guess it did exactly that for you."

Mia studied the lipstick her mother had pressed in her hand at the airport before dropping it back into her purse. Today was not the day to take risks with new cosmetics. "Not my whole future, but important pieces of it. Even if it doesn't do the same for you, it's a pretty place where you could slow down and clear your mind. You could try painting. Jordan texted that the Wi-Fi speed is exceptional at the Majestic. What more could you ask for?" Her mother's chuckle helped Mia relax. "Think about it."

"You'd be okay if I followed you down there for a stay?" her mother asked.

Mia stared at the boxy office building that sat in front of a small water feature and a lot of neatly arranged landscaping. There were a couple of smaller buildings ranging out on either side, but Sadie's headquarters stood tall in the center.

"I really would. You could help me research." Mia checked her borrowed briefcase and wondered if she was going to look like a little girl in her mother's high heels when she walked into the lobby with the expensive briefcase...borrowed from her mother.

"Maybe I will. Call me when your meeting is over. I know how it will turn out, but I want to celebrate with you

and listen nervously while you maneuver LA traffic back to your hotel by the airport."

Mia shook her head. "I will definitely call you as soon as I'm done."

They ended the call, and Mia considered sending Grant a text. Talking with him, seeing his face had boosted her certainty that she was on the right path. Every step felt more solid.

"But the sooner you get a contract, the sooner you'll be back in Billings." Mia opened the car door and slid out, being very careful not to ding the expensive SUV parked in the next spot. She had always been lucky enough to have nice things, but there was something about this vehicle that convinced her that the owner took serious pride in the ownership. That had something to do with the high gleam and crystal clear finish. The image of her dusty car, after less than a week in Prospect, flashed through her mind.

It had never occurred to her to be bothered by the dusty film.

"Another sign you'll fit right into small-town life, Mia." She gripped the briefcase handle firmly and strode toward the revolving door. It was whisper quiet as it moved, and Mia was standing in a tall, modern lobby in an instant. As she waited for the receptionist to end her call, Mia studied the furnishings. There was a photo of Sadie behind the reception desk, her warm smile inviting, as it was in every photo Mia had found. She was seated behind a desk and the large mountain vista currently hanging behind the Majestic's check-in desk was her backdrop. Below that were photos of the Cookie Queen Corporation's current board of directors and Michael Hearst, the CEO she was here to pitch to. She was happy to recognize Patrick Hearst, Sarah and Jordan's father, who she'd met in Prospect.

"Michael's in another meeting, but he said he'd be down

to meet you soon." The receptionist stood and pointed at the hallway. "If you'd like, he suggested you tour the displays of Sadie's memorabilia, which we've been in the process of adding under Sarah's direction. Would you like water?"

Mia nodded gratefully. "That would be wonderful. Nerves give me dry mouth, which makes it difficult to speak."

The receptionist's expression flashed confusion before she smiled and then produced a bottle of water from a small refrigerator behind her desk. She offered it to Mia.

"That was too much information, wasn't it?" Mia waved a hand between them. "Nerves."

The receptionist shrugged. "No one holds onto their reserved professional demeanor here for long. Some companies say their employees are family, but Sadie Hearst lived it."

Mia nodded. "Good to know. Did you work with Sadie long?"

The receptionist paused as she calculated. "I've been here nearly five years, so I was lucky enough to get to know Sadie well. She was exactly as you'd expect her to be from her shows. There was no acting. That lovely personality was real."

"I've gotten to know Sarah and Jordan. I believe you." Mia moved toward the display as the receptionist stepped away to answer the ringing phone. The first display case was filled with a couple of mannequins dressed in Sadie's line of Western wear and images of Sadie's life arranged in a timeline from when she launched her TV show until her death. It was an impressive visual of how quickly Sadie made each step. She didn't hesitate.

Before Mia could look at the other memorabilia, the elevator dinged and the doors opened. Michael Hearst stepped out. He was escorting another man who Mia would

have bet her entire paycheck was the owner of the spotless SUV outside.

His suit was expensive. Mia didn't know much about men's suits or designer labels in general, but the fit was perfection.

When the two men shook hands, Mia noticed a tattoo across the top of one of the man's hands, which revised her assumption from international royalty to... Well, she had no idea, but he was a handsome one, whatever he was.

He was no Grant Armstrong, but there was only one of those.

"You must be Mia Romero." Michael Hearst held out his hand and shook hers before pointing at his associate. "This is Brian Caruso. He's the executive chef and owner of Rinnovato. Have you heard of it?"

Mia's eyebrows rose because the restaurant was one of the most exclusive in LA, known for serving truly decadent Italian cuisine.

"I know you by reputation, of course, but I've not been lucky enough to eat in your restaurant." Mia smiled politely, curious about what was happening but always ready to pick up tiny bits of interesting news here and there.

"Mia's been in Prospect with Sarah and Jordan." Michael patted the chef on the back. "Brian is working with us to produce a web-streaming show coming from the lodge for the Cookie Queen website. This is something new. We're trying to keep traffic coming to the Cookie Queen website now that we won't have Sadie providing recipes there. Sadie kicked around the idea of producing her own series, but we could never agree on a budget or a concept. I'm sure you've heard Sarah and Jordan plotting their next phase of expansion at the Majestic Prospect Lodge." Michael shoved his hands in his pockets. "Brian's helping us identify two competitors for this web-streaming competition. The win-

ner will get a nice prize and the chance to run the lodge's kitchen for a year. Brian is also going to lend some of his star power as a judge."

"If you're in town this weekend, drop by Rinnovato." Brian rubbed his hands together. "I'd love to pick your brain about what I'm getting myself into by agreeing to spend a couple of weeks in the mountains at a fishing lodge." He said the last words slowly as if they were unfamiliar. "I don't fish. I don't mountain much, either."

There was no need for him to confess that. She could have guessed from his shiny car and his equally shiny shoes, but she wasn't picking up a snobbish vibe. Uncertainty made sense. So did investigating to find out, before he rolled into town.

She might go with the flow and depend on the kindness of strangers when the only bed-and-breakfast in town was fully booked and she had no reservation, but it was more than fair that others preferred to plan their trips more thoroughly.

"One of the prettiest places I've ever seen, and I'm a travel writer. You'll be impressed," Mia said. "I guess you'll be leaving for Prospect soon if this is happening before Western Days. I'm on my way back, too."

"Yes, we're going to take advantage of a school break. My daughter is also coming. If Sadie loved the town, I expect I will, too. I owe her so much that I'm happy to expand my horizons."

Mia immediately wanted to ask twenty questions, but Brian checked his expensive watch. "I better hit the road. I have to pick my daughter up from her mother's house soon."

Michael nodded and then motioned Mia toward the elevator. "I hear you have a business proposal for me. I am intrigued."

While he showed her to his office, Mia realized that she had been turning this way and that to see as much of the Cookie Queen offices as she could and immediately reminded herself that she should try to act like someone who had either a business degree or a journalism degree, at the very least.

Now, situated in Michael's cool office, she calmly opened the briefcase and pulled out two folders. "I have two pitches today. They are separate but related." She straightened her shoulders as she slid the first one across his polished desk. "Inside, you will find a proposal for a biography of Sadie Hearst. Written by me. For the Cookie Queen Corporation. Or not. You will have the right to approve the manuscript and ask for revisions. We will work together to locate the right publisher." Mia clasped her hands together tightly. "I have been lucky enough to spend time where Sadie grew up. I've read her cookbooks and even some of the recipe files Sarah and Jordan have on hand in Prospect. I've created a chapter-by-chapter outline. My initial concept is to use her most popular recipes as the introduction to each period of Sadie's life. You see the first chapter features her famous Cowboy Cookie."

"The one that started it all out at the lodge," Michael murmured as he scanned the first page.

She forced herself to pause to give him time to read the pages she'd roughed out as an example of her style. There was very little doubt in Mia's mind that she'd nailed the exact mix of information and comfortable tone that reflected Sadie perfectly.

"A biography. And you've listed how it would be marketed and sold along with Sadie's cookbooks. Did Sarah put you up to this?" Michael smiled slowly. "It's exactly the kind of thing she would do, eliminate any question I might ask in order to assure a victory."

Mia sat taller in her seat. "I will take that as a compliment. It's the first book proposal I've written, so I was following my gut." It was good to know her gut had good instincts, and that the time she'd spent suffering through college courses she did not enjoy could possibly return dividends at this late date. Who knew spreadsheets had so many good uses?

"It's a good idea." He leaned back in his cushy chair. "I need to do my own research, because we've been publishing Sadie's cookbooks for some time, but this would be a completely new direction. Figuring out the pay structure and the legalities of the contract won't be simple."

Mia still took that as a win. "I'm going to start this project as soon as I get back to Prospect. I'm excited about it."

He frowned. "You aren't a great negotiator—are you aware of that?"

"I've had a strong suspicion that was true," Mia said slowly, "but I believe Sadie and I are connected somehow. You wouldn't want to disappoint her by offering a subpar contract."

He chuckled. "You never met Sadie, right?"

"Not in person." Mia had met so many people who knew Sadie, though. She'd walked in Sadie's footsteps here and in Prospect, and she wanted to be friends with Sarah and Jordan. Mia would say she knew enough about Sadie Hearst to trust that her memory would convince her great-nephew to deal fairly and honestly with her.

"Sadie was tough on me." Michael smoothed his tie. "We knew I was going to be sitting here someday, but I struggled to figure out how to be good at this job. Sadie? She didn't cut me any slack while she watched me like a hawk. This place, these people, they were her family, too, so she had high expectations for me." He shrugged. "And I'm glad, especially now that she's gone. I feel the weight

of responsibility of keeping this business healthy. Sadie taught me how. I just have to follow her instructions." He tapped the proposals in front of him. "And lean heavily on Sarah."

Mia smiled. "I'm going home to Prospect. When you're ready to talk about what the contract looks like, we can iron it out, but…" She slid the second folder across the desk. "This is going to be important, too. Are you familiar with *The Way West*?"

He nodded and pulled out the advertising fee structure for the magazine. "I am. I don't know if we advertise in the magazine."

"You should. The next issue will feature Prospect, Western Days and the new Sadie Hearst museum, prominently." Mia grinned. "Advertising in the issue makes sense, but you should also consider coming in early on the digital platform my mother is planning to launch after the magazine's print version folds. With a long-term agreement, I can see plenty of opportunity for hosting Cookie Queen Corporation content and providing fresh material for your websites, possibly produced in Prospect." If Mia got her way.

Her mother would surely see the benefits of moving her work to Prospect once Mia got through listing all the reasons to do so. "I expect that will be a late summer or fall project, but you could discuss advertising terms for the magazine and any savings that might come from signing before the website launches." Mia licked her lips nervously, relieved to have gotten every single bit of that out without stumbling or blacking out from nerves.

Michael propped his elbow on the desk and rested his chin on his hand. "This might be the most interesting sales pitch I've ever experienced. Gutsy. Bold."

Mia gripped the armrests of the chair. She would have

chosen those adjectives for Sadie. He would appreciate them, right?

"More interesting than the biography you're going to buy that you didn't know you needed?" Mia asked.

"Yeah. Even more than that." He closed the folder. "I'll give your mother a call to see what terms we can agree to. Since you seem certain this is in everyone's best interests."

Mia was learning that the gifts of the universe sometimes depended on knowing when to make graceful exits, so she stood and offered Michael her hand. "My phone number is listed on both proposals, but if you need an alternate method to track me down, I'll be staying at the Majestic."

Michael stood as she walked toward the door. "Hey, Mia…"

She opened it and paused.

"Remind Sarah that she promised to reserve a room for me. I'm thinking I might need to see what Western Days is all about." He waved her folders. "I'll be in touch about Sadie's biography."

She nodded, exited his glass office and stepped onto the waiting elevator, poised and serene.

Her neutral expression held all the way through the lobby and out into the parking lot.

The spotless SUV was gone, confirming Mia's hunch about the driver.

But as soon as she was behind the wheel of her rental and the car door was shut, she did a celebratory dance to end all celebratory dances. Her faith in the universe was holding strong, and her confidence in her own abilities was growing every day.

Now all she had to do was enjoy it…within kissing distance of Grant Armstrong.

CHAPTER TWENTY

ON FRIDAY NIGHT, Grant was breaking down a cardboard box, and wondering how much longer his unpaid shift at the new Sadie Hearst museum was going to last, when his father inched up beside him.

"Don't let Sarah see us conversatin'," Walt said in a low voice through stiff lips. "I don't want to get my pay docked, but you doin' okay? How you're looking over your shoulder has me worried we're gonna be ambushed by that ol' scalawag Red Williams again. I'll create a diversion to distract Sarah if you need to escape out the back."

Grant grunted his amusement before shooting a careful glance over his shoulder. "She is determined to get this place set up tonight, isn't she?" He tossed the flattened cardboard on top of the stack next to his foot and picked up another box. "If Red shows up here, he'll regret it. Catching me out on the sidewalk in front of the Ace was one thing. No way would he wade into this herd of family and friends to try to take me on."

His father narrowed his eyes. "Shoot. I been working on my resting mean face."

Grant studied his father's expression. To him, it read more "the print's too small and I can't find my glasses" than a real threat, but he appreciated the effort.

He squeezed his father's shoulder. "Mia texted she was on the road early this morning. I expected her to be here by now, that's all. If Red's still around, we'll handle him."

Walt carefully stacked the cookbooks he'd been told to remove from boxes and place on shelves. "That Red Williams fella is a bushwhacker, riding into town with his own reporter. That's some grade A nerve right there. I'm glad you didn't mince words, son."

If he hadn't been surprised by running into Red on the street in front of the Ace High after an excellent dinner, he might have been more careful in how he'd handled the encounter. Shock and the immediate anger that welled up when he'd seen the man who had betrayed his trust had burned right through the polite restraint Prue had tried to teach him.

Grant didn't regret a single loud, honest word.

After that exchange, where Red promised he'd find a way to get even, Faye refused to serve him in the restaurant and Rose Bell had no room in the bed-and-breakfast. Red was either too smart or hadn't learned about the Majestic, because he had loaded back up into his truck and driven out of town instead of hanging around any longer with no place to sleep.

Prospect had rallied around Grant.

Even if he had gotten into more trouble than he should have growing up, his neighbors had stood with him.

That felt good.

For the first time in months, Grant was nearly relaxed. He didn't know what the final fallout would be from the Association's investigation yet, but his family and friends were nearby.

There was only one piece missing tonight: Mia.

Grant tossed the flattened cardboard down and took the box his father handed him. "How much trouble will I be in if I sneak away to call Mia?" No one was quite sure what the punishment might be for lollygagging, but the intense expression on Sarah's face had quelled even Jordan's usual

complaints. She had settled into a spot on the floor, next to the large display of Sadie Hearst merchandise, where she was grimly arranging DVD collections into her best artistic vision, which Sarah would undoubtedly rearrange while muttering under her breath. But the firm management style was getting results.

A couple of hours ago, when they'd walked into what was once the tailor's shop, the place had been full of neatly organized stacks of unopened boxes. But now…so much progress had been made. This would be an amazing museum. Even he could see it. The mannequins were arranged here and there throughout the space to showcase Sadie's glittery style. All of the memorabilia Sarah had chosen for the museum's opening collection was carefully lit in glass cases. Informational placards were attached. All in all, they were still looking at cleanup but the space had been transformed.

"I'm not sure I'd want to work for her long-term, but you cannot argue with the results," Wes said from Grant's other side.

Walt raised his eyebrows.

Wes chuckled.

"I love all of you," Sarah said as she stuck her head into the mix, "but if you have time to talk, you need more to do."

Wes pressed a kiss to her lips. "You're doing a great job, babe."

Sarah's expression softened immediately. "Thank you, babe. You are, too." Then she marched off in another direction.

Grant could see that his mother had been volunteered to work on the display at the reception desk. "This place is terrific. I hope Sarah can take a minute to enjoy what she's done."

Wes nodded. "Yeah, me too. She's concerned about Michael's opinion on whether she's spent the corporation's funds well, but most of all, I know she wants to make Sadie proud."

"Can't imagine anyone finding fault with this place," Walt said. "Not sure what counts as state-of-the-art in terms of museums, but the group Sarah's been working with has included some high-tech features, all controlled by an app. Can you believe that?"

It wasn't surprising that Sarah and Jordan would want the best for their great-aunt.

When Grant had pictured a Sadie Hearst museum, he'd expected the photos and pieces from Sadie's life that were on display, but the modern touches that Sarah had incorporated were a nice surprise. The rough walls behind the facades on Fashion Row had been covered in a large sepia-toned photograph that spanned three walls and depicted Prospect's Old Town. The cases blended in and every piece Sarah had chosen stood out, but also seemed to belong to the setting. It was jaw-dropping.

He pulled his phone out to check for a text but noticed that Sarah, Jordan and Prue had formed a committee in front of the large display of Sadie-inspired merchandise. Their heads were together. He couldn't make out the words, but they would converse, scatter to make minute adjustments and return to the center to repeat.

Eventually Sarah spoke up. "Okay, everyone. I can't tell you how much I've appreciated what you have helped me out with tonight. This place is…" She covered her face with her hands, overcome with emotion. "It's my dream and it's coming true and I miss Sadie desperately, but I love it and I love you and I…"

Jordan wrapped her arm around Sarah's shoulders and hugged her tightly.

Grant could hear boots shuffling nervously and wondered if Sarah was about to be mobbed by a group hug, but she waved her hands in front of her face and sniffed loudly. "I want you to be the first ones in town to see this."

Grant crossed his arms and leaned carefully against the counter as Sarah turned down the lights, using the tablet in her hand. Whatever came next, it was going to be special.

MIA PULLED THE door closed quietly so she didn't interrupt Sarah, who was speaking in the middle of the room. She moved in between Amanda and Lucky, who were at the back of the group facing the large screen on the longest wall of the museum space. There were shelves of Colorado Cookie Queen cookbooks and DVDs on one side and small housewares arranged on the other.

"We want this place to celebrate Sadie, but we know she would say she was nothing without Prospect. Amanda gave us permission to use a recorded greeting that Sadie did years ago for the Picture Show. Rose Bell and Prue Armstrong added local town color in the way of old photos and oral history, and the rest of this… Well, I hope you like it." Sarah tapped the tablet in her hand and then she moved to the back of the group. When she saw Mia, she immediately towed her closer to the screen.

She and Jordan stood on either side of Mia as the presentation started to play. A smooth narrator spoke over a changing slideshow of old photos, covering the foundation of the town, first as Sullivan's Post in the hills above the Majestic Prospect Lodge, and then after it moved and spread in its current location as Prospect.

Mia was entranced as antique stills of rough silver miners and finely dressed town politicians blended into color photos of the 1960s and 1970s.

"Cowboys in bell bottoms. I never would have guessed,"

Jordan murmured as she bumped Mia's shoulder. When they snickered, Sarah hushed them.

"We're getting to the best part," Sarah said sternly.

It was something to watch the transition go so smoothly, and when Sadie Hearst burst on the scene, the background music changed. The tone lifted, and the warm, happy buzz Mia experienced anytime she saw Sadie Hearst's smile returned instantly.

Sarah and the museum consultants had included publicity shots of Sadie on a TV set, but most of the photos were lovely candid shots. There was one of Sadie in a hammock with three little girls crowded in beside her and a sweet-looking woman making rabbit ears behind Sadie's head.

"We had to get our mom in there, too." Jordan blinked rapidly. "Brooke is going to kill us when she finds out we put that one in." Since the youngest girl's smile was ragged, thanks to a missing front tooth, Mia thought she understood why Brooke might not be pleased.

Then the video introduction started. Sadie was standing on the wood sidewalk in front of the Prospect Picture Show. She was wearing dark jeans, a red-and-white gingham button-down shirt, with white fringe forming a V on the front, and a bright white Stetson.

"Well, now, I was hoping we'd meet right here. You found me in one of my favorite spots, the Prospect Picture Show in my hometown, the prettiest place you ever saw. Do you like cowboys?" Sadie's sly grin flashed. "Don't we all? Whether it's a silver-screen hero or one a little more down-to-earth, betcha find that cowboy here because you are lookin' in the right place. Come inside, grab a treat and find your seat. Welcome to Prospect. We sure are glad to see you." The last frame was of Sadie standing, hands propped on her hips. When the presentation was over, the lights came up slowly.

Everyone was quiet until Prue said, "Hard to believe, but I miss Sadie more than I realized. Seeing her face like that, hearing her voice, is a gift. This is perfect."

Sarah sniffed and nodded. "Yeah, it's pretty great, and this is only the beginning. We have so many plans, things that needed more time to work through, but the future is exciting."

Mia spotted Grant's curls above the crowd and waited until he met her gaze to inch closer to him. Sarah exclaimed and grabbed her hand before she made it far. "Oh wait, the book. We're going to have a biography. Maybe even by next year's Western Days. Mia sold Michael on a book all about Sadie!"

A flush of embarrassment filled Mia's cheeks. It was tempting to downplay the whole thing, but she knew it was going to be fun to work on and wonderful when it was finally done, so she matched Sarah's enthusiasm instead. "I did! There's still so much to figure out, but this book is going to be awesome, I promise."

"A book! And I don't have to write it!" Jordan shouted as she hopped next to Mia.

When they were all laughing and out of breath, Mia shot past the congratulatory crowd to launch herself into Grant's arms. "Finally. I've missed you!"

He pulled her tight to his chest. "Not as much as I've missed you. It's as bad as losing my cell phone when you aren't here."

She pulled back. "Work on your romantic metaphors, please."

"It's like I was missing my favorite pair of boots?" He motioned toward the door and they stepped out onto the quiet sidewalk. "I will definitely need coaching on metaphors in general, but I promise to get better."

Mia pulled him away from the window and pressed her

lips to his. "Lucky for you, I intend to stick around Prospect. I can coach you every day if you need it."

"I am a lucky, lucky man." His sweet smile filled her with a wild fluttering in her chest, the butterflies she'd heard of so often. "Not sure who is happier to hear your long-term plans, me or Jordan."

Mia rested her forehead against his chest. "Wait until I propose working part-time at the Majestic in exchange for a place to stay for a bit."

He laughed. "They need lots of help, inexpensive help. Jordan may get down on one knee and propose marriage."

Mia stared at him. "You think? I wouldn't mind a proposal."

He dropped a kiss on her nose. "Way ahead of you. I was considering the when and where of it just now."

"Oh, I can wait for the right time." Mia smiled. "The universe hasn't disappointed me yet."

EPILOGUE

Western Days Weekend—
Cowboy Games Winners' Ceremony

GRANT SMILED AS Mia hugged Annie Mercado and accepted the third-place trophy for the overall score of the coed teams in the Cowboy Games. The award—a bronze-colored bucking bronco with a plaque on a wood base—would be a great reminder of a great day, and he was gratified to see both of their names listed.

"Not too shabby a finish. You and Grant make a good team. Mia, you looked like a champ in the saddle during that relay race. Prue just edged you out by a nose, dropping her last boot in the bucket seconds before yours."

Annie was right. Mia had ridden almost as well as his mother through the relay that had all the women racing to drop a total of ten old boots painted in their team colors in a bucket in the fastest time.

As soon as he got Mia alone, he'd tell her she'd managed that perfectly to earn his mother's undying love. Although Grant was certain Prue Armstrong and Mia Romero were family already.

Annie shook his hand with enthusiasm. "Next year, work on your coffee-brewing skills and I bet you move into second." Her lips were twitching as she added. "At least."

He deserved the ribbing. He and Mia had been neck-and-neck with his mother and father in the standings until

the cooking competition. Their teamwork through the timed mucking out of the stalls, washing laundry by hand and hanging it to dry, and the three-legged hay bale race had been impeccable. His steak seared over the campfire had been fine, but the coffee unfortunately was as strong as battery acid and the judges had given him zero points for that round.

"Come back next year. These games will be bigger and better," Grant told her. "My coffee may be the same."

"Wouldn't miss it. Call me when you want to schedule some time for me to work with your club." Annie moved on through the crowd to where a group of young women were waiting for her to sign autographs.

Mia's arm slipped around his waist and she stood on her tiptoes to press a kiss to his lips. "Sad you didn't crush the competition? We'll demand a rematch."

He turned to stare into her eyes. "How could I be sad when you're here? Our team… I never knew to wish for someone like you."

Mia blinked before she touched his chin. "All I did was play a few silly games with you and laugh my fool head off while I did it. I can be so much more for you than that."

And she already was.

Grant shook his head. It was important that she understood how much bigger today was. "First, you gave me peace. You tackled my enemies head-on when you didn't have to. Because it was the right thing to do for all of us." He smiled down at her. "That was huge. For a lifetime, I struggled to find that peace, and then there you were."

Her forehead wrinkled as if she wanted to argue.

"But today…" Grant's voice dropped to a whisper. "There's no other word. I'm happy. You're amazing, Mia. One of a kind and so much fun. That laugh of yours was

better than a first-place finish. I can't imagine ever feeling more love and more happiness than I do right now."

Her eyes teared up, which wasn't his intent at all, so he immediately added, "Unless we win the whole thing together next year, of course. That might top this."

Her snort of laughter sent a fizz of joy through his veins and he held her tightly to his chest. "I love you, Mia Romero."

Her adorable grin as she stared at him from under her Cookie Queen Western Wear hat would stay with him forever.

"I love you, too, Bad Boy of Bronc Busting." She traced her fingers over his jaw. "When we met on the side of the road that day, I was pretty sure you were too handsome for my own good, as well as kind and loyal and… You just get better looking, better everything, unfortunately. You're stuck with me now. There's no running away."

As Grant watched Damon and Micah make kissy faces behind Mia's back, his mother and father smiling and looking on, he realized coming home to Prospect had been the best decision he could have ever made. The universe had been drawing them both here.

Grant grinned. "With you by my side, there's no other place I'd rather be."

* * * * *

Don't miss the stories in this mini series!

THE FORTUNES OF PROSPECT

The Right Cowboy
CHERYL HARPER
July 2024

Courting The Cowgirl
CHERYL HARPER
September 2024

MILLS & BOON

WESTERN

Rugged men looking for love...

Available Next Month

The Maverick Makes The Grade Stella Bagwell
The Heart Of A Rancher Trish Milburn

....

Nine Months To A Fortune Elizabeth Bevarly
Hill Country Hero Kit Hawthorne

....

LOVE INSPIRED

A Companion For His Son Lee Tobin McClain
Hidden Secrets Between Them Mindy Obenhaus

Keep reading for an excerpt of a new title
from the Special Edition series,
HER FAKE BOYFRIEND by Heatherly Bell

Chapter One

"Hey, isn't that your *girlfriend*?" Noah Cavill said.

Finn Sheridan looked up from scrubbing the floor of their catamaran. He saw Abby a few feet away down the dock in a clinch with an unfamiliar man.

"Yep, that's Abby."

He recognized the tight jeans, the long blonde hair. She was definitely his type. Beautiful, carefree and fun. Never worked *too* hard but just enough to be responsible. She knew how to unwind and relax. And she'd been exactly what he'd needed at the time.

"Hey, I'm sorry." Noah threw aside the rag he'd been using to polish the guardrail. "If I caught Twyla with some other guy like that, I'd have to kill the dude."

Finn chuckled. "I should have clarified. Abby's my *ex-girlfriend*. And she can do whatever she likes. I'm not going to *kill* anyone."

"Wait. What? Since when is she your ex-girlfriend? Just last week you two were at the house with me and Twyla, watching the game. You looked...happy."

"I was happy. It was a good game." Finn shrugged.

"I'm not talking about the game! I mean you and Abby. Weren't you into her? She seemed to really be vibing with you."

"Yeah, she was great. She is great."

"Then I don't understand." Noah froze as if he'd just re-membered he left the oven on or had another thought that disturbed him. "You're kidding me."

"When I'm kidding you, you'll know." Finn straightened, sliding his hands down his board shorts.

Life as part owner of Nacho Boat might sound glamor-ous to some, but the truth was far from it. Sure, he got to be on the water every day, but he also had to clear and clean the deck after taking a group of men fishing for marlin. Still, the work was exactly what he'd wanted and came at a good time when Noah suggested that Finn invest in the business alongside him. A few months ago, he'd bought Nacho Boat Adventures from the previous owner and al-ready had plans to expand. Like Finn, his oldest friend Noah was no stranger to boating.

For Finn, investing in the business with his family's help was a nice change from constantly being in competition with someone else. He'd already experienced the peak at the Olympics and had the gold medal to prove it. Well, in theory he had the gold.

He still missed having the medal with him some days and the memories of the life of a competitive athlete that came with it.

Point being, now he only competed with himself and that's the way he liked it.

"Okay, so you and Abby are finished. Please don't tell me you're still having these two-week-long relationships and moving on," Noah said.

"Okay, I won't tell you. And it's not two weeks. Not that I've been keeping track."

"That's okay, Twyla and I do it for you."

"Don't. It's not true." But Finn counted quietly in his head.

"It is." Noah sat on the bench and started to name the

women Finn had recently dated on one hand. "Since you started dating again, every two weeks, almost like you set an alarm. Next!"

Hell, maybe it only took him that long to figure out whether he wanted to spend more time with a woman. He was fast and efficient in more than one way, apparently.

Finn faced Noah. Behind him, the beautiful Gulf Coast sunset was beginning to crest in hints of red, purple and gold. The salt air filled his lungs and brought about faint memories of over a decade of training and racing. Sailing.

"Maybe I can figure out whether a relationship is going to work out sooner than most people do. That's all. I didn't realize it was exactly two weeks but whatever."

"And how can you figure this out in only two weeks' time? You haven't even met her family in that short a span."

"Experience."

Finn didn't want to ruin Noah's day, but a divorce taught a man a lot about who would and who wouldn't make the distance. If it wasn't going to happen, why waste his time?

"Okay, I get it. Your divorce was a romance killer. You two wound up hating each other. But what was wrong with *Abby*?"

"Nothing. She's just not right for me. We're not right for each other."

"Huh."

Noah seemed to mull this over as if he couldn't figure out if Finn was a genius savant in terms of relationships, or if he was simply commitment phobic after a bad divorce, as he'd often been accused. But he wasn't, and also it wasn't just a *bad* divorce. His divorce had been like *The War of the Roses*. Like World War III. Until he'd finally given up and let Cheryl take everything she wanted. By then all he'd really wanted was out.

He'd lost something that meant a lot to him in the process: a gold medal and a relationship he'd thought might last forever. Love, gone. Friendship lost too.

"Look, we can't all fall in love with our best friend."

Sure, Finn wanted what Noah and Twyla had. The assurance that no matter what happened between two people, they'd never *hurt* each other on purpose. Noah and Twyla loved each other far too much for that, with a love that went deeper than physical attraction and magnetic chemistry.

But they had that, too, damn overachievers.

"I think the divorce is still playing hockey puck with your brain."

Finn didn't want to believe that, because it meant Cheryl had taken far more from him than a medal he'd earned due to years of practice and commitment. It meant she'd taken his peace of mind and the chance of any future happiness with it.

"Look, I obviously know it's tough for me to consider anything long term with a woman. I can admit that. But I'm not hurting anyone. All of the women I date want temporary, too. And that works for me right now."

"Okay," Noah said with a sigh. "As long as no one is getting hurt."

"Wow." A lightbulb went off in Finn's head. "Don't tell me you're worried about *Michelle*."

"I'm sorry, but I still feel guilty. I didn't mean to hurt her, and she moved here from Austin because of me."

"You didn't ask her to move here."

"No, of course not. I was trying to break up with her."

"Guess she didn't get the memo."

Were she not Noah's recent ex, Finn might like to get in line to enjoy two weeks or however long of Michelle La-Croix. She was beautiful, smart and funny with long legs

and an amazing figure. But she wasn't dating anyone, because clearly, she was still not over Noah. Nothing less attractive to a man than someone still pining over her ex.

"She got fired from her job!" Noah was still going on, trying desperately to expunge his guilt.

The problem was, Noah had always been in love with Twyla but until recently, he'd had no idea she felt the same. Once he did, well, that was all she wrote. No other woman stood a chance.

"Not your fault. Plus, she landed on her feet. She's found a new home over at Pierce & Pierce."

"Twyla calls that place P&P, after Pride & Prejudice. Says it sort of redeems the whole divorce attorney thing."

The same law firm his ex-wife had hired to fleece Finn of everything he owned but his underwear. The little shark Arthur, Jr., had been Cheryl's attorney. Finn's attorney was a nice woman who thought they should mediate and try to part as "friends."

She was a dreamer, in other words.

And that was the other, much bigger problem with Michelle LaCroix. She was a family law attorney.

One of the best.

Michelle LaCroix stood from her desk and stretched. With a sedentary job like hers, she had to remind herself to get up every twenty minutes or risk heart disease. Sitting was the new smoking, after all. She'd never smoked a day in her life and if she died of coronary heart disease, she was going to be very pissed.

Closing her laptop, she strolled to look out the window of her office. In the distance to her right, the lighthouse appeared in the fading rays of the sunset. To her left were the bright lights of the Charming, Texas, boardwalk twin-

kling like matching stars. Across the street was Once Upon a Book, the bookshop her former nemesis, Twyla Thompson, owned and managed.

Even if Michelle was unhappy that she'd had to start over after working for years to make partner at her law firm in Austin, she had to admit Charming was the perfect place to do it.

The town was well named—a picture-postcard place situated along the Gulf Coast of Mexico. When she'd arrived here six months ago, Michelle had driven along the curvy coastline in her rental, taking in the views. Her ex-boyfriend Noah's hometown was everything she'd expected from a bucolic coastal town with a converted lighthouse, piers, docks, and sea jetties. She'd found a temporary rental in a row of private and secluded cottages along the beach, owned and managed by some retired rodeo cowboy who loved to surf.

Foolishly, Michelle had actually come here for another chance with Noah. She'd had no idea he'd been in love with his best friend for over a decade. To be fair, even Twyla had been unaware. Still, it was neither Noah nor Twyla's fault Michelle had been fired from her old law firm. The entire reason had been professional jealousy, the kind a woman in her field met with far too often.

Gus O'Connor, former friend and associate, had taken it upon himself to forward a private email meant to be only between the two of them. She'd complained about a senior partner, and he'd forwarded that personal email to everyone in the firm. That's how her former law office staff learned Michelle believed Richard Styles walked as if he had a stick up his butt.

Stupid, stupid, stupid. She knew better than anyone how dangerous and exposing email could be. But she'd been

off her game, heartbroken over the breakup with Noah. She'd then made the colossal mistake of venting with a colleague who often made his own jokes at Richard's expense—though he'd been clever enough not to put anything in print. But no one cared to hear that, because while she was in Charming on the first vacation she'd had in years, the shit hit the fan. Texas was an at-will work state, and Richard didn't need a reason to let her go. He used the fact she'd taken too much time off, and promptly fired her.

She'd landed on her feet as she always did. Agile. Like a cat. Arthur Pierce Sr. adored her and had hired Michelle on the spot.

"You're just what this firm needs. A breath of fresh air."

A *woman,* in other words. The firm hadn't grown much over the years and now consisted only of a father and his son, Arthur Jr., hence the highly *original* name of Pierce and Pierce. Snort. Arthur Sr. was nearing retirement, and Junior was a real piece of work. Every morning he'd grin at her lasciviously as he walked by her office on the way to the better corner one.

"Already here?" He'd chuckle all the way, knowing he'd never have to work hard a day in his life because of dear old dad.

But Michelle told herself that Junior was good for her. He reminded her to never let her guard down again. She worked harder because of him and was highly motivated. Right now, this was a good thing because she vowed to make partner one way or the other. If nothing else the name needed some originality, and LaCroix was a fine name.

And would it be good to make partner here in Charming? Yes, yes, it would. Noah and Twyla would finally stop feeling so damn guilty. She'd send news of the promotion to everyone at her former Thomas and Styles law firm in Aus-

tin and tell them all to eat her dust. Especially Gus. She'd have the last laugh. Success was always the best revenge.

"Are you still here?" Arthur Sr. stood in the frame of her door, glancing at his watch. "It's seven o'clock. Stop trying to impress me! I already can't love you more than I do, or my wife will get jealous. Go home to your boyfriend and take the poor man out to dinner. You rarely see him."

Oh, yeah. That. Arthur had implied that were she to ever make partner, he'd need to be assured she had deep ties in Charming. He had to know that with a family law firm he'd built from the ground up, he could trust that she wasn't going to go back to Austin. In a weak and rather stupid moment of which she'd had far too many lately, Michelle told him she had a boyfriend. She also told him they were getting quite serious.

She'd pictured Noah, of course, but hadn't given him a name. Good thing because Noah was no longer a possibility. He was, in fact, quite engaged. As in to be married to someone else *engaged*. So, she kept calling her imaginary guy "my bae" and "my boo," even if she wanted to throw up every time she said it.

"As a matter of fact, we're going out to dinner tonight." She started to shove papers in her briefcase. "I better get going or I'll be late. Thanks for reminding me."

Work-life balance was important to Arthur. With a son like Junior, at least he'd never had to worry that his own son would work too hard.

"I'd like to finally meet him," Arthur said. "Lynn and I want to have you both over for dinner."

"Oh, sure. I'll tell him. Let's talk about it and arrange a date."

She'd been stalling for weeks, and she could stall a bit longer. Eventually, she'd find someone to date, even if it

was casually, and she'd introduce that man to Arthur. No one had to know their relationship was new.

Arthur left before she did, and Michelle brought up the rear not long after, shutting off the copy machine, coffee-maker, and lights before locking the doors. A burger from the Salty Dog Bar & Grill sounded good tonight, which she would eat alone in her little beach shack while listening to the waves. And watching her true crime shows. She got in her sedan, called in her order for pickup, and drove the short distance from downtown to the row of restaurants on the boardwalk.

Twyla wasn't a social butterfly, so Michelle rarely ran into her and Noah here. The one time she had run into them a couple of weeks ago, Twyla had waved her over. She was trying to be friends. Trying *too* hard. Michelle wound up pretending there was a work emergency. Someone who wanted a divorce, like, immediately. They bought it somehow.

Tonight, the place was slammed, filled with couples. Glancing at her watch, Michelle realized it was actually already Thursday. Damn. The weekend again. After tomorrow, she'd have no work for two days. Last week, Arthur had sent an email to the three other people in the office: no more working on the weekends. Their clients would survive their divorces without them. They were attorneys, not counselors. Except the truth was in many ways they were both.

"Believe me," Arthur had once said to Michelle, "I made the mistake of working too much and losing sight of what's truly important. Now I'm on my third marriage and I've learned a few things. Family time is crucial to a success-ful life."

Michelle had nodded at Arthur's wisdom while simulta-neously making the decision she could just as easily work

at home on the weekends. She'd been bringing files home ever since. Her work was consuming, passionate, and she loved it that way. Nothing was more dramatic than two people who'd decided to end a marriage. On her client list now, she had a poor man whose trophy wife had cheated on him repeatedly and had the nerve to fight the prenup due to her own "pain and suffering."

She'd married a seventy-five-year-old man, after all, so how could she be blamed for getting her needs met elsewhere? She'd actually tried that defense, and her lawyer should be disbarred for allowing it. That case would wrap up soon, and the woman would get her settlement and not another cent. Zip. Zero. Nada. Michelle was a good attorney, thank you very much.

As her bad luck would have it, Noah and Twyla were here tonight. She spied them holding hands and sitting on the same side of a four-person booth. They hadn't seen her, and she hoped she might be able to get out of there before they did. She took her spot in the long pickup line and averted her eyes from anyone else she might know.

But just then she heard the sound of a booming voice she recognized.

"Michelle!"

Holy legal briefs, it was Arthur Sr., sitting at a nearby booth with his lovely wife.